Bad Lands

USA TODAY BESTSELLING AUTHOR

STACEY MARIE BROWN

ALSO BY STACEY MARIE BROWN

Contemporary Romance

How the Heart Breaks

Buried Alive

Smug Bastard

The Unlucky Ones

Blinded Love Series
Shattered Love (#1)
Broken Love (#2)
Twisted Love (#3)

Royal Watch Series
Royal Watch (#1)
Royal Command (#2)

Paranormal Romance

A Winterland Tale
Descending into Madness (#1)
Ascending from Madness (#2)
Beauty in Her Madness (#3)
Beast in His Madness (#4)

Darkness Series
Darkness of Light (#1)
Fire in the Darkness (#2)
Beast in the Darkness (An Elighan Dragen Novelette)
Dwellers of Darkness (#3)
Blood Beyond Darkness (#4)
West (#5)

For everyone calling me names,
I bathe in your curses...
with Jason Momoa.

Bad Lands

I heard the last bell of the midnight hour strike in the distance.

An explosion popped behind my lids, funneling from the nectar, tangling with the thick magic still in the air. Electricity scorched up my throat and down my veins, burning everything in its wake. Energy surged my spine, the nectar's force powering through me.

It did not speak the words, but it told me what I was.

I was nothing and everything.

The bridge between life and death.

The in-between.

I was *The Grey*.

Chapter 1

The slight sweetness of magic seared up my nose, the taste of decay coating my tongue while life shot through my veins, leaving charred marks in its wake. Lightning fractured the sky, rolling and spearing my body with electricity.

It crackled in my ears, and screams of agony echoed in the night with the ringing of the midnight bell.

The nectar pulsed in my real hand while my shadow hand rested over my uncle's chest miles away through Scorpion's link. The power consumed me. Dominated. Piercing me so deeply, my insides twisted as if they were burning into ashes.

The nectar had been waiting years to be united with me again. It was overzealous and eager to be let free.

It was so familiar, marking my bones, but at the same time so foreign, like a twin I never knew about and just met for the first time. Awkward. Stumbling as if I was a newborn, I had no understanding of how to control it or what it did. My emotions were the only things swimming up to the surface, directing my focus to Uncle Andris.

His dead body lay crushed under the wreckage, his blood smearing over the rubble. The small underground base was now in ruins, with dozens and dozens of other corpses scattered around. I could feel their souls cry, confused and scared in death. But only one held my focus, tapped on my grief and fear. Andris was my family. He protected me, loved me, and had been there for me growing up. Even my blood uncle, Mykel, could not claim the same.

I would not lose him.

"Nagybácsi... Please, don't leave me." The plea bubbled in my gut, panic shooting down my arms, while Maddox and Wesley reached for Andris, trying to remove him from the rubble. To them, he was already dead. They could not hear or see me, but instinct dug into my bones, pushing through the connection I had with Scorpion.

Wind swept through, whipping up my hair and brushing energy across my skin.

A possessive snarl clashed through my teeth. *"Don't touch him!"*

White light flared from me.

A roar ripped from Warwick, echoing through the thick night air surrounding the castle while Scorpion bellowed beside my shadow, each one feeling the link sizzle and blister. Lightning continued its dance through the sky, striking with savagery. Wind tunneled through me like a conduit.

It burned.

It shredded.

Andris's eyes burst open as his heart sputtered with life, the thump of it vibrating against my palm. His body seized with a harsh scream as I tore him away from death's grasp.

The group surrounding him stumbled back with a cry as the human they were certain was dead stared back at them with wide, confused eyes.

It was a split second. A moment hung in time, where physical distance between us did not matter. I was in the room with him, not miles away in a rundown castle on sacred fae land.

My uncle turned his head, his eyes finding mine. He looked right at me.

Then the light around me snapped off. Darkness grabbed my legs, yanking me back. Pain wrenched through every fiber of my being as blackness swallowed me. My mouth opened to scream, but instead, Warwick's roar thundered through the night, and Scorpion cried my name.

Warwick! I reached for him, but consciousness slipped through my fingers and let me fall into the darkness

Devouring and cauterizing what was left of my remains.

It scorched.

It destroyed.

Magic tore from my body, leaving behind a vicious throb of pain spearing my muscles, gnawing on my nerves. My lids fluttered, and the shallow breaths that pulled at my lungs locked me in place, frozen in torment.

I swallowed the bile down, trying to keep it from rising back up, slowly becoming aware of my surroundings. Of myself.

On my hands and knees, I shuddered, the agony so deep, my body instinctively tried to numb me, to not let my brain understand the true depths of its pain.

Cold air burned my heated skin, and the silence pulsed in my ears. Not even a cricket or lap of water from the river below. Dead silence.

I pulled my lids open slowly, staring at my hands, the crumbling cobble path denting my palms. I was fully back at the High Castle. I sensed the figures around me, but emptiness still burrowed deep past the pain I felt, pounding in my heart.

Something was wrong.

Licking my lips, I lifted my head, turning to see a massive figure on his knees right behind me.

Warwick heaved in and out, sweat dripping down his face. His expression was stone, but his aqua eyes searched mine like he was trying to communicate something. Something deep in my gut coiled, and if he was, I couldn't feel or hear anything.

Glancing away from his penetrating gaze, I saw Ash, Kek, and Lukas standing there, their faces a mask of horror, awe, fear, and confusion.

Kek's regard went to the group in front of me, her lips parting, her eyes widening. Her response snapped my head back to the seven necromancers. Their faces were still disguised by their hoods, capturing the darkness under the fabric, but I watched the six behind their leader move, lifting their hands with awed reverence.

Terror hitched in my lungs.

Their hands were still slim and boney, but now plump with flesh. Necromancers weren't skeletons, but their physiques were so pallid, skinny, and mummy-like they could almost appear so. They needed to feast on dead souls to keep themselves strong and powerful—the rulers of the in-between.

All but the leader lifted the hoods from their heads.

A guttural noise tore from my throat as I scrambled to my feet. I rammed into Warwick as he rose. He gripped a gun with one hand, the other curling around my hip protectively.

"Holy shit." Lukas balked, shuffling back, pointing his gun at them.

My blood pumped so hard my ears only heard the pulse echoing in them.

Tall and short, light to dark skin, their faces were distinguishable. Almost human. Emaciated, but *alive*.

3

"What the fuck?" Warwick growled, pulling me tighter to him.

The leader stared at her hands, the hood hiding her face, flipping her palms around with astonishment.

"I don't understand." Kek's lips were parted with shock, a look I had never seen on her, and it unsettled me. "What the fuck just happened?"

"She did this." The leader's voice came out soft and broken, as if she wasn't used to speaking.

Necromancers didn't talk as far as I knew.

My head jerked to her as I watched her skinny fingers reach for her hood. The dark hair, which had been dry and lifeless, now shined in the bright moonlight. Slowly, she tugged the large hood from her head, the moonlight reflecting off her pale skin and dark eyes.

"No…" My head shook, knocking back harder into Warwick. He held me firmer as my legs dipped, panic and terror dimming my senses and spinning my head. There was no way. It wasn't possible.

The woman stared at me, her tongue sliding over her dry, cracked lips, opening her mouth.

"It was you, Brexley."

My entire world flipped in that single moment. All I knew or understood disintegrated under my feet.

Sickly and gaunt compared to the woman I had seen in the vision on the battlefield, it was the same face I had been staring at all day in the picture. The one still in my back pocket.

Eabha.

"Mo-mom?" My vocal cords wrapped around themselves, barely making my voice audible.

Her head cocked as if I spoke a foreign word. A moniker she had never been called because I had never gotten the chance to call her that.

Making a hum in her throat, she stepped closer to me, her bare toes knocking into my boots. I couldn't move or breathe. I barely felt Warwick's grip on me. My body jerked at her nearness, caught between thinking this might be a dream or the fact it was real. Both scenarios were terrifying. My mother, who I thought had been dead for twenty years, was alive.

Sort of…

She had been a necromancer. All of them were, so how was she standing before me, blood pumping through her veins?

"Ho-how is this possible?" My gaze ran over her, drinking up every inch. She was slightly shorter than me, but similar dark hair fell to her waist, and the same black irises as mine stared back at me.

Even withered, my mother was beautiful. I had imagined her so many

4

times in my head growing up, how she looked, spoke, and moved. Nothing came close to the real thing.

"Because of you." Her voice was deeper than I expected—lyrical. A drop of an Irish accent wound softly through her pitch.

"Me? What does that mean?"

She peered back at the box, drawing my attention to it, noticing the nectar was now dull and grayish. The pulse and life I had seen earlier was extinguished. "You feel it as it feels you. It's part of you. Weaved through magic. It is the essence of life."

"Essence of life?" I echoed.

"Your life."

"I don't know what you mean." I blinked, staring at the lump of matter. "Did I break it?"

"I don't know." She seemed unsure of how to move her mouth; her speech was slow and broken. "You used a lot of power to bring us back." She motioned to the group behind her, their eyes on me with cautious admiration.

"Bring you back?" I repeated, my gaze snapping around to all the figures standing around her, still gazing and touching themselves in awe.

I did that? My power brought them back?

"H-how?" Though I already knew. It was the same power I had used when I brought Andris back to life. The power I had when touching the nectar was so vast, and I had no understanding of how to use it. I yanked someone from death's hands when I wasn't actually there while bringing back seven necromancers.

What. The. Fuck?

My eyes drifted to my mother, a stranger to me, not sure how to react to her. She hadn't touched me or moved to hug me, so I didn't either.

"You look so much like him." I expected her tone to be tender, overcome like I was, but it was reserved. Detached. "You are more beautiful than I could ever imagine," she said evenly. "Strong. Fierce. Your father did well in raising you."

I sucked in sharply at the mention of my father. Did he know about her? What had happened to her? Is this why he left the coordinates to this place?

"I have found leads. But eyes are watching me. Always watching."

"I understand now…"

Is this what he meant?

"Did—did dad know? Did he find you?" I whispered, tears burning the back of my lids, trying to ignore the pain and queasiness rolling inside me.

5

"Yes." Her head dipped. A wobbly smile stretched her lips, like a memory had come to her, but the gesture seemed unfamiliar to her mouth. It quickly faded. "He discovered our coven before he died."

"He didn't know what you were before, did he?"

A slice of shame flicked at her brow. "No."

I rolled my lips together, trying not to cry. What heartbreak and devastation my dad must have felt finding out the love of his life lied to him about who she was and had been only miles away from him all that time.

"You talked to him?" Ash's pitch mounted with confusion. "Necromancers don't speak. It is said the clans communicate with each other through a link."

His words sent an electrical shock into my system.

Through a link...

Holy shit...

My head whipped around to Warwick, his eyes filling with the same wonder.

As if hands wrapped around my throat, air tried to squeeze into my lungs, the understanding striking me over the head like a club. Is that why I could do it with Warwick and Scorpion? They're my clan?

I struggled to breathe, terror racing up and down my spine. "Am... am I a necromancer?" I croaked, nausea climbing up the back of my throat.

Eabha pushed her shoulders back, her movements stiff.

"Necromancer is not a race of beings. It is a curse." The group shifted behind my mother. "An ancient one when there was yet to be a difference between Druidism and Wicca. Once we were all witches, but the Fae gods favored some of these witches, gifted them with real magic. After centuries, some clans did not want to be slaves anymore, beholden to the Fae kings and queens. They refused and were punished for it. In death, they would walk the earth forever—tortured in purgatory—not alive, but not dead. Feeling nothing but emptiness, always hungry, and never satisfied." She placed her palms on her chest. "But I feel..."

"What?" I whispered.

"Life." She dropped her hands away. "Now I can smell the air, feel the cool breeze on my face, crave real food." Her eyes watered. "All because of you."

Shock at what I had done—what I was capable of—was keeping everything in a strange haze.

"Can necromancers bring people back to life?" I peered around at my friends before directing my question at my mother. "I thought they could only reanimate skeletons." At the end of my statement, my eyes shot to the shadows behind them. All the skeletons lay on the ground in a heap, no longer in the thrall of necromancers.

"We can't." Eabha watched me for a long moment. "What you did…" A look of pride and relief hinted on her face. "You are not one of us."

A hiccup balled in my throat. "Then what am I?"

"I don't know. You might have traits that came from me, as you would from your father, and the circumstances you were born under, but you are completely unique. There is no name, no race, no one else who came before you. It is you who decides what you are."

"I don't understand." A memory of something grazed my mind, a moment when I had been touching the nectar. I felt an absolution and power within me, a name, but I couldn't remember, couldn't reach what stayed just beyond the shadows.

"In time, you will." She reached out, her hand grazing mine, forcing the sob up to my tongue. Her fingers felt boney, but a warmth absorbed into my skin.

My mother was really here. Alive.

"Come." She took my hand, pulling me toward the other six necromancers.

My group lurched with me, Ash and Warwick instantly stepping forward to protect me.

Eabha paused, peering at Warwick. "I know who you are." She inspected him. "The great legend… *the Wolf.*"

"Glad my reputation precedes me." He showed his teeth. "Then you know what I am capable of."

"You have walked among us, Wolf. A shadow of death—touching the darkness but also drawn to the light." My mother's eyes flicked to me. "Depended on it."

Warwick growled, inching farther to her.

"Warwick, stop." I tried to reach out to him, but it echoed in my head, going nowhere.

"Hey." I touched Warwick's shoulder, trying to move around him. Something felt off. Missing.

My brows furrowed, my gaze darting to him as I passed. Was he blocking me?

His expression mirrored mine, tightening a knot in my stomach.

"Brexley." My mother's voice jerked me away, causing me to push off the sick sensation and focus on her. "I would like to introduce you to your family. Meet your Aunt Morgan."

A woman with dirty and stringy reddish-brown hair stepped forward.

Her skin was pallid, but it was the same stunning face I recalled from twenty years ago. It was the woman I remembered from my vision.

"I can't believe it is you." She wrapped her arms around me awkwardly, her mouth wavering under the smile she was attempting. But her brown eyes glittered with awe. "You are so beautiful."

"Thank you." My own eyes filled up with tears.

I had an aunt. One I could see the family resemblance through. Neither Morgan nor my mom had aged a day from the night they died, making them appear more like my sisters than their true age.

"Your cousin, Liam," my mother continued, motioning to a tall man with green eyes and reddish-brown hair like Morgan's. He stared at me with steady regard.

Eabha pointed at the others, and I followed her hand, nodding my head in greeting to each. "This is Sam." Tall, fit, chiseled cheekbones, with beautiful black skin and caramel eyes. "Roan." White, freckled skin, short and stocky with blondish hair and hazel eyes. "Breena." She had the same striking features as Sam, making me wonder if they were related, if not twins. "And Rory." Pale, petite, brown hair, with huge blue eyes.

"This is my coven." Mother stared at me. "Your family."

The color of their skin, hair, or eyes didn't matter. Coven was family.

My family. I had aunts and uncles besides the ones who actually shared blood with me. I had grown up alone with no idea I had kin.

"I can't believe this." I shook my head. "You've been here the whole time?"

"Yes." Direct. To the point.

"So, Dad made it here? Did he know anything about what you really were?"

Eabha's mouth pinched. "No," she said quietly. "He did not. I never told him I was a witch or about my family, or the curse."

I waited for her to continue.

"I loved your father so much, but I kept a lot from him. It was safer."

"Safer?" I was confused by her admission. "Why safer? Aren't witches human?" Doubt colored my query. The way I grew up, humans still had strict societal norms. They might be snubbed if a factory worker and an elite mixed, but it was begrudgingly accepted because it was a human-to-human relationship.

Witches, artists, or anyone who didn't follow society's rules weren't looked fondly on in HDF, but it wasn't forbidden, like associating with a mixed-breed or fae.

"Yes." An odd note hung in her tone. "*Witches* are. My coven was quite…" She cleared her throat. "Well-known at the time." She glanced back at her family, Liam and Sam scoffing under their breath. "When I met your father, we were being hunted by our enemy. I should have stayed away, but I couldn't. Instead, I kept him protected the best way I knew how. Ignorance and secrecy."

"He thought you died in childbirth… at home." I gestured, hearing my voice rise. "But you were here…" I moved my hand toward the field behind the castle where so many died. "Why? The nectar showed me, and I heard you say if Aneira died, something happened to you guys as well." My throat clogged, my words squeaking out. "So, was I not the reason?"

The guilt I bore on my shoulders for thinking I was why my mother died that night crashed down on my chest.

"No." She swung her head vigorously, a flicker of grief crossing her face. "You are not to blame. Our fate was already sealed. My death was not your fault, Brexley."

I inhaled a sharp gulp of air, my eyes burning. "Why? What were you doing there—fighting *for* her?"

"It is a complicated story meant for another time," she replied.

My head whirled with emotions, questions bubbling on my tongue.

"I don't understand. If you weren't actually dead, why did dad think you died in childbirth?"

"Someone we trusted took you from here and delivered you to your father with a note saying I had perished in childbirth the night of the fae war. Which was not a lie. I *did* die on that night giving birth to you," she said flatly.

"And yet here you are." A spark of anger tingled in my mouth, ire for what both my father and me were led to believe. The pain and agony he struggled with because of her. What I had dealt with.

"A necromancer does not love, does not feel or care. We are bound to our nature. I was as good as dead to both of you."

Overwhelming emotion punched at my heart, dividing me into fractions. It was too much; my mind clogged with questions and thoughts. If I didn't step back, take a moment, I would break. I was already shutting down, turning off, compartmentalizing my grief, and focusing back on the mission.

Easy. Cut and dry. No convoluted pain.

"I can't do this right now." I swallowed, my head wagging. "We came to get the nectar."

Eabha's form stilled, her demeanor shifting, hand wrapping around her scythe.

"I can't let you do that."

9

Chapter 2

"What?" My heart jerked back at her sudden shift. "The nectar is mine." It was part of me… it *was* me.

"It belongs here. I cannot let you—" Her words were drowned out by a stream of piercing gunshots resounding in the far distance, bouncing off the sky like tiny balls of thunder.

My heart tripped. Air caught in my lungs as my eyes searched the horizon toward Budapest. Samhain was known for chaos and commotion, but my gut twisted as I wondered if it was my uncle's base getting attacked again. The first explosion would have sent the survivors out like rats to gun down. Was my uncle okay? What about everyone else? Were they alive or dead now?

Reaching out, I couldn't even feel the buzz from Scorpion, sinking my stomach further.

"We have to go." I still faced southeast. The pull to Sarkis's base was overwhelming.

I glanced at the nectar, laying there with no pulse or magic.

I moved toward the container. Liam, Roan, Breena, and Rory stepped in front of it quickly, blocking my way, making me stumble back.

"What are you doing?" My forehead crinkled, my regard darting to my mother. "I need the nectar."

"No." Liam's fingers wrapped tighter around his bardiche, his green eyes watching me coldly.

My attention flicked to my group behind me, then back to my mom, my mouth going dry. Eabha moved in next to Liam, Morgan next to her. All of them building a wall between me and the nectar.

"What do you mean, no?" My shoulders rolled back, my hackles rising. "Lives depend on me getting it."

"And many more lives depend on us keeping it safe," my mother said evenly, taking a slight step forward, showing her leadership. "We stole it from those who did not understand what power it possessed and have kept it hidden for fifteen years. Around us, it cannot be seen or felt. It is safe."

Ash let out a dry laugh, his hand rubbing at his face like something finally registered with him.

"What?" I asked.

"It's why the fae book stopped recording events right after those pirates stole the nectar. It was you guys waiting in the shadows? Who stole it from them?" Ash indicated to my mother.

She dipped her head. "We had been tracking it for a long time and finally found it."

"What does that have to do with anything?" I glanced at Ash.

"Remember when I told you the book can only document life? It only records the living."

"Yes?"

"They aren't—or weren't—*living*." He nodded to them.

Holy shit. That's why the book cut out the moment they robbed the pirates. Why nothing showed for the last fifteen years. Because it had been here, in a well, guarded by necromancers.

"That is why we cannot let it leave here," Eabha stated, her accent growing a little stronger, her voice coming out clearer after 20 years of not speaking. "As witches or as necromancers, we have sworn to keep it protected from both human and fae. From those who cannot withstand its magic and will crumble under the weight of greed and power. It seeks it too much. Desires it. *Her* power is too much part of it, and it is not safe to be out of our care."

"What do you mean, *her* power is still too much a part of it?" I tipped my head, knowing they weren't referring to me.

A sad smile touched my mother's mouth in response. "I'm sorry, you cannot have it, daughter. We swore by blood magic... it is no longer even a choice. We will keep it hidden no matter what."

"Witch magic?" Kek snorted behind me, taking a step up to me, looking her usual bored self. "That's like Ouija boards, naked circles, and cute little séances, right? Can you call that *real* magic?"

I shot Kek a warning look.

"What? It's true." She rolled her eyes with a shrug.

Witches were human and held no "real" magic. Druids had gained the favor of the fae gods and were given true magic and long lives—but in exchange, they had to work in service of the high Fae rulers. No matter if they were treated well or not, it was still servitude.

Things changed as druid power grew and fae realized they couldn't control them. Propaganda spread far and wide, especially during Aneira's reign, when druids were slaughtered by the thousands.

What did my mother's witch coven have to do with any of this if they weren't considered powerful? And how did witches become necromancers?

"Don't forget, *demon*," Liam sneered with disgust. "Your bones are just as easy to rise and play my bitch as any human."

Kek lunged for him. Their side reacted, drawing their weapons on us as my group did the same.

"Stop!" Eabha held up her hand, stopping her clan in an instant. She might not have magic like a fae, but you could feel power and strength resonate from her. The quality that made people listen and want to follow her.

Ash grabbed Kek, tugging her back as she scowled and hissed at Liam. A smirk curved Liam's mouth, forcing Ash to hold her tighter.

"We aren't leaving without it." Warwick stepped past me, his shoulders widening, making his threat clear. "No matter what." He repeated her oath back, his lip curling. There was so much riding on this nectar, but it was *his* family who Killian was using as collateral.

Roan's lucerne hammer jabbed a hair away from Warwick's throat. The Wolf's eyes dropped to it with a snort.

"You think I'm afraid of death? I've walked straight into it, and it spit me back out." He smacked the sharp blade away from him like a fly, stirring up the coven, all their weapons directed at the legend.

"Then we are at a crossroads." Eabha's chin lifted as she peered up at him, then over to me. "As much as I wished in those final moments when you were being born that I'd have a chance to know you, to hold you…" I swear I saw a flicker of grief and love hint in her eyes, but then it was gone, leaving me to think I imagined it. "But our oath is binding. I do not want to fight you, daughter." Her manner was so matter-of-fact. "But I will."

The fragile thread between our groups snapped, hurling the opposite sides at each other in a clatter of metal. A whirlwind of energy and determination erupted, both sides believing they were right.

My head churned in the opposite direction of my heart. To find my mother after all this time… to discover I had family, and I had come from a line of witches. My mother was human, as my father was. We should have been hugging, rejoicing in this moment, catching up on lost years. Instead, I faced her on the other side of the conflict, her terrifying but beautiful war scythe pointing at me. I yanked out a smaller saber from my hip, the clash echoing in the night.

"I'm sorry." She twirled, her scythe crashing into my saber, making my bones rattle. "But I can't let you have it. This goes beyond your needs."

I gnashed my teethed together, our weapons knocking together. "You don't know why I want it. You know nothing about me."

The tip of her blade nicked my chest, reeling me back.

"And you know nothing, daughter." She grunted, coming for me again. I spun away. "You have no idea what power it holds."

"Does it?" I countered. "It looks useless now."

She shook her head, almost in pity at me. "Don't ever underestimate it."

Grunts and clanks of metal rang around me. Even if they had two more than us, our side was mainly fae. We should have them down in seconds. The coven might be struggling to be human again, to move and talk, but they had no problem fighting. It was as if they trained all day for the last twenty years. Fast, precise, and strong, they wielded their weapons with deadly strength.

I peered over at Warwick, watching him fight. Something rubbed me wrong. Granted, he was fighting three at once, but he seemed a bit slower, not as brutal as he could be. I mean, I witnessed him topple a giant in less than a minute.

I felt stuck in the middle. My mother wouldn't let us take the nectar, and he would not leave this place without it.

"Warwick?" I reached for our link.

BOOOOOOM!

A tremendous explosion detonated in the air, stopping us all with a gasp. Our heads snapped in the direction of the city miles away. The ground vibrated under our feet, our eyes reflecting the fire and smoke billowing into the sky.

I knew in my gut this was no Samhain prank. It was too vast, the glow of fire igniting the sky all the way over here. This was something massive and deadly.

"Scorpion?" I tried to connect to him, but I got nothing. Not even a hum, which usually told me if he was alive or not.

Nothing.

Oh gods… was he dead?

"Noooo." A deep bellow rang from my chest. I couldn't think; my need to get back dominated everything.

Nothing else mattered.

"Scorpion?"

Again, nothing.

"Andris?" I wasn't sure if I had any connection to him, but I felt nothing.

Panic sizzled and cracked my legs, directing me back to the river, to our home.

"Brexley?" Lukas yelled as I darted past, but my singular thought was getting back to my family and friends. I no longer cared about anything else.

Boots pounded the earth behind me, and I hoped they were all following me back, because I wouldn't wait. Not even for Warwick.

Kek helped me shove the boat off the bank, and I leaped in, starting the engine. The boat lurched, the motor churning the water as Ash, Lukas, and Kek jumped in.

Warwick wasn't with them.

I searched for him, finding only the absence of the energy that thrummed through our connection instead of the buzz I always felt and had grown accustomed to.

Dread plunged my stomach into the waves, the boat moving farther and farther away from shore, but my determination was set. Getting back to those who might need us, who may be already dead, was the priority.

I pushed the throttle, the boat picking up power and gliding us through the water. When we cleared the embankment where we had docked, my eyes snapped back, hoping to see him standing there.

It was empty.

Hurt knotted in my gut, though I understood why he chose the nectar instead. It represented freedom for his family.

Hitting the accelerator again, I felt desperate and terrified of what horror lay miles away.

My body stumbled as the boat tipped to the side. Then, like a creature crawling out of the depths of the swamp, a massive form heaved himself into the boat.

Soaking wet, pissed off, and sexy as hell, Warwick rose to his feet, his gaze set on me with intense fury. His boots and pants sloshed as he stomped in my direction. Water from his hair dripped on my cheeks as he loomed over me, the icy wind curling between us.

His lids narrowed, and something flickered across his face, but I

14

couldn't read it before he was gone, stomping down the steps into the small cabin below.

I blinked as a gasp stuck in my throat.

Terror gripped my lungs because I knew Scorpion wasn't the only one I couldn't feel.

The link between Warwick and me…

Was as silent as the dead.

"*A manóba!*" *Into the goblin!* Kek hissed, her nose wrinkling while Ash wrapped up the deep cut across her bicep.

"Hold still," Ash demanded.

Kek hissed at him again. "That little Wiccan fucker was faster than I thought he'd be."

"Maybe you need to start working out," Lukas retorted.

"Fuck off," she sniped. "Unless you want to work out with me? How about all three of us?"

Ash snorted, working on her arm, but his eyes slid to Lukas, then back to her.

They continued to chatter, their murmurs carrying over the wind.

I stood at the front of the boat like some carved figurehead at the bow; my nerves wound tighter as every minute passed, and I felt no closer to our destination. The scenery went by at a glacial pace. It seemed like forever until we hit the outskirts of the city.

After coming up from the cabin with a towel, trying to dry himself off, Warwick took over steering the boat. I hadn't been able to look at him, not ready to confront the truth, another thing that had gone wrong tonight.

When the ghosts back at Povstat sucked out my energy, I still felt Scorpion and Warwick. Like a fly landing on one spider web, vibrating through the others, telling you it was somewhere there.

Now… nothing.

Checking my bag, I found it empty, like it had been the first several times I looked. Hopefully Opie and Bitzy were safe, probably ripping up someone's curtain somewhere, parading around in leather chaps.

"Holy shit! Look!" Lukas yelled, his hand pointing. My head snapped up, the bag in my hands dropping to the floor, a cry catching in my throat.

My brain expected to see fire billowing from the Savage Lands, the base near the old market a war zone. I even half expected to see HDF bombed out, but my old home shone brightly in her full glory as we sailed by.

Lukas pointed to the opposite side of the river. To the fae palace.

"Oh, my gods..." My hands went to my mouth, my gaze taking in the scene, my heart screaming.

The grand palace, the symbol of the fae dominance, sitting high on the hill, was aflame. Smoke mushroomed from the debris on one side. The left wing was in ruins, fire stretching up to the dome like it was trying to grow as tall. I had stayed in one of those rooms, now destroyed. It was the side of his personal quarters.

Killian!

A sickness knotted my gut. Was this my uncle's doing? He told me they wanted to let Killian and Istvan know they were here and getting stronger. This seemed extreme for him, though he was the one who blew up Halálház. He had the resources, army, and ability to do it.

Why Killian and not HDF?

"Fuck!" Warwick bellowed, snapping the wheel toward the destruction. The realization it wasn't just Killian in there hit me hard.

Eliza and Simon.

The boat rammed into the dock in front of the castle. The heat reached us far below the wreckage, the flames kissing my frozen skin. Warwick leaped out, his feet already pounding up the jetty to the street.

Without a word, I tore after him, doubling my speed to catch up. His head darted briefly to the side, seeing me next to him, but he paid no other notice to me as he sprinted for the stairs leading us up the hill.

With a sick déjà vú, I realized it was the exact path we took when he broke me out of here a few months ago. Now we were running straight back in.

My legs burned and my lungs ached, my body still weak from what happened earlier, but we didn't stop. Pure adrenaline spurred us on.

The heat grew intense when we reached the palace grounds, pooling sweat on my lower back. Screams blended with the lash of the flames. Figures who worked there ran by, heading for safety. They gave us peculiar looks as we ran straight into the destruction.

The moment we entered, smoke swarmed my lungs, the taste of ash coating my tongue, making me cough.

Warwick and I pulled our shirts over our noses and darted through the wreckage of the first story, my eyes watering from the thick plumes.

"Eliza! Simon?" Warwick bellowed out their names, only for his cries to get swallowed up by the chaos.

"How do you get down to the prisoner cells?" His look was wild, his muscles tight with fear... and I couldn't feel one ounce of it.

Swallowing back more of my panic, I searched the place for stairs. I knew very little of the actual palace, spending all my time either in the labs, cells, or for one day, the luxurious bedroom upstairs. Bile burned the back of my throat.

"Oh, no." Frantically, I turned toward the grand staircase, panic rushing me up the steps.

"Kovacs!" Warwick yelled. "Where are you going?"

I didn't open my mouth to respond, pushing my legs quicker to my destination.

For once, I wanted my instincts to be wrong about Killian, though I knew they weren't. As much as everyone painted him a monster, he wasn't. They were leverage, not prisoners. He would have given Eliza and her son a bedroom. A guarded one, granted, but he wouldn't put them in a cell.

Reaching the upper landing, I turned right, down the hazy passageway, the dense air clawing at my lungs, the smell singeing my nose, the heat burning my skin.

It was a second before I noticed the floor disappeared. A cry sprang from my lips, my feet backpedaling as my boots started to slip off the precipice, my stomach dropping with terror.

Warwick's arm looped around my waist, yanking me back from the rim, pressing me into his body. Our chests heaved together with fear. We both stared in silence at the remains. From the boat, you couldn't see how extreme the damage was. The entire wing was gone. Gutted, burned, and decimated, barely a skeleton remained of this side of the building. Ashes rained down like tears.

The once-prized beauty was now nothing but cinders and rubble. No human or fae would have survived.

Was Killian underneath there? Eliza and Simon?

"Warwick." The whisper barely made it from my throat, grief coiling around it like a snake.

"No," Warwick growled in my ear. Fury stiffened his form, his arms dropping as he stepped back. I twisted to face him. "You don't know they were there." He shook his head, retreating farther, rage filling his eyes, daring me to defy him. "They're safe... in some cell below."

"No. They aren't in the cells below." A woman's deep voice spoke with vicious giddiness behind him as his body started to convulse, his eyes going wide. "There were in the room he had designed for *you*."

"Warwick!" I lurched for him as a woman stepped from his shadow, holding a device against his spine, electrocuting him into paralysis. His body continued to shudder, his jaw locking as a jarring noise gurgled from his throat.

My feet came to a halting stop, the oxygen knocked from my lungs. Terror crashed down in my gut seeing her face.

Nyx.

I reached for my gun.

"Don't." She sneered, pointing a gun at me with her other hand. She was tall and broader than a lot of the guys here. Quick, trained, and out for revenge.

A deadly combo.

Using him as a shield, she stood slightly behind him, smeared with soot and blood. Her eyes were bright and almost crazed. She kept the device on his neck and moved the barrel of the gun to his temple.

"You make one move, and you'll be picking your lover's brains out of your hair for months." She rammed her gun harder into Warwick's head. A muffled grunt came from him, but his body didn't move.

The device she was using was a type of stun gun from the West. A newer gadget that was only issued to the Unified Nation's private bounty hunters. Istvan had been searching the black market for them for years to no avail. Very rare and grotesquely expensive.

And Nyx had one.

"Warwick?" Our link was empty. My call fell into a black hole. Biting on my lip, I swallowed back the trepidation soaking in my skin, not wanting to think about what it meant.

"You touch him—"

"And you'll what?" Smugness shone through her features. "What will you do? You may have fooled my lord, but I instantly saw what you were— a lying, deceitful, treacherous bitch. And now you will pay for what you did." She zapped him again, his nose flaring, his teeth gritting through an agonized growl.

"Stop!" My body jolted, a small cry sliding through my teeth. My eyes met his for a moment, but I got nothing but a stony expression back.

"Mmmm… the sweet taste of revenge." She glowered at me. "How does it feel to know *your own* army did this… killed *his* family?"

Warwick jerked with a grunt at her statement, his eyes turning darker, nerves down his neck dancing.

"You're lying." Was it true Sarkis's army did this?

"I'm not." Nyx let out a dry, demented laugh, leaning in closer to Warwick. "Your sister and nephew are dead, Farkas. Crushed and buried under the rubble there. And Kovac's to blame… not that I didn't enjoy every second knowing how much pain this would cause you as well." Cruelty widened her mouth. "How does it feel? To lose everything you love because of her?"

A low vibration came from Warwick. The Wolf. The beast. His shoulders twitched, his chest pumping in and out, his eyes on me. Furious and brutal.

"What do I have to do with this?"

"Everything!" Nyx screeched, sounding more like a hawk. "It all leads back to you. From the moment you stepped over the fae line, you've brought nothing but death and destruction. You are a cancer to us. You've destroyed everything," she squawked, her voice rising with emotion. She was a moment away from snapping. I could feel her frantic anger building. One twitch of her finger, and Warwick's brains would be spilling on the floor.

Something deep in my gut was scared this time that he might actually die.

"*All* of them fell on their knees for you," she spat at me. "What was it about you? You made them all blind and stupid. And all you did was lead them to their deaths."

"What are you talking about?"

Another manic grin seized her lips.

"The one guarding their room." She pushed the barrel deeper into Warwick's temple, making fury scorch from his eyes, a sound huffing through his nose. "Another who was enamored by you. A *spy* among us. I knew something was going on when I caught him in your room. Traitorous horse-shifter. He was under your spell too. Well, he got what he deserved. He's nothing but ground horse meat now, buried right under your feet."

Vomit sizzled up my throat.

Oh gods… Zander.

"No," I whispered, my head shaking, pleading for her to say it was just a cruel joke. I could picture his soft brown eyes, the kindness he showed me in Halálház—an anchor in hell. The way he kissed me, the risk he took to get me out of the palace, knowing he could be caught at any time.

Agony ruptured in my chest, a crack across my heart.

"But you had to take everything from me, didn't you?" Her cruel smile faded, her eyes filling up with tears as something altered inside her mind. The gleeful malice shifted into a sorrowful abandonment, her pupils fully dilating, her fury pinning on me.

Her prey.

The energy changed in an instant, and I knew I only had seconds.

"You killed him." The gun in her unsteady hand tapped against Warwick's head, her finger curling tighter. She was losing control. Any moment she could pull the trigger, and he would be dead.

The knowledge I wouldn't be able to bring him back, that my quota was up, swirled deep in my subconscious.

I held up my hands. I needed to stop her. "Nyx..." I took a step, my gaze snapping to Warwick, trying to communicate what I was about to do. He watched me, the monster inside him contained against its will.

"Stop!" She zapped him again, his legs dipping, agony vibrating in his throat. She adjusted her hold on the gun. I stopped. "You have to watch him die. Feel the utter agony of losing everything," she shrieked, her hair starting to appear more like feathers, her fingers growing into talons. "You killed him!" I knew she wasn't talking about Warwick. "You took him from me... from us!"

My heart thumped in my ears, dread filling my stomach. "What are you talking about?"

"You are to blame!" Fury burned in her eyes at me. "And you will pay."

"For what?"

"For my liege..." She pushed the barrel into Warwick's head.

"Lord Killian is *dead*!"

Chapter 3

Her words sunk in slowly, but my mind rejected the claim, certain she was wrong.

Killian? A flash of his face, his seductive voice and beautiful eyes. The time we spent together in his labs, the man I kissed on the balcony.

"No," I whispered. Grief tore through my limbs, pounding in my chest. "I don't believe you. You're lying." My head shook vehemently. The Lord of the Fae couldn't be dead. He was too powerful, too strong. He was larger than life. One of the most formidable fae in the east. Pure fairy. Yet, I understood that immortal life didn't mean they couldn't be killed. And since the wall came down between worlds, they were a lot more susceptible to death.

Was it strange I never imagined Killian needing rest, his bedroom more for show? Even running up here, I didn't allow myself to think Killian would be in his quarters. He was always working in his office or far below in the labs.

"See for yourself." Nyx let out an eerie laugh, waving the gun toward the destruction. I turned my head automatically and peered behind me at the wreckage, at the aftermath the bombs left behind. Several floors collapsed onto each other, rubble and debris in a smoldering heap. No way anyone could survive.

"He was in his quarters when the bomb hit." Nyx's tone sounded more and more unhinged. "I was just heading there for my guard shift." I noticed more of the burn marks and wounds covering her face, the soot caking her uniform.

"This ends tonight." She held the gun to Warwick's head, and his eyes went wild, while his muscles were locked. "A king for a legend."

Her finger pushed harder on the trigger.

"No!" I screamed, leaping forward.

Bang!

The echo of the bullet and my scream bounced off the smoky air. My entire world stopped. My gaze went to Warwick. Our eyes connected. A lifetime passed in a millisecond, the horror leaving me frozen like him. Locked in time and space, knowing I could not save him, my soul shattered into pieces.

I drank him in as I waited for death to take him back for good.

Nyx's body dropped.

A yelp stuck in my throat, shock and confusion jerking my head to her crumpled form on the ground, then to the figure behind her.

Ash stood there, his gun still pointed at her, reminding me of the time in the alley when Warwick rescued Birdie and me from a similar fate.

This time, Warwick was saved.

"Hell! You two really do need around-the-clock babysitters." Ash shook his head, lowering his gun.

A choked laugh heaved up my throat, relief watering my eyes, loosening my chest with a sob.

"You okay?" I moved to Warwick, my scrutiny rolling over every inch, reassuring myself he was alive and all right. My fingers grazed his arm, and his shoulder jerked, but he wouldn't look at me.

"What the hell is wrong with him?" Ash came around, noticing Warwick hadn't moved or talked.

"She stunned him." I peered down at Nyx, her face planted in the burned rug, blood pooling around her. The device lay feet away from her body.

Warwick muttered something, stretching and curling his hands.

"Come on! What the hell is taking so long?" Kek's voice yelled from the end of the hall, Luk next to her on lookout. "We got more guards coming."

"Can you move?" Ash asked Warwick, his hands touching certain nerves in Warwick's arm, getting a reflex.

"Ye-ah." His head dipped, the word thickly rumbling from him.

"Let's get back to my place. I've got stuff that should help ease the numbness and stress on your muscles," Ash replied.

Shouts from below rang from the stairway.

"We have to go now," Kek yelled again.

Warwick stumbled as he started to head down the hall, Ash helping him get his footing. I took a step to run after them, but paused at Nyx's body. The shadow of the flames from the wreckage flicked her hair-like feathers, giving the illusion her body was heaving with air, like a dying animal. A stab of guilt tapped at my conscience, knowing I did take everything from her in some way: her love, her king, her revenge... and her life.

Then it was gone. I swiped up the stun gun, stuffing it into my jacket pocket, and ran, leaving the fresh graves of family, friends, and enemies in my wake.

My body shivered, but I didn't feel the cold. Or anything.

The boat ride back toward Savage Lands was silent. An endless hole of darkness.

Anguish and wrath were shrouded and cloaked in our silence.

The intensity of Samhain was slowly dissolving as dawn approached. This day felt like a never-ending horror. The Grim Reaper's version of the Games, where he devoured a gluttonous feast of souls.

Happy birthday to me.

Warwick paced the front, the moonlight shadowing his outline. His movements became sturdier, though his muscles stayed locked and tight.

Not in shock, but in fury.

Everyone in the boat could feel it pulsate off him, his silence growing more deadly as time let him absorb the truth.

The loss.

My mouth couldn't seem to open, to say anything which might help ease his pain. I couldn't ease mine. I felt like nothing more than a burned-out shell. Empty and vacant.

Lukas steered us to the dock, Warwick leaping off the second he could.

"Warwick!" Ash yelled after him, worry in his tone.

Nothing would stop him. His shoulders curled slightly, set on his mission.

"Fuck," Ash hissed.

"What?" Anxiety bubbled in my stomach.

"I haven't seen that look in twenty years." Ash's green eyes filled with a panicked horror. "It's like *he's* back…" He continued to watch his friend move up the dock, licking his lip.

"Remember when I told you after he returned from death, his personality intensified? He craved death, lived for revenge, felt nothing unless he killed those who wronged him?" He briefly glanced at me, then back at the road. "It seemed to change when he met you. Whatever connection you guys shared calmed him. He *felt* again…"

My neck snapped to Ash, the base of my head prickling with alarm, not able to speak or move. Our link had been severed.

"Looks like the legend, the *Wolf*, is back and seeking revenge."

"Revenge? Who could he?" I tapered off. There was only one he could blame right now. One who ordered the attack on the palace and killed Warwick's family.

Andris.

I took off running, fear pumping my legs, dread slamming my heart against my ribs. I had already lost Andris once tonight, had ripped the shreds of space to bring him back. I would not lose him again. If Warwick hurt him, there would be no coming back from it—for either of us. There would be no us.

My boots slapped against the ramp, moving to the street toward the old marketplace, which was still standing. The block behind it was not. I knew it had been blown up. I'd seen it through Scorpion, but observing it in person was like a punch to the stomach. Figures milled around in the debris, digging up dead bodies and attending to the hurt.

What was left of the rebel army? The base suffered the same level of devastation the palace had. Only parts of its shell remained, while most of the block was no more than rubble.

Strange both the base and palace were bombed tonight.

The same way…

Something connected in my brain as my eyes roamed over the devastation, spotting my uncle in the distance, giving orders and trying to help his people.

I couldn't even enjoy the relief at seeing him alive and well before I spotted a massive form striding up to Andris, a large hand wrapping around his throat.

"Warwick!" I screamed, clambering over blocks and cement, trying to reach them. "No!"

My palms scraped over the wreckage, my pants shredding at the knees as I rushed to them.

"Warwick, Stop!" I scrambled up, grabbing Warwick's arm. "Let him go!"

"No." He drew my uncle's face to his, baring his teeth. "You killed my family."

Andris's mouth opened and closed, but nothing could come out, his skin turning a deep red as he struggled to get away.

"No, he didn't!" I yanked and tugged at his massive bicep. I tried to push deep, see if I could use his energy against him. But there was nothing there. "Warwick, please!" I begged, my nails digging into his hand. "Let him go! He didn't do it!"

Warwick's gaze darted briefly to me, then back to my uncle, squeezing tighter.

"He ordered the attack on the palace."

"Let him go." Scorpion stepped up to us, yanking out his pistol and shoving it into Warwick's face. "Now!"

Warwick grabbed the gun with his free hand, flipping it and pointing it at Scorpion, ready to pull the trigger.

"No!" I bellowed, shoving myself in front of Scorpion, the barrel of the gun hitting the middle of my chest.

"Get the fuck out of the way, Kovacs."

"No." I snarled, my chin high, pushing my ribs against the barrel. "You want to kill someone here? You have to go through me first."

Warwick hesitated, an emotion I couldn't decipher fluttering through his eyes.

"My uncle didn't kill your family. Nor were they the ones who set those bombs." I reached out, my fingers pulling on the ones still wrapped around Andris's throat. "Think about it. This place was bombed *before* the palace, and HDF is left alone? That's not a coincidence. Plus, to do so much damage, they would have to get close. It had to be an inside job."

"Exactly. Zander," Warwick growled.

"And Zander's plan was to die with them?" The simmering grief over his death, over Killian's, drifted closer to the surface. I had no time to really mourn or accept either one.

"Zan—Zan—dead?" My uncle's voice was strangled. He jerked his head as he took in the news, shock and sorrow filling his eyes.

"Warwick, it wasn't Andris." I gently touched his arm.

Warwick growled, his hand squeezing tighter, fury riding his shoulders. My uncle's eyes started to pop, breaking blood vessels staining them red.

"Stop!" I could feel he needed someone to blame, something to hurt before his grief destroyed him. "Let. Him. Go," I demanded, moving more in front of Andris. "I will fight you, Farkas. And you will have to kill me too."

Warwick's gaze jerked to mine, his chest heaving, a noise working up his throat. It was a full fifteen seconds before he dipped his head, sucking in air, then dropped his hands and stepped back.

Andris bent over, coughing and gulping for air. Ling rushed to his side, trying to soothe him. I hadn't noticed the group that had circled around us, many with guns pointed at Warwick, ready to shoot him if I hadn't interceded.

Spitting on the ground, Andris slowly stood, still struggling to breathe, his hand on his throat. His voice came out low and harsh. "I didn't order the bombing at the palace."

"You had something planned." Warwick's shoulders drew back again.

"We did, but we got attacked before the mission even left here. And it wasn't at the palace." He hacked, clearing his throat. "We were going to plant something back at the old prison. A reminder we had eyes on him. That we could get to him again if we wanted."

Warwick's brows furrowed, doubt creeping in.

"It wasn't us," Scorpion growled.

Oxygen huffed through the Wolf's nose, his head turning away.

"Is Zander really dead?" Andris looked to me.

I nodded in affirmation.

Andris's face crinkled with grief, his throat bobbing as he absorbed the news. He gave himself a moment, then he lifted his head, the commander of Sarkis army back in control. A leader had no time to mourn the dead. They had to lead the living.

"We heard the bomb go off across the river. I'm sorry for your loss." Andris dropped his hand from his neck, peering around. "But right now, we have our own worries, our own bodies to bury. I don't have the time to care about Killian's troubles."

"Killian's dead," Warwick replied, emotionless. He might as well have dropped another bomb. Hearing it out loud knifed my heart, the emotion I was still holding at bay creeping up higher.

"What?" Andris stilled, his pink face blanching, though I noticed how healed his wounds appeared, when only hours ago he had been dead and buried under wreckage too. "Killian is dead? Are you sure? How do you know?"

"We were there." I bit down on my lip until I tasted blood, my mind still not allowing his death to sink in. "It was his private wing that was blown up."

Killian seemed invincible. Impervious to death. He was the fae ruler. Beautiful in his cruelty. Sexy in his deceit. Powerful. Aloof, but under those formidable layers, he was also caring and, in his own odd way, kind of sweet.

"*Az istenit!*" *God damn it!* Andris ran his hand through his hair. Why did it look a lot less gray than I remembered? "How could this happen?" He started to pace frantically. "This is extremely bad."

"I thought you'd want to get him out of the way," I replied.

"No, I wanted to unite us." Andris stopped right in front of me. "Killian was far more likely to change the status quo. With him gone, this country is even more unstable. Dangerous. Making it clear for—"

"For Istvan to come up and take hold of the power," I finished for him.

"Yes," he agreed. "With the fae side in disarray, trying to figure out who will lead, it opens up an opportunity for Istvan."

"This was planned and coordinated to make sure it would take Killian down. Istvan wouldn't leave it to chance. Which means—"

"Which means Zander wasn't the only spy infiltrating Killian's circle." Andris pinched his nose.

Before the idea had fully developed in my head, my gaze was snapping over my shoulder, searching. "Where is he?"

"Who?" Andris asked.

My boots were already crunching over the debris, my head snapping around, spotting who I was looking for in the distance. He was tucked up against a bombed-out building, several guards surrounding him, his wrists cuffed.

"Did you know about this?" I seethed, rushing up to a person who held me so many nights growing up, who used to be my entire world.

Caden's brown eyes tapered on me, his jaw clenching. He was covered in dirt, blood, and cuts. His eyes were puffy with exhaustion, but he pulled himself up when he saw me.

"Did you?" I hollered, my hands slamming into his chest, cracking his head back against the wall. "Tell me!" My fingers rolled into his shirt, throttling him.

He only glared down at me with disgust.

"Did you know your father was going to bomb Killian and us?"

Again, Caden didn't answer, his jaw grinding tighter, his glare going past me.

"Tell me!" I slammed him repeatedly against the wall.

"No, I didn't know." His lip curled. "But even if I did, I wouldn't have told you. We now have fewer fae and human traitors in this world."

Red bled into my vision, and something snapped inside me, my fist finding its target. The night's events, my heartache, and my grief severed my control. Fury fired my anguish, and I released it on Caden, striking again and again.

So much had happened tonight, and not just the bombings and deaths. My mother was a necromancer and was now alive because of me. I brought her back, along with Andris. And I wasn't just connected to this mythical nectar… I was it.

I had no clue exactly what I was, but the moment I felt myself discovering it, it had been ripped away. And now all those things which hummed in my veins and whispered in my ear, telling me I was different, were dead, floating down the river with the rest of the carcasses.

I never felt more human and lost. Angry and scared.

"Kovacs." Warwick's hands grabbed for me, but I couldn't stop. Anguish flowed from me like lava, burning and blackening what was left inside. Hollowing me out. "Stop."

He yanked me back, holding me tightly to his chest. Heaving, my blurry gaze cleared on Caden. His half-conscious body slid to the ground, blood gushing from his wounds, red liquid coating his teeth, his eye blooming with bruises. His face was a bloody pulp.

Shock and horror knocked me back into Warwick.

I had done that. Caden and I sparred all the time, but this was different. I had never attacked him. Never purposely hurt him, especially when he couldn't fight back.

This was the me who survived Halálház, ruthless and callous. The one who killed Aron in cold blood.

I never thought I was capable of turning that monster on Caden.

My body went limp in Warwick's arms. The walls protecting me from the impending emotion exploded. But instead of crying, I went numb.

Drowning in my grief.

People wondered why I didn't like my birthday.

It meant death.

Chapter 4

The sun started to rise, the hazy November light barely brushing at the buildings as they appeared like a Monet painting, but underneath the strokes were more of a Picasso. Broken up and stitched together in pieces, colored with blood.

Bodies still lay underneath the remains, trapped in a tomb where they would stay. Life in the Savage Lands meant no time to mourn or bury the dead. You had to keep going to protect those who were still alive.

In the distance, hyenas sang their warrior cry, their howls a warning they would be coming to pick off the weak and claim our dead.

"Fuck," Warwick grunted, his warning shooting to Andris. "We have to go."

"Zuz, Maddox, Wesley?" Andris whistled, motioning for his men to start moving. "Head for the new base."

"It's not ready yet," Zuz replied.

"Doesn't matter. Get everyone going, quickly!" They reacted instantly to Andris's order, helping those in need and rounding up what was left of the army.

"Scorpion. Birdie. You are in charge of them." Andris motioned to Caden and a figure a few yards away, and I did a double-take. I hadn't even seen Hanna there, but the way she watched me, I had no doubt she saw my assault on Caden, who was her friend and the boy I was supposed to love.

Covered in dust and wounds with her hands cuffed and her wavy blond hair matted in a ponytail, she glared at me with utter abhorrence, knotting my chest with shame. Scorpion pushed her to get moving, her feet tripping over each other, then she finally looked away from me, rolling her head high.

A young fae assisted Birdie, both helping Caden up and getting him moving inland.

"If Istvan is the culprit…" Andris turned my attention back to him, his feet retreating as Ling came up to him, his hand touching hers. "He'll be sending out people soon to do a sweep, making sure the explosion did the job, and if it didn't…"

"He'll finish us off." Warwick peered in the direction of HDF.

A sweep. Both Andris and I were familiar with those. In training, Bakos had us simulate doing sweeps for months. How to split up and come in from all sides, what to look for, what dangers and situations to expect. How to pick off the survivors.

We were sitting ducks here. Weak and vulnerable.

"Just imagine if he finds we have Caden," Andris added before taking off after his army, heading for their new location.

Istvan would rain down unimaginable wrath on us if he discovered we were holding his only son hostage. Two reasons I knew Istvan didn't know we had Caden: First, he would have never risked his son by bombing the building in the first place. Second, Istvan wouldn't have waited this long to do a sweep. This would have been a recovery mission. They would have descended on us with a full sniper team coming in to take Caden back.

Howls of the hyenas grew louder, their bloodthirsty cries licking the air with their proximity.

"Guys?" Ash yelled, tugging his pack straps tighter, the fae book safety on his back. I could see him, Kek, and Lukas over Warwick's shoulder, waiting on us. "Decide."

Without a word, Warwick grabbed my arm, tugging me toward Ash, in the opposite way Sarkis's army was traveling.

I yanked my arm free with a violent jerk, stopping him. His brow lowered as he peered back at me. He didn't even bother asking what I wanted or where I felt I needed to be. I was not his chess piece to move around how he saw fit.

"What are you doing?" His nose flared, annoyance and rage shooting from his eyes.

I glared back, my stance burrowing into the ground. Defying the mighty Wolf.

The tension between us weaved and expanded. It was living and breathing, while the link between us was lifeless. Was it gone for good? Another victim, burned and buried with the other bodies we lost tonight?

"I'm going with my uncle. They need me." *Need us*, but I didn't say that. "You can go." I laid the challenge down at his feet. "But I'm not leaving Andris or any of my *family*."

Warwick's expression turned to stone, but I could sense the fury under his skin. The way he breathed, how his hands curled and shoulders inched forward.

Lukas and Kek came to my side, their path with me, but my eyes stayed locked on the legend, neither one of us giving an inch.

"Come with me or don't. You're *free* to do what you want." The jab hissed off my tongue. The truth feeling like a cut across my chest, making it hard to breathe, which caused my anger to swell.

There was a good chance the feelings he thought he felt for me were only from the connection. Now it was gone.

Before he could see my emotions, I turned away, jogging after my uncle, the demon and half-fae beside me. We turned the corner out of sight, and more of my heart shattered when he didn't follow.

The touch of morning light drew deep-shaded curtains through the streets and alleys, presenting easy hiding places and blind spots. Half of what was once Sarkis's army moved through the silent streets, the hour still too early for many to be up, and making us even more of a target.

The back of my neck prickled. The sensation of eyes on me from the buildings had my gaze darting around with my gun out, primed to shoot. The howls of the hyenas in the distance spread goosebumps down my arms.

Though, it wasn't them that had my heart beating in my ears; they would go straight for the easy meals. The ones that were already dead.

It was something else.

Intuition. A decade of training. Knowing the enemy so well I could feel them creeping in.

Surrounding us.

Lukas's head snapped to the side, his muscles constricting. His reaction needed no explanation. He could feel it too. Besides his fae senses, his training was laced into every fiber of his being, ready to respond to a threat.

A disturbing growl emerged from Kek, her eyes darkening as her demon senses picked up on the danger.

Shit.

My mouth opened, ready to warn Andris, but it was too late.

A zing swooshed through the air, the sound of metal splintering through flesh and bone as one fae in the very front went down without a sound. The bullet went through his brain, killing him, before he could even cry out.

The reaction was instant. Andris's soldiers dove for him, shielding their leader. Yells and commotion pinged off the buildings on either side. Weapons drawn as our group condensed together, trying to find the source of the threat.

It was silent for a moment. Even the air seemed like it was holding its breath as all of us coiled together.

Pop!

A girl behind me dropped to the ground, a bullet between her eyes.

Pop!

A shot came from one side. Then the other side. They were moving in, but able to hide among the narrow alleys.

Another one of ours dropped.

They were picking us off one by one.

"Go! Go!" I screamed, motioning everyone to head down a passage. We learned to sweep in training, but Bakos also had us do simulations where we were the ones being surrounded. To flip it around and get them all on one side, you had to break through one way hard and fast, spilling out of their circle like liquid, forcing them to regroup behind you.

Our movements flipped everything into chaos. Gunfire and figures darted everywhere, the shadows easily fooling the eye. Our group barreled forward, trying to break HDF's line.

"Help! They have me and Caden as hostages. Help!" Hanna's voice spiked up with the barrage of bullets bouncing off the buildings. Scorpion grabbed her, covering her mouth with his hand. She struggled against him, but he kept her pinned to his chest, trying to move her down the path, kicking and flailing against him.

"Stop shooting, or I blow your pretty prince's head off." Birdie shouted, clean and sharp, her words somehow making it above the pandemonium. Her gun cocked, the sound snapping loudly as she pressed the barrel to Caden's temple. "Make a move, and you will be scooping up his brains with a shovel."

A muscle under Caden's puffy eye flexed, his jaw clenched so hard I could see the veins in his neck.

The firing stopped. The silence was louder than the volley of bullets.

I had no doubt they were struggling with what to do. We were taught to sacrifice ourselves for the greater good. One soldier was not worth the lives of our mission, but Caden was no ordinary soldier. He was HDF's prince. Their future leader. Istvan's only son and heir. They would not risk him.

Taking up the cue, our group made our escape down the alley, forcing Andris to move, though I could tell he wanted to be the one to make sure all his people made it first.

"No!" Caden bellowed. "Shoot now! Kill them!" Fury danced in his eyes, and I knew he hated that they waved the white flag for him. Caden was proud. He never wanted to be treated differently from the other soldiers. He wanted to earn his place, even if it didn't really matter if he did or not.

"That is an order!" he screamed as Birdie and another guard yanked him back, practically dragging him. "Shoot them!"

They still hesitated.

Caden fought against Birdie and two other guards trying to silence him and move him away. "Sarkis's ex-general, Andris Takacs! He's alive! A traitor working with the fae. Kill them now. I command you!"

My stomach sank, knowing Istvan would learn his old friend was still alive—not only alive but leading the insurgent group against him and detaining his son.

Caden's last instruction did the trick. Shells lobbied into the passage, zipping by my ear as I saw HDF uniforms hiding behind dumpsters and walls, progressing toward us.

Kek grunted next to me as a bullet nipped across her arm and blood began pooling out, her eyes going down to the injury. "Your little boyfriend is starting to piss me off." She frowned at the wound. "And I liked this shirt."

Another shell skimmed her blue hair.

"Oh, hell no." A growl crawled up her throat, scraping fear into my spine, the sound more like some unearthly beast. Her eyes turned black, then her arm waved toward a dumpster. The entire thing skidded across the cobble, revealing a handful of HDF behind.

Their eyes widened, startled and scared.

I knew all four. One had been in my class, Rafe, the other three had been in Caden's. Their eyes found me, rage and hate filling their features.

"Fucking traitorous bitch," one yelled.

"Get them," another added, not realizing they were about to face a demon.

"Go, little lamb." She waved me off. "My demon wants to play with your friends."

"You sure?"

She rolled her eyes at me before curling her finger at the men, her lips spreading into a chilling grin. "Come here, little boys."

"Come on!" Luk yanked me with him as shots whizzed by, forcing us to duck. We weaved through the tight passage, spotting some of our group ahead, fanning out into the main streets, escaping the noose around us.

Luk was ahead, his long legs scarfing up the distance, while I struggled to keep up. I was normally a lot faster than this, but my body felt like it was stuck in slow motion, struggling to pick up speed no matter how much I pushed. Luk curved around a corner up ahead out of my eyeline.

"Lu—" My cry to him cut off.

Wham!

As if a train smacked into me, the impact sent me flying. Twinges wrenched through my nerves as my bones crunched onto the concrete, my gun skidding across the ground. A heavy body landed painfully on top of mine, a cry puffing from my lips. My legs and arms thrashed against my assailant, my elbow ramming back into his face with a crunch.

"Fuckin' bitch," he snarled, grabbing my arms painfully and pinning me down. "I have fought you so many times. I dreamed of taking you down one day." The familiar voice vehemently hissed in my ear.

Rafe. A massive guy from my class, who I defeated almost every time. He was arrogant as the rest, but quieter. Socially distant. He kept to himself. I never thought much about him either way, except when he was across the mat from me. But I always felt him watching me, pissed every time he lost to me.

"You know, all the guys used to bet about you... who would fuck you. Though, Aron bragged all the time he got in there first, popped your cherry." Hate and shame sizzled up my esophagus, knowing Aron had. "We also bet who would beat you in practice, put you in the clinic... or who could get your mouth around their cock first." It was the most I ever heard him say at once, and suddenly I missed his silence. "The *teacher's pet*. You are the last person I ever thought would become a fae-lovin' traitor. Vile bitch. You should be taught a lesson." He grabbed for his belt, spearing ice down my veins.

No. I thrashed against him but couldn't seem to wiggle away or tip him over. What the hell was wrong with me?

"Stop fighting me." The barrel of a gun jammed into the back of my head while he tugged at my pants. "You deserve everything you get, fae-lover," he seethed in my ear, pushing down my underwear.

"Try again, *faszszopó*." *Dicksucker*. A feral growl thundered before Rafe's body was torn from mine. I flipped around to see Farkas lift the big guy off the ground by the throat like he weighed nothing. Ruthless. Vicious. The legend I remembered who killed the bull-shifter with one hand was in front of me. Warwick throbbed with pitiless anger, his eyes dark, sparking with revenge and death.

"It's you who will be taught a lesson." He squeezed his fingers around

Rafe's neck, making his eyes bulge. My classmate's legs kicked frantically, his hands clawing at Warwick, every second growing weaker. "A deadly one."

Like crushing a tomato, Warwick's hand clamped down, and the blood vessels popped in Rafe's eyes as the snap of his neck cracked off the stone. The Wolf snarled as he let the body drop in a heap, staring at the corpse as if he wanted to bring him back to prolong the kill this time.

Eventually, he twisted to stare down at me with a sneer. "You're welcome, princess."

Gashing my teeth, I climbed to my feet, forgetting the leap in my heart from thinking he came for me. That he followed me. "Fuck you."

"Looks like I have to get back in a very long line if I want a turn again."

Rage fueled me forward. *"Eszem azt az ici-pici szívedet!"* *I'm gonna rip your heart out and feast on it!*

"Whoa! Whoa!" Ash stepped between us, his hands on my arms, pushing me back. I hadn't even noticed he was there until now, the mythical asshole always seeming to dominate my focus. "Just calm down. This is not the time or place. You can kill or fuck each other later. We need to get out of here."

"Brex?" Luk's panicked voice came back around the corner, his shoulders easing when he saw me and who I was with. "Don't do that. You scared the crap out of me. I turned around and you were gone."

Warwick puffed up, stomping for Lukas.

"Next time, keep your fucking eyes on her at all times, asshole." Warwick got an inch from his face, fury streaking his features. "If you leave her again like that, I won't hesitate to gut you."

"Warwick!" I tried to shove him off Lukas, not even moving him an inch. "Back off."

"Fucksake, I leave you guys alone for a moment, and everything goes to hell." Kek strolled up to us, blood and gore streaking her cheeks, and tinting her blue hair red, her eyes back to normal. "That was fun with your little friends. Got a little rush there." She licked her fingers as her gaze drifted to Ash. "Always makes me extremely horny."

A slight smile hinted on Ash's mouth before he turned away. "We need to go. The hyenas aren't too far behind, and there could be more HDF."

Warwick, still in a stand-off with Lukas, curled his lip, his shoulder ramming into Luk's hard, almost knocking him to the ground as he passed, following Ash.

"You okay?" Luk asked me, his glower still tossed back at Warwick.

"Yeah, I'm fine." I touched his arm, reassuring him. "Ignore him. He's being an asshole."

"Hard to." Luk shot another glare at Warwick. "I'm sorry. I didn't realize I was so far ahead."

"I was extra slow for some reason. Don't worry about it."

"I worry about you anyway. But I don't think he's the kind to lay down false threats."

Walking with Kek and Luk, Ash and Warwick were a few yards in front of us.

"Like I said, ignore him. His ego is all puffed up and obscenely massive." I rolled my eyes.

"And if you recall, princess." Warwick peered over his shoulder at me. "So is my dick."

The new headquarters was a row of neo-classic buildings on Kürt Street. Boarded up and long abandoned, the buildings were condemned, and even the homeless avoided them. But whatever it looked like on the outside, the underground area was vast, reinforced, and secure enough. It was clear Andris had found this property a while back and had been preparing it. The space was very basic, but there was the computer room with a few screens up, a workout and training space, canteen, and an entire wing for the sleeping quarters, some with beds and some still empty. The place was up and running enough for Sarkis's army. What was left of it.

The main underground space was filled with the wounded: gunshots, broken bones, burned, bloody, beaten. Their eyes were swollen with grief, pain, and exhaustion, their shoulders sagging with misery. We had taken a huge blow, and by the faces and quiet mutterings, you could feel the loss echo in the room.

Deflated and dejected.

"Brexley." Andris came up to me, not looking at Farkas. "So glad you came with us."

"I couldn't leave. Not now with so much going on." Exhaustion started to weigh heavily on my bones. "Are Hanna and Caden… ?"

"They're fine." Weariness rode over Andris's expression. "But now HDF knows we have them. Knows about me. We thought we had a target on us before. There's nothing Istvan won't do to track me down now."

"I know." And it was all on me. I was the one who forced them to contain Hanna and Caden, and it was now my fault HDF knew they were alive and being held by Istvan's ex-general.

"Well, we can't think of it now." Andris sighed. He would never say it, but he had to blame me too. No apology in the world was good enough for all the danger I was putting them in. There was a good possibility I was the reason the bunker had gotten blown up. This was twice now the base had been discovered since I had shown up and put his army in harm's way. That was not a coincidence. "Other things take precedence."

"There's still so much we need to talk about. Not just about Istvan or Killian." I swallowed at saying the fae ruler's name, my lids burning. "But what we discovered at Visegrád." The discovery of my mother and the nectar already felt like days ago, not just last night.

Andris dipped his head. "We do, but right now, my priority is with my people. Making sure this place is guarded, safe, and everyone gets settled in and taken care of. We lost a lot tonight." He rubbed at his face, his eyes bloodshot. "I guess there was a moment everyone thought they lost me." He slid his hand over his head. "It's so strange. I even feel like I died. I think I did. But..." Andris tapered off.

Warwick and Ash's heads snapped to me, eyes searing in with sharp wonder and perplexity. It felt so long ago now that I forgot I never discussed what happened with them. Everything occurred so fast, spiraling into more chaos, never giving me time to work it out myself.

Andris studied me for a moment, his eyes going back and forth between mine like he was trying to figure something out. "I thought I saw you..." He laughed dryly. "Never mind. It's nothing. Simply crazy rantings of an old man." He patted my arm. "I need to go deal with everything first. We can meet later." He strolled straight into the throng of the wounded, talking with his fighters and giving orders to protect us.

The guys still stared at me. Warwick's intensity multiplied, but it was Ash who spoke.

"*Brexley*. What was he talking about?"

Taking a deep breath, my lips rolling together.

"The necromancers weren't the only ones I brought back to life tonight."

Chapter 5

"Start from the beginning again." Boots clipped the floor in a steady beat, and my scrutiny centered on the deep scuff mark and dried blood on Ash's boot as he paced from wall to wall, which wasn't very far in the small cube-shaped room. Big enough for two cots, but the rest of the room was bare. Nothing else had been placed in here yet.

I folded my arms tighter against my ribs, using the corner to keep myself propped up, exhaustion nipping at my legs like a pack of hounds.

Licking my lip, I exhaled. "The nectar... it's me."

Warwick dropped his head, pinching his nose, leaning against the wall parallel to mine. Lukas and Kek sat on the opposite bed from me, looking utterly confused. It was my decision to bring them into this conversation. They were part of it now, and I wanted them to understand the real stakes. The danger they were putting themselves in being associated with me.

I had already rushed over a condensed version of everything so far, like the link between me, Warwick, and Scorpion. Given their expressions, they were struggling even with the minimal information I gave them.

"What do you mean you?" Ash ran his hands through his grimy hair, continuing to pace.

"The nectar is my afterbirth." I tugged on my lip. "My mother was on the field giving birth to me the moment the wall fell. All that magic..."

"Absorbed into it like a sponge." Ash stopped, eyes wide with disbelief. "Absorbed into you." He dropped his head back. "Holy shit."

"I'm so confused. Why was your mother there?" Kek absently stroked her braid. "And how did necromancers turn into living, breathing witches before my eyes?"

"Me." I dipped my head, pulling my neck tighter. "I was holding the nectar, and it was showing me what had happened on that field. I even saw the moment the Seelie Queen was killed. That is when the wall completely dropped and magic flooded Earth. But then I was suddenly linked with Scorpion, and I saw my uncle's bunker get blown up. Saw the devastation and death…" I swallowed over the lump in my throat, the images flashing back through my mind like a movie.

"I couldn't lose him," I croaked.

"So you brought him back." Ash shut his lids briefly. "And with all the power, you brought them back as well."

"Wait. Wait." Kek held up her hand. "You were able to bring *seven* necromancers back to life, while miles away you were also in the bunker, and because of some bizarre ghost link to Scorpion, you were bringing your uncle back to life?"

I flinched, realizing how utterly absurd and insane it sounded. "Yes."

Kek's jaw dropped, her navy eyes wide. "What the *fuck* are you?"

The lump in my throat expanded, almost choking off my air. "I don't know." My voice came out so quiet it barely carried to them.

"There is no name, no race, no one else who came before you. It is you who decides what you are."

The room was quiet, all eyes on me, while I stared at the bloodstain on my pants. The dirt and tears proving the night was not a dream. This was all happening. Only last spring, I was happily ignorant of what lay ahead, the domino effect about to totally flip my entire world and beliefs. Sitting on the roof of HDF with Caden, drinking Pálinka, the scent of the Danube in the air, the wind blowing in my hair. My one problem was wishing Caden would kiss me, and I was oblivious to the thorny web snarling around me. The lies, deceit, and truths were weaving my story way before I was even born.

"Hey." Ash strolled up, rubbing my arm. "I told you, you are not alone. We're going to figure this out, okay?" His head dipped, trying to connect with my eyes. "I mean, you literally aren't alone." He motioned back to Warwick, who hadn't moved from his position on the wall. "Though I'm not sure that asshole is in the plus column."

My chin lifted, Warwick's emotionless eyes on mine. He shifted against the wall, turning away.

Distant.

Cold.

"What?" Ash's look ping-ponged between us, his forehead wrinkling, his demeanor shifting as if he could feel the icy tension prickling between us. "What am I missing?"

"It's gone," I whispered, finally saying it out loud.

"What is?" Ash whipped back to me.

"The link." I swallowed. "It's gone."

Ash blinked several times, confusion twitching his cheek. "What do you mean *gone*?"

My attention fluttered over to Warwick again. Gaze on the ground, his arms were crossed, shoulders up high. Defensive. Guarded.

It happened once before when I used up all of his energy in the fight at the train station. This felt very different.

Absolute.

"I think something happened when I brought everyone back." I dug my shoulders further into the cement wall. "The magic running through me…" My vocals gave out. Why was I getting so emotional over this? "Saving my uncle. I don't know. It was like it fried me from the inside out. I didn't realize it for a while. I mean, so much was going on. But it's gone."

Warwick shifted again, his attention still not meeting mine.

"The nectar as well," Ash replied, his mouth bunching together. "That's why it was dull after." He bobbed his head, putting pieces together. "You burned through it, bringing them all back."

My emotions only skimmed the surface now. "I think so." I tucked loose strands of hair behind my ear. "Do you think it's gone for good?"

Ash huffed, scouring his hand through his hair again, looking suddenly tired. "Possibly. Magic, like nature, is a balance. It's a give and take. Like any natural resource, there is an end to it. If you used it all up, it might be extinguished forever."

Crunching my molars together, I nodded in understanding. Did I destroy the object so many had spent their lives trying to locate? Did I kill a little piece of me along with my connections to Warwick and Scorpion?

I had no clue how I was supposed to feel about any of it. Especially since the treasure that people would kill for was me.

"I'm sorry, I'm still stuck on her being able to save General Takacs though she was miles away." Lukas leaned over his legs on the cot. "I may just be a half-breed and raised mainly by a human, but I know that's not possible. The only connections I've ever heard of even close are through mated pairs or the same species, usually by noble fairies. And neither of those sounds like what you are talking about. So how the hell was she able to be with us at the castle, but back in Savage Lands saving her uncle at the same time?"

"How was she being born and saving his ass too?" Kek snorted, thumbing to Warwick.

"*Pokol,*" Ash muttered. "Of course."

"What?" I straightened off the wall.

"Think about it. It was twenty years *to the night* you brought Warwick back to life, without actually being there."

My brain stumbled over all the other incidences, I hinted at bringing people back, but each time I was there in person. Only the freak time was Warwick, Scorpion, and now Andris.

"Yeah."

"Both times you were holding or coated with the magic-infused afterbirth."

"But I went through the book to save Warwick," I replied.

"In theory, yes." Ash tapped on his chin. "But now we know you were actually there. The infant was you, and you were the one who had the magic. The older version of yourself was simply a conduit. The magic you absorbed the night of the fae war is the same magic you used tonight to save Andris."

In its confusing way, it made sense, and the significance of it sat heavy on me. I was capable of bringing people back to life.

"And the necromancers?" Luk asked. "Or whatever they are now."

"They are basically like Scorpion." Ash smiled at me. "Just lucky bystanders in the moment."

They weren't my targets but were in the path of magic, becoming recipients of it whether they wanted it or not.

"Damn, little lamb. I knew there was a reason I liked you. Got some kink under that hot human façade. You're like a really fucked up reverse necromancer." Kek winked at me.

Her words hit deeper than she expected, carving into my chest.

My mother was a witch. Human, yes, but cursed. I still knew so little about what led them to be necromancers. Why they were blighted in the first place, going from Wiccans to cursed necromancers. It seemed insane. The day before, my mother was feeding off souls from corpses and reanimating skeletons. Now she was alive.

The shock of finding my mother again was like a blast of freezing air. Shocking. Brutal. It left me numb. I had an entire family I never knew about, just miles from me, and I had no clue how to even wrap my mind around it. To come to grips with how I felt, especially when so many other things were colliding in, crushing me.

Killian's piercing eyes and beautiful face entered my mind, right after the softness of Zander, the way he tipped his head when he looked at me.

They were gone. Dead.

Oxygen evaporated from my lungs, my spine curling as I tried to get my breath.

"Brex?" Ash came up, his voice sounding further away than it should have, his hand touching my shoulder. "You all right?" Concern shaded his timbre. Full of compassion and attentiveness.

I was being smothered. Everything was closing in on me, scratching at my skin, making me want to claw my way out. To run and never look back.

"Brex?" Ash rubbed my arm.

"Get out." I tried to breathe.

"What?"

"Everyone out." I curled over more, my voice hissing. "Please… get out."

Ash hesitated, the empathy in his expression strangling me further.

"Go!" I needed air. Space. I wanted to be left alone.

Ash nodded, "We'll be close by if you need us." He waved for them all to leave the room.

Sucking in gulps of air, I saw Kek and Luk follow him out of the corner of my eye.

"Warwick?" Ash called to him.

Warwick pushed off the wall, heading for the door, but instead of stepping through it, leaving me in peace, he slammed the door in Ash's face, closing us in the tiny room.

My chest clenched, sweat beading my hairline as his massive frame towered over me, choking me in his shadow, stealing more of my air.

"Kovacs…"

"Get the hell out," I seethed. I couldn't take anything more. *Especially* him. Because deep down, all I craved was to hear his voice skim up the back of my neck through our link, easing the panic building in my chest, the feel of him keeping the pieces of my broken soul together. The fact I yearned for it, *needed* it, tapped at a raw nerve of resentment and fury.

He didn't budge, his stony expression gazing down on me, taking me back to how he had looked at me at Halálház.

Detached. Cruel. Empty.

Like I was nothing.

It lit the fuse in my body, detonating through my bones.

"I said, get the fuck out!" I screamed, my palms shoving at his chest, creating more fury when I didn't move him an inch. The power to take his energy and use it against him was gone. All the magic I hadn't even realized stirred in my veins was burned up, leaving soot marks inside and outside.

We were no longer on equal footing. I was also not the girl I once had been. I was stripped to the bones, burned, and left in a heap of fiery anger.

"What are you waiting for?" I seethed, pushing at him again. "You are finally free. You got what you wanted all along. The link is broken. So go!"

A rumble came up his throat, his body moving closer to me. Caging me in. Trapping me.

And the sickest thing was I wanted it. I wanted him to hurt me, to make me feel something other than grief. To slam me up against the wall and fuck me until I forgot how to breathe. To think. To move.

Make me forget.

Except forgetting would take away my most prized possession.

Anger.

I bared my teeth, inching up on my toes, getting close to his face. "Don't tell me this isn't exactly what you wanted?" I growled.

His nose flared, but he didn't respond.

"Right?" I spat.

"Yes." His low, harsh growl barely constructed a word, but it hit my chest like an arrow.

"Good." I nodded, a malicious smirk upping my lip. "We're both free now."

"Princess—"

"Don't fucking call me that." I sneered. "I'm not some spoiled, fragile girl. I am a monster just like you."

"You are *nothing* like me." He moved closer; our bodies pressed together.

"You're right. I'm worse. You may enjoy death, but *I am* it. Everything I touch crumbles into ruins. Everybody close to me dies. I'm like the fuckin' plague."

"Don't say that," he growled. Grabbing my arms, he slammed me up against the wall, the strike of pain spreading through my body like wildfire. It felt good. Anger made you feel alive.

"Why? It's true. Admit it, I've done nothing but wreak havoc on your life since I entered Halálház."

"You think my life wasn't like that before you?"

"Only of your making. This is all me. Look around you. Look at the lives I've destroyed. Where are Eliza and Simon now?"

Warwick jolted at their names, the muscles in his neck plucking like violin strings.

"Get the hell away from me and never look back."

"Think it's so easy, princess?"

"Yes," I snarled. "Because we both got what we wanted. We can finally walk away. No hard feelings. *Free* of each other."

"You want to be free of me?" His hands tightened around my biceps, his hips pushing into mine. Desire flamed into more resentment as his hardness pressed into me.

"Be honest, Farkas. Without that connection, you'd feel *nothing* for me. You think you would have looked even twice at me at Halálház? Saved my life in the Games?" I snorted sardonically. "You're not the type to stick around for happily ever after. So don't pretend you were ever going to."

His jaw cracked together, his lids lowering, and he stared at me, expressionless. His silence broadcasted everything he didn't say.

It had never been about *me*. His interest was because of the connection, and now it was gone. I rolled my jaw, my anger gliding into the darkness. I wanted him to hurt as much as I did.

"Exactly what I thought," I derided. "Now get the hell out. Go back to Kitty's and fuck your nymphs and sirens. I couldn't give a shit."

"That *really* what you want, Kovacs?" He snarled back, grabbing my chin and forcing me to look right at him. "I don't play games. So be *certain* you mean what you say."

"Yes."

No. But I let that word get drowned in my anger.

He watched for a long moment, my resolve refusing to break.

Rage burned through his eyes before he pushed off me. "*Fine.*" His shoulders expanded, shaking his head slightly, and without a word, he stomped out of the room, slamming the door behind him.

A sob hiccupped in my chest, and I struggled to fight it back. I couldn't stop it. The tsunami barreled down on me, my body sliding down the wall, and I crumpled into a ball. My heart broke into a thousand pieces for my mother, my father, for Killian and Zander. For Eliza and Simon and all those we lost tonight.

For letting him walk away.

For one moment, I had a taste of what had made me different. What I was.

The power of the in-between. I always thought of gray as a blend of black and white, but it wasn't. What I had felt tonight was a mix of all colors of life and death.

Now I wasn't any hue.

I was nothing.

"Seems extra gooey and crusty around the edges." A voice stirred me from my moment of peace, my nose tickling. "Like a pie."

Chirp!

"Ooohhh, apple pie does sound good. This even has chunks in it, like fruit pie."

Chirp! Chirp!

"Don't blame me. I didn't force you to try it." Opie's voice rang in my ears, cracking my salt-encrusted lashes apart, my head instantly pounding. "So, that's a no on it tasting like pie, huh?"

Chirp! Chirp! Chirp!

"Not even pecan?"

Chirpchirpchirpchirpchirp!

"Ugh... ." Jerking my head back, I batted at my face with a groan. I wasn't ready to surface into reality and longed to surrender back into nothing, where for one second, I could breathe.

"Master Fishy!" Opie's palm tapped on my cheek, splinting my lids more. "You're awake."

I didn't want to be. When I had finally fallen asleep, my body was so wrung out that my sobs turned into whimpers. Nightmares and imaginary screams for help kept me from truly letting go. Sometime during the night, I climbed onto the cot, curled into a ball, and succumbed to it all.

My tired eyes scanned over Opie, the tiniest spot of happiness in my grief, taking in his outfit. He'd dissected pieces of a lifejacket, and the bright orange weather-resistant material was wrapped around him like a long dress. The black buckle was cinched around his waist and up around his throat like a halter neck. What I recognized as the boat's seat cushions was made into a sailor-style hat. Floatation foam covered his feet. Bitzy had more of the seat cushion textile designed into a onesie. With floatation foam for a belt and a smaller sailor hat as if they were ready to sail away to some tropical island.

"You okay, Fishy?" Opie tipped his head, concern written on his face. "Bitzy said your nose tastes extra salty today. And you smell less fishy."

"So gross." I sighed, but there was no energy behind my words. My body felt heavy, worn, and achy, all my energy sucked out of me. I felt wrong. Itchy in my own skin, but I had no strength to move. "Less fishy?"

"Yeah." He tapped at his nose. "I couldn't smell you today, which worried us." He motioned to Bitzy, who looked away. "Right, Bitzy?"

Chirp! She flipped us off, and something in that comforted me.

"See? She said she was totally worried about you."

I huffed, "Sure, that's what she said." I rubbed at my face, feeling the grime coating my skin. "Glad you guys are okay."

"We sub-fae are far smarter than they like to believe. We know when and where to get in and when to get the hell out. And necromancers..." Opie shivered. "Yeah, no thanks. They are scary. So boney and creepy."

I tucked my hands under my cheek and licked my split lip. "And one of those is my mother."

"Master Fishy has a mum fishy who's a bonefishy who controls dead fishies?"

One eye squeezed together, his statement doing aerobatics through my sluggish brain. "Um… yes?"

"Wow." Opie's eyes widened.

Chirp! Bitzy plunked down on my pillow, sucking on the tips of her fingers.

"Bitz says you even taste less fishy."

My lids shut, and I let out a shallow groan before I pitched myself up, my muscles quaking with the effort. Never had I felt so weak before. Even after getting my ass kicked in training, I'd only be in the clinic for moments before I'd bounce right back up and head back to training.

Now my entire body didn't just hurt; it seemed anemic.

Is this what it feels like to be totally human? The thought vaulted into my head. All the times people eyed me with shock when I'd pop up and head to the mat from the hospital unit. Caden used to tease all the time. *"You are like fire, Brex. People try to put you out, but you come back with a roar. You amaze me."*

I never thought about why I recovered so easily or why I moved as fast as I did. I just did. It was my normal. Now, with every crack of my bones and every stinging wound still cutting painfully deep across my flesh, I understood how different I had been.

Because now I felt… human.

Still fully clothed and dirty, my boots hit the floor as I twisted to sit up. Pain wrenched across my nerves, and I paused, sucking in sharply. The simple movement had me wanting to lie down again. It was tempting, but I needed to speak with Andris. We had so much to go over and discuss.

"You all right?" Opie's little hand patted mine.

Flinching, I nodded, trying to breathe through the agony, both inside and outside. I never got that moment of complete serenity in the bits of sleep I had. The screams and losses were always there, cracking more of my soul into pieces. I couldn't forget for a moment what had been lost last night. So many deaths. Killian hung on my heart like cement. A sob lodged between my ribs. It seemed impossible. Not him…

But loss came in all varieties, and one penetrated so deep, I stopped breathing every time my mind brushed over it. *Him.* The loss felt worse than death. I shoved the memory of him walking out of this room into a box I locked away.

Compartmentalized.

"Special smell or not, you are still our family, Fishy. You always have us."

The lump grew in my throat, peering down at the sincere brown eyes gazing up at me.

"Right, Bitzy?" He looked at her, jerking his head toward me.

Bitzy rolled her huge eyes to the side, her mouth flattening.

"Riiiight?" Opie's voice strained.

Chirp. Bored, she flung her middle fingers at me like a solemn teenager, making a true smile hint on my lips.

"Thank you," I croaked.

"Just a warning, the food here is bad and dreadfully limited. I mean, they didn't even have tea biscuits or extra sugar packets. What kind of place doesn't have tea biscuits?" He threw his hands up. "Like we're back in prison."

"I'll see what I can do." Snorting, I stood up. My head spun as my frame tipped. I grabbed onto the wall, my skull pounding harder.

"Think you need tea biscuits too, Fishy," Opie added. I was extremely dehydrated and lacking nutrients, though the thought of food sounded revolting. Even the idea of taking a shower seemed too much. My body hurt, my heart cried, and my soul was screaming.

Inhaling deeply, I re-centered myself, limping as I made my way to the door. Pausing, I looked back at my friends, the question coming out before I even realized I had thought of it.

"Is it gone?" I whispered hoarsely. "My fishiness?"

Opie tipped his head, sorrow filling his eyes, understanding exactly what I was asking. He let out a heavy sigh.

My teeth crunched together, tears burning the back of my lids. I never realized I had this gift until it was gone, and now it was a void in my soul.

"For good?"

"I don't know, Fishy."

I knew he wouldn't, but I felt desperate. Aching for someone to tell me it was going to be okay. That I would feel whole again. Not able to talk, I nodded my head and went out the door, needing to run, craving something—*someone*—and it sent me reeling in circles.

Duty first, Brex.

It was my only escape from the pain. Focus on action, doing *something*, and fighting. Because what was out there, barreling toward us, was a lot bigger than me.

It was between survival and death.

The main areas had quieted down and cleared out, though it still bustled with activity. People were setting up the command room, taking supplies to and from the new clinic space, which was filled with the most people. Healers were working mostly in the dark, with few beds and not enough supplies. Small groups sat in a mess hall with a handful of tables and chairs and a single fold-out table holding limited food and drink.

The place hadn't been ready to move into. The water hookup, wiring, and lighting still not fully functional in some areas. It seemed all those who were capable were trying to help get this place operational.

For our safety, the command/computer room was the first priority. It was where I found my uncle, helping Ling get her station up and running.

Neither one of them had changed or gotten a chance to clean up; they might not even have slept yet. I had no idea what time it was.

"Brexley." Andris's eyes softened at seeing me, though a flicker of worry twitched in his eye. "You're hurt."

Peering down at the various wounds decorating my frame, still oozing and stinging, they felt like a taunt to all that was lost. And what I no longer was.

"I'm fine." My throat was thick. How blind I had been before, how easily I had healed, how confident I had been about my skills. *Untouchable*.

The fall was brutal and hard.

He stepped closer to me, hand touching my cheek, his thick brows meeting together.

"What?" I rasped.

"I don't know. Something feels different."

My chest surged, my jaw locking down. I couldn't get my tongue to move, fear tangling my vocals.

"I couldn't sleep last night, but when I drifted off..." Confusion pinned his mouth together. "I kept seeing you. Your eyes... And I would burst awake." His subconscious knew and was trying to tell him about what he probably considered impossible, even for me.

I had been the one to save his life.

"We need to talk." I swallowed.

He nodded, dropping his hand away from me and turning to Ling.

"Sweetheart, you good here? I'm gonna go talk with Brexley."

Ling's eyes went to me, watchful, insightful. From the day I met her in Halálház, I felt as if she could see right through me. The words she spoke to me there still rang true.

"Danger and violence want you. They hover around you. And you welcome them."

Her gaze softened on him, and she gave a curt nod before going back to her workstation.

Andris showed me to his small office area. Nothing here besides a desk and two chairs.

"Have a seat." He motioned to one, settling himself behind his desk. He leaned back, scouring at his face. He looked exhausted. He had bloodshot eyes and dark circles, but not one scratch donned his skin.

Not one.

The man had been crushed under cement.

I watched him with reverence, knowing he was my one good thing yesterday. If I hadn't done what I had, I would not be looking at him now. I would be mourning his death. But the man I considered my uncle all my life, the last of my childhood family, sat across from me.

Alive.

I gripped that small gift with all my might, letting myself feel the joy for a second. A tear streamed down my face.

"*Drágám.*" *My dear*. He reached his hand out for me, and I laid mine in his. "Are you okay?"

"I still have you." Another tear fell down my cheek. "I don't know what I'd do if I lost you."

"You didn't. I'm here." He squeezed my fingers to reassure me, hiccupping another cry up my throat. "I'm fine, *drágám*. Besides being a little tired, surprisingly, I feel great. Maddox and Wesley keep telling me they swore I was dead, but I guess my time wasn't up yet. I still have things to do."

"Your time wasn't up with *me*." I extracted my hands from his, wiping at my cheeks and nose. "I wasn't willing to let you go."

"What do you mean?" He cocked his head, shifting in his seat like he could feel something in my tone. Something he already knew deep down.

"I found the nectar last night."

Andris's eyes went wide, his head jerking back. "What?"

"It's been hidden up at the High Castle for a long time."

"You found the nectar?" He lurched from his chair, not able to sit still, his mouth hanging open. "You sure?" My head nodded at his inquiry. "I mean, how? How has it not been discovered until now?"

"It was being guarded." I paused, my eyes meeting his. "By a group of necromancers."

"Necromancers?" Andris blinked at me in total shock.

"Yeah, but that's not all." I licked my lip. "The necromancers guarding the nectar," the declaration rode up my tongue, the secret I was about to reveal humming in the air. "Are my mother and her clan."

Andris went still. Not a breath or twitch. He stared at me, unresponsive. Aloof. Although, I could sense the turmoil of my statement erupting inside his mind, spilling and flipping as it soaked in.

A full thirty seconds passed before he breathed out. "Your mother?" He still didn't move, shock locking him in place. "You must be mistaken. I met her briefly. She was full of life... human. No, it can't be."

"She kept the truth from dad. He never knew she was Wiccan. Her whole family—*my* family—are witches."

"But—"

"She said necromancers weren't a race, but a curse. The night of the fae war, she was there, on the battlefield."

Andris's head jerked again at the claim. He and my father had both been somewhere on the field that night too. And little did they know, not far from where they fought against the Seelie Queen, my mother was fighting *for* her and giving birth to me.

"The entire clan died that night and became necromancers."

Andris's eyes ping-ponged around while he started to pace. "I still don't understand. You aren't a necromancer." He motioned to me.

"No." I still didn't know what I was—or what I had been. "But I might have some of their abilities."

"Necromancers aren't really alive. They don't even talk or think like people do. They rob graves and reanimate skeletons. They feed on souls and are *pitiless* creatures."

"No, they're not!" I stood up, rage weaving through me. "They are people who used to have lives, who loved, and cared. They communicate through a link, one I used to have too.

"Brexley." Andris said my name with concern and alarm. "They aren't people anymore."

"But they are now."

Andris's brow crunched again.

"You know how you saw me bring back Aggie?"

Andris's chest clenched, his head moving slightly in acknowledgment, recalling Rita's cat.

"I brought them back like her." I swallowed, lifting my chin to him. "Just like I brought you back."

Andris slumped in his chair, his legs no longer able to keep him up. What I had thrown at him, going over the night until we got here in specific detail, pretty much melted his brain.

I was wrung out and drained. My own head struggled over the events of the night before. It was too much to fully wrap around.

"The nectar is back at the castle?" He took a large swing of Unicum, the dark liquor rolling down his throat with ease, his third refill since I started talking. My glass sat full in front of me, my head hurting and my stomach rolling with the idea of putting anything in it.

"Yes."

He downed the rest, frowning at the empty glass. "I'm not feeling anything. I don't even feel a slight buzz." He set the cup down, pinching his brows again. "I don't have a single wound from the bombing. I have no aching back or hurt knee." He inhaled, peering up at me. "When you brought me back,"—he licked his lips—"when I came back to life, was... was I changed?"

"I think so." The words came out so softly I barely heard them.

"I still don't understand how this is possible." He dropped his head back into the chair. I told him all about the links and bringing Warwick and Scorpion back, as well. "It shouldn't be. It's so ridiculous and farfetched, but yet, something in me is saying it's true." His Adam's apple bobbed. "I feel it. Everything is sharper. Smell, hearing, taste... colors are brighter. I'm tired, but I've never felt more alive. Strong. Youthful. My joints no longer ache or groan. I feel like I'm twenty again."

He swiveled his chair to face front, sitting up, his gaze meeting mine. "I'm fae, aren't I?"

I held a pocket of air in my lungs before releasing it. "Sort of."

"The nectar was said to be a lot like fae food, which gave humans fae-like abilities." He folded his hands together. "Basically, they were fae, but with slightly shorter lifespans." Which were still thousands of years.

I had read all about the power of fae food. It only existed in the Otherworld before the wall came down. Humans couldn't leave the Otherworld once they had it. It was like the worst drug in the world. It was all they craved or thought about, and they would starve themselves to death in the most horrendous agony if they went back to Earth.

When our worlds became one, it was destroyed.

"Istvan has been searching for the nectar for at least fifteen years, and he's not alone. Millions of people would kill and destroy nations to get their hands on it. And if it fell into the wrong hands…"

"Yeah." The weight bore down on me again.

He rolled his bottom lip between his teeth, his eyes on me.

"We need to destroy it."

"What?" I jerked upright. Possessiveness curled around my spine. "No."

"Brex, it's beyond dangerous. This tiny substance is the most powerful thing in the world. Think of the damage it can do. Do you know what could happen if people found it? What if Istvan discovered it?"

"They haven't found it yet."

"It's no longer safe, and you know it. A wisp of a word, a single hint that it might be out there, will rip this world apart."

"No." I stood fully up. "We find another way. I can't destroy it. I won't let you." I bared my teeth. It was me, part of me. I couldn't let anything happen to it. "Plus, it's useless now. I used it up bringing all you guys back to life."

"I'm not willing to take that chance." Andris watched me, tension growing.

"Lieutenant?" A rap on the door broke us away from each other as a guy popped his head in, his eyes darting straight to me, his frame stiffening.

I sucked in.

Scorpion.

"Yes, what do you need?" My uncle waved him in.

Scorpion stepped in, his eyes wary on me, before forcing himself to look at Andris.

"We are out of supplies in the clinic. Herbs and medicines. It wasn't ready at all for this level of wounded at one time."

"I know." Andris stood up, tugging on his filthy and burned jacket. "Gather up a group and head out as soon as it's dark."

"Yes, sir." Scorpion dipped his head, turning for the door.

"I'll go with you," I spoke up, both men twisting to me.

"No, my dear, it's too dangerous. If you are seen..." Andris shook his head.

"It will be dark, and I'll wear a hood. I'm good at stealing."

Andris frowned, about to say no again.

"It wasn't a question," I stated firmly. "I'm going."

I had to do something. Stay busy.

Or I would fall apart.

"What the hell is going on?" Scorpion hissed, his hand circling my wrist, tugging me out into the hallway the moment we stepped out of Andris' office. "I tried to reach—" His attention darted to all the figures mulling around within earshot. He pulled me deeper down a quiet, dim passage.

"I tried to reach you through the link a hundred times now," he whispered hoarsely, still looking back over his shoulder to make sure there were no eavesdroppers. "What the hell happened? You brought Andris back to life, didn't you? Like you did me. I could feel the magic, hear the lightning. I mean, you fucking lit up."

I shifted on my feet, the aches in my body throbbing louder. I never was someone who needed painkillers, almost bragging about it. Now I yearned for anything to take the edge off the gnawing discomfort.

"Well, you brought me here, and through you, I could save him. Without that link,"—I swallowed—"he would be dead."

"You can do that? I know you saved me and the other douchebag, but to experience it, the energy..." He shook his head. "I've never felt anything like it. And then it was gone." He looked away. A fleeting second of vulnerability shone through and then vanished. "*You* were gone."

Biting my lip, I bent my head. "By saving him, I think I burned it all up."

"You mean it's gone?" He peered down at me, his expression unreadable. "This link between us is gone for good?"

My shoulders lifted. "I don't know. I think so. I took too much. Drained it... it wasn't just Andris I brought back."

Scorpion opened his mouth to respond.

"Hey! There you are." Maddox came around the corner, his regard jumping between us suspiciously. "You talk to Andris? We going?"

"Yeah." Scorpion took a huge step back from me, and I realized how close we were and what it must look like to Maddox.

He turned away, marching toward his friend, his voice gruff. "She's coming with us."

"Is she now?" Maddox's lips curved a little, peering back at me. "And here I thought it was the little blonde making you jerk off earlier."

"Shut the fuck up," Scorpion growled, knocking his shoulder into Maddox, making him laugh.

"Someone's a bit sensitive." Maddox snickered, following behind his buddy.

"Hanna," I said her name, feeling it like a blade, while catching up to them. "Is she... is she all right?"

Maddox and Scorpion looked back at me.

"She's fine," Scorpion huffed, his response widening Maddox's smile.

"Though I would hold off seeing her for a bit." Maddox winked back at me. "Think she had some choice things to say about you... or was it about you?" He nudged Scorpion. "Oh right, she wanted to cut off your dick and stick it up your ass."

Scorpion snarled, his strides getting faster. "Just shut the hell up."

"For god's sake, will you stop flirting with each other so we can go?" Birdie stood at the entrance, shoving a knife into her sheath. Wesley stood next to her, loading his gun.

"Oh, someone get jealous?" Wesley tugged on her ponytail.

"Ugh!" She hit him. "You're so annoying."

"Admit it. You love my youthful charm." Wesley prodded her again, like a pesky sibling.

"Juvenile is more like it." She rolled her eyes.

"Ahhh, now I see..." Wesley tapped on his lip.

"See what?"

"Why you keep asking to guard that human who barely has pubes yet."

"I do not." Her shoulders jerked back, her defenses going up.

"Oh, come on." Wesley laughed. "Henrik told me you took over his shift. Twice now."

"It was that or help in the clinic. I'll guard a pretty boy over playing nurse any day."

"Not like Birdie has the best bedside manner," Maddox huffed with amusement.

She glared at him.

They were all so close, acting more like siblings, and it made me envious. I used to have Caden, but I was always enamored of him in some way, so there was never a "sibling" thing there. I grew up very much in an adult world, alone, and never with any of these types of relationships. Even as we got older, we were taught more to compete than to help each other.

The closest I had were Caden and Hanna. Two people who despised me now.

"We ready to roll out?" Scorpion shoved his loaded gun into his holster.

"Yep." They all nodded, twisting for the door, already knowing what the plan was. I had no idea what the strategy was, but I figured I could learn on the way.

"Brex?" Hearing my name, I whipped around to see Ash.

"Hey." I took him in, tangled hair, dirty, ripped clothes, and ragged. He jogged up to me, looking like he hadn't slept well, if at all. "You look like shit." I tried to joke, but the sentiment was hollow, the playfulness not even reaching my face.

Ash scoffed, his eyes going over me as to say, *same to you.*

"Where are you headed?" I realized he was carrying his backpack, the one with the fae book inside. I tried to reach out to it, see if I felt anything. Not even a tiny buzz or pull. My feet shifted underneath me, the knot in my stomach braiding tighter.

"I was going to head back to my place for supplies. I have some rare healing herbs." He tugged the bag straps tighter. "Grab some clothes, maybe a shower. Like you should." He winked at me. I knew he was trying to lighten my mood, so I forced a shallow smile on my lips, but it quickly went limp, my head bowing.

The elephant danced between us, the subject both of us were hoping we could avoid.

"He's not here," Ash whispered.

Swallowing, I lifted my head, my expression blank, my eyes not able to meet his. "I figured."

"It's his way." Ash tugged on my chin, forcing me to look at him. "It doesn't mean he doesn't care. It's how he handles emotional situations."

I pinned a detached expression on my face. "He can do what he wants. He's no longer tethered to me."

"Brex." Ash tipped his head, his tone sorrowful, showing off the deeply bruised and bitten skin along his neck.

"Holy shit." My finger immediately went to the spots, my eyes widening in shock, realizing what they were.

"Yeah, it's how *I* deal with emotional situations." He pulled his jacket collar up, glancing away. "It was a rough day."

"Someone here?" My mouth parted, glancing over his shoulder as if his bedmate would pop out. My mind reeled with prospects.

He shrugged with one shoulder, a strange blush dotting his cheeks.

"Oh, my gods." My mouth dropped. "Kek? Lukas?"

Ash stared at me.

My eyes widened. "Both?"

"X, if you're coming with us, hurry up," Scorpion's voice yelled down the stairs.

"Saved just in time." Ash bumped my shoulder, strolling past me.

"You are not getting off so easy." My voice trailed after him.

"Actually, I got off easy *several* times." He grinned at me before twisting away and charging up the stairs.

The fog was thick as it advanced over the city, rolling and wrapping itself around buildings and the darkness. Bundling deeper into my coat, I shivered with cold. It was the kind of night you'd want to spend indoors by a fireplace, eating something rich and creamy.

Cries from livestock and howls from feral animals haunted the skies, prickling the back of my neck as we moved through the streets on foot. Those not searching for trouble huddled close to their camps, the moist air strangling the bit of warmth they could get from the fires and dampening their thin blankets. The weeping of hungry children cut across my heart. I wanted so badly to help fill their bellies and find them a place to feel warm and safe.

I used to steal from Istvan to help Maja's family, thinking I was doing some big, heroic thing. It wasn't even a crumb. Our country was so broken, and what was worse was the hopelessness strewn across their faces, the awareness that this hell was all they'd know.

The five of us kept a tight formation. Scorpion and Birdie were on lead, Wesley and I in the middle, and Maddox watching our backs.

"Where are we going?" I whispered to Wesley.

"The old Lehel Market," he murmured back.

My boots made a squeak on the cobbles when I stopped. "What?" I blinked at him. "Lehel?"

I knew that building. It was an old indoor marketplace located in what we now called the North Léopold district. Istvan privatized it for the elite of Léopold and those in North Léopold who could afford to shop instead of work there. It was an exclusive bazaar holding the best household items, produce, medicines, and meats, along with hard-to-get things and imports from the Unified Nations. I knew it was guarded twenty-four seven, not that I ever went there. The servants for the elite would most likely be seen shopping there. Maja told me it was where she could sometimes meet up with her kids, visit, and give them the products I stole. A neutral ground between the world she lived in and the one they did.

"It's the only place that carries the items we really need." Wesley's attention was still out on the night, securing every alley and corner. "You gonna get a conscience on us?" He glanced back at me, my feet rushing to catch up to the moving party.

"Why would you ask that?"

"Need to know if it's going to bother you that we're stealing from your ex-daddy."

"He's not my dad." I gritted my teeth. "And I've never had a problem stealing from him." I had been since the age of seventeen.

"Good thing," Wesley muttered in my ear as we rounded a corner. Scorpion's arm went up, telling us to stop.

Yards ahead, the block-long, three-story marketplace came into view. It was a bizarre building, a mismatch of styles and juxtapositions. The now fading primary colors gave the construction a pre-school feel with a splash of an Eastern vibe.

The gates were rolled down, the glass doors long gone. The market was locked up for the night. A dim streetlight, still working in this area, cast an eerie glow through the mist down on the pavement. Four guards milled around under it, smoking, laughing, and chatting, not giving much care to watching it. They were treating it like a shit job, probably because it wasn't killing fae or being some hero to the human race. HDF put heavy weight on your role, and this wouldn't be considered heroic or pride-worthy.

Our group padded quietly the opposite way of the guards, passing a rundown park. The street was darker here. The only other streetlamp working was at the opposite end of the building, lighting the two entrances and exits open to the public. We huddled close to the structure in the shadows, right next to what used to be a parking garage. The ramp from the street heading up to different parking levels was now lined with more vendor booths instead.

"There are four guards here and four at the other end." Scorpion motioned down the block. "Every hour or two, they make their way around the building to do an overall check. But it's not consistent," he whispered, explaining it to me. The others all seemed like they had done this before. "It's why we need to hurry and be ready to run at a moment's notice. X?"

He pointed to me. "You will be on watch. The rest of us will split up. We know this place and know exactly where to go to get what we need. Birdie, you are on medicine. Wesley, you are food. Maddox is on medical supplies, and I will get us a portable generator and gas. Grab what you can and get out. Got it?" All our heads bobbed in unison. "The car entrance is gated, so we climb up." He pointed up. "Okay, let's go."

Scorpion scurried to the fencing built up the side of the ramp area and used to keep people out. You could see a thin gap between the roof and fence. A sliver of space we could slip through.

One by one, we quietly climbed up slowly, trying not to clank the metal while we scaled the chain-link fence. My throat knotted at the hum of the guards chatting around the corner. They were so close on this end. At any moment, one could come around and see us. We were defenseless. Targets on a wall.

My heart thumped loudly in my ears, stopping dead when a pitched holler spiked the air, sounding like it was right below us, my head darting around to see if we had been caught.

Wesley shoved at my feet below, telling me to keep going. Sweat was dripping down my back.

I easily slipped through the slot, descending to the other side, waiting for our last person to join us. Peering down the car ramp, I could see through the gate. The guards were a few yards away, their cigarettes glowing like fireflies, the dim streetlamp shadowing their forms. One of them could look up and notice movement in the shadows. Every breath felt precarious.

If Istvan knew how careless they were with their job, how easy it was to slip in, he would probably shoot every one of them in the head for disloyalty and indolence. Nothing pissed him off more than laziness and incompetence.

Even as we slunk up the rest of the ramp, staying low and near the wall as we heading toward an entrance to the market, I felt the instinct to run to Istvan and tell him of this weakness. To prove myself his faithful soldier. The best of them. It had been ground into me for years to prove myself to him. It would take a while to fully reprogram that, no matter how much I understood, he was my enemy now.

Scorpion waved everyone through the door, but his hand stopped me, rearing my attention to him. His brows furrowed with concentration before he shook his head.

"It's really gone, isn't it?" he muttered, frustration lining his forehead.

"Yeah." I knew he was talking about our link. The strange connection neither of us asked for nor wanted, but in a short time had grown accustomed to. I missed my bond with him, but it was nothing compared to the gaping hole someone else left behind. How had he dug such a fissure into me, marking me, carving my bones and muscles?

I bit down, shoving out thoughts of Warwick. He was probably elated it was cut. Finally, he could return to his life of fucking and killing.

"Would be very convenient to have right now," Scorpion grunted. "You stay on watch here and whistle or something if anyone starts heading this way." He patted my shoulder, disappearing into the building along with the rest, making me realize how flimsy and dangerous this plan was. Sarkis didn't have the means as Povstat did to buy high-tech gadgets like ear comms. And now I didn't even have the link to Scorpion.

This entire venture was dancing on a string.

Hunkering against the wall next to the door, I stayed on alert. Every sound. Every movement. The guards' words were low and muffled, but I could make out some of their conversation.

"*Tesó,*" Bro. "I had the sweetest fuck the other night. The bitch had my eyes rolling back into my head." A guard groaned, like he was recalling the moment of pure pleasure. "There's a reason that whorehouse is the best." My head popped up. There were plenty of whorehouses in Savage Lands, but only one was considered the "best"—Kitty's. "That *kurva* did things I didn't even know were possible. Freaky shit."

"Fuck man, you're gonna come right here just thinking about her, aren't you?" another laughed.

"I might. I'm telling you, she was unbelievable."

"She was fae, wasn't she?" A third spoke up, making them all give him shit.

"You're a *fae fucker*, Kristof?"

"No, *tesó,* she's fully human. Pretty, with full lips, and huge fuckin' boobs, and this long red hair I wrapped around my hand while she sucked me off like a vacuum. They call her the English Rose. Like giving her a pretty name makes her anything more than a warm hole to stick my dick in."

Searing hot anger bloomed up the back of my neck and across my shoulders, my teeth grinding together. It took everything in me to keep from running down the ramp and shooting this Kristof right between the eyes. The protectiveness I felt for Rosie shuffled my feet, twitching my trigger finger. Not only did I most likely know this guy, at least by face, but this piece of crap had another connection to me, to my friend, and he had no clue what she had gone through in her life to survive. His spoiled, entitled life held no understanding of how hard the real world was outside HDF. It made me want to show them all exactly how horrible it could be.

"Szar!" Shit! One of them hissed, and I could see his outline push off the lamp post he was leaning against, tossing down his cigarette. "They're here!"

"Fuck." The Kristof guy exclaimed, stomping out his as well. "They weren't supposed to be here for another few hours."

All four straightened up, their demeanors shifting into serious soldiers, cascading prickles down my spine. Something was coming.

"Get the gate. Hurry!" Kristof ordered two of them, their forms jogging for the locked entry down the ramp.

Fear grated down my chest, splicing itself between my ribs. My head darted back inside the market, none of my comrades anywhere nearby. Before I could even whistle, the gate peeled opened, the metal shredding over the cement as the men dragged the gates open. Blinding light from car headlights slammed me back into the corner, trying to dissolve into the darkest shadows.

Panic clogged my airways, paralyzing me as the windowless van came up the ramp, curving around only feet from me. Two guards followed close behind, the two others staying back to keep watch. I could tell it was the guy Kristof who had spoken about Rosie and the other one who was leaning against the lamppost. They seemed more in charge than the other two.

The closer they got, the more I recognized their faces. Both graduated a few years before Caden, and they were so unmemorable and low rank, I had no clue what their names were. Kristof was tall and stocky, not at all fit, but large enough he might look intimidating. The other one was shorter but trimmer, with a buzzed haircut and a deep scar above his lip.

They followed the van to the far side, parking in front of another pair of doors, to what I would think would be a utility/electrical closet or a room for supplies.

A middle-aged, lean blond man climbed out of the driver's seat. His face immediately made me press harder back into the wall.

"Captain Kobak." Both men went straight, saluting him. "You're early."

"And you're a disgrace." His pinched brows didn't move, his long, skinny face displaying nothing but annoyance. He opened the sliding door of the van, and two more soldiers climbed out.

Kobak was well known at HDF. Cruel. Solemn. Detached from any emotions which made someone human. No family, friends, or pets, his lone focus was rising through the ranks. He had Bakos's job for a while until he had an overabundance of complaints about his brutality, even sending trainees to the clinic himself and getting off on beating them within an inch of their life. Istvan had to remove him, put him in a different position.

The passenger side door slammed, and the other man waddled around.

It took everything in me not to gasp.

Dr. Karl. The last person I expected to see tonight.

He was dressed in his white lab coat, his protruding stomach straining his shirt. My gut twisted with warning. Why was he here? What the hell was going on?

"We don't have all day," Captain Kobak snapped, motioning for them to move.

"Of course, sir!" Kristof and Buzzcut dashed for the door, pulling out a set of keys. The two other soldiers followed them, just out of my eyeline.

Drawing in a breath, I inched closer, slanting my head to see. All their attention was focused away from me, but if any of them turned around, they would be able to see me.

Kristof unlocked several bolts before the door swung open. He stepped into the room, the three others following, telling me either this room was a lot bigger than I thought, or it was connected to a larger one.

The strike of my heartbeat counted the seconds they were gone, until I saw Dr. Karl lean into the doorway.

"Oh, these look like much better specimens than the last ones. Maybe they will last a bit longer."

"Like we can't simply get more. They're cockroaches," Kobak sneered, stepping back as two guards dragged something out.

It took me a moment to make out the shape in the dim light.

A man.

Young and tall, he sagged over like he couldn't stand up, his feet barely able to move. The guards carted him to the van. He was dirty, emaciated, and beaten, but I had no doubt he was fae. His hair looked almost like feathers, so dark it looked iridescent. His nose was sharp, like a bird's beak. Beautiful. Regal.

And appearing to be drugged.

He swayed and stumbled like he could barely stay conscious. The two sentinels roughly flung him into the van, and the sound of his bones thumped hard on the van floor.

"Make sure he's cuffed," Kobak ordered. "Last one was able to get loose, and I had to shoot him before we even arrived."

"Yes, sir." They climbed into the van while Kristof and Buzzcut dragged out another one.

My hand slapped over my mouth, swallowing back my reaction. I recognized her. One of the workers I had seen in Carnal Row, still half-shifted into her bunny form. She was also gaunt, beaten, and drugged.

Dr. Karl's beady eyes watched her as the men tossed her into the van, forcing her to cry out.

"Shut up, you fucking fae *kurva*." Kristof spat at her.

"Please be gentle with the stock. I need them in somewhat good condition." Dr. Karl strolled around to the passenger side, climbing in.

Kristof huffed, sliding the van door, the two other guards already inside.

Captain Kobak turned to Kristof and Buzzcut. "Don't think I won't mention to General Markos about your abhorrent lack of commitment to your job. Now get back to your posts."

"Yes, si—"

Crash!

The sound of something falling onto the tile in the market below echoed out, turning everyone to the door. To me. It was a second, my reflexes moving slower than I was used to, not ducking away fast enough. Kobak's eyes landed on mine.

Recognition widened them.

One beat, and everything turned to hell.

Chapter 7

"Traitor!" The claim rang through the garage like a death sentence, Kobak's hand going to the Glock in his sheath. "Get her!"

Whirling around, I tore for the entry of the market right as bullets kissed the ends of my ponytail, the crack of the gun piercing my ears, my legs pumping, my mind zeroing in on survival and reaching my friends.

It was deep inside me. An instinct, a reflex, which shouldn't be so imprinted in my DNA, but I felt myself instantly reaching for him. Calling. I had been in danger a lot in my life and got myself out. This wasn't because of the need for him to come in and save me. It was deeper. Not just the high at borrowing his strength, but the connection of power we shared. The line of life and death we walked together. Having Warwick with me no matter how far he physically was from me.

Nothing was there. No buzz or life. The link I claimed to hate was the only thing I wanted.

Bang! Bang!

"Allj!" *Stop!* The demand from Buzzcut and Kristof bellowed behind me.

My boots struck the stairs, taking me down to the lower level. Birdie and Wesley ducked behind a food stand in the middle, shooting back at the men. Shouts and gunfire pinged off the red painted railing, the open stairway making it too easy for them to target me.

Without thinking, I grabbed the handrail, flinging my body over it and dropping a full story. I hit with a bone-crunching thud. Pain sheared up my nerves, my ankles, wrists, and knees, cracking into the tile, popping and screaming in agony, leaving me momentarily immobile.

Another kick to my gut when the realization hit me. I was feeling normal pain for any human who jumped down a story onto a hard surface would feel. But I had never known I was abnormal. Never knew how fast I rebounded was peculiar, or how much farther I could push my body than others.

Now I no longer knew who I even was. The very thing I believed I was, even hoped I was, I no longer wanted to be.

"X!" Birdie's body slammed into mine, propelling us both under a booth table as shells rained down on us. Wood splintered off the thin table, hurling in the air like feathers. "What the hell, girl?" Her head darted around, trying to find another place we could run to. The table wouldn't hold out much longer. "You okay?"

"Damn, that hurt," I grunted, spitting through the throb in my ankle and pangs in my knees.

"Can you walk?"

"Yeah." I gritted, a bead of sweat trailing down my temple. Adrenaline coursed through me, keeping the debilitating pain back for now. Pulling out a second gun, I breathed through the aches. "I'm fine."

A squeal of metal jerked our heads toward the sound. The gate at the front entrance was rising. The shouts of more guards coming our way infiltrated the mall.

"Fuck," Birdie hissed.

"B? X?" Scorpion's voice pulled our attention over to a newspaper stand where he was hiding with Maddox across from him. "Come on! I'll cover you."

"You ready?" Birdie started to crawl out.

"As much as I ever will be." I slunk right next to her, my finger on my trigger.

"One. Two. Three!" She and I darted out.

Blasts reverberated around us, licking the back of my neck, as we sprinted for Scorpion, his gun firing round after round, guarding us.

Fruits and produce burst like firecrackers around us. Juice sprayed across my face, and bits of food tangled in my hair while we ducked and weaved through the stands.

A scream belted through the building right as we scrambled into the newsstand, twisting my head, fearful it was one of us.

Buzzcut's body tumbled over the top railing, his head hitting the ground first with a wet crunch. Like a watermelon smashed into the floor, its red juices leaked out, with bits of seed and meat of the fruit splattering over the light tile.

"What the fuck happened to warning us?" Scorpion shot at me, tucking further behind the stand.

"I didn't have time!" I volleyed back. "And I couldn't link to tell you."

"Link?" Birdie frowned between us. "What are you talking about?"

Both of us shook our heads, irritation heightening the already tense situation.

"What is going on with you two?" Birdie motioned to us.

"Nothing." Scorpion's tone went cool, his attention back on the fight. "And not at all important right now." He filled his chamber with more bullets.

"How the hell are we getting out of here?" Maddox yelled over to us from his hiding place, his backpack barely containing all the items he stole.

"The only way is out the front door," Scorpion replied. "We let the guards come farther in, and we slip out the front."

Like a leaking hole, the only way was to get them deeper into the market so we could break through.

"I'll go first. Everyone ready?" Scorpion peered over at Wesley, seeing him nod his head. "Leave what you can't carry on your back. This is all about survival now."

Guilt swelled in my throat. I was starting to feel like a bad luck charm. So many items we needed would have to be left behind now.

"Birdie, X, you guys flank me. Maddox and Wesley, take the rear," he ordered. "All right, go on three."

He counted down, all of us leaping into action the moment he uttered the last number, our guns primed and ready to kill.

The four guards in the front were heading straight for us. The excitement of seeing real action, of playing soldier, was written naively on all their faces. The other ones were quickly coming from behind. With no other exits, we were pretty much surrounded.

Everyone in my group, minus me, had strength and speed over them, but HDF's fae bullets could kill all of us just the same.

"It's her!" one shouted, my eyes locking on the familiar guard. "The fuckin' fae traitor! Kill her!"

A shot whistled by my ear, grazing my skin, his disgust and anger directed at me. I knew their orders were to shoot to kill. If they brought me in dead or alive, it no longer mattered.

Scorpion didn't hesitate, his bullet finding the middle of the guy's head. His body crumpled to the floor as he moved us forward. It was only a matter of time before they would have reinforcements here. The call would already be out. Our window to escape was closing in on us.

Gunfire volleyed from both the front and back of us, but when Birdie took out another one, the truth of their situation was sinking in, fear in their voices mounting as they called back and forth to each other.

As we advanced, both of my hands held guns and aimed at anything that moved. Casings dropped on the tile, the sound like wind chimes.

The two who were left in front retreated. Their dreams of being a badass gave way to the truth. They didn't want to die.

"Go! Go!" Scorpion motioned for us to run. We didn't hesitate. We burst out, bullets and shouts thundering behind us inside and from the roof. Twisting my head, I spotted Kobak glaring down at me as we slipped out into the dawning morning, hiding in the deep shadows still looming across the city.

We escaped with our lives, but those fae I saw being put in the van wouldn't.

The truth of what Istvan was doing had faces now. Beings who didn't deserve to be caught up in Markos' sick methods—a farcical dream of ensuring human supremacy.

"Tell me again what you saw?" Andris paced behind his desk, his question directed at me.

The five of us were spread out through his office. Birdie and I were in the chairs while the guys leaned against the wall or sat on a filing cabinet made of crates. The mood was low. Our plunder half of what it should be, which I took on my shoulders. Even if Wesley had knocked something over, they could have hidden. the guards chalking it up to a rat or wind, but when Kobak saw me, the game was over.

"They put two fae into a van. They were beaten and clearly drugged. They were taking them somewhere else to experiment on them. This place was some kind of holding location."

"You're positive about this?" Andris stopped, placing his hands on the desk, leaning forward.

I hesitated for a second. "Yes." I nodded, rubbing at my throbbing knee. "Seeing Dr. Karl there makes me certain they were moving them to a place where he could test them."

"Dr. Karl?" Andris stepped back, air sucking in. "He was there?"

I had gotten so used to him in this world, I sometimes forgot Andris knew all the players in HDF too.

"And Captain Kobak."

"Shit." Andris hissed through his teeth. "Karl is far too intelligent, ambitious, and greedy for his own good. And we both know Kobak is a sick son of a bitch." Andris ran his hand over his hair. Everything about him felt youthful and energetic. For a man in his early fifties and going on no sleep, he almost looked fae. "You didn't see which direction the van was headed?"

"No." I cupped my kneecap, feeling the swelling underneath. "They hadn't left yet, before everything went to shit."

"That was my fault." Wesley held up his hand, his own guilt straining his features. "My bag hit a stack of wood boxes full of apples." He rubbed his eyes, probably picturing himself watching them fall and not being able to stop it.

"You guys are safe. Alive," Andris replied. "That's most important."

"And I got us the medicine we needed," Birdie claimed proudly. "Food we can get other places."

Andris nodded in agreement, leaning over his desk again. "Well, if anything, this is the break we needed. We've been searching for the testing location for weeks now. This at least gives us a lead. Tonight we stake it out again. Watch and follow."

"You think they will use it again?" Scorpion pushed off the wall. "They know we were there… that *she* was there and saw them."

Andris sighed, his lids shutting briefly. "There is a good chance they won't, but we have no other tips." He sat down in his chair. "It will be highly guarded now, but we don't need to break in. Just follow the van to see where it goes."

"I'll go." Scorpion nominated himself. "Maddox, Wesley, Birdie, and I can go out again tonight."

"I want to go too." I straightened in the chair.

"No." Scorpion shook his head. "You seem to draw too much attention and…"

"Danger." I rolled my eyes. "Yeah, yeah. But I also know these people. I could have insight." My head darted between Scorp and my uncle. "I need to do this."

So much was out of my control right now. I hadn't even wrapped my brain around the fact I had found my mother, Warwick was gone, but I still wanted him, and we lost Killian and Zander. The panic bubbling in my chest, fear of being left alone with my thoughts, made me desperate.

"Please."

"No." Andris jerked his chin to where my hand continuously massaged. "You need someone to look at your knee and ankle first."

"But—"

"Brexley, you will slow them down if you are hurt," he said plainly.

Flinching, I dropped my head away, the comment cutting deeper than he meant.

I had always been the strongest and fastest in my training group. I killed fae and fought my way out of Halálház, but now I was fragile. A sprained ankle and twisted knee from something I wouldn't have even thought twice about before.

Andris returned his attention to the group. "Devise a plan and check in with me later." He dismissed us, the guys already heading for the door.

"Come on, girl." Birdie helped me up. "Next time, why don't you leave the flying to me." She nudged my shoulder. "Is hanging around us making you think you're fae too?"

Not fae, but what I used to be. Whatever that even was.

"You want to get something to eat? Think it's about breakfast time." She motioned to the minimal canteen area. What Wesley was able to get wouldn't even feed half the dwindled group for one meal.

I felt like a failure. "No, I might get some sleep first."

She grinned. "Is that code for finding the massive legend's dick and riding it until you pass out?"

The walls I was trying to keep up around me splintered in thin fissures, letting pain seep through. I bit down on my lip, swallowing it back.

"No. He's gone."

"He's coming back, right?"

"No." I stepped back.

"What?"

I motioned behind me. "I should go check in with a nurse to look at my knee." I turned, hobbling away.

"Wait, X, what happened? Where is he?"

I acted like I didn't hear her, slipping down the hallway.

"Brex?" A different voice called my name, swinging my head to the side. My shoulders sagged at seeing him, like being near him I could let down my walls. He appeared as if he had just gotten back too, his backpack full. Ash strolled up to me. "Hey, what's wrong? You're limping."

"Sprained it." I realized I had never sprained or broken anything in my life, this frailty making me itch in my own skin.

"Hey." His hands cupped my face, tipping it up to look at him. "What's wrong?"

A crazed laugh came up my throat. "What's not?"

"Fair enough." His brows crinkled with worry. "But did something happen on your mission?"

"Yeah, I sprained my knee and ankle."

"Well, you're in luck. I brought many miraculous herbs and painkillers."

His lightness caused my face to crunch up.

"What?" He tilted his head in confusion.

"I never sprained or broke anything before," I whispered.

"Ah." He pressed his lips together, getting my meaning.

"I may have not known *what* I was, but I knew *who* I was."

"And now you don't."

Gritting my teeth to keep from crying, my head danced up and down.

"You are still the girl I met over a month ago. And like I told you then, and I will say it again, you are not alone. I am here." He tipped his forehead to me. "Whether you want me or not, you are family to me."

"But why? You've *only* known me a month." Was it really just a month? I felt like I had known Ash my whole life.

"Because you're *his* family. That makes you mine."

"But—"

"No." He cut me off. "Whatever that asshole needs to work through, he will come to the same conclusion. I'm not saying you should give him a pass, not at all. On the contrary, I hope you kick his ass for a decade. *But* Warwick does not understand love in the conventional sense. He doesn't know how to let someone in. I've known the bastard forever, and he still keeps me at arm's length. He protects and cares for people, not the other way around. But he transformed with you. I've never seen him the way he is with you. Ever."

"Doesn't change anything. He doesn't want to be here."

"We all know that's a lie. And eventually, he'll see it too."

My hands rubbed over his, my lids squeezing shut, so thankful I had Ash. He was wrong, though. Warwick was stubborn, and if he didn't want something, he would not bend.

"Now, let's go see if we can heal your knee." He kissed my forehead, then turned down the hall to the sleeping quarters. We entered a room with two beds. Both mattresses had been placed on the floor together. They appeared to have been slept in. Maybe not slept in, but *used*.

Vigorously.

The sheets and blankets were in complete disarray and twisted up. One pillow was ripped, and a sheet had some kind of stain I didn't even want to think about.

My brow lifted.

"You have no room to talk. I heard what you did to the room at Kitty's… and at Povstat."

"Gonna tell me who slept over?"

He grinned mischievously, motioning to an empty cot for me to sit down on, not answering.

"Boy? Girl? Boy and girl?" I prodded.

He chuckled, sitting down next to me, pulling stuff out of his bag. He yanked the fae book out, placing it down between us.

My question forgotten, my focus was entirely on the book. My breathing faltered. I stared at it, trying to feel or sense something, any tiny hum or pull to it. Reaching out to touch the book, fear shook my hand, not wanting to acknowledge what I already knew.

My fingers glided over the cover, my lips pinching together.

No hum, no voice in my head, no magic.

Nothing.

My lashes fluttered, feeling Ash's gaze on me. My eyes drifted to see him watching me intently.

I shook my head, my voice hoarse. "I can't feel it."

Ash reached over, covering my hand with his, placing it on the book. "Hmmm." His brow furrowed. "It's like you aren't even here. I could always feel it calling to you. Wanting you. Now…" His shoulders slumped. "Nothing."

I yanked my hand away, staring at the wall, trying to let the strange loss wash off me and not settle in.

"What do *you* feel?" I asked.

"You mean toward the book?"

"No." I pushed my back against the wall, licking my lips. "Toward me." I folded my hands in my lap. "You said you were drawn to me before, could feel death and life around me."

Ash didn't say anything, his green eyes watching me.

"It's gone, isn't it? The attraction."

He let out a huffed chuckle. "If you're asking if I'd still love to fuck you, the answer is yes."

"That's not what I was asking."

His humor quickly dissolved. Somber and uncomfortable, he looked away. "Yes. It's gone."

Sucking in sharply, I gnashed my teeth together. I knew it, but to hear it out loud was something else.

It was *what* I was which drew people to me, not really me. Like fae glamour.

"Stop." Ash hit my leg. "I know what you are thinking."

"How can I not?" I flung up my hands. "It wasn't me they wanted at all."

"Believe me, it's still *you* we are enchanted by. It's *you* I'm here for, with or without it. And if some can't see it, then fuck them. You'd know who is real and who isn't then."

I blew out my lips, slinking back into the wall. "Thanks."

"If you want me to prove it, this bed hasn't been used yet."

Snorting, I tipped my head back, quickly going somber. "I guess you're right. We'll see who is real." I blinked back moisture in my eyes.

Both of us knew who I was referring to.

Ash moved the book lying next to me, staying quiet, putting it back into his bag.

"Will it come back?" I whispered.

"I don't know. As I told you last night. Magic is a give and take. You might have taken too much."

Still staring at the ceiling, I nodded.

"We'll figure it out." He squeezed my good ankle. "Okay?"

My head bobbed, still not looking at him.

He sighed, turning back to his bag.

"FUCK!" Ash bellowed, jerking me to him. "Those little assholes!"

He shoved the cotton bag at me. Peering in, my hand slapped over my mouth.

Among some remnants of mushrooms were Opie and Bitzy, asleep at the bottom. Bits of mushroom stuck to their faces, tongues hanging out.

Bitzy's eyes cracked open, her middle finger flipping me off, a happy smile on her face. *Chiiiiiirrrrpppp*. Her eyes closed, passing out again.

I fought back my laugh.

"It's not funny. I just filled the entire bag." Ash barked out.

"Oh, come on. Don't be upset." I leaned toward him, rubbing his arm. "Be a—"

"Don't say it."

"Fun-guy."

Ash groaned, freeing a deep laugh from my chest.

Even if it was brief, it felt good to laugh.

To feel like me.

Chapter 8

"Nothing?" Andris perched on the lip of his desk as he addressed the group who staked out all night. I slunk into the room when I saw they had returned, curious to hear any news.

"No," Maddox replied, appearing completely exhausted. "Triple the guards were there, but not a thing moved in or out all night."

"Then we try again tonight." Andris folded his arm.

"Sir, I think it will be a waste of time, and I think you know it. They understand it has been compromised." Scorpion was in the same position as yesterday, leaning against the wall, his eyes bloodshot, but of course, it worked on him. "They won't be using that place again. We lost our chance."

Andris let out an exhale, his shoulders dropping with frustration, scrubbing his hand across his bushy brows. Begrudgingly, he concurred, his disappointment screaming over his features.

"We'll start from scratch again tonight. We have to find this place and shut it down." He rose from the desk, strolling around to the other side. "All of you, get some rest. Send in a few who can do a market run. We are already low on food."

"I'll do it," I spoke up, every head twisting to look at me.

"Fuck, no." Scorpion huffed. "You are not exactly anonymous. You're still on the cover of every newspaper and on the most wanted list."

"Scorpion's right." Andris was already going through the files on his desk. "You're too noticeable. And with your leg…"

"It's fine. Ash put some herby-crap on it, and it feels better." I crossed my arms, my stubbornness ticking back my shoulders. "I will wear a hood and be careful. I didn't leave HDF to sit on the sidelines. I'll take Ash, Kek, and Luk with me. Let me do something." *Or I'll go insane.*

Yesterday, I ended up sleeping most of the day. After Ash rubbed some magical herbs on my injuries, I crashed in his room because I was too afraid to be alone. My mother, the nectar, Warwick, Killian, Caden and Hanna, Zander, Simon and Eliza, all the things I couldn't solve or fix, rolled round and round in my head until Ash had me drink something stronger so I'd sleep. I woke to Opie braiding my hair with Ash's herb leaves and Bitzy still high, trying to catch dust.

Andris tapped on the files, and I could see he was on the verge of breaking. His stress was on high, and the fourth day without much sleep was getting to him. And I was not above using it.

"Please, *Nagybácsi.*" I exploited the voice I used on him a lot as a child to get what I wanted.

His lids shut for a moment, and I knew I had him.

"Fine," he replied curtly. "But you better be so cautious and careful."

"Of course."

"I mean it, Brexley. You stay hidden, and if there is any trouble, and I mean a whiff, you get the hell out. Do you understand me?" He came back, using a tone I heard a lot from him as a kid, my method biting me in the ass.

Touché.

"Yes."

"Are you serious?" Scorpion flung up his hands in disbelief.

"She'll be fine." Andris defended me. "She was raised to be a strong soldier. One of the best."

"Don't be a douche, Scorp. I've seen her. The girl can take care of herself." Birdie leaped off the cabinet she was sitting on. "Now, *this* girl needs some food and sleep." She high-fived me on her way out. Everyone followed her.

Scorpion stopped in front of me, his cheek twitching.

"Yes?" I arched an eyebrow.

"You're not..."

"What?" I tilted my head, aware he was probably going to say I was just a human now, but he shifted on his feet.

"Just be careful." He grunted and stomped past me, knocking my shoulder.

Andris smirked, his head shaking.

"What?"

"I think I've heard Scorpion talk more since you arrived than I had in the five years I've known him. He was always an excellent soldier, but now he's becoming a great leader."

"And you think I had something to do with that?"

"I do." Andris didn't hesitate. "And maybe I don't know Warwick enough to say, but I think you've done the same to him as well."

"Done what?"

"Found life in them. Their soul," he said to me. "Made them better men."

"You know I could take this." Kek tossed up a bruised apple from her palm. "Just put on a little demon show and walk right out of here with a box full of these crappy things."

"But you won't." I dug into my pouch, taking out some coins to pay for the bundle I got, smiling at the old lady working the stall.

Kek groaned, rolling her eyes, frowning at the rain clouds moving in on the cold day. "You are taking all the fun out of this."

"I never said it was going to be fun."

"It was implied." She huffed like a surly teenager, turning away from the fruit stand. "You said we're going out. Which I thought meant something like taking me to that whore house with you this time."

I rolled my fist around the bag, forcing myself not to look in the direction of Kitty's. We were only a few blocks away. And even though I couldn't actually feel Warwick, his presence was still there, making me constantly think I saw him out of the corner of my eye.

"Here." I shoved the apple bag into Lukas's hands.

"I'm starting to think you brought us to carry shit." Lukas and Ash were already loaded down, their bags stuffed with items as Kek and I continued to add more.

"Like a donkey," Ash grumbled.

"More like two firm asses." Kek glanced over her shoulder, winking at them, her blue eyes darkening with lust.

I wasn't sure if I was reading into it or if there really was a lot of tension between them, but everything they said felt like some double meaning. Kek was always like that, but something was different. I couldn't tell if it was between two or all three of them. They did a good job of hiding any signs of their fun marked on their skin under their clothes and hoods.

"We need potatoes, onions, and meat," I stated, checking off our shopping list. So far, the trip had been seamless and quick.

"I'll get the meat." Kek ginned, turning around to face us, walking backward. "Which one of you wants to come with me?" She cocked an eyebrow. "Ash? How sweet of you to volunteer."

He chuckled, the side of his mouth tugging up, his head wagging as he stepped up with her. She looped her arm in his, craning her neck back to us.

"Don't wait up, kids."

"Be back here in ten minutes." I pointed at the spot.

"Thirty." She shot back, their forms getting lost in the busy market throng.

"Ten!" I shouted. "I'm not kidding."

I heard a cackle of laughter only Kek could make. Shaking my head, I chuckled too. "Kek." I said her name like it explained everything as I tucked my own arm in with Lukas's.

"Yeah." He breathed out as a slight pink colored his cheeks.

"Lu-kas?" My voice was full of meaning and suspicions.

He didn't look at me, acting like he didn't understand, but by the twitch in his jaw, I knew he did.

"Come on, tell me." I shook his arm. "I know something is going on."

"I have no idea what you're talking about."

"Seriously, how dumb do you think I am?"

He huffed out a laugh, still not answering.

"Please. Right now, there is not much good around. I need a little happiness." I prodded him in his side, tapping on his healing wound. "Something juicy and naughty."

He laughed louder, his head falling forward as he sucked in a breath.

"Tough day. Things needed to be let out." He shrugged, walking toward the stall, making me recall it was pretty close to what Ash had said to me.

"You and Ash?" I stood in shock, gaping. "And Kek?"

He continued to walk on, not saying yes, but not saying no, either. He was suddenly very interested in the produce.

"Holy shit!" I was right. I had teased Ash, but I didn't know I was actually right about the who. Plural, in this case.

Reaching his side, I couldn't help but bob on my toes, clapping giddily. The feeling was euphoric in all the heartache. "I can't believe this."

"Stop." He pushed down my hands. "It was nothing." He muttered, glancing around cautiously. "A one-time thing. A lot of emotion and loss that night."

"Oh, yeah. Of course." I replied in a mock serious tone. "Sure. Will never happen again."

"Nope." He picked up a bundle of onions, putting them into our pouch.

"So?" I rolled a tomato in my hands. "How was it?"

"Brex," he warned.

"I'm just asking. I mean, you were with a girl too."

"I've been with a girl before."

"What, when you were hitting puberty? This is different. Or was she not in the middle?"

He breathed out, giving money to the seller and turning away, his mouth brushing my ear when he strode by me.

"We took turns."

A squeak came out of my throat. "Damn, that's hot." I breathed out, realizing how tense I was. The need for my own release pulsed my thighs. But the thought instantly dropped me back down. There was only one I craved, just one my body even wanted now. He ruined me and my ability to desire anyone else.

Twisting to follow Luk, a shoulder slammed into mine, stumbling me back on my ass onto the cobble.

"Ouch."

"Oh, I'm so sorry." A woman, her face mostly covered by a dark wool cloak, reached out for me. "Let me help you."

She yanked me up, pulling me closer to her than was normal. Her voice hissed in my ear. "Meet me at the Lantern Pub. I have information about the warehouse you seek, Brexley Kovacs."

I sucked in when I heard my name, freezing for a moment in fear. Then she was gone.

I whipped around, searching the crowd for the woman, but the sea of dark clothes and jackets blended her into the tide of bodies.

"Hey? What's wrong?" Lukas came back up to me, taking in my expression, the frantic movement of my body.

"That woman, did you see where she went?"

"What woman?" His brows furrowed, his demeanor shifting into defense, his instincts taking over.

"The one who helped me up."

"I didn't see anyone."

"She knew me." Panic fluttered in my chest. "Knew my name."

"Like she recognized you from a magazine or paper?"

"No." My gaze still darted around the crowd. "It felt different. Like she knew who I was and purposely knocked me down."

"What do you mean purposely?"

I faced Luk. "We need to find Ash and Kek now."

"Why?"

"Because I think she knows something about the fae experiments."

Along a shadowy back street, a single worn iron door with a faded painting of a lantern next to it almost disguised what it was. Amongst boarded-up shops and dilapidated buildings, the existence of this place would never be noticed by anyone who didn't already know it was there.

Luckily, Ash did.

"I really don't like this." Ash pressed me deeper into the shadows as two horses and their riders trotted by. Their confidence and interest in everything suggested they were out looking for trouble. It was late afternoon, and the lowering sun hidden by the angry clouds was already heavily shading the alley into twilight. "This isn't a place you go unless you're looking for conflict."

"And funny you know it so well," I challenged back.

Ash lowered his lids, not amused. "I'm not kidding. It's underground, which makes it a perfect place to trap someone. It's for those who are looking for cheap drinks and dirty dealings."

"Sounds like my kind of place," Kek replied dryly next to me.

"I have to go. If this person really does have information…"

"They knew who you were, which clearly means they've been watching you." Ash hitched the heavy bag up higher on his back, uneasiness riding his brow. "This is such a perfect setup. Dangle something they know you want and trap you."

"I agree with Ash." Lukas gestured to him. "It seems too convenient. It has to be a trap."

"How would they know I was particularly looking for this warehouse, though?" I argued. "Istvan wouldn't know. He doesn't know Sarkis has been searching for them. I feel it in my gut. I need to do this."

"Brex." Ash rolled his hands in frustration. "I'm not sure I trust… you're not—" He broke off, his head bowing.

"What?" I challenged, hurt curling into anger. "I'm not what? Special anymore? Able to make a call because I'm an ordinary human now?"

"That's not what I mean, and you know it." Ash snapped with exasperation. He took in a huge gulp of air and let it out slowly. "I'm just worried." His moss irises met mine. "With or without the magic, you are one of the smartest, fiercest people I know. I trust you implicitly. But I won't pretend you not having those powers doesn't worry me. Humans are fragile; your lives can be taken in a blink compared to us. So yes, I fear you going down there is outright stupid and dangerous. And if something happens to you? I'm dead. *He* will kill me. And I like my life."

"No, he wouldn't," I scoffed.

Ash, Kek, and Lukas burst out laughing.

"You serious?" Kek chuckled. "He would string us all up by our intestines."

"Which, I've seen him do, by the way." Ash's lip lifted in a grimace. "More than once."

"Well, guess what? Warwick isn't here." I pushed off the wall I was tucked into, moving past them. "And no one is *letting* me do anything. I'm going." I heard their rebuttals, my hand going up to stop them. "I'm not stupid or a newbie at fighting my way out of deadly situations. And lucky for me, I have three badass fae at my side." I turned to face them. "You guys spread out through the bar, and if anything goes sideways…"

"I'm sitting at the table with you." Ash stepped closer to me.

"But—"

"That's where I draw the line." His expression was firm. Ash was easygoing, so when he said that was the line, he meant it. There was no swaying him. He would be by my side, no matter what I said. "And if they've been watching you, they already know we are with you."

"Fine." I nodded. "Let's go."

The four of us crossed the dirty street, dodging a few motorcycles and horses, making our way to the entrance. Ash and I went first, appearing like patrons after a day at the market, looking for a drink to ease our tired feet and ebb the weariness of our lives.

My stomach knotted as we descended the stairs to the decrepit basement pub. My trigger over small, windowless underground spaces saturated me in panic, adding to my anxiety.

The dimly lit place looked like some underground tunnel with brickwork and sloping ceilings, ready to crumble at any moment. Low murmurs from the patrons bounced off the walls like white noise. The tight space was pretty full for this time of day, but I guess in this world, they had no societal rules about what time of day you could drink your life into numbness. HDF had a more uptight notion of drinking in the day, though I knew many wives who filled their tea with alcohol to forget their own boredom and unhappiness, plastering on a happy smile for their husbands.

At least these people were honest about it.

A mix of ages, races, and genders, mostly hidden under hats and hoods or stuck in the shadows, made it hard to define between species. Most didn't glance our way, but I still felt eyes on me. Keeping my hood up, I peered quickly around the space, trying to pick out the woman in the marketplace, knowing the longer I stood here, the more notice we would receive.

My focus landed on a single form in the corner. I couldn't see a face, just a hooded figure, but the short, curvy stature told me it was a woman. Taking a chance, I weaved through the tables, Ash close behind me. She watched us sit down across from her, our backs to the door. Her silence and unsurprised reaction to us suggested I chose correctly.

"Were you followed?" Her voice was low and controlled.

"No," I answered.

"Except there were four of you," she replied.

Twisting slightly, I watched Kek and Luk stroll in out of the corner of my eye, one sitting at the bar and one grabbing a small table near the front.

"They're around." Ash's tone implied we were not unguarded.

"Good." She dipped her head. "Do not trust anyone."

"Yet, you are asking me to trust you by coming here." My muscles coiled, ready to respond to any attack coming.

"I owe it to you. To my mother. I have much to thank you for, Brexley Kovacs."

"How do you know my name? Who are you?"

The woman reached up, pulling her hood down, exposing her face. She was in her mid-thirties, her naturally curly, dark hair spang from the hair tie. Her brown eyes and round cheeks were so familiar.

A breath caught in my lungs, her appearance shifting me back in my chair.

A thin smile curved the woman's face, her head dipping. "I am Lena, and my mother Maja worked as your maid for the last five years."

"Maja," I heaved out, connecting the resemblance now. To me, she was far more than a maid. She was like a mother, friend, and grandmother rolled all in one. "You are Maja's daughter?"

I had never met either of her grown children, although I heard much about them. I felt a connection to them even though we didn't know each other.

"Yes." She nodded across the room, and I turned to see a balding man at least in his late thirties with the same brown eyes rise from his stool at the bar, walking over to us. He slipped into the chair next to Lena. "And this is my brother, Emil. We just wanted to make sure you were really you."

She had the same idea we did, someone watching her back if anything bad went down.

"It's odd to finally meet you in person. Especially here." Emil dipped his head in greeting.

"I've heard so much about you both." I shook my head in awe.

"As we did you," Lena responded, her eyes still darting around, on guard. "We are taking a huge risk—our lives and our families are on the line. But what you have done over the years to help us…"

"I realize now how little I did. What it's really like out here. How arrogant and sheltered I was."

"No." Lena's hands cupped over mine. "You saved my baby girl from death. We were able to sell the items and get money for a healer." She blinked the tears away. "I owe you everything."

"I wish I had done more." What I stole was so little in the scheme of things. So many were starving and dying while the rich got richer.

"It may be small in your eyes, but to us, it was the difference between life and death some days."

Liquid burned the back of my lids. She squeezed my hand again before letting go.

"Besides, our mother adored you. Considered you another one of her children. She wanted us to do this."

"Maja wanted you to come to me?" I pointed at myself in shock. I was a traitor now. She always seemed very faithful to the Markos family, to HDF.

"She was the one who told us about the incident at the market. She overheard a conversation with General Markos about you being spotted there and what you saw, afraid of what you might know. My mother was very worried about you. Knew none of the rumors they were saying about you were true."

The greatest spies were those who the arrogant people overlooked, like a sweet, older lady who cleaned their home had access to everything and everywhere.

"Okay, but what does that have to do with you two?" Ash motioned between them.

"Because." Emil leaned closer, his voice going so low only we could hear. "Lena and I work at the factory they are using for their fae experiments."

Shock slammed into me, dropping my jaw. "What?" I belted out, instantly slamming a hand over my mouth, peering around to see if we grabbed anyone's notice before whispering hoarsely. "You work there?"

"For twelve years." Emil's guarded focus went around, leaning even closer. "It's a normal factory by all appearances, and most of those working there don't know what's going on below their feet."

"How do *you?*" Ash laid his forearms on the table, his lids tapering.

"Lena and I have kept our heads down, done our work, and been there every day," he defended. "We have been faithful employees no matter how many times they cut our pay or docked us. We were promoted one day out of the blue about a year ago. To do clean up." He swallowed roughly. "What we saw down there. What they were doing to fae. Men, women... *children*."

"But you stayed." Ash sneered.

"We didn't have a choice," Lena snapped back. "I'm a single mom of two kids, one sickly. If I lost my job, my family would starve."

"It's not that." Emil patted her arm consolingly. "They threatened us. Our families... *our kids*... if we spoke one word of what we saw." He gulped, his Adam's apple bobbing. "We would receive extra money for our silence. To keep from living on the streets and watching your kids suffer would silence the most honorable of men trying to survive in this land. But someone like you might not understand true destitution." Emil's censored gaze drew over Ash.

"You have *no* idea what I understand or don't." Ash sat back, his arms crossing in front of him.

From what Warwick told me, he did know what it was like. He lived it daily as a child. All three of them did.

"We took this chance to meet with you. I'm sorry we can't do more, but our families' lives are at stake." Lena slipped a piece of paper to me. "There is a door we use on the northwest corner to take the trash out. It's always locked and alarmed by magic, but it would be the only way in." She stood up, her brother joining her. "That is all we can do."

"Thank you." I tried to express my gratitude in two words.

Lena bowed her head, lifting her hood back on, Emil doing the same before they slipped through the dusky pub, and up the stairs, out of sight.

Ash and I watched for a while to see if anyone followed them before turning to each other.

"Well, I was not expecting that today." Ash's head wagged. "Gods, Brex, even without your magic, danger still seems to be *drawn* to your ass."

I unfolded the paper Lena gave me. An address was written out roughly.

The location of the factory.

I exhaled, folding it back up.

"Like a fuckin' G-string."

Chapter 9

The dark skies rolled with cantankerous clouds, threatening at any moment to spit more rain down. Mist slithered off the Danube only yards away from our hiding spot.

"You sure they weren't setting you up?" Scorpion peaked over a small barrier wall in front of the collection of factory buildings on the street. Even at this hour, smoke billowed from the chimneys, and dim light came from inside. "This was one of the first factories we checked out. Many nights we staked out this place and saw nothing. The factory runs twenty-four seven. Day shift and a smaller night shift."

There were no laws or unions giving workers' rights or controlling how many hours they worked. It didn't surprise me they were forcing people to work all night or all day.

"No, this is not a setup." I really hoped I was right, that this wasn't some trap to get me, while they got a handsome reward for leading me here. "This has to be the place."

The address Lena gave me was on the other side of the Rákóczi Bridge. The old industrial area in the 9th district had been gentrified at a time before my birth, but now it was back to manufacturing in rundown buildings, pumping waste into the river, and polluting the air with black smoke.

It was a perfect location—close to the river to dump bodies and sewage, and right by a train station used solely for factories to load cargo to export their product to other countries before continuing to a pedestrian hub.

"You guys in position?" Scorpion muttered into a walkie-talkie device he stole from Lehel Market. An item only the uber-wealthy could afford, brought in from Unified Nations.

"Yes." Birdie's muffled voice responded on the twin gadget.

Birdie, Maddox, and Wesley were on one team, scouting the other side. While Ash, Lukas, Scorpion, and I were on the other, coming up the west side of the brick building.

Built for function, not beauty, the long, unappealing rectangular box seemed too ordinary to have such horrors hidden beneath.

"Lena said there is a door on the northwest side they used to take out the trash. It must be there." I pointed to an overgrown area with stairs leading down into the ground. The basement door was so hidden it could easily be missed unless looking for it.

"You said it was magic-locked and alarmed?" Scorpion asked, his attention still fully on the building, a frown on his face.

"That's what she said," I replied.

Andris wanted tonight to be merely a stakeout mission, gathering more information about possible guards, trip alarms, entries, exits, and what the place was being used for. In the meantime, Ling was trying to get more black-market items for the base, like fae lock picks and the earpieces I told him Mykel had at Povstat for larger missions.

I needed to get word back to Mykel soon, letting him know everything that was going on here and what I had found out. He didn't even know Tracker and Ava were dead, or my mother was alive. Sort of.

I was unsure about telling him we found the nectar. My trust in Andris was complete, but I didn't know Mykel enough to think he wouldn't use it. Even if it started out for good, things like that seem to corrupt people easily.

"Let's get closer." Scorpion gestured with his gun for us to follow. Skulking through the darkness, only the light from the factory guiding us, our boots made the smallest shuffling sound as we moved together. Ducking behind brush, we listened for anything that told us we tripped a wire or our presence was known.

"I don't see any cameras or guards," Ash whispered to us. "Doesn't mean they aren't somewhere around."

"Istvan would want to make this appear like a normal factory. Anything noticeable like guards or high-tech gadgets might attract attention. If he has them, they will be well hidden."

"Which is not a plus for us," Scorpion muttered, pulling up the walkie-talkie to his mouth. "Anything?"

"No. So far, nothing to report," Birdie retorted through the device.

"Why does that make me more nervous?" Scorpion muttered under his breath, and I concurred. The more everything seemed mundane, the more I felt this might be a trap.

Time ticked by painstakingly slow, with no movement or any guards making rounds on the outside.

"This is pointless," I finally huffed out. "We're not learning anything from here."

"Lieutenant said specifically not to engage tonight. Surveillance only," Scorpion curtly replied. I could see his own restlessness and irritation growing.

"Never took you for one to follow the rules," I scoffed, my brow lifting.

He shot a glare at me, but it had everything to do with his ego and not what I was proposing.

"No," he grumbled. "Whatever you're thinking. No."

"Just Ash and me," I countered, giving Ash a look, hoping he wouldn't nix this idea. He rolled his eyes as if to say *like I could stop you.* "You and Luk cover us. I want to get a little closer. See if there is any other way inside. Anything that might tell us something more than this."

Scorpion exhaled through his nose, not looking at me. He had to know I wasn't really asking for permission. He was our superior tonight, and I wanted his approval, but there was a good chance I'd go anyway. Otherwise, this entire mission was for nothing.

"You know I'm right," I said matter-of-factly.

He dipped his head with a grunting sigh. "Fine." He clipped back, pointing to both Ash and me. "But the moment you see or sense anything, you get the fuck out of there. You got it?"

"Yes, sir," I mimicked his tone.

"This is not funny, Brex." Irritation flicked over his face. "I don't have a way of knowing you are okay now. If something happens to you…"

"I know." My gaze met his somberly. I understood all too well what he meant. The lack of connection between us, between Warwick and me, bristled at the back of my neck. I hated I couldn't even feel if they were in danger. The gap where both had been in my soul, even if it hadn't been for very long, felt hollow.

Another thing I shoved into a box to deal with later.

Lukas and Scorp got in position, their guns aimed, while Ash and I slipped out of the brush, clambering closer to the building. Leading, I darted toward the back of the building, toward the door. Ash glanced around, his body low and defensive. Because my senses were ordinary now, dull and limited compared to his, I depended on him to detect anything off or wrong while I hunted for ways in.

Lena had been right. Besides the front entrance and the utility door, the place was impregnable. All the doors and windows that once had been there were bricked over, allowing only those permitted to go in and out.

Controlled.

"Brex!" Ash hissed in my ear, his arms wrapping around me, yanking me behind the corner of the building into the dark shadows. Ragged breath pumped in my ears, his form tense behind me, causing mine to bobble and leap all over the place. "A camera is hidden by the rain duct in the middle." His voice was hoarse in my ear. "It looked to be scanning both ends."

Relief and panic dug through my lungs when I exhaled. Thank the gods for Ash. I hadn't seen anything. "I really hate being human," I mumbled.

"And just think, not long ago, it was all you wanted."

True. I had. Now I wanted nothing more than to be me again.

"Let me check it out." Dropping his arms, he crept in front of me. With stillness only fae were capable of, Ash inched his face out just enough to peer around the corner. Seconds ticked by slowly before he so gradually pulled his head back. It was undetectable to a human eye or camera.

"Thirty seconds on each side before it starts sweeping back."

"Thirty seconds to get in that door?" I huffed. "I can do it in my sleep. I used to hop trains, break inside, find and steal product, and hop off in under three minutes."

"Not a chance." He shook his head. "This is simply surveillance. Plus, we don't have the means to get through the door. Andris will be satisfied with what we found."

"Oh, Bitz, when will these stupid fae-brains ever learn?"

Chirp.

My hand slapped over my mouth, holding back the scream as a small voice came up behind my ear. The feel of bare feet climbing onto my shoulder shot adrenaline into my system until my brain clicked in, understanding who it was.

"Fuck." Ash breathed out heavily.

"Not sure if it's an appropriate time, but sure, I'm game." Opie grabbed onto my hair, coming into my peripheral, Bitzy in her pack.

Chirp.

"Oh, I didn't mean me." Opie coughed. "I meant them two. Certainly, *I* wouldn't find this tree fairy with golden hair and a dick the size of a tree trunk *at all* appealing. I mean, gross. And that big war man? Even grosser." He stuck out his tongue. "Blah."

Chirp!

"I did not!"

Chirp!

"That was a total misunderstanding."

"Shut the fuck up." Ash hissed, his attention darting around. "You two are going to get us killed." He pointed at Opie. "Though you are not wrong, I'm seriously disturbed you know anything about my dick."

"You sleep very soundly."

I groaned, my face planting in my palm.

"I'm not going to think about that right now."

"You, sir, don't think at all. Any of you." Opie sighed. "How many times do we need to tell them, Bitz? Larger they get, the less brain power there is?" He motioned at Ash. "Locks mean nothing to us."

Lifting my head, I blinked.

"No." Ash instantly shook his head. "It's too dangerous."

"When is it not?" I opened my arms.

Ash let out a quiet scoff. "Fair point, but there are alarms on this door."

"Oh, alarms-salarms." Opie batted his hand. "Those are cake."

"You sure?"

"Yeah… like ninety percent sure."

"Ninety?" I peered at him.

"Yeah, ninety or at least eighty percent."

"I'm not liking the way this is trending." Ash's nose wrinkled up.

"Get the broomstick out of your ass, fairy. I totally got this."

Chirp.

"Yeah, maybe you're right."

"What?" I asked.

"Don't worry, Master Fishy. Seventy-five percent is still really good." He threaded his fingers together, cracking them. "Magic fingers are ready. Bitzy and I knew you might need us tonight. Have them all warmed up."

Chirp!

"It was the only warm place to stick them. They needed to stay nimble."

Ash and I cringed, both knowing what that meant.

"Even more of a no," Ash uttered to us.

Folding my arms, I saw Opie copy me, our heads tilting at Ash.

"No." He shook his head vehemently. "We should get back as it is."

"This might be our one chance."

"Plus, tree humper, I didn't warm these fingers for nothing." Opie held up his hands, wiggling his digits.

"No."

"Yes," I countered. "Every moment, another fae is being tortured, and most likely killed. I'm not saying we go down there and blow the whole operation. We aren't ready for that. But I do want to know if we are even at the right place. If we aren't, we don't waste any more time here. But if we are, we need to know what is going on down there so we can put an end to it."

"This is completely stupid." Ash gritted his teeth. "And totally dangerous. We have no plan."

"And would we have a plan later? We have no idea what is below. We can't have a plan if we have no understanding of what this place even looks like."

"There could be an army down there." Ash shot at me.

"There could be nothing," I volleyed back. "Do you sense anything on the other side of the door?"

He closed his eyes, letting himself reach out, feel life humming in the earth. "No, not right there—but I do feel something down there."

Staring at Ash, I waited for his answer.

"This is so reckless." He pinched his nose.

"Yes, it is. But are you in?"

He huffed and puffed, shifting around until he finally grunted.

"Fine." He held up his hand. "But you go on my word, what I say. You don't have the awareness you used to, and if I say run, you don't question me. You run. Got it?"

I nodded. In that moment, I felt an inkling of understanding Istvan and his desire to elevate humans on the food chain, which greatly unsettled me. It sucked being so fallible and unbalanced to the fae. Now that I was without power, I identified a little more with the need to be equal.

"Be ready to go." He then gestured to the two on my shoulder. "You get the door unlocked as fast as you can. Less than thirty seconds."

"Yes, sir!" Opie saluted Ash.

Chirp! Bitsy flipped him off.

"I'm so gonna regret this," Ash muttered, turning back around, inching a breath away from the corner. "Ready?"

I glanced out toward the brush, knowing Lukas and Scorpion were about to lose their minds.

"Go!" Ash whispered.

Turning away from where they were, I ran. Bounding down the steps to the wide, solid door, my heart drummed in my ears with a fevered melody. Opie darted down my arm as I reached out, holding it near the seam in the door above the handle. Opie's little hands patted around the surface, searching.

"Hurry," Ash commanded, his gun up, watching the camera and any activity which might come up behind.

"Keep your dick in your pants." Opie snapped back, his palms finally landing on a spot, cringing. "Ohhh."

"Ohhh, what?" My voice squeaked. "What does ohhh mean?"

Chirp!

"Okay, so it was a soft seventy-five percent."

"What?" I blinked.

A grunting sound came from Ash behind me.

"Hold your tree limbs." Opie's tongue stuck out of his mouth, his hands tapping and fidgeting around the spot. "This one is tighter than Master Finn's ass."

Chirp!

"I would not know. It was an expression."

Chirp!

"That was a total misunderstanding."

"Guys!" I hissed.

"You don't open it in ten seconds, we are aborting." Ash hissed over his shoulder.

Opie's tongue switched to the other side, his brow furrowing.

"Eight... seven..." Ash counted down.

Anxiety compressed my breathing, panic clawing and biting at my nerves.

"Getting closer." A bead of sweat formed on Opie's forehead.

"Closer is not good enough. Hurry." Forcing my legs to stay steady for him.

"Five... four..."

Bitzy reached over Opie's shoulder, her lids shutting briefly, her face strained.

"Three, two... one!"

Click! The lock snapped.

My body slammed forward as the door was ripped open. Ash shoved us in with a jarring force, shutting the door behind him.

Our breaths pitched together in gulps, my body leaning back into his. Adrenaline pumped frantically through my veins. Peering around, I noticed the space was dim with a few fire bulbs leading into a long tunnel. It was a typical industrial basement with cement walls, floors, and ceilings lined with water and gas pipes. The ceilings were a few feet above Ash's head, and it was wide enough for a large truck to wheel through, like the one I saw parked next to the door.

Large enough to carry several bodies in.

Ash slipped away from me, taking lead, his gun up.

Motioning for Opie and Bitzy to get into my pack, I matched Ash's steps, my weapon swiveling behind us as well to guard. Both of us on high alert, our footsteps were precise and silent.

The tunnel sloped farther down, gradually taking us lower into the earth. Passing a few doors that appeared to be utility closets, I noticed everything was very ordinary. Nothing you wouldn't find under any factory.

That quickly changed.

Bright light shone down at the end of the tunnel. Noise from machines and movement reached us, each of us tightening our grip on the trigger. Ash and I moved on opposite walls, and the more we neared the end, the less we could hide in the shadows.

Peeking out where the passage split to the right or left, more fire bulbs flickered in the space, machines and equipment lining one side of the wall. Nothing I recognized or understood, but their noise hummed through the air.

"Which way?" I whispered to Ash.

He shrugged, nodding at me, telling me it was my choice. I forced this on him, so it was my decision to be right or wrong.

Inhaling, I motioned to the left, going with my gut intuition. Stepping out, we were no longer hidden by any shadows. The long corridor was like a bowling lane. If we were found, we had nowhere to hide.

We scuttled down, the tunnel curving, and climbed down metal stairs, running into another pair of magic-locked doors. A card scanner was next to it.

"Shit!" I bit down on my lip. I knew it wasn't going to be so easy; Istvan was far too paranoid and smart. "What do we do?"

"Card scan?" Opie was back on my shoulder. "Easy-peasy."

"Really?"

"Of course." He started down my arm. "A strong eighty to thirty percent."

"Wait... thirty?"

Chirp!

"Twenty-five the lowest." Opie motioned for me to move my arm to the card scanner. "They're a little tougher, but I'm their bitch."

I tilted my head.

Chirp!

"No, I meant they're *my* bitch." Opie huffed, his hands on his hips. "I'm *the* bitch! No, no, that doesn't sound right."

Chirp!

"Fuck my life." Ash waved at the scanner. "Shut up and do something, both of you, before we are all dead bitches."

Opie promptly went to work while Bitzy flipped Ash off, chirping in a low, continuous noise.

"You want mushrooms?" Ash slanted his head at her.

Instantly, her mouth clamped shut, her enormous eyes blinking.

"I will get you a full bag of mushrooms if you shut up and get us in."

She blinked once more before climbing out of her bag and over Opie to reach the scanner.

I twisted my head to peer at Ash, his expression in disbelief. "My life is now bribing a three-inch imp with hallucinogenics so she will listen to me."

"Father of the year." I winked at him.

"Fuck." His finger dug into his eyes, rubbing fiercely, then snapped back into defense mode, his muscles tensing.

"What?"

"Voices." Ash's head tweaked toward the stairs. I strained my ears to listen, but heard nothing but the humming of the machines. "They're coming this way."

Terror flashed through me, my head feeling dizzy, but after years of conditioning, I quickly locked it up, searching for anywhere to hide.

"I think he will be pleased." This time, I heard the male voice arising from the passage before the physical forms followed.

Their footsteps were seconds from turning the corner to the stairs, leaving us right in their eyeline.

Panic bubbled in my stomach, my gaze darting over the space. There wasn't much between the stairs and the door. We had one possibility.

Clutching Opie and Bitzy in my palm, Ash and I scrambled for the stairs, slipping underneath the open treads as shoes hit the metal. Ash pressed me into the corner against the back wall, his body almost covering mine. We didn't move or breathe as we watched three sets of legs move down, their chatter blocked by the pounding of my heart. The moment they reached the ground and came into view, I recognized them: Dr. Karl, his assistant Dr. Stefan, and the man who was Istvan's right-hand man, Lieutenant Andor, another one with too much greed, misogyny, and entitlement. Faithful to Istvan to a fault. He didn't care about right or wrong; he only believed in following Istvan.

He, like so many, wouldn't hesitate to kill me. And all it would take was one of them to look back, and we would be as good as dead.

"The last batch had much better numbers. Also, the younger ones seem to produce better results. I think we are getting closer. Now that we've updated the science of Rapava's theories and tweaked the water tanks from the plans General Markos obtained from those lost records, the results have been much better," Dr. Karl said to Andor, searching his pocket and pulling out a card.

"They better be. General Markos has not been pleased with the progress so far."

Dr. Karl's fingers slipped, the card falling from his grip. It felt like slow motion as it hit the ground, Dr. Stefan twisting to pick it up. It would only take one side glance, and we'd be caught. Deep fear rooted me in the spot, not even daring a twitch of my lungs. Sweat pooled at the base of my spine as Stefan picked up the card, his head lifting.

Oh gods… we're dead.

"Give me that." Dr. Karl snapped at him, yanking the card and Dr. Stefan's attention to him. Away from us. A minuscule ounce of relief pressed into my lungs. "You are so slow. Lieutenant Andor doesn't have time to waste." He belittled his assistant, even though it was his own fault.

Karl swiped the card over the scanner, the door unlocking and sliding open.

"Come, we should be getting the new shipment in soon." Dr. Karl motioned Andor in, following in behind him. Stefan was on their tail, disappearing to the right.

From here, it appeared there were no guards or anything waiting on the other side.

The door started to shut, and the instinct to run and block it from locking rattled through me. I locked myself in place, watching our way in close on us.

Something caught my eye, tearing across the floor to the door. It looked like a rat with a backpack and a mohawk.

Huh?

For a second my attention snapped down to my empty hand. I hadn't even noticed when Opie and Bitzy slipped out. This time when I blinked at the form, it looked more like a tiny man in a black bodysuit with pink tassels and a similarly dressed imp on this back.

Right as the door was sliding closed and would lock, Opie propped his body in the opening, the door squashing into him until his mouth and cheeks puffed out.

"Now would be a good time," he muffled, the door groaning, trying to close all the way. "Before this brownie becomes a pancake."

Ash and I darted to him. Ash pried open the doors, letting Opie free, peeking his head and gun through. "All clear."

"Wow. I think I'm thinner now. And much taller." Opie padded at his body. "Do I look thinner?" He stretched his form like he was doing a photo shoot. "I'm like a model now. Handsome, thin, tall with impeccable taste."

91

Chirp!

"Okay, but I'm at least taller?"

"We don't have time for this." Ash jerked his head as he opened the door wider. "Go!"

I snuck through the opening with my gun raised, ready to shoot, while Opie and Bitzy climbed up to my shoulder. Ash slipped in behind. The door hissed shut, locking. The sound hit my stomach with dread.

Trapped.

Underground.

"Looks like we don't need a card to get out," Ash whispered, nodding at the button by the door.

"Let's hope." I took a step forward, my gun following my gaze, searching every corner. The men were nowhere to be seen. The space was the same cement and machinery, but a dome like-structure dominated the middle of the area. Like an observation point, cement went to waist level, then clear plastic panels curved over the top, light glowing from below.

Tentatively we moved toward it. The distant sounds of talking and machines itched at my ear, keeping me on guard.

Finally reaching it, I peered down.

And I knew I was looking at the deep pits of hell.

Chapter 10

Dr. Karl, Stefan, and Andor descended steps on one side of the vast room below. A handful of other people in lab coats milled around. Whether scientists or doctors, I didn't know or care. If they looked up, they could see us, but they were all far too busy with what they were doing to notice the voyeurs above.

Half a dozen bodies were strapped to tables with strange machines or equipment next to them.

"Oh gods." My hand covered my mouth, bile burning up my esophagus when I spotted one victim, no more than ten years old. Tubes were in her veins and nose, dried blood smeared across her tortured expression. Her body continued to half-shift into a buffalo, then stop, reverse, and start over again.

"My sister was just a calf, but they had no problem kidnapping her, experimenting on her, and then taking her life." The memory of Rodriguez, what he said to be moments before I killed the bull-shifter in the Games crashed down on me like a brick. My knees wobbled, and my head spun as I choked down vomit. His anger and rage, the need to kill me... in some way fight for his sister, honor her. I understood it now. This little girl was like her, was possibly someone's sister. Someone's daughter. She was innocent. A child, but because she was fae, HDF treated her as if she were a rabid animal. A soulless creature who needed to be put down.

For so long, I thought as they did, believed the propaganda, not wanting to actually look past what they told me and see they had all the qualities our side deemed were worthy. Humanity. Those claims we were righteous and better because of that single word. They were not *human;* therefore, they must be evil. When all along, we were the evil hypocrites. Rotten to the core.

Dr. Karl gestured past the tables, strolling to the farthest wall. Leaning over, my lids squinted trying to see what he was monitoring, what took up the entire wall.

"Holy fuck." Ash's tone made my stomach twist more, taking me a little longer to see it clearly.

Holy fuck was right. Water tanks. We had overheard Dr. Karl mention them, but this was nothing close to what I had thought he meant.

Approximately seven-by-four see-through water tanks lined the wall. Twelve of them, filled with some kind of thick liquid, and floating inside were people. Young and old, women and men. Their mouths fastened to a breathing device, their eyes shut, tubes pumping something into their veins. The same machines the fae subjects had attached to them at the table were beside each tank. It appeared one was pumping fae essence *out,* and the other seemed to be pumping *in.*

"What is that?" My voice barely made it out, my eyes rising to Ash, hoping I was wrong.

"I have no idea. But I think we both know whatever they are doing here, it's not good."

"They're killing the little girl, aren't they?" The lump in my throat barely let me swallow.

Ash's expression pinched, his head bowing. "Yeah. She's too young for her body to endlessly change like that. I mean, an adult would die after that much stress to their body. I've been told it takes a lot of magic to shift."

"They're taking her essence every time she shifts?" It wasn't really a question.

Ash nodded again. "That's when magic is at the highest. Shifters use the purest magic in the transition between the animal form and their 'human' one."

They wanted the most powerful and richest magic, which is why they weren't allowing her to fully change either way.

True fae essence.

A clank came from behind us, the door unlatching, jerking my head with a snap, a gasp rising in my throat. Ash moved before I could even blink. His arms wrapped around my torso, yanking me down behind the dome on the other side of the door.

Footsteps hit the ground a few feet away from where we were hiding.

"Tell Dr. Karl more shipments are coming in. I'll prepare the side bay for their arrival," a man's voice spoke.

"Will do," another one responded.

Peeking over the half-wall, I watched one go right toward the stairs to the lab, and one went left down another corridor.

"There's another entrance in here?" Ash said the moment the guys were out of earshot.

I shrugged. "Makes sense."

"Probably a tunnel leading here from somewhere close by, so they don't stir up notice," Ash answered, tapping my arm. "We've got to go." Ash, low to the ground, started heading for the door we came through.

I glanced down again, the young man reaching Dr. Karl, but it was the young girl on the table who pulled my attention. Agony warped her adorable features as she shifted into a buffalo before going back, and every time she did, I saw more liquid pump out of her, travel down the tube, and into a clear bag. Forcing her to change over and over while tearing her very being from her. Her soul.

They were monsters.

I was empathetic to her pain, the loss. It wasn't being torn from me, but it was taking part of my soul, and that loss hurt deeper than I ever imagined possible.

"Brexley." Ash frantically waved for me to follow him. Giving the little girl one last look, I made a vow I'd get her out, and then I turned and followed him.

We shuffled to the exit; Ash hit the button next to the door. My heart tripped over itself when voices came down the passage, and the door didn't budge.

"Oh, hell no." Ash stabbed his finger into it again, the voices growing louder. Closer.

The door jolted, slowly opening like we had all day to wait for it.

Ash slammed his palm against it, tearing it open. While I watched to see if anyone came up behind us or was walking up on the other side of the door.

The moment it was wide enough, we darted through and up the stairs. We raced down the corridor, about to turn down the tunnel leading back to the door we originally entered.

Two men stepped around the corner, HDF insignia branded on their black t-shirts and cargo pants. HDF-issued guns with walkie-talkies were attached to their gun halters.

Two more I knew by face, but not by name, but I was certain they knew mine.

The shock of seeing us, their eyes landing on me, gave them pause for a moment before they snapped into soldier mode, reaching for their guns. Ash didn't hesitate to take advantage of their shock. He sunk his fist into the taller guy's face, the power making him stumble back. The guy's gun fell to the ground, snapping the rest of us into action.

I leaped for the shorter one. My knuckles skated across his cheek, into his nose, tipping him to the side with a crack. I didn't give him time before I punched hard at his eardrum. A spot that could mess with your equilibrium.

A grunt barked from him as he swung back for me. I couldn't get out of his line fast enough, so his hand drove into my gut, heaving me over. Biting back the pain, I gripped his arm and swung my body till he stood behind me, his arm bent the wrong way. Using all the momentum I could, I flipped him over on his back with force.

The other HDF member was flung by Ash and landed on his face right beside his partner. They weren't out cold, but out enough to escape.

"Come on!" Ash wouldn't want to waste any more time on them while others could be coming for us. We sprinted around the corner and down the tunnel, no longer caring about being quiet, our boots striking the ground with heavy thuds.

"Stop! You traitorous fae-lovin' bitch!" one of the guards screamed from behind us. "Or I'll shoot!"

"Don't threaten me with a good time." My words barely made it out before bullets were being shot down the passage.

"You had to encourage him?" Ash griped at me.

"Like they weren't gonna shoot at us, anyway."

Picking up our speed, Ash still had to keep himself from zooming past me, my legs not carrying me as fast as he could go.

"Code red! Code red. Intruders in the west tunnel. Brexley Kovacs confirmed. Need backup." I heard one soldier speaking into his walkie-talkie.

"Damn," Ash spit through his teeth. "They really don't like you, do they?"

They hated me more than they hated the fae next to me because being a traitor to them was worse than being the thing they hated.

Reaching the door, we didn't have the luxury to check for threats before bursting through it. My lungs happily soaked in the cold air of the night, happy to be out from the underground.

Ash and I barely made it up the stairs when shouts and orders rang through the air, whipping us faster toward our comrades. I knew Lukas nor

Scorpion would leave, though if we got out of this, one or both would most likely kill me.

Racing toward the brush, they leaped up. "What the utter fuck did you do?" Scorpion roared. "I'm going to fucking kill you."

"Not the time, man." Ash waved them on as he kept going. "Let's get the hell out of here first."

Louder voices and commotion flipped Scorpion and Luk's focus to retreating with us.

"We got them, X. Get out now!" Scorpion ordered through the device while he picked up pace, the brush forcing us back onto a path.

A burst of light beamed on us from behind. Twisting my head, I saw car headlights and then heard the roar of an engine coming to life. The car squealed as it jolted toward us at full speed.

"Fuck! Run!" Scorpion bellowed, waving us on.

We tore around the corner near the water, running on an old bike trail and walking path, but the car didn't care, jumping onto the path, the engine roaring louder with momentum, nipping at our heels. Passing under the bridge, we cut across train tracks and brush, hoping to lose it.

The shout of guards and the sound of horseshoes clicking on the pavement clawed more terror down my nerves.

"Split up!" Scorpion shouted. We all knew us being in a cluster was perfect for them. We needed to divide their attention and sources, though I was really the one they wanted.

I dragged up my hood, needing to hide my features the best I could.

Lukas and Scorpion splintered, one along the river and one heading northeast up a side alley.

"Ash, go. I'll be fine."

"I'm not leaving you."

"We're too noticeable. They know you're with me."

"If anything happened to you... No." He shook his head. "I'm not leaving you."

"I'm not asking."

Ash would stay next to me even if he knew it would be his demise. Not just because he was a good guy and my best friend, but for his brother, too. He had some warped idea that when he protected me, he was protecting Warwick as well.

"No." He grabbed my arm and pulled me down a street. The pounding of horses and boots echoing in the air, bouncing off the deteriorating building. The area was more modern than most of the city and didn't have as many nooks and areas to hide in.

"There they are!" Someone shouted from behind, his nasal voice arrowing through my spine, his bloodlust and excitement pitching it even higher.

"Shit!" Ash hauled me faster down the lane, gunfire ringing out behind us.

The wide path let us see the soldiers moving in to block us from the other side, peeling us off across an area of land now used for livestock. Weaving and darting through the sheep, cows, and pigs, we slipped across the road.

My breath was heaving so hard it hurt, but my shoulders eased, thinking we finally lost them. But the piercing sound of tires squealed across the pavement, headlights blinding my vision for a beat as the car came for us.

"Move!" Ash screamed, shoving me out of the way, my body flying back as the car plowed into the tree fairy. My bones hit the ground while I watched Ash's form sail into the air, crunching hard on the top of the roof and rolling off on the other side as the car came to a squealing stop.

"Ash!" A guttural cry ripped from my gut.

I didn't have time to get up before the man behind the wheel stepped out, his gun pointed at me, a sneer on his face.

Kalaraja.

"Finally," was all he said before his finger tugged at the trigger. Scrambling up, I dove behind a bin as the bullets bounced off the spot where I just had been. "I always get my mark. Always. And I no longer have to bring you in alive." Bullets hit the metal, the sound forcing my hands to clasp over my ears. His boots moving closer.

I was dead. This was it. How I would die. Behind a smelly dumpster.

The gunfire suddenly stopped, replaced by the thud of bodies hitting, bones cracking. "Brex, run!" Ash's voice strained out. "Go!"

"No!" I scrambled out, seeing my friend holding down Kalaraja. Bruised, bloody, and torn up, but alive. In the distance, shouts of soldiers were heading right for us.

"Go!" Ash ordered, struggling with Kalaraja, his fist cracking across the older man's jaw so hard Kalaraja's head went limp. "Just run! I'm right behind. Go!"

A shot zipped through my hair, making me duck down, and seeing Ash appear to be getting up, ready to run with me, I twisted and tore down the street, running as fast as I could and cutting down an alley. I paused behind a wall, sucking in gulps of oxygen, turning back to see if Ash was following.

I felt it too late. The form slipped in behind me, grabbing me firmly.

"N—" Before I could even try to fight, a rag slipped over my mouth, and a shot of adrenaline zipped up my spine, knowing exactly what toxin covered the cloth. I couldn't stop or control it.

Warwick! On instinct, I felt myself reaching for him.

As my eyes shut and my body went limp, I thought I felt a hum of something, but I was wrong.

It was just empty darkness.

Awareness rushed at me with a start, my lungs gasping. I tugged against the binds around my wrists, my head throbbing painfully. Bile coated my throat.

Blinking, I tried to clear the thick haze from my eyes. I realized there was a reason I couldn't see. A cotton sack was over my head, only letting in filtered shadows from a crackling fire near me. I could feel I was in a small space by the way the single fire warmed the room. The smell of old wood and potato soup made it cozy.

My fuzzy brain whirled with fear and confusion. I knew HDF's prisons. They were cold and sterile. I even knew the smell of Istvan's office, his cologne.

This wasn't any of them. Where the hell was I?

Any HDF soldier would have me taken straight to headquarters. Or did Istvan want to torture me in private? Didn't seem like his MO. He'd want to publicly execute me to make it clear what happens to traitors of HDF.

Several pairs of footsteps clipped the wood floor, moving closer to where I was, my body stiffening. My shoulders pitched back, my body fighting the need to vomit and curl into a ball from the effects of the drug.

My heart thumped, my fingernails digging into the rope with every step as the group drew closer. *Clip. Clip.* The steps paused, and the air in the room shifted, adapting itself to the addition. Whoever captured me was now in the room.

Holding up my chin, I prepared myself.

"Gods…" I heard a voice mutter. "I told you to bring her here. Not tie her up and blindfold her."

The voice was familiar, striking something in me, but my clouded head wouldn't allow me to fix on it. To believe.

"She's here, isn't she?" another smooth voice retorted.

The first guy didn't reply, but the second one grunted, marching over to me.

My muscles locked up, feeling a large physique looming over me.

The bag was ripped from my head, my hair crackling with static. I flinched, my vision adjusting and blurry while it took in the familiar beefy figure with caramel-colored hair and violet eyes, tripping my brain up even more.

What I saw and what I was expecting did not click together.

"Sloane?" I stammered, my forehead wrinkling, not understanding why the high-ranking, elite fae soldier was before me.

His expression stayed blank, stepping around me, revealing the figure behind him.

Everything stopped.

"Oh, my gods." Hoarseness strangled my throat, my lids prickling, hoping I wasn't totally losing my mind.

"Why is it always you, Ms. *Kovacs*, causing so much trouble?" Smooth like honey and wine. His voice punched a hole through my chest. A dark eyebrow cocked up over his bright violet eyes.

"Killian!" I didn't even notice Sloane had cut my binds. I was flying out of my chair, crashing into the warm, solid form, tears already spilling down my cheeks with happiness as he pulled me in. My arms wrapped around him so tight, making sure he was actually there.

Alive.

"Missed you too," he muttered in my ear.

Sobs hiccupped in my throat as I smelled him, felt him. "How?" I leaned back, my eyes gobbling up every feature. He appeared tired and ungroomed compared to what he usually looked like; his scuff was more like a beard, his hair unkempt, but to me, he was even more sexy and beautiful. "Y-you're alive. I thought you were dead. How? Oh, my gods." I hugged him again, not letting him get a word in. I hadn't even let myself feel the pain of losing him; the hollowness was too much. The heartache too great. Even if we were on different sides half the time, he had become very important to me.

He held me tighter, tucking his chin into my hair. He sighed against me, squeezing tighter before he pulled away. This time when I peered up at him, a smile still curved his mouth, but his forehead furrowed.

"What?" I asked.

His eyes scanned me like he was searching for something. "Nothing." He shook his head, stepping back, pinning his smile up higher. "It's nothing."

"I don't understand. How did you escape?" *He's alive. He's right here and alive.* My heart kept looping over and over with pure joy.

"We will get to that." He rubbed at his chin, the fire reflecting off his silky dark hair. I finally took a moment to notice his casual outfit of dark green cargo pants and a black t-shirt with boots, appearing more a soldier than a king. It was sexy on him, but it didn't "fit" him like his suits did. Killian held too much grace and nobility to think he ever actually got down in the trenches.

I also took in the small cottage we were in. This room held a sofa and chairs facing the fireplace, a small, round table with four chairs not far behind it. A doorway opened to a hallway, which I figured lead to a kitchen, bathroom, and bedrooms.

"But first, Ms. Kovacs." His eyes glinted, stepping to the side. "I thought you'd want to say hello first." He held his hand up at the doorway. Three figures stood around the hallway entry.

It was the one in front who held my focus.

A repressed cry rose in my throat, my hand clapping over my mouth, tears no longer staying back as I ran across the room, jumping into his arms.

"Z-Zander." My heart cracked open, letting everything I had kept at bay out. The horse-shifter neighed, tucking me in tighter to his chest.

"So good to see you." He whispered against my temple, holding me until I was ready to step back.

Wiping the tears away, I retreated to look at him, to double-check that he too was alive and healthy.

"I can't believe this." I sniffed, glancing at the others behind him.

Eliza and Simon smiled back at me.

"You are all alive." Eliza didn't know me, but I gripped her hand, touching Simon's head. "I saw it blow up." I shook my head. "We went to the palace... saw the devastation. No one could survive that. How?" I faced back to Eliza. "We need to find Warwick. He needs to know you are all right."

"That will have to wait." Killian gestured to a chair. "There is a lot to catch you up on."

"He needs to know."

"Ms. Kovacs." Killian lifted his brow again, insisting I sit down. Eliza nodded her head in agreement. Wearily I went back to the chair where I had been tied, watching the room. I felt like I was missing something.

102

Zander indicated for Eliza and Simon to take one side of the sofa, Killian on the other. Zander and Sloane stayed standing.

I rubbed my head. I tried to center myself, my elation ebbing enough for the sickness to come back. "People really do love chloroforming me," I grumbled.

"I apologize for that." Killian folded his hands together on his knees, shooting Sloane a sharp look. "It wasn't supposed to go like that."

"I personally wanted to knock you out." Sloane shrugged one shoulder.

"Why did you need to do anything at all? I would have gladly come."

"Easier," Sloane replied. "A lot less chatty my way."

"Right now." Killian pulled my attention to him. "We can't trust anyone. I can't have anyone, including *you,* know where we are hiding. Plus, you wouldn't have left without your tree fairy sidekick. I only wanted you."

"Why can't you have anyone knowing you're alive and well? Aren't you leaving your side vulnerable? So many people are devastated, thinking you are dead."

"They need to remain thinking that way for a while longer. Until we find out more." Killian loosened his hands, glancing at the fire. "The bombing was from inside."

"I know, I saw it."

"No, I mean, someone *on* the inside. One of my own men." Killian peered back at Sloane again, causing him to move closer.

"I found Vale and Conner dead. Discovered their bodies minutes before the explosion. They were on duty, watching a private back entrance which leads straight to the private chambers." Sloane spoke, lifting his chin, strain along his jaw, appearing to fight the emotion at losing his two comrades. "Their necks were broken and sliced open. There is *no way* a human could breach our fae lines and also sneak up and kill two of the best soldiers in the world." Emotion flickered in his eyes before it was gone. He cleared his throat. "Whoever killed them was someone they trusted. Someone part of the palace." Sloane nodded at Killian. "They were not the targets. They were in the way."

"If this person could get straight to you. Why didn't they just do that?" I bounced between Sloane and Killian.

"More destruction. More devastation. It also looks more like an attack on the fae than a personal job."

"The buzz around is it was Sarkis' army." Zander piped up, his hand on the sofa right behind Eliza.

"But it wasn't." I shook my head. "They got bombed too. It had to be Istvan."

Killian sat back on the sofa, his expression distant. I could see all the questions going round and round in his head, probably on an endless loop, never quieting.

"Two bombings that night, and the humans aren't touched? It's so obviously Istvan. Why has no one gone after him yet?" Asking that question coiled fear in my gut. Between what I saw earlier and this brash arrogance, Istvan was showing more and more. I wondered what it all meant. Why he was feeling so bold.

"Another thing I'm trying to figure out." Killian rubbed his head, pushing back his hair. "All I know is someone wanted me dead. Someone powerful enough to sneak in with enough C4 to blow up half my palace, which has magic protection on it. This individual or group had to be very aware of that magic and how to counter it and also be known and unquestioned by the staff. Only those within my palace know information like that." He sighed. "Until I know more, the best thing for me is to pretend I'm dead and let them poke their head up and start declaring themselves the new leader of the fae."

The fire crackled and popped, all of us trying to put the pieces together.

"Anya?" Mom? Simon peered up at his mother. "Can I get a cookie?"

She smiled warmly down at him, her hand brushing over his dark mop of hair.

"Of course. Only one, *Édesem."* *My sweet.* The pet name hit right in my heart; my father used to call me the same thing. "Just be quiet. Don't wake him." The boy smiled, tearing off down the hallway.

Wake him?

"I am so happy you are both okay." I looked at her. "Warwick is going to be ecstatic."

"On the inside." She chuckled, brushing her dark hair back, the ends skimming Zander's hand. "As my brother never shows emotion any other way."

"Yeah." A laugh bubbled up, my head lowering, remembering all the ways that man showed me emotion. Wild, raw, and fierce emotion.

"How did you guys escape?" I inquired.

Killian headed for a table against the wall, filled with whiskey, Pálinka, and glasses. "Sloane got to us in time." He picked up a bottle, pouring liquid into several glasses. "He sensed something was about to happen. We were in the tunnels when the explosion hit." Killian picked up the glasses, handing one to Eliza but skipping Zander as if he knew he'd didn't want one. He distributed the others to Sloane and me before taking a sip of his. "This was the one place I knew of where I trusted we'd all be safe."

Two things danced around in my thoughts: not only did the Lord of the Fae serve us himself, but Eliza had no fear or resentment toward him in any way. She didn't at all act like a person being held against her will for ransom. All of them seemed comfortable and at ease with each other.

Interesting.

"Why did you kidnap me?" I sipped at the whiskey, the rich taste nipping a little at my pounding head. I really hated chloroform.

"Kidnap?" Killian leaned against the mantel. "We borrowed you, Ms. Kovacs." He winked at me.

I snorted. "Fine, why did you *borrow* me?"

Killian opened his mouth to speak, but a grunt had both our gazes darting toward the doorway to a man shuffling into the room.

"Oh, I hope Simon didn't wake you up." Eliza twisted around, reaching out to him.

"No, I was already up hunting for cookies myself." The old man chuckled, patting her hand. His clear blue eyes darted up, realizing an unknown person was in the room.

"Tad," I whispered. Taken back, I gaped at him, not expecting his presence. It was nothing compared to his response to me.

A mix of disbelief, terror, confusion, and shock stumbled the man back into the wall, his wide eyes set on me. The entire room reacted rushed to him, but I stayed pinned in place, dread circling through my lungs, sinking into my stomach like a stone.

"It can't be." He shook his head, Zander and Salone on either side of him, trying to steady him on his feet.

"Are you all right?" Eliza took his hand, worry etched on her face. The only other person not helping him was Killian, whose heavy gaze danced between us curiously.

Tad didn't answer her, his focus entirely on me. He used her arm to move closer to me. His Adam's apple bobbed. "This cannot be." He shook his head.

I wanted to ask what couldn't be, but my mouth would not open, would not utter the question. Deep down, I already knew.

Zander and Eliza helped him waddle closer to me, their expression full of bewilderment.

"Do I have an aura now?" I tipped my chin up, my voice coming out weaker than I hoped, scared of what he'd say.

It was like he didn't even hear me, his hand shaking as it reached out for my face. "How did I not see it? It's so clear now."

"What?" I swallowed.

"You're Eabha's child." His fingers took my chin, searching my face.

"I can see her in you. How did she hide you from me all this time?" His head shook with turmoil. "You've been right in front of me this whole time. How was her magic able to block me from finding you?"

The memory of what the nectar showed me came back, reminding me of when Tad came upon my mother and my aunt on the battlefield. The words she was murmuring before the magic hit, sailing Tad back.

They were not friends.

But enemies.

Was he my enemy?

Leaning out of his reach, I shifted my jaw. "Why did you try to kill my mother?"

His lids narrowed on me, clearly curious how I would know such a detail.

Boldly, I stared back, letting him read it on me. On my face.

"You have no idea what your mother really was."

A knowing twist of my lips jerked his hand back.

"You do," he breathed, as if he could read my thoughts. "She's alive."

My lips pursed, not answering either way.

"How is that possible?" He muttered. "How is she still alive? How was she powerful enough to hide you from me?" He mumbled something under his breath. "Ah... it wasn't just her, was it? It was the magic from the Otherworld which had hit the same moment she cast that spell." He still watched me in reverence. "Whatever invocation she had on you broke. I can see you so clearly now." He blinked at me, feeling he was peering deeper into my soul than just skin deep. "You are..."

"Ordinary." I gritted my teeth.

"Oh, my dear, I wouldn't call you that." He shook his head. "You wanted to know about your aura?"

"Yes?" It was crazy that now I wished he didn't see one, the opposite of what I wanted when I first met him.

"I've never seen anything like it." His hands ghosted the space around me.

"What do you mean?"

"It's the most iridescent gray I have ever seen. I have only seen one being in the world who came close to this, and it was only a fragment of her aura and certainly not as bright."

"Who?" I rasped.

Tad regarded me with a fright I had never seen on his face before.

"Queen Aneira."

The silence in the room might as well have been the loudest screams in the world. The impact punctured my ears and captured the air in my lungs like a thief.

No one moved or spoke. Most in this room had known her, lived under her reign, been branded by her cruel authority. I had only heard stories, glimpses through my father and the history books.

"What are you talking about?" Fear and shame rocketed up my defense. "You are wrong, old man."

"I am never wrong." Tad swallowed, gawping at me like I was some fearsome science experiment.

Searching the room, everyone stared at me with the same expression, making me feel even more like a feral animal. "That doesn't mean anything." The words fell flat on my tongue, tasting of ashes. "Right?" The pitch of my voice escalated.

"I remember now," Tad whispered. "So vividly. It had been hidden from my mind until now. I remember her giving birth to you on the battlefield." His mouth opened more as if each memory was coming back to him like a book, and he was flipping the page, learning more. "What happened before I was knocked back." He reached around, touching his t spine as if something in his memory revealed itself.

"What do you mean, Druid?" Killian was rigid. His tone was smooth like glass and could cut as deep.

Tad dropped his hand, his scrutiny snapping up to me. "I might never be wrong, but I'm finding I do not know everything. I do not see the future with this one. She is like a ghost who lives in the gray area."

His words burned with truth down my throat.

Tad strolled closer to the fire, holding himself up by the mantel.

"It makes sense. The moment you were born, you were infused with Otherworld magic. With Aneira's entire family line. Fire and Wind. Her family line was the one to create the wall around the Otherworld when fae had to go into hiding thousands of years ago. Protecting and keeping fae safe from persecution. Their bloodline fused that barrier, and when she was killed, the wall dropped fully. Babies are like sponges, soaking up everything around them, but an adult's body would defend itself and die against the surge of magic. Proof of what we unfortunately saw happen across the world."

"But human babies died that night," Killian countered. "Some fae children did as well."

"That's because she is not either." Tad turned his head, powerful blue eyes drilling into me. "Her mother was a witch."

"A witch?" Eliza sputtered. "But aren't witches human?"

"Yes." Tad sighed, turning to face the room. "However, the O'Laighin clan was unique." He reached out, Eliza taking his hand and helping him sit. He huffed, and his face pinched with pain. He took a heavy breath, his regard back on me. "Your family has lineage back to the days of old. Working for kings and queens when we ruled Earth's realm."

"Wouldn't that make them Druids then?" If I remembered correctly, the fae gods and goddesses elevated a group of witches, giving them real magic and longer life. They called them Druids, while witches stayed without true magic.

"Glad you know some history." Tad dipped his head, shifting on the chair, seeming never to be comfortable. "That is true. Your family line at one time were Druids."

"What?" I balked. "But—?"

Tad held up his hand, and I slammed my mouth shut, letting him finish.

"Not all Druids were happy with their new role among the fae. Some were treated kindly and became very powerful. Too powerful for some. Other Druids were not treated so well and were forced to help advance ambitious leaders and were treated like slaves."

"After centuries, some clans did not want to be slaves anymore, beholden to the Fae kings and queens. They refused and were punished for it. In death, they would walk the earth forever—tortured in purgatory—not alive, but not dead."

"O'Laighin was one clan forced into servitude. Over time, Balfour O'Laighin assembled a group of Druids who felt the same, an underground rebellion, plotting to overthrow their cruel masters. That group grew more radicalized and turned to black magic. To hate. Everything we Druids are against." Tad touched his forehead, grief hinting in his shaking hands. "One night, they put their plan into action. O'Laighin slaughtered his fae lord and the entire fae household, including servants and the king's children."

"What?" I breathed.

"They ran, but were caught by another high king. Someone who was the enemy of the family they murdered. So instead of having them killed, because the king benefited greatly from the death of his foe, the king instead stripped them of their title. This was a great humiliation among my kind, to become low-bred witches again and have a curse placed on them, forcing them to work for his family line until the end of theirs. A curse which had you fear death far more than servitude."

"Necromancer is not a race... it is a curse." My mother's voice came into my head again.

"A curse?" Killian asked. "What kind of curse?"

I bit down on my lip, realization hitting me. "In the death of their monarch, they become necromancers."

"Necromancers?" the entire room repeated in shocked unison.

Neither Tad nor I looked away from each other, understanding far more than anyone else.

"That man, O'Laighin..." Tad stared right at me. "He was *your* grandfather."

Gasps fizzed in the room, bouncing off me as the information sunk in slowly. Everything I saw in the vision of my mother in the war, Tad coming in, all made sense now. And it was why my mother and her clan had to fight in the war for Queen Aneira and became necromancers when she died that night.

"The curse was supposed to continue on in the O'Laighin family line until they died out." Tad gripped the armchair. "But you carry no such curse. I don't understand, but you are different. And oddly absent of magic now."

My heart sunk.

"So what does it make her? Druid? Witch? Human? Fae?" Killian asked. "I can't sense any of those."

"Me either." Tad eyed me curiously. "You don't seem to be any of them."

"Then what am I?"

"Nothing I have ever come across before." Tad shook his head. "But this is even different from when I first met you... what did you do, my dear?" He leaned forward, his voice barely above a whisper. "You had magic before. Why don't you now?"

The story clogged up my throat, not making it past my tongue. I used up the magic saving my uncle and bringing seven necromancers back to life.

The treasure everyone had been searching over a decade for was an empty shell now. Nothing.

Just like me.

"Is it gone for good?" My throat squeezed, my nails digging into my palms. If anyone could see, it would be a druid. "My magic is gone, isn't it?"

Tad slanted his head, really digging into me, frustration marking his expression. "Like I said, I can't see anything inside you, girl." He shook his head. "Only gray. It's like this strange reflective shield. As if you are still shielding yourself, even though your aura is right there for me to see. It's so peculiar."

Folding my arms, I let my hair curtain around me, my emotions almost suffocating me.

The room was silent for a long time before Tad spoke softly.

"Do you know the original meaning of your family's name?"

I raised my head to Tad in curiosity. "No."

"It means The Grey."

The Grey.

The name called to me, not in voice, but like a summoning. Deep in my bones, it carved and marked itself, then fizzled out before it could even whisper its truth to me, before I could sense if I imagined it or not.

Eyes watched me from around the room, their curiosity and caution tapping at my skin. I could choose to tell them everything or not. Trust was a fragile thing. Even if we thought we were on the same side, everyone was out for their own, with their own goals and agendas.

Compartmentalizing the information I had just learned from Tad, I abruptly turned to Killian.

"I'm guessing you didn't 'borrow' me for a fun sleepover?" The accusation was direct.

Killian shifted back at my sudden turn in conversation, his arms folding. "No."

"You want the nectar." It was not a question. His new circumstance had sped up his need for the substance. For power.

Killian's mouth pressed together, his shoulders tilting back. "Every-one, leave us." His voice was silky and low, but not any less authoritative.

Zander and Sloane were the first to respond, Sloane helping Tad up, shuffling him out of the room. My gaze caught Zander waiting for Eliza, his hand gently touching her lower back as they both exited. He gave me a glance over his shoulder, a soft smile.

I could see it in his smile, his eyes. Whatever little thing he had for me was no longer. A whisper in the wind evaporating into nothing. I didn't doubt he still cared for me, might even claim more, but the spark was no longer there. Reminding me it had not been me they were drawn to at all. My power beckoned them. *A queen's* power.

When they all left, I faced Killian.

"Still the lord of your domain, I see?" I locked my arms tighter to my chest.

His violet eyes scoured over me, his jaw tight. "I am *always* the lord of my domain. Wherever I am. You best not forget it."

"Or what, *Killian?*"

He didn't even flinch when I said his name, binding fear around my lungs like rope. Doubt. Insecurity. Hanna had once accused me of wrapping men around my finger. Consciously, I never thought I had, my focus too much on Caden. Though subconsciously, I must have understood my power, the attention I received, and if I put effort into it, the result I would get.

And when you no longer got that result...

Shifting on my feet, I nipped at my lip, barricading myself more.

"We made a deal." Killian stepped closer.

"My month is not up yet."

A nerve along his jaw twitched. "Things have changed." Another step, his high-ranking fairy magic pushing against me.

Telling myself to hold my ground, fight back, I could feel his dominance shove at me... and I bent to it without a chance. My spine smacked into the wall, my chest rising at how easily he could move me. Grinding my teeth together, anger flared into my muscles.

Was this how it was for all humans? To be so easily overpowered?

"Hmmm." Killian lifted his brows, his boots hitting mine, his frame a breath away. "Interesting."

Locking down my expression, I stared back at him.

"Something's changed in you, *Brexley.*" His voice felt like it slipped between my thighs, the vibration sliding into me.

A gasp parted my lips, my head slamming back into the wall, my entire body shivering with a response. The unbelievable power he had in merely saying my name.

His head tipped in curiosity. "Something has *definitely* changed." He knew I had never responded like this before. I had been able to block his power and glamour. "Makes me curious what else I can do to you now."

"Is that your kink, Killian? Doing things to me unwillingly?" My brain was rattled by the force coming off him, the sexual energy he always had but had never affected me like this before.

"Would it be, though?" He moved in closer, his breath skating down the curve of my neck. "Would it be unwillingly, *Brexley?*"

Pleasure fluttered my lashes, and I felt myself growing wet in response. My breath faltered, my hips curving forward. Which really pissed me off.

How fast he had flipped everything on me. How quickly he could have me pleading.

"Stop it," I growled, trying to curb my response.

"Why don't you make me?" He studied me. "You always have before, *Brexley.*"

My mouth parted in a moan, my skin tingling, my nipples scraping across my sweater. My brain was starting to lose the will to fight back, craving more, needing the release he was tempting me with.

"Block me, *Brexley.*" He intentionally said my name low and dark, the tone driving into me. His mouth didn't touch me, but grazed along my neck. My body curved into his, the taste of an orgasm on my tongue. It would only take a handful more times of hearing my name on his lips. The power and intimacy of it were addicting, and he wasn't actually touching me yet. I could see why so many humans craved this. Sought it out like a drug. How many snuck away from Léopold to visit the back alleys or dens of iniquity to feel this high. To feel fae magic.

It had always escaped me before why humans pursued this, not realizing it was because I could fight it. Now I felt weak and exposed. At *his* will, not my own.

"I can't even place what it is, but there is something missing." The vibration of his timbre danced along the sensitive part of my ear. "I used to be able to sense you without even seeing you."

"You don't feel it anymore?" My voice came out breathy and coarse. Afraid. For some reason, the thought of Killian only being attracted to my power cut far deeper than Zander.

"What?" He leaned back to look at me.

"*Drawn* to me?" I looked straight into his eyes, watching every nuance.

His eyes went back and forth between mine. Inspecting. Searching. Peering deeper in.

"If you are asking if I am attracted to you? Want to fuck you against this wall." He pressed in closer, making my body beg for him to crush me under his weight, to feel his magic drive into me. To do what he said and fuck me against this wall. He grunted, leaning his free arm on the wall next to my head, his hand curling into a ball, his nose flaring like he could smell my arousal. "The answer is yes."

"That's not what I was asking." Ash had the same response, but they both knew that was not my meaning.

He stared at me, a realization dropping on him, pinching his mouth. The truth was sharp and painful. A cascade of hurt and disappointment rushed through me, flicking over my face before I shut it down.

"That's what I thought," I growled, pushing against him. "Get the hell off me."

"That's not it at all." He grabbed for my arms, pinning them back.

"Get away from me." I thrashed. "Let me go."

"*Brexley*, listen." My name glided through me again, dipping to my knees, my bones sagging against the wall.

"Please," I croaked, fighting back the tears, not sure what I was pleading for.

Killian pulled his head back, actually looking at me. "You really can't fight me, can you?"

Emotion crinkled my face, my throat full of tears. "No." The single word barely made it from my mouth as I dropped my head.

"What the fuck happened?" Fingers slid under my chin, propping my head back up. "Why can't you block fae glamour anymore?"

He didn't need to know the why. He only wanted to know one thing. Staring at him, my emotions cut off and tucked away, I responded.

"I know where the nectar is."

He jerked, dropping his hand from me, taken off guard by my response.

"Where?"

I rolled my jaw.

"Tell me where it is."

"It won't help you now, anyway."

"Why?"

"Because I burned out all its magic." I swallowed. "And mine. It's gone."

"Don't fucking lie to me, *Brex-ley*." He gritted angrily through his teeth, pushing his energy harder against me as punishment.

"I'm not." A whimper hissed between my teeth, my breath panting, taking all my self-worth and stubbornness not to rub against him or demand he to take me right here.

"I don't understand." Fury bristled under his skin. The man who always got what he wanted twisted his power deeper into me. "It's one of the most powerful objects in the world. How could you burn through it?"

"Because." I ground out as his powerful fairy magic switched from pleasure to pain. "*Stop.*"

"Stop?" He lifted his eyebrow. "Wouldn't stopping be more of a punishment? For those I want to cruelly reprimand, I stop at the cusp of their release. I've been told it is *excruciating*. Do you like pain, *Brexley*?"

"At least it would be in *my* control, *Killian*." I gnashed my teeth at him. Honestly, it would be a cruel punishment. I needed the release so badly it hurt. But I didn't like it being forced on me. It reminded me I was no longer strong enough to play at fae level.

I was a mere mortal.

"Fine." Killian stepped away, curbing his power. I slumped into the wall, sucking in air. Holy shit, I was about to take it all back. My body clenched, feeling like every muscle I had, especially my core, was experiencing the spasms I used to get as a growing child. I was denied the pleasure of a mind-blowing release, and now every nerve in me struck back in mutiny. It was worse than torture.

"Fuck," I hissed, taking deep, controlling breaths. I lifted my head to see Killian's expression was taut and his cargo pants showed he was experiencing painful tension as well.

"Now talk." His hands on his hips, veins danced in his neck and jaw. "And don't lie to me."

"I'm not lying to you," I spat, standing up fully, though the agony didn't recede. "The nectar is useless now."

"That's impossible," he shouted, moving around the room. "How did it burn out?"

"Because of me."

"You?" He jerked his head my way. "You think you destroyed it?" He paused, then let out a laugh. "Ms. Kovacs, you may not be human, but you are certainly not powerful enough to annihilate one of the most powerful objects in the world. Some of the most formidable fae have tried to own it, use it, and never could. I doubt *you* could simply come along after decades and turn it obsolete."

"Don't underestimate me." Pushing off the wall, I strolled to him, my spine unyielding.

"You can't even fight off fae glamour." He motioned to me. "How could you supersede a fae treasure?"

A wicked smile teased my mouth. "Don't you get it?"

"Get what?"

"*I am* the nectar."

The crackle of the fire was the only sound, Killian going utterly still, though I felt him in every fiber of the room. His energy popped like the flames.

"Excuse me, Ms. Kovacs?" His voice cut through like a sharp blade with deadly precision. Not one syllable was afflicted, though danger lurked under it like lava.

I didn't flinch or buckle. "More accurately, the nectar is me."

One nerve jumped in Killian's jaw.

"Did I not warn you?" He stepped for me again. Slow. Calculated. Everything about Killian was smooth and controlled. Graceful in his fury, it did not make him any less dangerous than someone who barreled for you. If anything, it made him more so.

"I do not take kindly to liars." The ruthless lord watched me with no sentiment. The ruler who could be fair and kind could also slit your throat in a blink.

"And I'll tell you again. I'm not lying." I stood my ground, fighting the impulse to drop to my knees and beg under the wrath wrapping around me. Most would. But with or without my powers, I would bow to no man.

Ever again.

Women have always had to apologize or bend to their will. We were punished for their weak character. In doing so, we helped them keep us down like pitiful creatures they claimed us to be. When in truth, we were the dragons.

Even in death, I'd go down with talons and flames.

"I don't know what you are gaining from this." Killian's eyes burned bright. "If this is some trick. But you took an oath. If you break it." He gritted his teeth. "I will make sure torment and suffering rain down on you for a century."

He reached for me, his magic already knifing into my skin. My chin ticked up higher.

"She's telling the truth." A voice came from the doorway, jolting our heads to it.

Tad stood there, his cane in one hand, helping him balance out his twisted back.

"What?" Killian faltered back.

"She is not lying to you, my boy." Tad huffed, slowly hobbling into the room. "She is what she claims."

For the first time ever, shock came over Killian's features, his head darting back to me with awe.

"How—how is that possible?"

"Sometimes this thing still works." Tad grinned at me, tapping at his head. "Took me a moment to find those lost memories. My mind does not work on the same timeline as others. When your mother did a spell right when the wall fell, she blocked my mind from anything that had to do with you. The veil has now been lifted. I can see it all." He wagged his head. "She was deviant and smart enough to piggyback on the Otherworld's magic with her own, understanding the force that was coming. There would have been no other way to do a spell that could obstruct me from seeing even when it was in my hands."

"What are you talking about?" Killian folded his arms.

"The nectar is part of Brexley." He confirmed. "It's her afterbirth."

"Her afterbirth?" Killian blinked, a frown crinkling his lip.

"It is more like a sponge, soaking in all the magic, becoming one of the most magically infused substances in the world—as powerful as the four treasures of Tuatha Dé Danann. Even more so because on top of that, she has magic from a druid."

"But I thought you said my mother was a witch again."

"In title, yes. And they lost potency of their magic, but high kings and queens don't have the power of the gods and goddesses. They can't strip them completely. Your mother's clan still held special magic. Human witches, remember, can't do any *real* magic or be cursed in their death to be necromancers."

The memory of my mother and my Aunt Morgan fighting in battle came back to me. I recalled them being able to lift people off the ground and break their necks with a spell.

Human witches couldn't do that.

"So you're saying this afterbir—nectar." Killian quickly jumped back to the original name, his head ticking like it was gross. "Is holding both fae *and* druid magic?"

"Yes," Tad affirmed. "Not simply holding, but merged together."

"How is it possible?" Killian exclaimed. "They don't mix! The fae and druids have always had contention between them."

"Not completely true." Tad adjusted his weight. "The Druid Queen of the Unified Nations is mated with a fae dark dweller, and has kids… both have dual abilities, which is a first in existence. Though I think their powers are still separated by which form they are in. They can't use druid magic in their dark dweller form, and they can't use their dark dweller abilities when using druid magic."

"Because they don't mix," Killian stated again, arms flaying about.

"Well, in this one case." Tad gestured to me. "They did."

My mouth hung open. "But I don't have powers of both druid and fae." I shook my head. *I didn't, right?* "Even when I had it, I wasn't that powerful. Not what you are suggesting."

"I think you were a lot more formidable than any of us understand, including yourself. However, for a true blending of both, *no* physical form could handle that amount of magic. Not the level I felt that night." Tad's skinny fingers squeezed my wrist. "The afterbirth has no such boundaries. It is still you. Your power, except kept on the side. Sort of like a familiar."

A familiar? A familiar was a witch and Druid term, usually an animal companion with supernatural abilities, which was exactly what it felt like when I touched it. Part of me, but its own entity. Capable of even more greatness... and destruction.

In my case, because nothing was ever normal with me, my familiar was my pet afterbirth.

I shall name him squishy.

"Fuck the gods..." Killian's head dropped back. He rubbed at his face, his legs starting to move back and forth. "If this stuff is so powerful, how is it worthless now?"

Tad cocked his head in my direction.

"Well..." I nipped at my bottom lip. "I kind of brought my uncle back to life... along with seven necromancers."

The stunned silence and blank stares from the men almost made me laugh.

"Didn't expect that one, did you?" I tucked hair behind my ear, shifting on my feet, their weighted gazes making me nervous.

"No." Tad's hand dropped away from me. "And there is not much that ever surprises me. But you, girl, seem to be the one thing I can't foresee."

"Explain," Killian commanded. He didn't like being shocked by anything, either. He wanted to be the one in control, the one who could see everything coming.

I was not one of those things.

Inhaling, I watched the flames reflect off my boots and started telling them. It seemed pointless to keep the information from them now. We were all in too deep. I gave them the highlights of the night at High Castle, finding my mother, the nectar, and the commotion raging past the stone wall in the heart of the city.

They took it all in, not questioning me on much... until I had to explain how I knew my uncle's place had been bombed, how I saved him when I wasn't there. The connection between not only Warwick but also Scorpion tangled them up.

"I knew you had a special connection to Warwick, but also this other guy too? You saved both that night in the fae war?" Tad stepped back, lowering himself down on the sofa.

"Yes."

"But she was just born." Killian's confusion was making him angrier.

"Oh, deities." Tad's head raised. "The fae book. It took you back."

I didn't have to respond; he already connected the dots.

"The fae book... it wouldn't let me in, but it wanted you. Still, I've never heard of one letting anyone be more than a viewer. I am a high druid, and I've never been more than a spectator of history. It let you *become* history. You should not hold so much sway over a fae book." Wide-eyed, Tad gulped, his lids shutting as if something was dawning on him.

"What?" I whispered, my heart tapping rapidly against my ribs.

"Do you know anything about the first fae books?"

"Ash told me they were made by druids for their masters. The old kings and queens."

"Yes." Tad nodded. "And those books were bound to that family line. Most books aren't now, but then the nobles wanted to own everything... including books. Druids had the rulers' signatures magically laced in with the binding. Every person has a special signature of magic, and every family has one too."

"Ash mentioned something like that. He also said they all had been destroyed by now."

"I thought so too." Tad absently rubbed at his shoulder, his gaze faraway. "I didn't pay attention that day, but now I can feel it."

"What? What day?" Fear tickled at the base of my spine.

"The day you came down into the tunnel... when we went into the book... or at least I tried." His dazed expression sharped, stopping on me. "It kept me out. It wanted only you."

My chest went concave, waiting for him to finish.

"Because you are its owner."

"What?" Killian and I spat out at the same time.

"Have you lost your mind, old man?" Killian barked. "Books aren't owned anymore."

"This one is different. This one is old." Tad gripped his cane. "It is one of the original fae books. And can you guess to which family it belonged?"

My lids shut, already knowing the answer.

"Queen Aneira."

My head dipped forward more, letting it sink in.

"It recognized her signature in you. To the book, you are part of that same family, its true owner now."

It was why it picked me over both Ash and Tad. It called to me. At least it used to. *"Brexley Kovacs, the girl who defies nature."*

"It knows what I am... was." I shook my head. "That I'm not right."

"Doesn't matter. Aneira's magic is part of you; her family line is in you. It bows to you."

"Doesn't Aneira have actual family out there, a niece?"

"Yes. And if the book was in her hands, it would do the same. It's owned by the family, not the person. And whether it likes it or not, you have slipped under that umbrella."

"Great." I huffed. "I have one of the most evil queens to ever exist as part of me."

"First, there were plenty of evil rulers before her, but her magic wasn't necessarily evil, nor her family line. I knew Aneira as a child. As well as her sister, Aisling, who was kind and full of life. Her power was fire. Aneira was always jealous of that. Circumstances, isolation, and her father's severe strictness are what turned Aneira petty, jealous, and cruel. Especially watching her sister be pampered and adored. Free to love and be herself, adored by her father and mother. Aneira was always treated like a future queen, not a daughter." Tad tapped his finger against his cane. "Though in that great power, are you as capable of such evilness? Oh yes, my dear. All power can be. It's up to you how magic is used."

"Moot point anyway." I shrugged. "I don't have it anymore."

"We shall see, won't we?" Killian stated.

"What does that mean?"

"You are taking us to the High Castle," Killian stated. "You are getting me what you promised."

Chapter 13

Tucking deeper into my hood, my breath billowed in thick condensation, the clear starry sky plunging the temperatures. Water lapped against the stolen boat as we sailed steadily down the river. Killian took the helm and surprisingly proved himself a very experienced sailor. He knew exactly how to catch the light breeze to double our speed, making me recall the scene the book took me to in the tunnels and his mysterious past and relationship with the pirates.

Imagining Killian as a pirate just didn't sit right. He was entirely exquisite suits and fine brandy.

Tonight, you wouldn't know the sexy fae lord was under the hooded cloak, dirty cargo pants, and worn boots. There was not one face here that wasn't immediately recognizable. Tad, the oldest and most known druid alive in the eastern bloc, the fae lord himself, me the infamous HDF traitor, and even Sloane, for his Norwegian features, big build, position as an elite guard, and handsome stoic face.

Not a group built to go unnoticed.

Sloane kept watch at the stern for anyone following us while I stayed up at the bow, keeping an eye out for trouble, as there were plenty of river pirates taking their booty from anyone who passed by, like toll roads. Tad huddled in the cockpit, wrapped in cloaks, the icy temps harsh on his old bones.

The wind beat against my face as the bow cut through the water like butter, heading for the cursed lands of Visegrád. My stomach bounced and weaved, which had nothing to do with the swaying vessel. I was going to see my mother again. This time, I knew what I was stepping into, but I still didn't know how she'd respond to me. Excited? Blasé? This trip compared to last time was so different. None of the previous group was with me again, not even my two tiny friends.

I would never admit this, but to wake up without a finger up my nose and an obscenely dressed brownie in my face felt wrong. I guess Tad's magic secured the cottage and property line from everyone, including sub-fae. Without even understanding why, people would veer far away from the property, get confused, or be stopped by the invisible barrier.

Without my little duo being able to find me, I knew it would send Ash into a tizzy. *Would Ash go to Warwick and tell him I was gone?* I shook my head before I could think about it. I was trying to keep my mind off that man, though it was hard to do when you shared space with his sister. Even if they were only half-siblings, she had so many expressions that reminded me of her brother. And Eliza bringing him up earlier in the evening didn't help either.

"Hey." She had come into the tiny kitchen where I was nursing my second coffee, even though it was hinting at dinner time. Grabbing a cup of tea, she peered over at me. "How are you feeling?"

"Better." My chloroform headache had finally subsided.

By the time Killian, Tad, and I had talked everything out, dawn was peaking over the mountains, showing me nothing but trees around the cottage. Killian had us sleep most of the day to get ready for our mission.

"I'm surprised my brother isn't with you." She tucked her long, silky, dark hair behind her ear, the same shade as his. "I got the distinct feeling he doesn't venture too far from you."

Gulping down my sip of coffee, I coughed. "What makes you say that? You saw us together *once*."

Eliza leaned back on the counter with a scoff. "Because *I know* my brother." Her eyes were light brown, but she gave me the same hard stare he did. "Warwick is a real son of a bitch."

Coffee choked my throat, my hand clasping over my mouth so as not to spray it out.

"He's a pain in the ass. Impossible. Stubborn. Brutal. Aloof. And sometimes way too overprotective." She took a sip of her tea. "But he's only overprotective of people he loves. And I could count those on one hand. Ash, Kitty, Simon, me... and now you."

"I don't think I'm in that club." I shook my head. "Not anymore."

"You are," she said bluntly. Her energy was kind, but it seemed she had no time for bullshit. "He may be a stubborn ass, but it didn't take me but a moment to see you were different. Or more like, he was different with *you*. I had no doubt he would have stood in front of a bullet to protect you." She set her cup down. "Warwick has two levels: I don't give a shit, and I care too much. He keeps himself walled up and protected, only letting a very few slip into his second level. I'm blood, so he's got no choice with me and Simon. And Ash and Kitty, well, they are his family too. But you…" She lifted a brow. "He let you in."

"He didn't have much choice with me either." I sat back in the chair, brushing the bits of biscuit from my hands. "It's not what you think."

"There you are." Zander strolled in, the smile hinting on his lips as he took in Eliza faltering when he spotted me over at the table. "Brexley, hey." He dipped his head.

"Did you need something?" Eliza's voice sounded formal.

Too formal.

"Um… yeah." A bashful grin swept over his mouth, making him sexy and adorable at the same time. "Simon wanted to go for a ride." He motioned to his back. "Beautiful sunset tonight… just wanted to see if you wanted to join us? I can easily carry you both."

"Oh? Um…" Eliza peered over at me.

"Go. Have fun." I stood up from the table. "I need to get ready for tonight's task."

She nodded at me, turning to Zander. "Okay, sounds fun."

I definitely saw a look between them, blushing of cheeks, and shy smiles.

"Be careful tonight, Brex." Zander hugged me tightly, kissing my temple, before trotting out of the room. There was no doubt I had been friend-zoned. He was staying back to watch over the cottage, but I had a feeling he was watching something else entirely.

Eliza reached back, squeezing my hand. "I know what I saw. You might have to kick Warwick's ass to wake him up a bit, but you are part of us now."

"Oh, I think he's going to be too busy kicking someone else's ass." I snorted, my head shaking, gesturing to where Zander went. "Your brother is going to flip out. Do you like horse meat patties for dinner?"

"What, Zander?" She waved her hand, not able to stop the pink hinting at her cheeks. "There's nothing there. We're just friends. He and Simon have become buds."

"Sure." I flicked my eyebrows.

"It's true."

"I know what I saw." I taunted, knocking into her shoulder as I strolled out, winking. "Have fun on your *ride*. Stay safe. Have him wear a saddle."

"I take all the nice things back," she shouted down the hall, making me laugh.

"Brexley?" Killian's voice broke through my reverie, whipping my head back to the captain. The biting air burned the end of my nose. "We're coming in. We need help with the anchor."

My head jerked back to land, seeing the cadaver of the castle up on the hill, shocked we were already here. Scrambling back to help Sloane drop the anchor, Killian glided us the closest he could to the shore without getting stuck.

We trudged to the embankment, heading up the steep steps to the crest, Sloane carrying Tad on his back.

"All your power, old man, and you can't fly us up to the top?" I breathed out, my legs burning.

"Not how my magic works, plus it's good for you, keeps the youthful glow on your face," Tad heckled us.

"It's called sweat," I grumbled.

Finally, we reached the top, and I led them through the grounds to where the well was. With every step, my stomach rolled into tighter knots. This time there were no skeletons lurking in the shadows, guarding the castle, though I still couldn't escape the feeling scraping down my spine that this place—including the inhabitants—was fully aware we were here. My mother's clan couldn't control the skeletons anymore, but it didn't take away from the feeling they were still here, waiting for their masters to raise them again.

"Death saturates this place," Tad remarked as Sloane set him down. "My senses are overwhelmed. It hard to pick up on anything else." Tad hobbled up next to me, his eyes darting cautiously around. "It lives deep within the land, rock, and stone. This is where even the dead come to die."

"Is that why you are here?" A woman's voice cut through the dark, her small frame stepping out of a crumbling archway. Six forms in robes behind her. I jolted back at my mother's sudden appearance, all of them slipping from the shadows like they were part of them. Cousin Liam, Aunt Morgan, Sam, Roan, Breena, and Rory curved around their leader.

My attention was purely on the person in the middle. My mom. She was still boney and painfully thin, but moonlight reflected off her dark eyes and hair, and I swear I saw some color in her cheeks, showing there was a little more life in her.

I hadn't dreamed it. She was real. They all were. I brought my family back.

"Brexley." She twisted her head to me, the sound of her voice still odd in my ears. I had imagined it for so long growing up. In real life, it was much deeper, with an Irish accent, as opposed to the one in my head. Her regard went back to the Druid next to me.

"I could smell your stench, Tadhgan, before you reached the shore. You smell like a dying corpse."

"At least I don't look like one." Tad gripped his staff, his throat bobbing, though disgust curled his lip. Killian and Sloane went on the defense as the seven circled around the well, guarding the prize inside as if it was still worth something. "Plus, wouldn't that be an aphrodisiac to *your kind?*"

My Aunt Morgan snarled, her grip on her bardiche tightening. "Nothing's changed, I see, still a righteous, insufferable *pet.*" She flicked her chin at Killian. "A druid still leashed by a fae king."

"If anyone has been the pet here, it would be you. Shackled forever, while I am the one free. I work for who I want. Can you say the same?" Tad snapped at all of them. "Your father is the one who locked the chain around your neck by turning against everything we stand for."

"Because he didn't want to be a servant to the fae." Morgan's shoulders drew up. "If black magic is what it took to free us—"

"But you are not free, are you?" He cut her off, stepping forward. "And to use black magic on a fellow Druid…" Tad was always so serene and calm, but now fire raged behind his eyes, making them glow. "On *me…*" He twisted to my mother. "Your spell is broken now, Eabha. I know what you did." He motioned to his bent spine. "This is from you. Your black magic."

My eyes darted back between them, trepidation fizzing in my belly.

No emotion flickered on her face, but I saw her rib cage move faster under her cloak.

"I held you as children. Taught you both your first spell." Tad's sentiment dripped with sorrow. "Your father's best friend."

What? How did I not know that?

"And you turned your back on him. On us!" Eabha took a step forward, her lids lowering.

"No. Your father turned his back on our ways. He betrayed *everyone.*" Tad stamped his staff into the ground.

"You blind, arrogant fool." Morgan moved up with her sister, tension rising quickly.

"Watch yourself, Morgan," Tad responded as if she were still a child he needed to scold, but his eyes were still on my mom. I couldn't fight the feeling there was a slight fear in his eyes.

"Do you even know what really happened?" Mother stabbed the handle of her war scythe into the stone ground, stepping closer to Tad. "What happened to this clan under Aneira's rule? What she did to Father?"

Tad tried to straighten his twisted spine, and his shoulders went up as if trying to guard himself, not against her magic, but her words.

"You've heard the rumors about her. Her sick, perverted ways of punishing. Of controlling."

Tad's head shook. "You have it all wrong."

"No, you do. You have no idea what he went through before he died." Eabha took another step forward. "You are nothing but a coward, Tadhgan. A back-stabbing traitor."

Tad's eyes flashed, and he lumbered over until they were only a few feet apart.

"I have done a lot of things in my life I am not proud of, and I regret the situation with your father the most. If I could go back, I would. But he made his choice, and no matter what I said, he was willing to risk his family for the cause. For *her*!"

"Because he wanted us to have freedom." Morgan joined them.

"No!" Tad barked. "Your father killed that fae king and his entire family *for Aneira*."

The entire group sucked in violently, as if we all had been hit with force.

"You lying, disgusting troll!" Liam bolted forward.

In a blink, barely moving his lips, light funneled from Tad, flicking Liam back through the air, his body landing on the hard stone like he was a doll.

"Do not challenge me, *boy*," Tad grunted. "I might look old and decrepit, but I am far more powerful than all of you put together," he snapped. "And I am the *only one* who knows what actually happened. Your father's—Balfour's—cause did start out with good intentions, but as it grew, so did his influence, ego, and greed."

"Greed?" Morgan puffed up.

"Not for money, but for more power. For more results. He slipped more and more away from the original motive, dipping into black magic and violence. And then she came along, a very young, beautiful princess, and told him all the things he wanted to hear. How things would change when she became queen. It wasn't long before they became lovers."

"He would never do that. Our mother was the love of his life," Morgan hissed.

"She was. But your mother was four months in the grave. He had two young girls to raise and was lonely and heartbroken. She worked it to her advantage."

"No. No, I don't believe it." Rory shook her head. "Balfour would never fall for her; he'd see she was evil."

"We did not know her as such then. She was a stunning, young princess, our future queen speaking of changes and hope, of modernizing the ways of old. He did not see how manipulative and cunning Aneira already was. How she wrapped him around her finger, got into his head. Sex is a powerful coercion tool, and from what I've heard, even young, Aneira was a master.

"I warned him. Told him to not do it, but Aneira had gotten in too deep. They planned for Balfour to kill his master and the entire family, including the staff. I feel it was always Aneira who pushed that. Then he would have his freedom, and when Aneira became queen, which was sooner than we all thought, they could openly be lovers. It was a trap. And when your father was caught, along with everyone involved, including his kin, Aneira stood by her father, declaring Balfour's druid powers had forced her against her will into bed, and his entire clan should be punished. For eternity."

Tad touched his forehead, his lids squeezing shut for a moment. "I can't imagine the betrayal your father felt in that moment. But instead of hating her, he still did her bidding. I've heard of Aneira's perverted control methods, but your father was not an unwilling player. Balfour was one she had hunting us down during the Druid Genocide."

I had read of this briefly in my books. Druids had created the four treasures of Tuatha Dé Danann, the old name for the Otherworld, and hid them away from the fae because of their power. Not even Aneira could break the spell, veiling their whereabouts. Only a druid could, so she set on a rampage of death and torture until one would break the spell for her. She spread the propaganda of their evilness, making it okay to kill them freely.

Not one Druid gave in.

Thousands and thousands were slaughtered in the process. She was the reason there was still a stigma surrounding Druids. Why there were so few and why they still chose to live quiet lives away from the public.

"No." Eabha's chest heaved. "No. He would never! My father was not a traitor!"

"He was, Eabha. You can call me one if you like, and there are things I've done which warrant that." Tad raised his head. "But your father slaughtered his own. And when he found our hideout..." Tad paused, lifting his head.

"I was the one who killed him," Tad stated. "But it was your father who placed that curse on you. Not Aneira."

Chapter 14

The declarations rang in the air, clanging with piercing blows, peeling from the sky and raining down on us. No one moved. Not a word was spoken.

Out of the corner of my eye, I noticed Killian tense, as if he could feel the shift in the silence coming. At one time, I might have been able to as well, but my senses were dull compared to theirs. They could smell adrenaline spike, feel the moment before someone moved. I knew because, at one time, I was able to pick it up too.

"Liar!" Sam and Breena were first to react, the twins in sync, their matching lucerne hammers swinging for Tad at the same moment. Liam, Rory, and Roan only a millisecond behind, their howls of vengeance and death resounding together.

Sloane and Killian countered with the same speed, grabbing for their weapons before my brain even registered what was happening.

"STOP!" Tad picked up his staff and slammed it into the stone with effort. The impact chimed through my ears and down into my bones, the force of the strike tossing us all up like feathers. Our bones crunched to the ground as everyone flew back, our bodies strewn around Tad in a circle.

"You have no chance fighting me." He directed his comments to the O'Laighin clan, their hisses of anger directed back at him as they rose. I scrambled to my feet, my head whirling with what I just learned. Tad had killed my grandfather, but my grandfather was also a murdering traitor to fellow druids, and possibly cursed his own family. "You were able to challenge me that night because of circumstances, Eabha, not skill." He tsked my mother as she got back up. "I do not wish to fight you. Too much blood has already spilled from us, don't you think?" He moved closer to Eabha, looking directly at her. "Your father's death sits on my soul and has marked it forever, but I will not apologize for saving the lives of those druids by hiding them with me. He was no longer the man I once knew, one I had called my friend. She twisted his mind and blackened his soul. She was the one who convinced him to curse your family."

"What? He would never curse us," Rory spat.

"Aneira had perverted his mind so much, he no longer had power over his own thoughts. She was in complete control. He was a puppet."

"No!" Sam shook his head. "I don't believe you."

"I know you always assumed it was her, but it wasn't. Think about it. Aneira was always afraid of druids because they held different magic, could challenge her. It was why she had us hunted down and slaughtered. Aneira knew any curse she put on could probably be unraveled by someone like me or broken in her death. So, she made sure that could never happen. Instead of her own magic, she used your father's. He made sure it was something I couldn't even fix." Tad rubbed his lips together. "Black magic."

I saw my mother swallow, her fingers twitching on her scythe.

"Father would never do that. He loved us. He would never curse his own family." Morgan appeared like she wanted to stab Tad, but Eabha touched her arm, telling her to lower her weapon.

"He's lying." Morgan shook her head, almost pleading. "Father would never do that."

"He is not lying, Morga," Mother replied in a low voice, calling her by a pet name.

"What?"

"I saw and heard things. Things I didn't want to believe." My mom's eyes were glossy, peering at her little sister. "Things I kept from you. You were so young, and I convinced myself I was wrong. Mistaken. I let you believe father was a hero. Believe in the man he once was, who I knew when I was a small child." Eabha lifted her gaze to Tad. "But Father was too far gone. He muttered to himself, would stare at the walls for hours, and only come to life when she was around." Mom croaked. "I want to believe somewhere inside if he did do it, it was because he was protecting us in some way."

Morgan and the rest of the clan looked gutted, their expression still hoping she was lying, that none of this was the truth. I also wanted to believe it wasn't true. That their own father wasn't the reason they walked the earth for the rest of their life in the in-between.

"After his death, she became even more unhinged. We were able to escape, flee here, and hide. That was until the fae war, when we became…"

"Became necromancers," I finished.

"Yes," Mother affirmed. "We had to fight for her. We had no choice; I had you to think of. I was willing to do anything to save you."

"Including using black magic on me to make me forget, to hide her from me." Tad gritted through his teeth, once again jerking every head toward him. "This…" He motioned to his bowed back. "Is because of you. This whole time, it was your signature on me. Your dirty black magic afflicted me, twisted and scarred me forever."

Another detail of the moment the nectar had shown me—Tad's spine was straight, his body strong. Now, because of whatever my mother did, he was coiled and stained by her mark.

"I would cut you down dead if I had to," Eabha snarled, glancing at me. "I was not going to let you touch her. Even know about her. I was protecting my family."

"*Protecting your family?*" Tad huffed. "Is that what you called using that poor human man, getting pregnant, knowing perfectly well what would happen if you ever faced him in battle? What would become of the child you had with him? Keeping him ignorant of the truth?"

"I loved him." Eabha got in Tad's face. "Do not for a moment make it sound sordid and false. I fell in love with him."

"Enough to blind you to your morals?" Tad did not retreat, challenging her back. "What would have happened if you had to face him on the battlefield? You would've had to kill him. The curse overrides *everything*, Eabha. Even affection. You would have killed your own baby's father? The man you say you love? Or let him kill you? And what about Brexley? You were willing to have this child and know the same would befall her? It was only by chance that made her different; otherwise, she would be just like you."

My mother's mouth quivered, emotions I had not seen so far filling her eyes. Her expression was a mix of shame, guilt, anger, and grief.

"But I'm not." My mouth opened before my brain totally caught up. "I'm not a necromancer, though I have qualities similar to them, but I'm not actually one. Why is that?"

Almost every head swung to me; their gazes were like stones piling up on my shoulders, full of confusion as if that revelation just hit them as well. Except the two standing in the middle. Tad and my mother didn't even peer at me, their heads bowing.

"Why?"

"Aneira." Tad slowly twisted to me.

Beads of sweat trailed down my back, my heart knocking against my ribcage. "What do you mean, Aneira?"

"It wasn't until earlier when I saw your aura that I started to put it together." Tad licked his lips, adjusting his stance. "At the moment you were born, she died, sending a wave of magic out, like an atomic bomb."

I recalled the moment when the book showed me Queen Kennedy killing Queen Aneira, slicing off her head. I felt her power shooting out, crumbling the last bit of the wall. Her energy struck lightning from the sky, and I watched it crash into the baby, feeling it surge through me while I was bringing Warwick back to life.

I knew what he was going to say, and my limbs started to shake.

"Part of her embedded herself in you, and with that, she changed you. The curse would no longer recognize you as the same as them. In the wave of their deaths, you were the purest of life. When they collided, I think somehow you fell in the middle."

The area between life and death.

The gray.

"You said my aura was like hers, and her magic was part of me, but she's not in me or anything? She can't influence me, right?" I gaped and peered around. "I mean, is she going to take over? Will I suddenly go batshit crazy and start killing people?"

Tad let out a soft chuckle. "No, my dear, that's not how it works."

"I don't know. I wouldn't put it past that tyrant bitch," Killian scoffed. "She would do something like that."

"Not helping." Tad shot him a look when I started to hyperventilate.

My mother stood awkwardly, as if she had no idea what to do, as Tad strolled over to me, his hands firmly gripping mine.

"Think of it as more of a trait. Something passed down to you, like your dark eyes from your mother or a personality trait. Aneira used her power for evil, but it didn't make her any less great. She was extremely powerful and smart. You are made up of those same aspects. It's how you choose to use those things you inherited. You might have a weakness for power as she did, but she is not inside you, waiting to burst out at any time. Aneira's magic is another quality you have that makes you who you are. She never had children, so maybe this is her way of continuing on her line."

"So, are you sure I'm not gonna suddenly turn evil, wanting to take over the world?"

"I don't think so." He patted my hand.

"Though if you suddenly want a kinky sex chamber—I heard she had a few—let me know." Killian winked at me.

"Enough from you," Tad shot over his shoulder with annoyance, though Killian's teasing heaved a breath from my lungs, curving a smile on my face.

"As confusing as this is, Aneira saved your life." Tad's statement dropped the smile from my lips. "No baby should have survived what you did, but you soaked it up and used it. Remember, if anything should show you are not like her, across the field at that time, you were saving two people's lives."

One knowingly and the other more a bystander.

"I brought Warwick back... did I pass on anything?"

"I'd have to see Warwick's aura now, but solely by going off what I saw between you two before." Tad dipped his head. "Yes. I think you both would be the same. You gave part of yourself to him. But now that your magic is gone..."

"Wait." Morgan held up her hand. "Your magic is gone too?"

"Of course." My mom looked at her. "They are connected. Their power is linked."

Morgan pinched her mouth. "I was still hoping."

My mother strolled over to me, timidly reaching out and placing her icy hand on mine as if to mimic what Tad did. She had never even held me before her emotions were ripped from her, becoming a necromancer. I could see she wanted to be motherly to me but had no idea how, the instincts not coming naturally.

"I know what you came for." She petted my hands before dropping hers away, awkward and stiff. She stepped back. "You cannot have it."

"What?" Killian barreled forward, ire lifting his shoulders. "It's part of her, right?" He motioned to me. "Then she has a say in what happens to it. And she promised it to me."

"And what do you seek it for, Lord of the Fae?" My mother took her stance, her clan flanking around her. "Do you not possess enough power? Or will you soon be just like the human side, filling the river with your dead? Sending more and more to us until this land is piled in bones, screaming for mercy, and we can no longer consume their pain and torment."

"Wait. What?" I blinked, my mouth dropping. My head snapped to the archway where I saw the skeletons come from last time. The army my mother had. Of course, they weren't there now, as witches had no power to aminate the dead. "Those bodies... they were from the river? You know they were from HDF experiments?"

"As witches, we can still sense their pain, feel their story. Dozens and dozens a week are coming from the city." Roan spoke for the first time. "They still seem to be attracted to this place, even if we can no longer call them to us." Strangely, it almost sounded like he missed being a necromancer.

There was a twisted strangeness in knowing every dead body Istvan's scientists were throwing into the river was coming here. To the sacred fae land of the dead, finding their way to my mother's clan.

"Humans too?"

"In death, we are all equals." Sam's deep voice cut to me. "Something the living could learn from."

"We still cannot let you have the nectar." My mother's voice was clear. "In death and now in life, we have pledged ourselves to guard it. Protecting it from those who will use its power for harm." Her eyes darted to Killian. "Even if they think they will not. Corruption and greed seep quickly into the souls of those who already have a taste for those indulgences. The four treasures of Tuatha Dé Danann proved that. This might be even more coveted."

Killian lifted his lip, showing his teeth. "But if it holds no magic anymore, what does it matter?"

"Exactly, what does it matter to you?" Mother traveled to Killian. "The distinction that you hold the most powerful object in the world?"

"I see nothing wrong with that."

"Wars have started for less. Great damage can come from merely having it and the fool who runs his mouth off."

Killian's eye blazed, his anger at her insult climbing over his muscles. In a blink, this could all go to hell. And as much as I cared for Killian, I would not let him lay a hand on my mother. He'd have to kill me first.

"Stop." I tried to step between them, my mind unstable in its natural zone. Both sides held weight for me. "You will not fight each other." My request was directed at Killian, pleading for him to back off. "Please."

"It's mine, Ms. Kovacs. You *promised* me."

"I made a deal." Slight difference.

"Humans," he snarled. "You stand behind no words your mouth utters."

"Technically, when I made it, I wasn't either a human or fae."

"You're acting *human* now." He lifted his brow.

Ouch.

I turned to face my mother, her head already shaking.

"As long as it is safe here, it will not leave this land. We are its guardians. Please, *Brexley*." Her dark eyes met mine, and for one moment, I felt like I was truly looking at my mother. The one I would've had growing up.

Then it was gone.

"But if you force my hand, we will fight you."

"And you will lose, my dear." Tad sighed unhappily.

He muttered words under his breath, none of them making any sense to me, but I could feel the power behind them. The rise of his staff, his determined expression. A force slammed into us, scattering us back like pebbles, tumbling and rolling away in all directions.

"No!" my mother bellowed, her voice absorbing into the funnel of energy whipping around. My nails clawed at the stone, trying to hold on, blinking against the debris beating on my face and into my eyes.

Pure light glowed from Tad, his focus on the well. Raising his cane higher, he muttered a chant I could not hear, the tornado he created flapping against my eardrums.

Every inch of my skin felt his magic. I had been around a lot of fae—powerful ones—and I had never felt anything like this. Druid magic unleashed was something else entirely. Fae were born with magic. It threaded through their very being, making it personal and specific to the person. It was them.

But Druids had a relationship with the earth, borrowing its raw power. You smelled the soil and vegetation, you heard the crackle of electricity, you tasted the water from the river and felt the wind bat at your skin, answering his call. Untamed energy being funneled into a command.

Battering at my face, I grunted against Tad's power. Untouched, he lifted his arms higher. So much magic swirled around me. I knew it was probably in my head, but I swore I felt a scrape in my belly, a fluttering deep in my soul, like a heartbeat, as I watched the box with the nectar in it rise out of the well.

It was suspended for a moment, then it floated down to Tad's arms. The moment it touched, the energy keeping us at bay vanished. The tornado winds evaporated; the sky, still and clear, blinked down on us peacefully.

My chest heaved, the sound echoing in my ears, my arms shaking and still clawing at the ground to hold on.

For a moment, no one moved, discombobulated from the intensity and the fact he flattened even the most powerful fae to the ground. Glancing back at Killian and his expression, this fact had not been overlooked. And I can't say he was thrilled at all by it.

"I warned you!" My mother lurched up, grabbing her scythe, the other six getting up, wielding their weapons of death. Our side reacted the same, getting to our feet with weapons drawn. "The nectar does not leave our protection. We will fight you to the death if we must."

"How kind of you to do all the work for us." A raspy, nasal voice came from behind us, and we all spun to face the intruder, horror flooding my veins. "Little did we know in coming for her, we'd find something even better." he motioned his gun at me.

Captain Kobak, the man too sadistic to train us for deadly combat at HDF. The man out hunting fae to torture and test stood with a troop behind him.

"And they say fae are hard to sneak up on." He pulled the trigger.

Chapter 15

A barrage of bullets came for us, pinging off the stone walls. Commotion exploded, figures moving and darting for safety, firing back.

"Brexley!" Arms came around me, hurtling me behind a wall, as several bullets zipped by my head. Our bodies hit the ground with a thud, Killian scrambling into a squat position, already firing at the attackers.

Ire coated over the fear raging inside as I moved up beside him. I was slower to react to them. I hated feeling like the weak link, which was why I worked so hard in training. At HDF, being a girl was already considered a weakness by so many, and I trained my ass off to counter it.

Peeking over the wall, I watched Tad tug away from Sloane, stepping back in the fray, his mouth moving with a spell, his shaky hand lifting his staff. White light started to come from him, but not fast enough.

"Tad!" I screamed as a bullet sunk into the Druid's shoulder, blood surging over his light-colored robe. I lunged toward him, the need to protect him overriding everything.

"Brex, no!" Killian grabbed onto me, holding me back.

Another bullet hit him, stumbling him back. Then another. The entire time, his mouth kept moving, still trying to protect us, but the bullets were faster. His head turned, his eyes finding mine. They said so much, filling my chest with emotion.

"No!" Panic wound through my muscles, seeing the old man being gunned down in front of me. Shoving off Killian, I lifted my weapon, ready to shoot my way to him.

A shell hit his chest, blood spurting out, the force flaying his back onto the ground.

I lurched out from behind the barrier, headed for him. My legs came to a halt when red light, the color of blood, shot out, slamming into the HDF soldiers, tossing them back, and walling around us like a protective shield.

What the hell?

My head jerked to the side. Six of my mother's clan grouped together, speaking in unison, something I didn't understand, their expression locked down. Focused. Casting a barrier around us.

I darted to Tad, my knees hitting the ground. Blood soaked the linen, his chest barely moving.

"Tad? No... please... no." I gripped his hand, looking up. "Please, someone help him."

"Brexley, you need to go." My mother ran up to me, holding the box.

"I won't leave him. He's dying."

"You must!" She shoved the box in my hand. "We will hold them off. But you have to escape now."

"But..." I peered down at the box, the nectar inside.

"I said it stayed with us until it was no longer safe." She curled my fingers around the edges. "It is no longer safe here. You must protect it at all costs."

My gaze went back to Tad, not seeing his chest move.

"We will take care of him if we can, I promise." She touched my face briefly, making me look into her eyes. "Please, my girl. You need to go!"

"Come on!" Killian grabbed my arm, yanking me to my feet. Sloane and Killian pulled me to the exit behind us. My gaze, not taking in anything, still latched onto my mother's eyes. There was love in them. For the first time, I saw it.

Then she rose and faced our attackers.

Sloane took the lead, Killian not letting me go, my feet stumbling over the uneven steps and crumbling trail. My fingers dug into the box, holding it tight against my chest as we descended quickly.

I was highly aware of the treasure I held, but it felt distant from me now, just an empty vase. Like sitting with someone you loved, but no one was inside them anymore.

When we hit the embankment, Killian picked me up and tossed me into the boat. They swiftly got us turned around and pointed back to the city.

The container pressed to my ribcage. I looked up at the castle on the hill as we sailed away. Gunfire and metal echoed down to me, the sparks of light and screams of death.

Did I leave my family to die? Was Tad dead?

Tad sacrificed himself to protect us.

To protect me.

I saw it in his eyes. He did it for me.

Taking a breath, I opened the lid, nerves dancing up my esophagus. The substance lay at the bottom. My eyes burned with emotion, seeing it so dull and lifeless. I had hoped I would be wrong, that it would be glowing and vivid with power. Telling me my magic wasn't gone forever, and I hadn't destroyed it. But it looked the same as when I left it last time.

Slamming the lid, I stared up at the sky, blinking away the grief I felt in my soul.

The trip back was tense. Sloane was on such high alert, every time I moved, he twitched like he might shoot me. Killian appeared calm, but I could see the muscles riding high around his neck.

When the boat glided into the city, I saw Killian stare up at the bombed and burned-out fae palace. His eyes tracked the ruins of his home. The site of his power. A sign that fae were at their weakest.

And Killian had to lie low until the person who wanted to fill the vacuum of the lord's sudden death showed himself. I had to give it to Killian. Most would not be so patient, but Killian played the long game. He wasn't just thinking of his power today, but his legacy for centuries.

Returning the boat to its slip, we disembarked on the Pest side, heading for the parked SUV Sloane had hidden near Elizabeth square. I had no doubt Killian would want to take us back to his veiled cottage, but being so near my uncle and my friends, a big part of me was ready to run for it. I had no hope of outrunning either fae man anymore, but I couldn't stop my compulsion to take this box to Andris instead.

Before I could decide either way, my stomach coiled with nerves, the uneasy sensation of being watched hummed at the back of my neck.

Killian and Sloane must have felt the same, their heads jerking, their bodies stiffening, weapons ready.

Killian took in a deep breath, his lids shutting briefly. "Fuck."

The clicking of dozens of guns scraped up my spine, flipping me around. Terror filled my throat, my brain already knowing who I'd see.

Smoke trailed up from his cigarette, his beady, dark eyes sparking with the joy of the hunt. He held his Glock casually, as if he had no reason to fear us.

"You are completely surrounded." Kalaraja stepped out of the shadows, taking another hit. The soldiers moved in around us, weapons drawn on us, ready to shoot. "Drop your weapons."

"I don't think so." Killian snarled, his gun still pointing at Kalaraja.

Suddenly, a gun muzzle pressed into the side of my head, a guard moving in next to me, taking my weapon.

Kalaraja's smirk grew as he stomped out his cigarette.

Killian glared at me like he was about to shoot me in the head instead of the man holding the gun to me. Exhaling, he dropped his weapon to the ground. Sloane begrudgingly doing it too.

"Kick them over."

Metal scraped the cement, sliding over to the enemy.

"You didn't think I'd have men waiting for you here too?" Kalaraja's smugness dripped from him, cold and calculated. "I have eyes everywhere in this city. Knew the moment you parked this shiny, fancy car here and which boat you stole."

And had us followed up to High Castle. That was how they found us.

"You've been a slippery one, so I waited here for you too." His cold, dead eyes met mine, and for a brief moment, his gaze dropped to the box. "What you got there? Bring me a going away present?"

Killian locked up next to me. Unnoticeable to anyone else, but I could feel his arm brush mine.

Kalaraja had no clue what I was holding. Not yet. The men at High Castle had come for me, possibly even to kill the fae ruler. Instead, they stumbled upon something far more valuable. But that had yet to be communicated, and no one knew if those men made it back at all.

"The dick of the last man who tried to capture me." I slowly tucked the box under my arm, wanting his attention off it. "So, I guess you're safe." I tipped my head contemptuously.

"A eunuch?" Killian grinned at me.

"That's suggesting he had one to begin with."

"Shut the fuck up." Kalaraja gripped his gun, aiming it at my head, glaring. "Take it." He ordered the guard. My stomach sank when the guy pulled it out of my grip.

"You like a box of dicks, huh? I see your kink now." I tried to act like I wasn't about to panic.

Kalaraja gritted his teeth. "Think it's wise to piss me off?"

"Think it's wise to piss *me* off?" The deep growl vibrated from behind us.

My lungs halted, the voice dragging my body down into the depths of hell. I had to scrape and claw my way back up, every nerve shredded and torn until nothing was left. I was stripped and flayed alive by just the force of his wrath.

My head turned, air fighting to be released from my lungs, my gaze landing on a massive silhouette. Aqua eyes illuminated the darkness like blue flames, ready to devour and kill. Even without the magic I gave him, Warwick was the stuff of legends. His physical body dwarfed the human soldiers, but it wasn't enough for him; he took up every molecule of air, stretching far past his body. Taking territory with brutal force.

Warwick's glare went to the guard holding a gun to my head. "I'd remove that hand now." His voice iced through the air. It wasn't a threat. It went way past that. The boy stiffened, his hand shaking with terror, but continued to follow his commander's order.

Taking in the boy's response, Warwick's eyes slid to me. I sucked in. He was cruel, cold, feral. His fury told me to drop to my knees and beg to be consumed quickly, and not even the gun at my head stood a chance against him.

Every soldier swung their weapons to the new threat as Warwick stepped from the shadows. The cleaver I saw him use at my father's cabin was strapped to his back.

His gaze slid from mine back to Kalaraja, his head tipping up.

"Don't move, Wolf." Kalaraja barked, his finger firm on the trigger. Far behind Kalaraja, I thought I saw something move in the dark, but when I looked again, it was gone. "This bullet is begging to drive deep into your skull."

"Really?" He rumbled. I had forgotten how deep his voice ground into me, cutting me over the rocks. "Most things are begging me to drive *deep* into them." His voice licked between my thighs, my eyes darting back to him, finding his attention solely on me. Heavy. Dangerous.

Crack!

Kalaraja was not one to wait for results. His gun went off, propelling a cry from my lungs. Warwick twisted, the shell pinging off the dual blades of his cleaver. His nose wrinkled with a snarled growl, his hands reaching for his weapon. Before anyone could react, he lurched toward me, the ragged mouth of his steel cutting down. Terror choked off my scream as the blade sliced by my head, grazing my ear.

The guard screeched, blood spraying my cheek, the clank of metal accompanying the thud of flesh hitting the ground. My focus snapped to the severed hand laying on the pavement, the gun next to it. The teenage boy on the ground, spitting and howling, tucked his bloody stump into his chest.

"I warned you," Warwick grunted down at him.

"Shoot them!" Kalaraja ordered.

The realization hit me that there was no cover near us. We were far outnumbered, and a bullet would be finding me tonight.

Istvan would win.

A single shot rang out, and then…

BOOOOM!

Killian's SUV exploded, the vehicle launching into the air like a fireball, the impact of the blast scattering us to the ground. This was the third time tonight my bones cracked painfully over the ground, skidding across the pavement. Heat from the blaze singed my skin.

I popped up to find Warwick lying next to me, his eyes catching mine, a feral smirk tugging on his mouth.

"Let me guess. Distraction." He did this. Well, it was his idea, and I had a solid suspicion about who his accomplice was. The figure I saw lurking in the shadows earlier.

He gave me a look, his hand wrapping around my wrist, pulling me up.

"Come on!" Ash bellowed from behind us. Killian and Sloane climbed to their feet as some of the soldiers near us rose as well.

"You fucking blew up my car." Killian waved at the flaming hunk of metal.

"I could have waited until you were in it." Warwick shot the fairy a glare. "Aren't you supposed to be dead, anyway? Should have known you wouldn't die." Anger bristled under Warwick's skin as if he hated Killian more for surviving and standing in front of him.

Because he didn't know Eliza and Simon were alive as well.

"Warwi—"

"Let's go." He cut me off. "And keep your faces hidden." Warwick huffed, jogging for Ash.

Not hesitating, I swiped up the box and the two guns left on the ground near the one-handed guard. Tossing an extra one to Killian, the three of us followed our rescuers.

Giving one last look, I noticed among the dead and wounded, Kalaraja was nowhere in sight.

The man of death seemed to be able to slip away from his maker as much as we did. One day, there would be a final showdown, one of us not able to sneak from its grasp.

With a limping jog, we ran into the night, disappearing into the slums of the Savage Lands.

My skin prickled; the sudden contrast from icy cold to the sticky warmth of condensed bodies rubbing against me had sweat pooling at the back of my neck, my nose running.

Carnal Row was the pinnacle of debauchery. Music slithered around, laced with erotic groans from the hammocks swinging from the roof, enticing the most resilient of visitors. Gambling, drinking, and the euphoria of sex seduced all with a promise of forgetting. Forgetting your aching back and weary body. Forgetting your starving belly or empty pockets. Forgetting the unbearable suffering of daily life. Ebbing the grief of your children eating scraps and sleeping on flea-infested mattresses. The magic of this place let you believe for one moment there was beauty and pleasure in the world.

The girl with striking split features wound her body around the hoop swing, bending and contorting into implausible ways while twirling firesticks. Many of the barely dressed fae, luring passers-by into a club, called out to Warwick by name, begging the legend to join them for the night or any time he would allot them.

Killian, Sloane, and I kept deep in our hoods, but I kept turning around, trying to catch Killian's reaction to this place. His expression remained impassive and unmoved by the countless offers and touches he received. Some even gasped when he walked by. They didn't need to see his face to know he was powerful; they could feel it coming off him as he passed. The Lord of the Fae would have magic some might never have felt before.

Killian's eyes met mine. "You have no idea what I've seen in my day. This is nothing." His tone suggested his past went far more into the seedy dark underbelly world than his position, as lord, indicated.

Sloane and Ash were hounded as well. The whole group, except me, had both men and women sensually and crudely begging them for pleasure while I was almost unseen. Like my iridescent gray aura reflected like an empty spot, blinding them to a person there.

As if I were a ghost.

"Where the hell are we going?" Killian hissed, our group quickly weeding through the throng.

"Sorry, *Lord*," Warwick grumbled, slowing us down when we got to the infamous cathouse. "You're gonna have to lower your expectations for a bit. No silk sheets and chocolates on the pillow here."

Killian's gaze danced over the front of Kitty's, the prostitutes hanging out of the window calling down to potential clients.

"You think you're the only one who suffered in life?" Killian shot to Warwick. "I worked and fought for where I am. I didn't come from money." He started to brush by the Wolf. "Just so you know, my sister was sold at the age of fourteen to work at a brothel."

The bit of information hit my lungs like a punch. I had assumed Killian came from noble birth, which was how most became noblemen and kings. Nepotism was the formula for becoming a ruler. To get a little insight on him and his family was rare. He had a sister. Did he still, or did something happen to her?

The five of us stomped up the steps and through the doors, Killian, Sloane, and I still fully hooded and hidden behind the other two.

"No." Madam Kitty stood in the middle of her lounge. Regal, beautiful, and pissed. Her arms crossed, and her mouth pinched. "One stray was bad enough. I put my foot down at three more."

"So now I'm a fuckin' stray?" Ash snapped, his lids lowering. "Good to know how you look at me."

"That's not—" She held up her hand, taking a deep breath. "I did not mean it like that."

"Then what did you mean?" Ash got closer, his chest puffing. Anger bristled off the easygoing male, their past bubbling up to the surface fast and hot. "Seems pretty clear how you feel about me. How you've *always* felt."

"Ash, stop." Warwick shoved his friend back. "Not the time."

"Never is," Ash retorted, though he eased back from Kitty.

Warwick turned to her. "Kit."

"Don't you dare call me that." Kitty pointed her long nail in Warwick's face. "You continue to take advantage of me, Warwick. This is *my* business. *My* home. I have built this place up with my own blood, sweat, and tears, and you waltz in, give me those eyes and cocky smile and think I will simply bend to your will. How many times now has something gone wrong, and I have to rebuild another room or lose business because you are hiding out here."

"I have always compensated you for it."

Kitty glared at him. "You have pushed me too far lately. Your mood has gone beyond *unbearable*, and I've known you when you were *only* a vengeful killer. This week, you have destroyed an entire floor, threatened my workers, and scared away clients. So, until you find that girl and deal with your shit, I need you to get out."

"I have no idea what you are talking about." Warwick ground through his teeth, the sentence sounding more like thunder than actual words.

"For someone as smart as you are, who has lived as long as you have, you are an *idiot*. You have your head so far up your ass, all you see is your own bullshit." Fury flashed in Kitty's brown eyes. I had never seen her lose her cool. "I love you, brother, so I say this from the bottom of my heart. Get out." She pointed to the door. "Go find her now!"

Warwick expanded with pure raw fury, appearing to want to demolish this room.

Ash's hand clutched my cloak, dragging me forward and yanking down my hood. "Found."

Kitty blinked at me. Warwick didn't move, his gaze straight, a nerve in his cheek twitching.

"Though I think you have a misconstrued idea that his mood is going to improve now." Ash scoffed.

"It can't get worse." Kitty stayed emotionless, but her lips pushed together, almost in a relieved smile, like she was actually happy to see me.

"I doubt that." Warwick huffed, still not looking at me.

Kitty ignored him, motioning to the men behind me. "And they are?"

Out of the corner of my eye, I watched Killian tug down his hood. His regal and sharp features couldn't be hidden under the dirt and cuts.

Kitty let out a small gasp, seeing the Lord of the Fae standing in the entry of her whorehouse.

"My liege." She stumbled for a moment but quickly gathered herself together, dipping her head in respect. "Y-you are supposed to be dead."

"Seems we aren't so lucky," Warwick muttered.

"Yes, I am," Killian responded, shooting a glare at Warwick. "And I'd like to keep it that way. For now."

His response finally twisted Warwick around, the legend's eyebrows scrunching together in confusion.

"We have a lot to catch up on." I glanced at all of them, then at the door. "But I think it's best if we move away from here."

Kitty's head jerked, realizing she had some of the most wanted and notorious individuals in Budapest standing in her foyer, where anyone could walk in and see them. She exhaled, her shoulders edging down, and with a slight nod of her head, she yielded.

"Upstairs, now," she ordered. "The attic has a large room with mattresses and a private bath."

"You're giving us the orgy room?" Warwick snorted, making Kitty's long lashes lower to the point of slits, threatening him if he spoke one more word.

"I will have someone bring everything you need," she replied icily.

Ash tugged on Warwick's arm, pulling him away before Kitty kicked the living daylights out of him. I would have paid money to watch that.

Ascending to the very top, Warwick pushed open a door at the end of the hallway. Another single door was at the other end, and I had a notion it one was Kitty's private quarters, given the complex locks on the lavender painted door.

Warwick burst through our plain entrance, flicking on a fire bulb chandelier hanging in the middle.

"Oh, wow." I came to a stop in the large room. The slanted attic ceilings were draped with fabric, and there were several swings and hammocks like you'd see down in Carnal Row. Mattresses, sofas, and lounges covered with pillows, faux fur, and fake silk filled the room. On one wall was a closed door, which I assumed was the bathroom. Next to it were shelves and racks of feathers, paddles, beads, whips, sex toys, and other paraphernalia, while on the other side of the room was a bar filled with alcohol and drugs. An old-time record player sat on a table near the arched window.

Everything a sex party would need.

Being the only girl walking into an orgy room with four intensely sexual hot fae, there was no stopping the ideas from brushing at my mind, heating my cheeks.

But that quickly changed when the door slammed shut and Warwick whirled on Killian, ramming the fairy back into the wall, his hand gripping his shirt, digging into Killian's throat.

"You fucking kidnapped her?" Warwick bared his teeth. "How the fuck are you alive?"

Sloane instantly reacted, grabbing the gun from me and pointing it at Warwick's head. "Let him go!"

Ash, responding to Sloane, cocked his gun at the soldier's head. "You drop your weapon first."

"I need a drink." I groaned, rubbing my temple. I made my way to the bar, setting the box with the nectar down on the end. "Before you go killing each other, how about we talk this out like rational adults?"

Ash chuckled.

"Yeah, never mind." I waved them off, pouring myself a whiskey. "Go ahead, kill each other. Istvan and whoever is trying to take over Killian's reign will highly appreciate all the work you're saving them."

The men shifted, no one willing to be the first to retreat.

"Fuck's sake." I hopped onto the bar, sipping the cheap whiskey, the intense aroma already spinning my head.

"I'm alive because Sloane saved me. Two of my *elite* guards were killed before the bomb even went off. He knew something was going to happen." Killian looked at Warwick. "He saved me... and I saved your sister."

"What?" Warwick jerked back, his nose flaring, rage streaking his features. "Don't you fuckin' lie to me."

"I'm not." Killian spat. "Your nephew and sister are alive."

Warwick went still, clearly not ready to trust his enemy.

"He's not lying, Warwick," I stated. "They are alive and well. I've seen them. They're fine."

Warwick's wild gaze went to me, his eyes taking me in. No matter what was going on with us, he knew I'd never lie about that.

With a deep breath, he stepped back, letting go of Killian, his body still tense, but if you knew Warwick, you could see something unfurling inside him. The single blink, the release of his fisted hand, the small exhale. A relief so concentrated and private, not many would notice. But for those who did, it felt like a tsunami of emotion.

"Lower your weapon," Killian ordered Sloane, and slowly his guard complied. Ash did the same.

Killian pushed off the wall, rubbing at his neck. "We've been at one of my safe houses in the mountains. I thought it was better if we all stayed dead for a little longer."

"Why?" Warwick barked, his relief covered up and buried deep.

"Because." Killian swallowed, exhaustion heavy on his shoulders. "Someone within my own house wants me dead and went to *great* lengths to make sure I was."

"Something I understand." Warwick folded his arms, his profile to me. I noticed he wouldn't really look at me. Not for long.

Killian frowned but ignored him, strolling further into the room.

"They aren't working alone in this coup. Though it is someone close enough to move within my palace with ease. Someone who knows my schedule and has connections to pull this off without anyone noticing. And with enough bombing material to take down half a magic-spelled palace. We all know it isn't the rebel alliance they are trying to pin it on."

"Do we?" Warwick sneered. "How sure are you? Of the men around you?"

"You mean Zander?" Killian raised a brow, peering quickly at me. Breath held in my lungs, my body going still. "I knew this whole time he has been working for Sarkis."

"What?" I gaped. "But…"

"You cannot be where I am without being ten steps ahead of everyone else. And I learned at an early age, you can trust no one, even those who swear loyalty. Zander was way too easy to read." Killian unbuttoned his jacket, throwing it on the chair casually, like a traitor among him was no big deal.

"You saved him. You have him in your hideout."

"Zander is alive too?" Warwick's eyes darted to me, then quickly back to Killian.

"Oh, yes." Killian's violet eyes darted to mine with a smugness. "Very much. He was of great assistance in getting your family out and safe. He has been most attentive to Eliza and Simon. Dutiful in making sure they are *comfortable*."

My lips rolled together, trying not to respond to his insinuation.

Warwick's eyes tapered, as if he sensed more meaning behind the statement.

"But if you want to know why I kept a spy alive and close," Killian tilted his head, the answer already in his statement. "A spy can become a great tool to have when they don't realize you have caught on. You can get information from them as well. Sarkis, as I learned, was never a genuine threat or enemy. If anything, I saw more of an ally in him." Killian turned to me. "Tell Andris he must get better spies next time. Horse-shifters are not cut out for deceit and duplicities. They are too honest and righteous for seedy work."

"I still don't understand. You are okay with him being with you in the cabin?"

"Zander is not even close to a threat. He only heard and shared what I wanted him to." Killian leaned on the back of a sofa. "He is aware I know now. We have come to an… *understanding*. And it's not me he needs to worry about."

Both Killian and I glanced over at Warwick.

"What the hell does that mean?" Warwick grew defensive.

I smirked into my glass.

Ash groaned under his breath, and I wonder if he caught on. He came to the bar, stealing my glass and taking a sip.

"Get your own." I glared, swiping it back.

"What's the fun in that?" He grinned up at me, licking his lips. "Plus, I like sharing with you."

A vibration sounded from across the room, pulling my attention to the Wolf. His scowl was focused on his friend.

Ash smiled more, leaning into me, egging on his volatile brother.

"Why the hell did you take her?" Ash took my glass again, downing more, then turning to Killian. "Could have helped us out, and both of us would have gone with you."

"One, I don't trust you. Two, I don't trust you, nor do I want you to know where my safe house is. Three, I don't have to help you with anything. And four, she made a promise to me," Killian retorted. "I came to collect."

"So, you fuckin' pluck her off the street and drug her?" Ash slammed the glass down, standing up straighter. "I could smell the hint of chloroform. I thought HDF or some other group captured her again."

Killian adjusted on the back of the sofa, not mentioning that Sloane was supposed to just retrieve me, not drug me and tie me up. I guess Killian left it open for interpretation.

"How did you guys know where to find us tonight?" I changed the subject, turning back to Ash and Warwick. How I was taken wasn't important anymore, and it only seemed to piss everyone off.

Ash's stance tightened. He gave a quick glance to Warwick, who stared at nothing, muscles in his jaw and neck straining.

"Since the moment you were *taken*, we've been scouring every inch of this city." Ash glanced at Warwick again, something I didn't get hung between them. "We saw HDF soldiers move into the square and figured something was going down." Ash shook off whatever heaviness was between them, snorting sardonically. "Not surprised to see you in the center of danger as usual."

"The one thing that hasn't disappeared from my life." I poured more alcohol into my cup.

Warwick's head whipped to mine, his eyes burrowing into me with no exposed emotion, but intensity cut through me. I swear I could feel a flutter of something against my soul, but I heard and felt nothing from the actual man. Just an impression making me believe I could still feel the mark he left on my bones.

"How did they know where to wait for you?" Warwick rumbled, jerking away from me, taking off the weapon strapped to this back.

"Ummm…" I knocked my heels into the bar. "Seems Kalaraja is still really good at what he does."

"He is not fully human," Killian said with conviction.

"Yeah, I felt the same thing," Warwick agreed. "But I can't figure out what he is. He seems to adapt and able to hide even from me."

"Like a chameleon," Killian replied.

"What?" Warwick and Ash both barked out in shock. "A chameleon?"

"I've known one before. She could slip away right in front of you, smell like a human or fae." A bitter, faraway expression fired in Killian's eyes, telling me there was far more to this story.

"Shit." Ash leaned more into me with an exhale. "Makes sense, though."

"Why?" I asked, not having the background they all seemed to have.

"Chameleon's shifters are *very* rare. They can change and adapt to *any* situation with effortlessness and escape just as easily. They can change their smell and blend if need be. They are very smart and devious."

"If he is one, it's understandable why he's been so hard to sense. Why it's been so easy for him to find us without us being aware. Slip away from us." Warwick's irritation coated his statement.

Holy barrel of monkeys. The *Lord of Death* could hide among us, and we might not know it?

"Can they change their appearance?" I tucked my tangled and dirty hair nervously behind my ear. "I mean, could he look like one of you?"

"No." Killian shook his head. "Just like the animal, they can't change forms. He will always look like him, but they can fool the eye, blend in with the background, be the human beggar on the street to a noble fae at a party. They weave a story that makes you trust whatever they are saying. They are con artists. The ultimate imposters. Impeccable hunters."

Which was maybe why he got in with Istvan, pretending to be a human who was particularly skilled at tracking a target.

"What he *is*, isn't important. How he knew where to find you tonight is." Warwick stripped off his coat, his massive biceps bulging tightly against his short-sleeve shirt as he folded his arms, the veins and muscles straining against his tattooed skin.

Not that I noticed.

Yeah, okay, I noticed.

Even at a distance, without our link, or even looking at each other, Warwick was like a punch to the face. Jarring, brutal, and painful. It made me realize as tempting as Killian and Ash were, when Warwick was in the room, they were watered down to nothing. He consumed my very being. Gorged on it with a vengeance and plucked at my rib cage like violin strings.

I didn't have to be an enemy for him to destroy me.

Inhaling, I stared at my boots, Tad's blood dried on the tip.

"We went back up to High Castle. We were followed by one group, while Kalaraja had another group waiting back here for us."

There was a beat before Warwick's boots thumped over the wood floor, his body becoming a threatening device. The man was no less dangerous without the magic I bequeathed him. Before me, he had still been powerful and deadly.

Even as I sat on the high bar, he still loomed over me.

"You went back up to High Castle?" It wasn't a question. "To get the nectar."

My head tipped back to peer up at him, my jaw clicking. "Yes."

Anger billowed off him, his massive chest rising and falling when our eyes met. He was within touching distance, my hand aching to reach out and trace the curves of his muscles, the heat of his skin, feel his anger burn down my arms and feel him tear through my soul. The absence of the link, our connection, wasn't just something missing; it was a physical pain. Torture.

At least on my end.

"You went up there to retrieve the most powerful object in the world."

He stepped closer, his body almost settling between my legs. "Guarded by necromancer-witches, who would fight to the death for it, with just these two?" Warwick's nose flared, motioning back to Killian and Sloane.

"These two?" Killian shot up. "I am *pure* fairy. A fucking Lord! I have more power in my pinkie than you have in your entire body."

"You want to have a go, fairy?" Warwick gritted to Killian, gaze still on me.

"Name the place, Farkas." Sloane rolled his shoulders. "I will gladly show you how fast I can put a wild dog down."

"Just try." Warwick still didn't look away from me, but I knew every muscle in his body was ready to respond if Killian came at him.

"I don't see the problem." I contested. "Would going with you and Ash be any different?"

"Yes." He growled as his frame inched closer.

Air caught in my lungs, forcing my voice out strong. "Why?"

"Me."

"Gods, your huge, insufferable ego," I snapped.

His mouth got within an inch of mine, his timbre scraping the ground. "Not too long ago, you had no problem with my *huge* insufferable *ego*."

My body instantly heated at his insinuation. The memory of how his body felt over mine… so deep inside I couldn't breathe. Shoving him away, I slid off the bar, needing to get away from him.

"Don't worry. We brought a Druid along with us too." I stepped away, retreating.

"Tad?" Warwick sputtered, running his hand through his hair. "*Bazdmeg.*" He reached for the glass I had set down, grabbing the remains and gulping down the rest before slamming it back on the bar. He turned, pacing a few feet. "So, you got it then." He flicked his chin at the box I set down on the corner of the bar. "The nectar."

"Yes."

Warwick strolled over to it, his fingers flipping the lid, peering down. He stared blankly at it, his teeth grinding together. I wondered if he hoped the same as I had that it would be brighter, showing it was returning, that possibly our magic would come back.

Or did he fear the opposite?

He had freedom now…

A wolf without a leash.

Chapter 16

Warwick slammed the lid back down when a knock tapped on the door. Killian and Sloane reached for their weapons.

"Calm the fuck down." Warwick strode to the door, opening it up to a redheaded girl on the other side.

"Rosie!" At the sight of my friend, I ran for the door, crashing into her.

She chuckled as she tried to hug me with all the stuff she was holding. "Oh, luv. I'm so glad you are back and safe." She squeezed me. Both of us pulled back, smiling at each other. "He has been absolutely dreadful since he returned here after Samhain." Her blue eyes darted to the man in question. "Seriously, he's no longer allowed here without you. So good to see you."

Warwick huffed and grumbled something under his breath, strolling back to the bar and pouring more into my glass before downing it.

"Good to see you too." I took some of the items she was carrying, moving out of her way. She strolled in, and out of the corner of my eye, I saw Killian's head jerk, pulling my attention.

He watched her intently, his brows furrowing.

Rosie set down the food, her eyes sliding to him, aware of his stare.

"Madam thought you would need clothes and food, but let me know if there is anything else I can get you," she said. Her eyes kept darting to Killian as he continued to stare boldly at her.

Rosie was stunning, the perfect mix of softness, beauty, and wit, but his look wasn't of lust, but one of perplexity.

"This is more than kind. Thank you," I responded, an awkwardness winding through the room.

She smiled, about to turn for the door.

"I know you from somewhere." Killian's voice stopped her.

"Pardon?" I could see her gaze comb over him, wondering if he had ever been a customer, but we all knew, no matter how many men she had been with, you would never forget him. *Ever*. Killian left his mark.

"Yes." His mouth parted with disbelief. "You are Nina Petrov."

Rosie lurched at her name, her breath stuttering, her eyes widening.

"You were that young leading actress." Killian shook his head, making the connection. "I used to go to many performances at the theater before they shut down."

Rosie's head lifted, trying to hide her emotions, but even I could see her stumbling, trying to find solid ground as once again her old life and new life collided together.

"Well." Her fake British accent thickened. "I hope you enjoyed them."

Killian snorted. "No, they were awful. Merely a bunch of preening, flouncing, overacting performances. But they made me laugh."

"They were dramas," she muttered, low and controlled.

"There was a difference?"

Her entire body jolted, inhaling as if he kicked her in the stomach. Her lids narrowed on him, fire raging behind her eyes.

"It's a good thing I can still use those overacting techniques now in my work." She cleared her throat, not bowing down to the fae lord. "Something you clearly have a lot of personal experience with, my lord." She dipped into a curtsy, then whisked around and stomped out the door, leaving all of us with our mouths open.

Did she just outright insult the fae lord?

Killian's tan skin turned a deeper color, his physique vibrating with anger, his jaw locking. He took a step, appearing he was about to fly through the door after her. No matter if they were fae or human, you cut a man below the belt, suggesting they couldn't please a woman, and they went ballistic.

But you slight a fae lord, that was a whole other level of brazen.

Possibly stupid and deadly.

"Killian." I stepped in his path, blocking him, his rage still on the door where she exited. "Leave it."

He rolled his jaw, his eyes finally lowering to mine, seething. "No one, especially a human *whore,* talks to me like that."

My hands pushed on his chest, my threat clear. "You touch her, and you deal with me."

"And what can you do, *Brexley*?" He sneered down his nose at me, my name plunging through me, forcing me to suck in. "You can't stop me. You can't do anything anymore. Your power is gone. The nectar is useless."

"Whoa, back the hell up." Ash started to come for Killian, but Warwick beat him to it.

With a roar, Kilian's body flew back into the sofa, his body tumbling over it into a side table, cracking his head against it.

In a blink, chaos erupted.

Killian leapt to his feet, charging into Warwick, both of them falling into the sea of blankets and mattresses, kicking and punching like two kids on the playground. Ash dove for Sloane, their fists cracking against each other.

I rubbed at my head with a heavy sigh. Another version of this might have been hot, a bunch of hunky men rolling around together, but all I saw were egos and tantrums.

"Stop." I folded my arms, yelling. No one heard me or took notice. Walking to the far wall, I pulled off an item from a hook, twisting around to the fighting men. The sound of the whip cracked in the air like a gun, halting them.

"I. SAID. STOP!" The demand echoed through the silent room as I cracked the whip again. Each head turned to me, bloody, bruised, and blinking at me with a strange, stunned expression. "Stop acting like children and be the ruthless fae you're supposed to be. Our world is on the cusp of collapse. Istvan is beating us at our own game, and right now, all you guys can do is fight each other, doing exactly what he wants.

"Sarkis is weak. The fae are kingless and unsteady, while HDF has been gaining power and alliances all over the eastern bloc. He is distributing weapons and perfecting the fae pills for a full takeover. Ash and I have seen their progress. And it's much further along than anyone anticipated. And could you imagine what would happen if he got his hands on the nectar?" I gestured to the box, taking a deep breath. "We are exhausted right now. How about we get some rest, and tomorrow we start making a plan to fight back before we lose everything." I glared at each one. "Do you understand me?"

They stared.

"I asked, Do. You. Understand. Me?"

"Yes." They all muttered under their breaths like sullen teenagers.

Warwick shoved off Killian, fury riding his shoulders as he stalked to the bar. He downed a huge portion of the bottle, not even bothering with the glass. Ash joined him. Slowly, Sloane and Killian followed, grabbing other bottles of alcohol.

My lids shut briefly as I set down the crop, my bones feeling the toll of the night. My stomach was empty, but the alcohol edged off the hunger. I needed a bath to wash all the dried blood off my body. Most of it was not my own.

Grabbing a few items Rosie brought in, I headed to the bathroom. It was nothing special, a sink, toilet, and bathtub, though the tub was big enough to fit several people in it. I didn't even want to think about what happened in here or what still stained the blankets on the beds. I lost that level of decorum a long time ago.

Taking my time and allowing myself a moment of selfishness to soak and scrub my body and hair, I let myself drift for a moment in the quickly cooling water.

It was a prickle of my senses, a hum deep inside that was probably my training kicking in. The awareness I had of my surroundings.

I wasn't alone.

My lids flew open, already sensing the silent figure leaning against the wall. His stormy eyes watched me intently, as if he could still trail them over my skin with his invisible touch.

Leaning up against the wall, his arms crossed, he must have been there for a while. His hair was loose around his face, and he had a cut under his eye, his jaw bruised.

Even without the fully powered wolf knocking around inside him, the man was feral and wild. A danger to any living thing.

Our eyes stayed on each other, words and emotions screaming through the silent room, but they didn't soak in, didn't graze my mind, nor touch my soul, though it still felt like he was there. A ghost haunting me. A phantom limb that was cut off, but I could still feel it.

His gaze raked down me, slow and deliberate, not caring how boldly his eyes took in my naked body. The tub was hard to fill because of its size, leaving the water well below my breasts.

Heat filled my veins, making my skin very aware of every patch his focus trailed over. He didn't move. Hunting me silently, ready to sink his teeth in for the kill.

I was not prey. Not anymore.

Standing up, the water sluiced off my long, wet hair reaching my back, though nothing covered up my sex, my breasts, or my scars. It was all there for him to feast on. No inhibition or insecurity of my less than curvy frame. What I had been through, I owned, and I took it on as my armor.

Warwick's nose flared, his eyes growing darker, but he still didn't move or speak. His muscles flexed and coiled under his skin.

Anger. Death. Revenge. It was all this man understood. It was his religion. His conviction.

"Go away, Warwick." I stepped out of the tub, reaching for the towel hanging next to him. "I don't have the energy to deal with you."

His hand shot up, wrapping around my wrist, stopping me from taking the towel. He breathed through his nose, running his tongue over his lips.

"Let go." My glare leveled with his, my own rage spiking up my vertebrae. He didn't recede, a nerve dancing along his cheek. "I said let go." I ripped my arm from his grasp. Grabbing the towel, I wrapped it around myself. "You made yourself perfectly clear about what you wanted. You got it. I have nothing more to say to you."

I opened the door, but his palm hit the wood, slamming it shut. His body moved close behind mine, so close I could feel the heat of him, his breath against the back of my neck, his arm over my head, making sure the door stayed shut. He enveloped me—drowning me in his presence.

"Move. Your. Hand," I demanded, forcing every word through like a cheese grater.

"No." His voice was gravelly and wild. The violence thrumming off him was like lighter fluid, ready to ignite a single spark with the gnash of his teeth or the friction of his clothes against my bare skin. My hand clutched the doorknob, my lids closing, trying to keep myself above water.

Whirling around, I faced him. He jerked at my sudden proximity.

"You don't get to do this," I seethed. "You don't walk away from me, kicking me to the side like a broken toy, and then act possessive when someone else wants to play with me."

Inhaling noisily, he vibrated with anger, his face getting barely an inch from mine.

"Who the fuck is trying to play with you?"

I snorted derisively. "Whomever *I* want."

The hand on the door shot to my chin, his fingers clutching, forcing me to look at him. "If you say Killian…"

Rage and annoyance buckled through me, my hands shoving hard at his chest. The fact I couldn't move him an inch, that I was no longer on equal footing, was like acid in my bloodstream, spurting a storm through me.

"Get the hell away from me." I shoved at him again. He stood watching me, only making me more frenzied. "We have nothing to say to each other, so leave me alone."

His hands slapped the wood on either side of my head, leaning in. "I won't play these little girl games with you. I said to be clear about what you wanted. You told me to walk. So I did."

Chagrin raced through me, burning my face and rolling my fists at his statement. In truth, I had told him to go and was mad when he did. It was immature. I rolled the dice on a hand I could lose.

But logic and anger so rarely cooperate.

"And you practically ran out." I seethed. "I don't want to be with anyone who doesn't want to be there."

His non-response, like I hit the nail on the head, seared through my lungs. The need to get away from him crawled over my muscles like bugs. My brain understood I wouldn't beat him with brute strength. I would need to cut deep.

"You have no say in who I'm with. I can fuck Killian right now… or I can go curl up with Ash." I twisted for the door. "*Again.*"

I knew what I was doing, playing more of those little girl games, seeing how he'd react, but I just didn't give a shit. I wanted him to hurt like he hurt me. He walked away. Left me when I needed him the most. So screw him; he could watch me snuggle in with Ash and deal with his choices.

"The fuck you will," he snarled, wrapping his hands around my arms. He moved me away from the exit, ramming me back into the wall.

A spark flared up my spine, starting a bonfire in my chest.

Pain exploded through my hand as my fist struck his throat. He barely reacted, but his hands released me in favor of his neck. Slipping away, I made it two steps before he barreled into me, flattening me into the opposite wall, my cheek flattened to the wood. His frame pressed into me, pinning me in place.

"You are not sleeping with anyone else," he growled in my ear.

"Fuck you." I spat. "I can do whatever I want."

"Can you?'

"Yes. I told you to go that night, but let's be honest, you've wanted an excuse to go *way* before then. You pretended to sleep with my friend to keep me away. Who is the one playing games here? You can't have it both ways. You wanted freedom? You got it. The link is broken." My nipples ground into the surface, his frame heavy against mine. It was an excruciating teeter-totter of pain and pleasure. Nothing outside hurt, it was all inside. "Leave me alone and let me be with someone who *wants* to be with me."

With a snarl, he flipped me around, pressing my arms back into the wall, his eyes blazing like a ferocious sea.

"You don't think I want to be with you?"

"No." I held up my chin in defiance. "Maybe as a possession, or when I had magic, but not the real me." Deep pain snapped through my teeth. "That fan club you loved to tease me about, well guess what, it wasn't real. They were only attracted to my power... to *Aneira's magic.*" I spat her name.

"Aneira?" Warwick blinked.

"Come to find out, all the magic funneling into my tiny baby body was from her." And my mother, using black magic. "The reason the fae book was open to me was that it thought I was part of her lineage. That's why the nectar was so powerful—it absorbed all her magic plus the barrier's power."

He shook his head as if he didn't want to believe it.

"The magic that saved you, brought you back to life, is because of *her.*"

"No," he seethed, his grip on me tightening.

"What's wrong? You don't like knowing you fucked someone who used to hold the power of a sadistic evil queen?"

"Shut up," he growled.

"It's the truth." I retorted. "Tad can see my aura now, and the one person in the world he saw with a similar one, at least a sliver of it, was Aneira. She could lure men in, make them bend at the knee, do anything she wanted." I tried to keep my emotions back. "It was never me you wanted."

"*Lófasz!*" He bellowed, punching his hand into the wall. "Don't you get it? It's all *you*, Brexley." My name thundered through me, not with magic, but with the way he used it. The way it sounded on his lips, curling over his tongue with power. "Look around you." He motioned to the door. "With or without the magic, every man here is willing to fight for you, stand next to you, *die* for you." He put his hands near my head, caging me in. "And it's not the bitch's power which makes us bend. It's all *you*." Ire strained his features. "I won't lie; I had hoped it was the magic, something that could be broken. Terminated. I tried to tell myself that with every step I took away from you, every hour I stayed away. But fuck..." He leaned his head down, his mouth barely an inch from mine, his form entirely encompassing mine. "It wasn't. Now the link is gone, and I got what I thought I wanted... my life back, to carry on like I always had." He lifted his lip with a snarl I could feel flutter through me. "Seeing you tonight made it extremely clear."

"What?"

"Before you, nothing I ate had any taste." His mouth almost grazed mine. "All I could smell was death. Nothing but killing made me feel anything. Then you walked into my life." His hand slid under my jaw. "And I don't see just gray. I feel, smell, taste, and want to fuck you in every color."

There was a small gasp of my breath before his mouth crashed down on mine, hungry and untamed. A single touch of his lips and he lit the match. He kissed me so intensely, my entire body felt it shudder through, dipping through my pussy as if he still had the ability to touch me inside and out, switching me from defensive to aggressive. Feral. Vicious. My deep-seated starvation for this man ignited me. Our mouths clashed, nipping, biting, and sucking, trying to devour to the bone.

"Fuck." He lifted me up, my legs wrapping around him as my mouth claimed his over and over, our bodies slamming back into the wall. "I went insane when Ash told me you were gone. The fact I couldn't reach you... find you." He growled, his fingers tearing at the towel, ripping it from my body. A noise came up his throat as his eyes feasted on me, his mouth covering my breast, flicking at my nipple.

A groan knocked my head back into the wall, my back arching with need.

"I was already walking a thin line of sanity." He knotted his hands through my hair, tugging hard. My naked body rubbed against his clothed one, needing him more than air. "And when I saw you tonight, I realized something."

"What?" His thumb slid over my lips, tracing them roughly.

"The wolf isn't leashed... and yet it still runs back to you."

His words burst through me, penetrating so violently all logic ceased. My hands ripped at his pants, yanking his shirt fiercely over his head, our mouths cruel in our claim. We had no need for foreplay here, for coy seduction. With us, there never seemed to be. Maybe we were built that way.

We were carnal and brutal.

He yanked me off the wall, tossing me onto the sink, spreading my legs.

"This is mine." His fingers slipped easily into my wetness, stroking my pussy, sparking fire. I no longer cared about my voice carrying or who could hear the desperation in my moans as he lowered to his knees, his hands running up my thighs, opening me for him. His mouth closed on me, sucking and licking deep into me, ripping any air from my lungs.

"Fuck," he groaned. "I forgot how good you taste." He clutched my hips, pulling me closer, his mouth devouring me. "Like every fuckin' color."

"Oh gods!" I bowed, my hands clawing at his head, my hips bucking ruthlessly against his assault. I felt every nerve he hit as his fingers thrust in, jackknifing me almost off the counter, my orgasm already burning my spine. "Warwick…" I needed more.

I wanted all.

Wild sounds rolled in my throat as he devoured me. The reverberation of him licking through my wetness had my body begging to be touched everywhere.

"Brexley." His moan vibrated deep inside me, my name tearing everything away. Every nerve thrummed like music, tripping over the wire. I heard myself cry out, my body convulsing as he continued to consume me, leaving me panting and sagging against the mirror.

He grinned wolfishly up at me, his tongue flat and licking through me one last time as he rose. Breathing heavily, we watched each other for a moment, his eyes hungry and primal.

Sitting up, I yanked on his pants, shoving them down. "I need more." I would never have enough, my body already craving him. I wanted him to lose control. To be so far gone, there was no way back.

"And I'm far from being even remotely done with you." He shucked out of his pants and shoes, standing there like the god of death, with his tattoos, scars, insane physique, and massive cock, ready to reap and destroy. The day he walked into the shower room at Halálház, I think deep down I knew I was done. He burned every bridge a guy before or after could cross.

"Kovacs." He gripped my face, an emotion I had never seen flicker in his eyes. A naughty grin tugged his mouth. "I fuckin' missed you."

He could write that on my tombstone, because with four words, he obliterated what was left of me. From him, those words were everything.

With a punishing kiss, he grabbed my thighs, pulling me to the edge of the sink. His gaze was unwavering and lethal. The tip of him hinted at my entrance, a cruel smile on his face as he toyed with me. The need for him to be inside me, to experience every inch of him sinking into me, had me clawing for mercy.

"Want this, Kovacs?" He pushed in a little before pulling back out.

A growl came from me, making his smirk widen.

"How bad did you miss my cock in your wet pussy?"

"Farkas." I ground out. "I'm about to fuckin' kill you."

His head tipped back in a laugh, the rare sound filling me with more crazed desire.

"Warwi—"

My sentence was cut off as he thrust deep inside me, all the way to the hilt, hitting every nerve like he was trying to obliterate me with one stroke.

A moan I felt from the depth of my toes rolled from my soul, stretching and filling me so deeply, the air dissipated from my lungs as my muscles squeezed around him.

"Fuck!" Warwick hissed, pulling out almost to the tip before driving even deeper. "How does this still feel so fucking good?"

I understood. Our link had made sex so unbelievable there wasn't even a word for it. Merging realms and time. Our bond shook the soil we stood on and the air we breathed. But while the connection was gone, it didn't seem to make it any less intense.

It was *us*.

The bond accelerated something that was already there. Our lives were linked with or without magic.

He pumped into me deep and steady, his eyes drilling into mine with a passion he didn't need to put into words. I could still feel the rage, resentment, but there were also a million other things there, thousands of emotions and connections that tied us together.

"Deeper." I tore at his skin, my hands curving over his firm ass, pushing him harder into me. "More!"

He pulled out, yanking me off the sink and twisting me around. He pushed one knee onto the counter, parting me so wide, I felt the cold air trickling from the small window glide through me, emphasizing the wetness seeping from me. A groan huffed from me, my need desperate and aching.

"Watch me fuck you." He gripped my hips, slamming back into me so hard a silent scream opened my mouth. My muscles quivered from the unbelievable sensation as I watched him pound into me, bouncing my tits, the sound of us slapping off the walls. A noise howled in my throat, not at all sounding human.

And in that moment, I no longer felt human. Something inside me snapped, and it roared with vengeance.

I became only need and desire, demanding carnage and blood. The connection might be gone, but it didn't change who Warwick and I were. We loved like a battlefield. Slaughtered and destroyed, taking no prisoners.

Warwick yanked on my damp tresses, curving me deeper into him, producing a growl so loud it vibrated through my bones. His eyes, bright and full of carnage, met mine, and I countered with "more."

His grunt was feral, as if something in him unleashed, spreading me wider. Unrestrained and so brutal, I felt frozen. The air propelled from my lungs, my entire body shaking as my climax came hurtling for me, though I wanted him to keep fucking me. Forever, if it was possible. To never not feel this real and feral. There was a power in being primal. Only fulfilling your basic desires and have no consciousness outside of that. It tapped into the basic drive of people, even when we were layered with emotion and context.

His free hand slipped over my hip, gliding through my folds. Snarling like a beast, he pounded into me so hard, his balls slapped my pussy, shoving me over the edge.

My climax crashed into me with force, my body locking down on him, taking it all. Warwick's roar was deafening as his restraint broke, losing all control, his hips pumping with bruising force, forcing another orgasm to burst through me as he released inside me. He filled me so completely, it spilled down my leg, branding me inside and out like a tattoo.

"Fuck." He growled deeply, his fingers sliding up my inner thigh, catching his seed and pushing it back into me, rubbing it over my clit, hitting the bundle of nerves. "This is fucking mine."

Everything blacked out as my body responded violently, my limbs quaking. My body physically was on earth, but I wasn't. As I burst into pieces, becoming part of every molecule, I saw a flicker—a girl with an iridescent aura around her, the grey, and a massive man by her side, the wolf, slaying everything in their path, their power unmeasurable.

It was only for a second, and I felt it more than remembered it.

All I understood was that Warwick and I walked the line, and even if we lived in the gray, we fucked in color.

Chapter 17

"It will be like waking up in a field of roses."

Chirp!

My body felt warm, cocooned in arms and legs, but my nose tickled, the diluted aroma of rose perfume and soap coaxing me into consciousness.

"Right? Though be careful, Bitz, you don't know where that's been."

Chirp!

"I did not try to put it up there. Not on purpose." Opie's small but loud exclamation fluttered my lids. "It slipped! Soap does that." He huffed. "A total misunderstanding."

Chirp!

A groan hummed in my throat, my nostrils itching. I batted at my face, my eyes opening to see Bitzy sitting on the lip of the tub right by my head, her prong fingers covered in rose-scented soap, her eyes wide, trying to look innocent.

"Stop sticking your fingers up my nose," I grumbled, stretching. Every sore muscle, bruised bone, and bit of chafed skin cried out, bringing a delirious smile to my face.

"I won't tell her the other places you stuck them." Opie skipped up beside her in an old loofah. Part of it he used as a hat; the rest was cut into a tiny ballerina-type skirt. The feathers used for pleasure were stuck into the loofah like a headdress, and sex beads hung around his neck. Bitzy was wearing another set of sex beads as a crown and pleasure feathers for wings. I didn't even want to think about where those things had been before they put them on.

"Fishy! So glad we found you. We were worried." Opie sat down, swinging his legs against the side of the large tub, using his skirt to start scrubbing it. "And why the hell are you sleeping in a dirty empty tub? Not that I care it's dirty. To each their own." His eyes twitched, moving down to clean another spot. "Doesn't bother me at all that you lie in filth. Nope. Not. At. All."

"Bazdmeg." The warm, huge form I was spread out over like a blanket moaned, adjusting underneath me, making me feel his hard length press against my hip. One hand scrubbed at his face, the other rubbing at my ass. "Now this I didn't miss." Warwick's lids opened, glaring at the two. "If any fingers were in any holes…"

"Please, massive one." Opie waved him off. "You loved it. Not like your fingers and appendages weren't in holes too."

Chirp!

Warwick breathed in, sitting up. He dragged me with him, tipping his head back on the tub we had slept in. The memory of what we did with and without the water hummed my body to life.

He meant it when he said he was nowhere near done with me. Like he was determined to find where my line was, how far he could push me. And I met his challenge with my own each time. I could still taste him on my tongue, feel him inside me, my nails dragging through his hair as his seed branded me like an iron. His mouth devoured me over and over, his fingers exploring every inch. Finally, too spent to move, he cleaned me up, drained the tub, and lined it with towels, where he fucked me slow and deep until I passed out.

The bathroom was the only semblance of privacy, and he wasn't one to have any of those men in the other room watch my pleasure break over me again and again. Though I had no doubt they heard us. There was a high probability the entire place did.

"Have anything to report?" Warwick lifted his head. "If not, go. I have more holes to stick things in." His hands gripped my hips, readjusting me on him. Hunger sizzled my nerves, the feel of his heavy erection pressed into me, making me bite my lip. One shift of my hips, and he would be inside me, fucking me until I lost consciousness again. The need to do it commanded most of my thoughts, which is why it took me longer to absorb his remark.

"Report?" Covering my breasts, I turned my head to peer at Opie and Bitzy, then back to the man I was straddling. "What do you mean, report?"

He reached over, grabbing a clean towel off the shelf, and wrapping it around me, taking extra care to knot it right at my breasts.

"When Ash lost you, I figured they could locate you, like last time." Warwick nodded to the pair. "And when they couldn't..."

"Ohhh, the big bad wolfy went rabid. Destroyed several rooms downstairs." Opie's eyes went wide. "Thought he was actually going to eat me."

Chirp! Bitzy flipped Warwick off.

"And yeah, not in the fun way."

I cringed, my features wrinkling up, trying to pass over the image in my head.

"I thought it might be HDF." Warwick's hands dropped to my thighs, rubbing them absently, like he didn't want to stop touching me. "Sub-fae could easily slip in there."

"And spy." I blinked at the revelation. Of course.

Warwick huffed a dry laugh. "As long as your spies don't get distracted by everything sparkly."

"Oh, my broomsticks." Opie's eyes glazed over. "That closet was like a treasure chest... a dream come to life. No one could be there and not be dazzled out of their wits."

"Wits?" Warwick sputtered. "You have to have those in order to lose them. You were gone for a day and came back telling me about diamond-encrusted shoes."

"Oh, those were soooo pretty."

Chirp.

"I will neither deny nor admit I licked them."

Chirp.

"I did not do that. Though I saw stars like the time the vacuum hose fell down my pants."

Chirp.

"It did too fall down there. It was an accident."

"Oh, my gods. Please stop." I waved my hand, getting back on topic. "Diamond shoes? Are you talking about Rebeka's?" She was the only one I knew who had pure diamond heels, like she stepped out of one of those old fairytales. It was a gift from Istvan after rumors of one of his many affairs spread within the high circles. She wore them as a power play when he started to deviate again. A subtle reminder. "Why were you in her bedroom?" She didn't even share one with Istvan. It was usual for the top wealthy tier not to share a bedroom with their spouse. Got uncomfortable when trying to sneak in a lover.

"I wasn't!"

Chirp!

"Okay, I might have been." Opie shrugged, going back to cleaning. "Not like she was there, and her dresses were too beautiful not to drool over before they got packed up."

"Packed up?" My head jerked with confusion. "What do you mean?"

"The room was filled with boxes, and some lady dressed in a maid's outfit was storing all the exquisite stuff away. Such a crime to hide artwork like that. Whoever wore them is a goddess. The sparkles, the gems, the fabric…" Opie groaned, making me flinch again. "To. Die. For. The costumes I could design from just one."

"I don't care about fuckin' dresses," Warwick grumbled while my mind glitched over Opie's claim.

Why would Rebeka be packing all her stuff away? It didn't make sense. And like Opie, Rebeka would never let one of those expensive dresses touch something as dirty as a cardboard box. I knew how precise and stringent she was when they even were carried out to be cleaned.

"Anything else to report?" Warwick motioned them to continue.

"No."

Chirp!

"Oh right, yeah, something about patrolling the streets for the hideout of some fugitives, blah, blah…" Opie rolled his eyes. "Boring."

"Patrol?" Warwick growled. "And you didn't think to lead with that?"

"Why?" Opie blinked. "I try not to start off the morning with dreariness."

"You really are the worst spies ever," Warwick grunted. "Fucking you later. Count on it, princess." He grunted in my ear. Shifting me, he stood, climbing out of the tub. Dammit. I was hoping for a morning orgasm to start my day.

"Whoa, whoa, bad wolfy! Be careful where you point that thing." Opie held up his hands. "That thing is a grenade launcher."

Warwick didn't even pause as I watched his firm, naked ass march for the door, swinging it open. "Ash! Get the fuck up."

"Now there's the way to start off the morning." Opie sighed dreamily.

"Yeaaahhh." I sighed.

Chiiiiirp.

"You aren't going." His deep, commanding tone suggested the topic was over. "That's final."

Cool and calm, I tipped my head, an eyebrow curving up.

"Don't give me that look." Warwick strapped his cleaver to his back.

"I'm just looking at an arrogant male who thinks he has the right to order me around." I crossed my arms over the worn sweater Rosie had brought, my tone staying neutral.

"You two are the most known faces out there." Warwick motioned to me and Killian, who took the order to stay back a lot better than I had. He sat dressed in items from the same pile, sipping his coffee.

Everyone was up and dressed, though no one in the room was happy with us. They complained they didn't get any sleep and were prevented from using the toilet. Ash ended up going downstairs and taking out his frustration on someone else.

"And yours is not?" I gestured to Warwick. "You're more recognizable than I am, just by your frame."

"She has a point." Ash shrugged. "Sloane and I are the least identifiable. We could check things out."

"No." Warwick bristled, his gaze sliding to the guard. "We can do a fast sweep and be back."

"I need to get word to my uncle. Let him know I'm okay." It felt like a thorn wiggling in my gut. Some of the things Opie said were not sitting right. I had the niggling feeling something was off, and it made me anxious to check in with my family. Andris had to be flipping out.

"I'm going," I stated firmly. "Plus, they might know something."

"We can't chance it." Warwick shook his head. "You seem to be taken every time you step outside now."

"Not *every* time."

"I'll go with her." Killian set his cup down.

"What?" We all turned to him in surprise.

"Might be odd when a *dead* fae lord visits an insurgent base," Warwick clipped.

Killian stood up, his grace like a panther. Meticulous and deadly. "You know, Warwick, most of us know how to slip in and out of the shadows, too. You aren't the only one who has survived on the streets."

Warwick looked at him dubiously.

"Plus, I think it's high time the leader of Sarkis army and I meet. It could be greatly beneficial to us both." Killian's suggestion made complete sense. If HDF was growing in power, we needed to join together and fight. The enemies of your enemy could be great allies.

"I'm not leaving that here alone, and it's too dangerous to take it." Warwick motioned to the nectar box.

"Sloane will stay and guard it. I trust him with my life."

"I don't trust him." Warwick gritted his teeth.

"You don't have a say." Skirting over to Killian, I stood next to him in solidarity. "Sloane will watch my nectar. You boys go investigate the streets while we go check in with my uncle. Meet back here later."

Warwick's jaw clicked, his laser focus on me.

"Kovacs…" he rumbled.

"You're not changing my mind, *Farkas*. And you certainly aren't keeping me here. You never could, so stop trying."

"Woman," he huffed, scouring his face. "You drive me insane."

"Yeah, we all know." Ash snorted. "We heard it all night long." Ash snapped his fingers, pointing at Warwick. "But thank you for that, because the snake shifter? Damn, what she could do with her tongue." Ash blew out.

"Ugh. Stop." I wrinkled my nose, frowning, hiding the intense jealousy bubbling in my stomach, knowing Warwick had been with her, too. I had watched.

Footsteps thumped across the floor, Warwick's boots hitting mine. His build completely enveloped us in our own world, his head dipping low. "Don't worry, there's only one tongue I want on me now." His calloused palm glided to the back of my head, pulling me into him. He kissed me with no inhibition, making me forget everything else and everyone else in the room. Searing hot, with the promise of more later.

"Be fuckin' careful," he muttered, his forehead against mine. The unsaid list of things to watch out for hung in the air, but he didn't say them, knowing I could handle myself.

"You too." My mouth brushed his again.

His mouth claimed mine one more time before he pulled away, his glower on Killian. "If anything fucking happens to her…"

"Yes, yes. I get it." Killian glared back. "But just a forewarning, Brexley's safety is paramount to me as well. You screw up again, I will be there." There was no subtlety—it was an outright challenge to the wolf.

Warwick bulked up, stomping closer to the fairy. I could see his need to tear Killian into little pieces.

"Go." I pushed Warwick to the door. "You know where we are if anything comes up."

Warwick still stared down Killian.

"Grab my bag. I left the fae book in my room under the bed," Ash said to me.

I nodded.

"Come on, man." Ash heaved Warwick toward the exit, the tree fairy winking at me before the door slammed.

167

"You really have a death wish, don't you?" I twisted to Killian, chuckling.

"I meant what I said." His violet gaze met mine. "But I can't say I don't also love pissing that fucker off."

With the crisp but mild temperatures, more people streamed out onto the streets, which helped Killian and me slip through the lanes with little attention. Killian had to keep himself deep in a hood and glamoured, as his power could be felt if he wasn't careful. By acquiring the title of lord, he gained magic which could be even be felt by humans. An electrical current warning you, this man was more than what he seemed.

My own face was deep in my hood as I led them to my uncle's base, both of us on high alert, making sure no one was following us.

"They know we're here," Killian muttered next to me when we came to a stop close to the rundown building being used as the base. He looked up toward the rooftop. "We have guns on us now."

Peering up, I tried to find the guards hiding along the roofline, my ordinary senses picking up nothing. Still, for some reason, I was certain Scorpion wasn't up there.

Keeping my face pointed at where Killian motioned, I yanked my hood down, letting them see me before stepping toward the hidden entry.

In less than thirty seconds, the spell-locked door burst open, and guards with guns grabbed onto us, hustling us in and slamming the door behind us.

A woman stepped up to me, her weapon pointed at my head, a snarl lifting her lip.

"You're back." She scowled.

"Good to see you too, Zuz," I lied.

She patted me down, finding several guns and knives, while Killian was being stripped of his.

"Gone a couple of days and treated like an enemy." I peered around. None of the guards handling us were ones I knew well.

"Routine for anyone who comes through here." She sneered, placing my weapons on a table. "My job is to protect *my* people."

Her sentiment was clear. She did not consider me one of them.

"What is your business?" She flicked her chin to my comrade. "Who the hell are you? Another shmuck she fluttered her lashes at?"

Killian slowly tugged at his hood, revealing his face and dropping his glamour.

The intake of breath from the soldiers was sharp, their forms jolting with the realization of who stood before them.

"Lord Killian." Zuz blinked, a deep instinct dipping her legs and head in a bow.

"I'd like to see your lieutenant, *girl*." His voice rung with authority, a command lesser fae would bend to, the power crushing down on them. "Now. I have little patience for catty imbeciles."

"Y-yes, sir," Zuz sputtered, motioning for us to follow her.

Peering over my shoulder, Killian winked at me, humor tugging at the corners of his mouth.

I rolled my eyes but couldn't fight the smile warming my chest, knowing he went "extra" for me.

We weaved through the maze of tunnels and dead ends, which would confuse any enemy trying to get in or out before reaching the main stairs down to the base.

The entry area was busy with activity and people going about their business. A class looked to be taking place in the training room, the café filled with more chairs and butts, which meant fewer were filling the clinic.

"Brexley!" Andris's voice barreled into me right before he did, his arms wrapping around me, his lean body squeezing me in tight. "*Dragam.*" Relief, pain, and joy filled that single word. "You are all right." He hugged me tighter before leaning back to look at me, his gaze full of love, his hand on my cheek. "I was going crazy when you didn't return. I had a team scouring the streets for you. I was so worried."

"I'm fine." I clasped my hand over his, smiling up at him. For a second, I swore I felt something hum at my skin before he pulled away. He appeared so youthful for his age, the nectar's power moving inside him, though he still looked exhausted. "Are you okay?"

"I'm fine." He waved off the question, rubbing his forehead. "I've just been so worried. I haven't slept any since you were taken. I'm so happy you are safe. Where were you this whole time?"

"With me." Killian stepped forward, his movement and voice whirling Andris away from me. Andris' spine went rigid, yet his expression stayed impassive. He was trained to not show emotion in any situation.

"Lord Killian." Andris addressed him with a nod.

"Lieutenant General Takacs." Killian returned the motion.

"I will admit you are the last person I ever expected to visit my base." Andris clasped his hands, his legs out in a dominant position. "Especially since you are dead."

"Yes." A smile hinted on Killian's mouth. "I've heard the same reports." He matched Andris's stance. "For now, it has been beneficial."

Andris's eyebrows went up with curiosity.

"I thought it was time you and I met and had a little chat," Killian declared, a hint of more behind his words. Fae were all about nuances. The tiniest ones could mean so much. People trained in battle were no different. A simple inflection could be the difference between life and death.

My uncle understood this. The underlying message rolled into him, his head nodding. "I think you are right."

Both men looked at each other with understanding.

"Please." Andris turned, gesturing to his office. "Join me."

Killian agreed, strolling toward the open door.

My feet automatically started to follow.

"Not this time." Andris shook his head.

I understood, but I guess I was getting used to being the girl in the room in the know.

"Of course."

My uncle squeezed my shoulder, warmth moving down my arm. He turned to his office and shut the door, leaving me staring at the closed door for a moment. Laughter from the mess hall lured my attention away. Strolling, I stopped in the doorway, my mind trying to grasp what I was seeing. Sitting around a table laughing and chatting was Maddox, Wesley, Luk, Kek, Birdie, and Scorpion, but it was the figures next to Scorpion and Birdie which stumbled my mind.

Hanna and Caden.

Their wrists were bound, but loose enough for them to pick up a drink and eat the food in front of them. Their eyes were watchful, their faces perplexed as they observed the fae around them tell stories and tease each other.

Like we did with our comrades at HDF. Just like normal people.

To Hanna and Caden, and once to me, the fae were soulless creatures. They didn't love or have friendships like humans did. In a way, they were right. The fae experienced love even more profoundly than humans did, and their friends went far beyond family.

"X!" Birdie stood up, seeing me first, her tiny body almost knocking me down when she collided with me. "You're alive!" Her excitement dimmed into anger, her hand snaking out and punching me in the arm.

"Ow!" I rubbed at the spot she hit. The girl had a wicked right hook.

"That's for me thinking you were dead." She huffed, trying to hide her emotion, which made me smile.

Luk shuffled around her, his arms looping around my waist, picking me up off the ground, hugging me tight. "Fuck, we were so worried," he mumbled into my neck, not letting me go.

"Missed you too." I held him firmly before he placed me down on my feet. The blue-haired demon stood right next to him.

"Don't fucking do that to us again, little lamb." She blew hair out of her face, her arms folded, appearing annoyed. "He became insufferable with all his worrying, which he wouldn't stop fretting about."

"That was you," Luk shot at her.

"Demons don't fret." She tugged on the ends of her ponytail, a habit she had.

"You were the one threatening to level the city if she wasn't found."

"I'd level a city for a slice of chocolate cake." She flicked her eyes.

Grinning, I leaned in and hugged her, knowing she'd never admit she was worried about me. "Thank you."

"Yeah, yeah," She stood stiffly, patting my back before I released her. "Well, it's obvious you found the legend again."

"Why?" I reacted.

"Because you reek of him. He's *all over* you. I mean, wow." She lifted her brow. "That good, huh?"

A blush burned my cheeks.

"Figured." She sighed, folding her arms. "Your smell is making me horny now." She tossed her strands over her shoulder. "So where is your other sidekick? I thought he'd be right next to you."

"You mean Ash?" I smirked.

"Is that his name?"

Luk and I rolled our eyes at each other, knowing perfectly well she knew it. She'd probably screamed it out before.

"So, the prodigal daughter returns," Maddox shouted, lifting his cup in the air, refocusing me past my friends to the table where everyone was gathering around it again. "Good to see you're okay."

Wesley lifted his cup in agreement. "Cheers to not being dead."

"Cheers to not being dead." Most joined in the sentiment, lifting their cups.

"Thanks." I laughed, though I felt eyes on me from across the table. The three people who did not add to the sentiment. I expected Hanna and Caden to be icy in their response, but it was the anger glaring from Scorpion that cut me.

He was furious with me, which I understood. I put them all in jeopardy when I opposed his authority and altered the mission, going inside the warehouse. I hoped when he learned what Ash and I saw, he'd agree it was worth it.

"You guys are out." I nodded at my two old friends.

"For their good behavior, they get a little field trip and treat today."

Birdie strolled for her seat, motioning to the food and drink in front of Hanna and Caden.

"I'm glad." I tried not to sound patronizing, but by Hanna's glare, I didn't succeed.

"Yes, we're the model inmates," Hanna replied coldly. "Guess we know what prison feels like now."

Fury charred up the back of my neck. The flood of memories from Halálház—the screams, pain, assault, blood, death...

"You have *no fucking idea* what prison is, little girl." Kek slammed her hand down on the table in front of Hanna, leaning over the blonde's shoulder, baring her dagger teeth. "What she went through and survived. What we all experienced in there. In comparison, this is a posh holiday, human. But I will be glad to give you a taste of what hell really is."

Hanna jerked in fear at Kek's warning because she was smart enough to know it wasn't a threat.

"Kek," I said her name calmly.

My friend's black eyes finally turned back to blue, easing away from Hanna, stomping to an empty chair, and plopping down.

Birdie settled back next to Caden. I observed him watching Birdie, his body not pulling away from where her arm brushed his, her long blonde hair trailing his skin as she joked with Maddox. He didn't even flinch at her nearness. To anyone else, it might seem like nothing, but I knew Caden. Even if he tried to pretend he wasn't bothered, humans overall were terrible at hiding their true feelings when you really looked. He would slowly ebb away, not wanting a fae touching him, like she had some disease.

"Sit down." Luk pulled in a chair for me. "Catch us up."

A noise came from my throat as I lowered down on the seat, my head shaking. There was so much. But every single person at this table, whether they felt the same right now or not, was my family. People I had come to trust. Love.

I wanted them to know everything, even Hanna and Caden. They especially needed to hear the truth.

Not a single bite of food or sip of drink was taken as I recited my story of what Ash and I saw far beneath the factory floor. Their emotions were mostly hidden, but I could feel them in the silence. Their disbelief, sadness, rage, and fear coated the room like paint.

The little girl was the hardest to talk about, and I had to bite my cheek to keep the tears back. The memory of her face, her tiny body going through so much pain. My emotions were high when I saw her—I made an empty promise. And that killed me the most, knowing I didn't stop her pain. I didn't help her, and she was most likely dead by now, like Rodriquez's little sister.

"It's true." Maddox leaned forward on his arms. "Under the factory, this Markos has people torturing fae for their essence and is already making this drug?" His dark eyes were incensed. We had seen the bodies, figured out what was happening, but I think deep down, many here hoped it wasn't true.

"And it looks like they are advancing quickly." I nodded my head.

Maddox turned slowly to Caden. "Did you know about this?"

Caden hadn't even had the opportunity to respond. In a breath, Maddox leaped at him, wrapping his hand around his neck and slamming Caden backward to the ground.

"Maddox!" Birdie and I cried out, both of us rushing to where he pinned Caden to the floor.

"Did you?" Maddox seethed, clutching his neck tighter, smacking his head roughly against the cement. With his arms cuffed, Caden kicked out, trying to fight back, his face turning red from lack of air. "You sick fuck. Torturing and killing children? You vile piece of shit! You're fuckin' dead, Markos!"

"Maddox, stop!" I crouched down, trying to get Maddox to loosen his grip.

"He can't breathe!" Hanna cried. "Stop!"

Maddox's wrath was so laser-focused it didn't even feel like he heard us.

"Maddox. Stop!" Scorpion's voice cut through the commotion, jolting Maddox. "There is no honor in killing the unarmed. No relief in the vengeance. Only more blackness on your soul to carry." He said it like it was a creed. A principle they knew between each other. Their longtime friendship seemed to be the only thing that brought Maddox back.

Sneering, Maddox huffed and shoved away from Caden. As he rose, he spit at him. "If you are part of this, I will kill you." He strode out of the room.

As he was hacking and gasping for air, I tried to help Caden sit up.

"Don't touch me," he croaked, jerking violently away from me, humiliation burning him with rage and resentment. But he didn't refuse Birdie's help to get him back up on the bench seat, his eyes watering, his skin patchy, a snarl on his lips.

The room stayed quiet. He rubbed his neck, gradually lifting his head to me. Hate shone from his eyes.

No, not just hate. Betrayal. "You are a liar."

Agony pinched my lips together. "I'm not."

"My family took you in, took care of you, loved you. *I* loved you," he gasped roughly over his words, not listening to me. "I thought you were my best friend. Someone with a soul, but I guess I was wrong. You do belong with *them* now."

I could see both Birdie and Kek wanting to intervene, but I held up my hand, stopping them.

"I have never lied to you." I exhaled, though there were a lot of truths I kept from him. "I know this is hard to hear. I fought it, too, not wanting to believe. It broke me in half, thinking the man who helped raise me the last five years could do this. But when I came back, I wasn't the same. I had been through too much, saw too much to believe what was instilled in us since childhood. Istvan also sensed it. He was planning to have me killed and then blame it on the fae."

"What?" Caden's brow wrinkled. "Why?"

"For you."

"For me?" He dropped his tied hands into his lap. "How is having you murdered for me? I barely held it together when I thought I lost you the first time. I wouldn't have handled it a second. That would have made me go off the deep end…" He tapered off as if my point was coming to him.

"Exactly." A closed, sad smile inched up my cheeks. "What better way to have you completely join the fight against the fae if you thought they were the ones who killed me. Your need would be for retaliation, to do anything necessary to avenge me."

Caden sat stiffly, his shoulders high, trying to block my theory, but his eyes tracked back and forth as if he was recalling memories of times with his father.

"He kept you mainly in the dark on this project, only telling you enough to ease you into the idea slowly. He found the formula to raise humans to fae level. He thought once I was dead, he would bring you in completely, telling you it was necessary."

Caden's lids narrowed. "How do you know this? You wouldn't know—"

"Unless I was hiding in his office like we did when we were kids." I tried to smile, but it fell flat. "I overheard him and Kalaraja, who, known or not by your father, is fae."

Caden started to shake his head.

"He's a chameleon."

"A chameleon?" Half the table responded in shock. "Seriously?"

I nodded to them, returning to Caden to explain. "Chameleons can adapt and blend into any situation, making Kalaraja an excellent hunter. The night I overheard them was the same night I found proof of what your father was doing. I found out Andris and my father had searched for Dr. Rapava's formula for Istvan for years. Sometime after my father died and Andris went into hiding, your father found it. He has already begun to manufacture the substance, sending it to other countries like Prague." I licked my lip. "The pills I stole the night we were on the train, before I was gunned down and taken to Halálház, were them.

"I've seen what they can do, what Istvan is hoping to do, not only to equal the fae, but to surpass them, rule over everyone, no matter the costs. That night I overheard him, I took one of those documents."

Caden's head tipped back. "The night of my engagement party."

My head lowered in agreement. "I had no choice but to leave you. I already knew his plan and how he'd make my death a martyrdom."

"He made it sound you were mentally unstable," Caden replied lowly. "That catching you was for your own good."

"Do I seem mentally unstable to you?" I arched an eyebrow.

175

Kek laughed-coughed into her hand.

"You shut up." I pointed at her.

"You were crazy from the day I met you, little lamb." She winked at me. "But my kind of crazy."

"Not sure you're helping me." I tucked hair behind my ear.

She laughed while I watched Caden's expression start to lock down. I knew that look. When he didn't want to face something, he shut off. He would double down and fight against whatever shifted his world or understanding.

"Caden…"

"No. You are wrong. Father doesn't even care about the formula anymore. He's after the nectar stuff."

I swallowed hard, my eyes catching Kek and Lukas. Scorpion knew the truth as well, but his eyes still didn't meet mine.

"Nectar?" Wesley snorted. "Your daddy is going after that? The substance that is supposed to give humans fae-like powers and life, like fae food used to?" He laughed. "That shit is *a myth*!"

"Really?" Caden snarled back. "Because they found leads to it in China."

"And I found the Stone of Fail hidden in my underwear drawer." Wesley chuckled mockingly. "You humans are so fuckin' gullible. Wanting so bad to be like us, you believe in these fables."

"We don't want to be like you," Caden spat.

"Then why else are you running after a fucking fairytale to give you powers like ours?"

The two debated back and forth, and I felt the words come out before my brain understood what I was saying. "Caden's right." I swallowed. "The nectar is real."

Wesley guffawed, his eyes rolling. "You believe in that shit, too? It was a story to make humans believe they had a chance against us."

"It's not," I countered. "I know for a fact it is real."

"I doubt—"

"She's telling the truth," Scorpion finally spoke, cutting Wesley off.

"What?" Wesley and Birdie both gaped, jarred by Scorpion's claim. He was not one to buy into that crap unless he knew it was accurate.

Scorpion's gaze quickly shot to me; the decision on what to share and how much was up to me.

"I have it." *I am it.* Folding my arms, leaving the last bit out.

"*WHAT?*" Another chorus rang out, even Kek and Lukas joining in, not knowing I had gone back and retrieved it this time.

"I'm not going to get into all the hows, just that I do. It's boxed up and safe right now." *And useless.* I faced Caden. "And I will do everything in my power to keep it away from your father. I've seen what he can do. The lives he's already taken and destroyed, fae and *human.* I don't want to imagine what he'd do with the nectar." Istvan was too warped with greed and selfishness to use it for anything but to destroy and conquer.

Caden sat still. I watched his demeanor darken, his head start to shake. He was burrowing in. Stubbornly resisting all the information dumped on him. Because if it was true, it would tip his entire world over. Throughout our childhood and teen years, I could get him to do a lot he declared he didn't want to do. But he had a line when he wouldn't budge. Like the night up on the roof. He could have kissed me, could have chosen me, and our entire future would have been different if he had.

Looking back now, I'm glad he didn't. I would still be a soldier in HDF, fighting against the family I have come to love.

That path wasn't meant for me.

Caden wasn't meant for me.

"No." He continued to wag his head. "My father can be a bastard, but he's not capable of *this.* And my father certainly wouldn't sacrifice humans. He's spent the last twenty years protecting us from the fae, keeping us from becoming complete slaves to them."

"There will always be sacrifices in war, but their deaths are for the greater good." I quoted a sentiment Istvan had drilled into us over and over, knocking against the claim his father couldn't kill humans.

Caden's head jerked up, and I knew I made a mistake. His brown eyes lowered, anger sinking into his bones. He stood up, his tall frame inching over mine. "I almost believed you. Trying to turn me against my own father… my own people. You are a disgrace," he snarled, his body lurching for me. Birdie snatched the hood of his sweatshirt, yanking him back. "You are a betraying fae-lover!" he bellowed with fierce anger.

"Okay, field trip is over." Birdie dragged him across the room and out the entrance.

Hanna shot up, glaring at me, speaking to Scorpion. "I'd like to go back now, too. I don't want to look at her fucking face anymore."

Scorpion breathed out with annoyance.

Hanna wiggled her cuffed arms. "The inmate would like to return to her prison now."

Scorpion rose, his eye twitching as Hanna headed for the door. He took a swig of his drink, then followed her out, the hostage leading the captor.

I knew this wasn't going to be easy for either one of them to hear. You can't be taught something your whole life, then be okay when you find it was all wrong. It was going to take some time for them to adjust. Especially Caden.

And time was the one thing we didn't have.

Reaching under Ash's bed, I pulled the bag out, the heavy fae book dragging over the surface, poking out from the top.

Sitting back on my heels, I stared down at the leather cover, convincing myself I sensed the dullest of hums coming from it. My body was so cranked up from the scene in the café, my arms and head quivered with energy. Maybe I imagined it, making something there that wasn't. Though I couldn't stop myself, my fingers stretching, only inches from touching the cover.

Click.

The sound of the door shutting behind me had me jerking around with a yelp. My gaze took in Scorpion standing a foot inside the doorway, his emotionless eyes on me.

"*Bazdmeg!*" My hand hit my chest. "You scared me."

He stared silently. The weight of it crashed down on me. No longer could I skirt away from my actions.

"Scorpion, I'm sorry." Rising, I brushed my palms against my pants. "I know you are mad. You have every right to be."

He didn't respond.

"I went against your order and put everyone at risk."

"At risk?" he uttered, his chest starting to move up and down. "Risk was just being there, knowing at any time, things could go bad without doing anything. What you did—" He took another breath. "Maddox and Wesley were both shot and almost captured. They escaped only because of Birdie and Lukas."

"Shot?" Guilt tightened my airways. Of course, they wouldn't show it now, their fae magic healing them fast, but that didn't take away from what might have transpired.

"We knew the peril going in, what might happen, which is why everyone needs to follow the plan to the T." He traveled to me. To anyone else, he would be terrifying. He wasn't as big or intense as Warwick, but even scaling back half, Scorpion was still dangerous and frightening.

"I know." I wadded up my hands. "It was dumb and reckless, but I had to take the chance."

His hands grabbed my shoulders, ramming me back into the wall.

"You were gambling with all of our lives, Brexley. On a chance," he barked. "On *your* life! Do you know what I felt when I couldn't contact you? Couldn't find you? I thought you were *dead*. I scoured this city, ready to kill whoever took you, and I..." he gulped, emotion washing over his features, and I could see the terror, sense his grief, before he zipped it all back again, stepping away. He peered to the side. "If you put any of our lives in jeopardy like that again, on a chance, I will kill you myself," he grunted. "This place is my family. It's all I have." He flung open the door, stomping out and slamming it behind him.

Air exploded from my lungs, rushing in a steady stream. I sagged against the wall. His words were harsh and uncomfortably accurate. Though it wasn't what he said so much as what I saw in his eyes.

I was part of his family.

"With or without the magic, every man here is willing to fight for you, stand next to you, die for you. And it's not that bitch's power that makes us bend the knee. It's all you."

Leaning over, I swiped up the bag, looping my arms through the straps.

Chirp!

"What the hell?" I jerked my head to see Bitzy crawling onto my shoulder from the pack. Her lids almost shut, a dreamy smile on her face, gooey grayish-brown pieces stuck to her lip.

"Bitzy, no! Come back here!" Opie's voice came from the bag.

"Oh, shit." I pressed my palm into my eyes.

"Hey, Fishy!" Opie popped up with a wave, trying to pull Bitzy back. "Look away. Nothing to see here."

Chirp! Bitzy wiggled away, her three prong fingers stroking my face with awe.

"Opie..." I groaned. "You didn't."

"Didn't what?"

"Eat Ash's mushroom stash, *again*."

"I didn't." He batted his lashes innocently, making my gaze catch on them and his outfit.

"Oh. My. Gods." My mouth dropped open. "Then please tell me you did not make that dress from the book?"

Opie peered down. The thin curled strips of paper he attached to his lashes fluttered against his cheeks. He brushed at the tiered ruffled skirt made from parchment paper. His top was a one-shoulder crop top designed from another sheet. A single page fanned out on his head, aligning with his mohawk.

"I did not make this dress out of the book." He looked up; his forced smile was all teeth.

"Are you lying to me?"

"Y-yes."

"Opie!"

"Not my fault! Bitzy was passed out, and I got bored."

Chirrrrrpppp! She waved her hands in the air.

"Yes, I agree it's all your fault."

Chirp! Bitzy batted at invisible objects and then made a giggling sound.

So creepy and cute at the same time.

"For your sake, that better be a very boring moment in history." I closed my eyes, taking a breath. "Why are you guys even here?"

"Last time we lost you, Godzilla Pants threatened to turn us into a brownie tartar with imp sauce." Opie put his hands on his hips. "Which scared the broomsticks out of me, though slightly turned on, but *mostly* scared me."

Chirpppp!

"No, I doubt he'd put mushrooms in with your sauce." Opie's paper lashes fluttered. "So, where you go, we go, Fishy!"

A sigh came up my throat, my head shaking. "You know Ash is going to kill you."

Chirp! Chirp!

"Bitzy!" Opie gasped. "You'll waste the mushrooms if you put them up there! Get lost in the dark cave."

Chirp! She wiggled her fingers, a strange smile on her face.

"Right! Not like they haven't been there before."

Damn! That had to come with images. I groaned as Bitzy hopped around, trying to catch things that weren't there. "Get her inside before she falls."

"Sure thing, Master Fishy." Opie grabbed Bitzy, taking her back into the bag.

"And no more mushrooms or using the book for outfits. I mean it this time."

Muttering was heard from the bag, and it didn't sound flattering.

Exiting the room, I noticed down the hall my uncle, Killian, Kek, and Lukas were in the main area talking with somber expressions.

"Hey." I strolled up cautiously, all of them turning to me. "What's going on?"

"Lord Killian and I feel our numbers can't compete with HDF now." Andris exhaled heavily. He had so much strain on his shoulders—the lives in his hands, those he already lost, and our situation continued to get more dire. "He feels he can't trust most of his fae soldiers after the coup, and we've been seriously weakened here." Andris turned to Kek and Lukas, understanding dawning on me.

"You want Povstat's help," I finished for him. "You want to align with Uncle Mykel."

Kek and Luk were his soldiers. They would be the best to go back to him with information and the offer. They knew firsthand how fast the city was falling here.

"We probably should have done this earlier," Lukas spoke. "Captain needs to be aware and up to date on what is happening here. And we have no idea what is happening in Prague."

"I can send soldiers with you, though we haven't many to spare," Andris said.

"No." Luk shook his head. "Be easier for just the two of us to get in and out." He peered at Kek, a strange vibe going between them. "Plus, I got a demon with me; who'd mess with me?"

"Damn right, pretty boy."

Andris grasped his hands together. "I'm afraid we don't have much time."

"We'll leave immediately, sir." Lukas bowed, in his soldier mode.

"Thank you." Andris patted him on the back. "Borrow whatever weapons you need. Have Zuz show you where our motorbikes are. You will need them more than us. And please be safe." He didn't say it, but I could hear the warning in his tone. Our world was on the brink right now, and at any time, it could come crashing down.

Luk and Kek moved for the exit. I reached out, halting them. My heartbeat stuttered at the notion of anything happening to them. My mouth opened with the same sentiment, my throat closing up.

Luk saw everything I was feeling. "We'll be fine." He hugged me. "You be safe too."

"You guys come back, okay?" I blinked away my emotions.

"Don't worry, little lamb, no getting rid of us now." She squeezed my hand before the two disappeared.

"Ms. Kovacs?" Killian's voice turned me around. "You ready?"

I nodded in compliance, strolling up to Andris.

"I hate that you are leaving again." Andris wrapped his arms around me, whispering in my ear. "Be safe, *dragam*. I love you so much."

"You too, *Nagybácsi*."

He kissed my head before stepping back. "Keep her safe."

"I will." Killian bowed his head. "We will speak again soon, I am sure."

Andris crossed his arms behind his back, dipped his head, and then retreated back to his office.

"Got everything you needed?" I advanced to Killian.

"You mean aligning with not one but possibly two rebel militias I considered an enemy only about a month ago because someone in my own house is starting a coup?" Killian scoffed. "Sure, it's all going splendidly."

I smiled up at him, our eyes connecting. His mouth stretched into a grin.

"Ko-vacs."

The sound of my name jerked my gaze behind me, the call so muddled and low, I peered around, second-guessing the noise. A jet of wind from the top of the stairs gushed down, chilling my skin, the howl filling my ears with the same pitch as my name.

"You okay?" Killian asked.

"Yeah." I shook my head, hitching the bag higher on my shoulders. "Let's get back."

Killian and I headed out, slipping through the now darkening sky.

I couldn't get rid of the eerie feeling crawling over me, like the clock had just run out.

Chapter 19

The sky was painted with rich, dark blues and blacks, the stars glowing above our heads like diamonds. It was cold, but not a gust of wind blew. Everything was still, as if the city was holding its breath.

The distressing sensation flourished in my stomach like weeds, wrapping and killing off the joy I felt at seeing my family. Hope was suffocated by my growing fear.

"Killian?" I whispered his name in the dark, knowing he could hear and feel the anxiety in my voice.

He turned to me, his eyes meeting mine. The slightest movement of his chin was enough for me to recognize he felt the same, his gaze darting around with wariness. Humans could feel magic, the air thicker with electricity, but this was different. It dug into my gut, itching from the inside out. Calling and repelling. Familiar but strange.

The uneasiness skated over my nerves, bending them into kinks. "What is it?" I asked.

His teeth were set, his senses alert. "I don't know." His brow wrinkled with annoyance. "And there's not much I don't know." His hand reached for me, hastening me along. "Let's hurry."

When the Lord of the Fae tells you to hurry because something is unsettling him, you fuckin' hurry.

We got back to Carnal Row quickly. I had no idea what day it was, but there was never a time it was not flooded with people and debauchery.

But tonight, it was almost a ghost town. There were only a handful of people in the clubs or loitering in the streets. It was as if everyone experienced the same uneasiness, instinctively seeking safety.

My stomach rolled with fear. An omen hung over the still night sky as Killian and I ran up the steps of Kitty's.

Many of Kitty's girls and guys were milling around the main room, restless and muttering loudly among themselves, everyone feeling the strange energy descending on the city.

"Luv." Rosie broke away from the crowd, coming up to me, her hand taking mine. "Glad you are back."

"Have you seen Warwick?" I asked, peering around, seeing Kitty in the background.

"No." Rosie shook her head. "I haven't seen him."

My nerves bundled tighter.

"Do you know what's going on?" She peered around, her eyes landing on Killian before turning away. "All the fae workers are freaking out, and even I feel something is off." She shivered.

"No." I pressed her hand in mine before letting go. "But I think everyone should stay inside tonight and lay low."

"Sweetheart, lying low is what I do every night." She winked, trying to be playful, but we were all too on edge for jokes.

Killian huffed through his nose, irritation adjusting his stance behind me.

"Is it a problem for you, *Lord*?" Her voice was sweet, but thick with contempt. "Too unbecoming for a human whore to say? Did I not flounce or overact it enough?"

He glared at her. She glared back.

"If you see Warwick, let him know we're up in the room." I grabbed Killian's jacket, leading him toward the stairs, wanting to part them before it got uglier.

"I will," Rosie responded.

Once on the top floor, we entered the room. Sloane was pacing back and forth.

"*Az istenit!*" Sloane pitched for us, his gaze moving over Killian, assessing his boss was all in one piece. I couldn't imagine it easy for Sloane to let Killian go without him. His duty was to protect him at all costs. He already lost two of his comrades under his watch. "About time! I was about two seconds away from hunting you down." He bristled.

"We're fine," Killian assured him, his eyes darting to the box still on the bar. Exactly where we left it. Safe.

"Something's going on. There is an odd energy." Sloane's hand ran over his weapon on his hip.

"I know," Killian replied quietly as I strolled over to the bar, my pulse tapping in my ears, my fingers grazing over the top of the box.

When I was a child, my father gave me one thing of my mother's. A tiny jewelry box with a ring inside she had worn. Young and careless, I lost the ring. I had been devastated. I wished for it back over and over and never stopped going to the box, hoping when I opened it this time, it would magically be inside again.

The nectar's power was like the ring. Even if your brain told you it wouldn't be there, and you felt the stab through the thin layer of belief you held, you had that moment of suspended hope.

I lifted the top, the solidified honey substance laying in the middle. Staring at it, my head tilted, blinking to clear my vision. Was it slightly brighter? My mind was probably trying to see something there wasn't. A trick of the light. My own desperate hope coloring my eyesight.

Something prickled at my skin right before the door swung open. Killian, Sloane, and I reeled as Warwick and Ash barreled in.

Warwick's eyes found mine, assessing and running over me.

"We need to run."

His words made me falter.

The wolf, the legend, looked at me with alarm. He had never run from anything in his life, diving headfirst into death and carnage. His weighted stare told me running was the only option... to protect me.

"What?" I dropped the lid of the box, rushing to him and Ash. "What's going on?"

"How many men does HDF have?" Warwick's almost demanding tone jumbled my anxiety even more. "Trained soldiers?"

"Oh, umm... several hundred, maybe. Over three hundred, including the men behind a desk who have been trained as well. But counting classes not yet graduated, probably four to five hundred, max. Why?"

Ash and Warwick shared a look.

"What the fuck is going on, Farkas?" Killian came up next to me.

"There are over a thousand soldiers out there," Ash spoke for Warwick, jerking our heads.

"Over a thousand?" I bellowed. "There's no way. We barely have over a thousand people in Léopold, which counts everyone, including kids."

"Well, they're there, and..." Ash tapered off.

"What?" Killian grumbled.

"Something's off."

"Yeah, we know, there's a thousand soldiers coming for us." I flayed my arms.

"No." Ash shook his head, his bright green eyes zeroing in on me deliberately. "There is something wrong with *them*."

Inhaling so sharply it hurt, panic started to ripple off me. "What do you mean?"

"I can't describe it. Aggressive, but very robotic. Controlled monsters."

I whirled to Killian, our minds going to the same place. "Have you—"

"No!" He shook his head. "I stopped all experiments not long after you left. It became pointless. None survived, except you. In a rage, I destroyed all of it."

"Right," Warwick growled, getting into Killian's face. "I haven't had time to thank you for drugging and almost killing my mate." He shoved at Killian.

My body stilled.

I blinked at the same time Ash echoed my thoughts.

"Whoa, hold on. Did you say *mate*?" His mouth opened in shock, but a gleeful smirk lit up his eyes. "Just want to confirm I heard you right."

"Yeah." I nodded. "Me too."

Warwick rolled his head toward us, giving us an annoyed look.

"Right. Not the time." I waved my hand. "But we are revisiting it."

"We get through this, princess," Warwick rumbled, his eyes heavy on me. "We can revisit it as many times as you want." His sexual implication was clear.

Killian elbowed Warwick, straightening his shirt. "This has nothing to do with me. Plus, all those I tested could never be trusted out of a cage. They were unpredictable. More feral animal than soldier."

I thought of the woman trying to attack me through the cage, her teeth bared, her eyes wild and empty at the same time. I was pretty sure she would have broken every bone and crushed her own head to slip through the bars to kill me. Much more a wild animal than you'd see dressed in a uniform, holding a gun.

"Dr. Karl said they had improved the formula." I centered on Ash, the only one who saw what I had.

"What scares me is it didn't sound like they weren't stopping there. They were hinting at something even grander."

Like pumping fae essence straight into humans.

Istvan was a scrupulous man. He would have strategies in place until his main plan, the nectar, came to fruition. He became the leader of HDF for a reason, and even if they were humans, my father, Andris, and Istvan had won many battles because of their meticulous tactics.

"We can't stay here." Warwick moved to the bar, grabbing the box and stuffing it into the pack already on my back, next to the fae book.

"Actually, it sounds safer to stay here if they are flooding the streets." Killian motioned to the outside.

"They are breaking down every door searching for us." Warwick bristled. "I will not put these people in danger. Not to protect us."

"Yeah," I agreed. "Kitty has too much to lose and has already risked a lot for us. I will not be the reason these people are hurt."

"And it only takes one to let it slip that we're here," Ash piped in, his gaze sliding to Warwick. "One who might be a little pissed and vengeful."

I tilted my head at Warwick. He grumbled under his breath.

"What am I missing?" I asked.

"Seems a certain siren was a wee bit peeved he turned her down, *several times*, and kicked her out of his room." Ash winked at me.

I won't lie. The elation I felt hearing that made me want to rip off his clothes right here and show him.

"Can we fuckin' focus?" Warwick barked. "We need to get out of here. Slip south through the city. After that…"

"We can hide out in my safe house," Killian declared. "It's protected and spelled. We will be safe there."

"Where Eliza and Simon are?" Warwick asked.

"Yes," Killian answered. "In the Gerecse Mountains. You will need me to get past the barriers and find it."

Warwick flicked his chin. "Guess you live another day, fairy."

Killian snorted.

"We need to find some kind of vehicle since you blew up mine," Killian added.

"So fucking worth it," Warwick smirked, tipping his head to the door. "Let's head out. I know a guy in Őrmező who can get us a few pre-war Harleys. They're shit but will get us there." Warwick glanced over Killian. "Though he'll take one look at you and charge us double. Hope you brought your pocketbook, *Lord*." Warwick's palm pressed into the small of my back right below the pack, leading me to the door. I swear the simple touch ignited my body with warmth, with the feeling of being safe, even if I wasn't.

The hammering of our feet descending the stairs sounded like the execution drum roll, signaling the convict's last moments before death.

"Warwick." Kitty stopped him right as we reached the bottom. For the first time ever, I saw worry and fear in her eyes. "Don't."

"We have to." He took her hand in his. "It's my turn to protect you. And that means leaving here."

Kitty's gaze darted from him to Ash. I kept seeing her try to speak, wanting to beg them to stay, but she knew this was for the best. To protect her family, we had to go.

"You better stay alive, asshole. I can't take you dying on me again." She gritted her teeth, peering at Ash. "Both of you."

Ash nodded his head as Warwick gripped her hand with a final squeeze before letting go. I gave her a bow of my head as well before we headed for the door.

The sound of glass shattering splintered through the room, jolting us to the side window. An object thumped to the floor near the sofa where most of the workers were rolling across the rug.

There was a moment we all took it in, comprehending what it was.

A bomb.

"Fuck." Warwick uttered under his breath before belting out. "Run!" Shoving me toward the door, he motioned for everyone to get out.

Screams of terror pierced the air as people scrambled for the exit, clawing and shoving to escape.

It was like I could feel the explosive tick against my vertebrae, nipping at the back of my neck like a taunt with no idea where we were in the countdown to its detonation.

"Go! Go!" Warwick rushed me out, only making it a few yards.

Boooooom!

The force and heat of the explosion slammed into us, flinging us in the air like dolls, the fumes burning my skin. My bones crunched, striking the uneven cobbles, the backpack softening the blow a bit before my head slammed into brick.

I don't know if I blacked out or not, but when my lashes fluttered open, the world felt like it was on fire. Most of Kitty's was destroyed. The outer brick structure was still there, but everything inside was blown out, gutted, and burning. My ears rang; the only sound I heard was muted screams and the crackle of flames. The smell of burning flesh and toxic flames scorched my nose.

Trying to push myself up, my muscles wobbled, feeling weak. "Warwick?" I tried to call out, but my voice crumbled and cracked. Terror wrapped around my lungs like a boa constrictor, my head feeling dizzy.

"War-wick!" I cried out again, but all it did was echo in my ears, not making much past my lips. Tears filled my burning eyes, half from the fumes and half from fear. Gritting my teeth, I tried to get myself to sit fully up.

"Kovacs!" I swear I felt his call more than heard him, but suddenly

he was in my face, bloody and wounded badly, his torn hands cupping my cheeks. A cry broke from my mouth, my arms grappling for him, wrapping around him with a relief I couldn't even explain. His mouth took mine in a vicious kiss, almost painful. His fingers dug into my skin, and he punished my mouth as I clawed to get closer. It was a desperate need to touch him. Pain meant you were still alive. You could still feel. This was a necessity. The hardcore truth was that if he were alive, I could survive *anything* else.

He broke away, his hand sliding down my hair, his eyes reconfirming I was in one piece.

"Ash? Killian?" I spoke, my voice a little steadier, the ringing in my head a little lower.

"Don't know." His voice was even more harsh and gravelly.

His hand firmly taking mine, he helped me up to my feet, scouring the scene. Bodies were scattered everywhere, bloody and torn into bits. And I knew even more were inside who never made it out.

Here and there, I could see heads and arms moving, a few sitting up, though very few.

My breath caught when I spotted Killian. Half his face blackened and burned, his clothes torn, but he was moving. Standing up, I noticed someone underneath him, protected from the worst of the blast.

"Rosie!" I bellowed, running over to them. Sloane was a few feet away.

Falling before them, I checked them over. Rosie was bloody and deeply scraped up, but nothing dire. She blinked, her eyes dazed, her fingers touching the blood dripping from her head.

"Are you guys okay?"

"I-I think so?" she muttered.

"I'll heal," Killian replied, making me exhale with a small sense of relief.

"Warwick!" Ash's voice brought me back up to my feet as I watched my blond best friend limping over to us, Kitty next to him. Both looked really bad, but fae could heal from this. Most humans would not.

Another wave of relief hit my chest as I dove for Ash, hugging him hard, blinking back the tears. I knew many died tonight, but selfishly, my group was alive. The people I cared about were all standing.

"We have to go," Warwick ordered, his head up and darting around.

"I can't leave. This is my home. My family!" Kitty's emotions were everywhere, her face streaked with burns, cuts, and blood. "Most are dead!"

"Exactly." Warwick huffed. "You can't help them now."

"I'm not leaving them," Kitty bellowed, about to turn away.

"Az istenit!" Warwick grabbed her arm. "You think you'll help them if you are dead too? This was on purpose, Kit! Your place wasn't bombed by accident. This is war."

"Fuck you." She shoved at his chest. "I want nothing to do with your war. I got out of that life."

"That's not how it works." He gritted his teeth. "You can close your eyes and pretend, but it doesn't change the fact you are part of this." He waved his hand at the destruction. "They know who you are."

"The only reason they know who I am is because of you," she screamed, shaking her finger at him. Then her head dropped, her voice quivering. "I don't want that life again. This is my home."

"I know." Remorse hinted in Warwick's voice, but his expression stayed stoic. "But they will kill you. Anyone who survived. They will be in here soon to finish the job. We have to go."

Kitty's chin dropped to her chest, her beautiful slacks and silk top in shreds, blood staining them. She exhaled, lifting her head with resolution.

"You good enough to walk?" Killian asked Rosie, his hand reaching down for hers

"Yes." She ignored his hand, rising on her own, but wobbled on her feet.

"Whoa." Killian grabbed her hips, holding her up.

"I'm fine." She brushed him away, moving toward me. My scrutiny silently asking if she really was. She responded with a slight nod, though her mouth was pinned with pain.

Warwick took the lead, the seven of us stealing away from Kitty's House. All I heard was the snaps and pops of the flames steadily devouring the infamous building and many of the lives within.

Chapter 20

The still night echoed our footsteps like a drum, no matter how quiet we were trying to be. All of us were wounded, some badly and just trying to keep breathing, to file away the people we left behind. Shock, grief, and fear tied off the wound like a tourniquet, keeping us from bleeding out from the agony.

Warwick's tense physique moved us through the shadows and alleys, acting as the first line of defense. Ash and I were close behind him while Sloane was at the rear. Kitty, Killian, and Rosie were in the middle.

Nearing the Madách Tér, Warwick stopped us behind a stone pillar under the huge structural arch. Hotels, cafes, and shops used to fill this square with life. It was hard for me to imagine. As a young girl, I hadn't even known what a hotel was until my father explained it to me after one of his journeys across the land. Now they called them lodging houses. I had no understanding of life outside the walls of Léopold.

The strange eeriness of the night pounded my pulse against my throat.

"It's not going to be easy to get us to Örmező," Ash whispered to Warwick, glancing back at our injured group.

"No, but do we have another option?" The legend grumbled.

"Go back to mine, have a hot shower, drink by the fire, and have sex with a couple of river fairies?" Ash shrugged, making Warwick scoff with a low chuckle.

"Or maybe a snake shifter?" Ash added.

"And here I thought you were getting a taste for demon sex." I nudged Ash. His body stilled, his cheeks flushing. "And blond half-breeds." I winked.

"What?" Warwick's brow rose in a high arch. "Don't fucking tell me…"

"It was a stressful night… and morning. Energy needed to be worked out." Ash's voice went defensive. Too defensive. "And maybe more than once."

Warwick huffed, his head shaking in amusement, his attention going fully back to the area. "Okay, looks clear, let's go."

We stepped out, starting to cross the square when a chill stroked over my soul, causing every hair to rise on my body. It was so soft I could almost ignore it, death's kiss brushing the back of my neck. It was familiar—the line between life and death. But what I sensed didn't belong to either, as if nature was clashing against it, refusing. Everything in me screamed, feeling wrong.

"Wait—" My mouth opened, my hand reaching for Warwick.

Hundreds of red laser beams vaulted around the darkness until they zeroed in on us. The air filled with the reverberation of boots hitting the pavement and the swish of fabric. Figures rushed from all sides, jolting me with terror. Quiet and meticulous, hundreds of soldiers filed out of the alleys and the street like ants in an unnatural collective harmony.

Holy shit.

My head darted around, the nightmare coming from all different angles, herding our group. With our backs together, we kept our weapons in hand, ready to fight. Rosie was shoved into the middle of us, keeping her walled in and protected. In my gut, I knew it was all for naught. None of us could guard against this many, no matter how powerful the fae within our group were.

There were too many with tactical lasers trained on us.

Intuition told me none of these soldiers were ordinary humans. Not with the way they moved, looking the way they did. Dressed in black fatigues and beanies, they stared at us with bloodthirsty eyes, their guns clicking off the safety.

Ash was right. They were robotic in their movements, precise and empty, but their eyes were feral, as if at any moment, they could flip.

It was unnatural and terrifying.

"This was much easier than I thought it would be." The voice cleaved through me like a hacksaw, gorging out huge chunks of my hope. Every muscle locked up, my mind fighting the urge to either throw up or stand at attention.

Air cut through my nose as my head turned to the silhouette strolling assertively through a gap between soldiers. Not one lifted an eye to their leader, their focus centered solely on us. Abnormally so. I recognized none of them, and I pretty much knew, by face at least, every soldier in HDF.

"Ah, Brexley." The man clicked his tongue. "What a disappointment you turned out to be." Cool blue eyes met mine, the man coming to stand right in front of his army.

"Istvan." His name barely made it out. The insecurity I had always felt in this man's presence quaked through me. An imprint. He looked the same, but I saw the cruelty in his eyes, a confidence that almost elevated him above all others.

Warwick lifted his gun with a growl.

"I wouldn't do that." Istvan clasped his hands behind his back, smirking.

"I can shoot you before anyone of your men can even touch their trigger," Warwick stated.

"You think so?" Istvan barely dipped his chin before a bullet cracked across the square straight into Warwick's shoulder with sharp precision.

Fast.

Fae-fast.

A cry barely made it to my lips, watching Warwick's body jolt from the force, his weapon falling from his hand. The bullet hit the exact nerve, cutting clean through. Warwick's hand went to the wound, coming back bloody, his expression creasing with a snarl. Even without our special link, he was still half-fae. He'd heal from this. But not if the shot was fatal. I understood in this moment—together, we had possessed the power to heal each other from fatal wounds.

We no longer could now.

Glowering at Istvan, I saw him smirk.

"Haven't taught your fae-lover to be obedient yet?" Istvan tsked me. "All the years I spent trying to mold and guide you into a leader." Genuine emotion flashed in his eyes. "You could have been on the right side, Brexley. The Queen of Romania, leading the people. Instead, you chose this." He waved his hand at my group. "Whores, thieves, and half-breeds."

I noted he did not seem to know the Lord of the Fae was behind me, hiding his face under the wounds and hood. I wanted to keep it that way.

"I'd pick them over that life any day." I shifted closer to Warwick, making clear where I stood. "And are you any different? You put on fancy clothes, but there is more corruption, thieves, and whores in Léopold. At least here, they're honest about who they are. You hide away in your gold-plated palace, pretending you are protecting and fighting for humans when they're nothing but political chess pieces to you."

"This is all for them." He gestured about. "I'm in it for the long game. You can't seem to see that. The fight gets messy, there are casualties, but in the end, *I* will become the legend." He glanced at Warwick, telling me he knew exactly who he was. "Because they will see I brought them freedom. Peace. Safety. Humans will rule again, and fae will go back into hiding. Our world is upside down, being ruled by a demon and a druid. I am here to restore the natural order to the world."

He sounded like a mad person, though I realized Istvan didn't want to just be the king of the eastern bloc. He wanted to take back the entire world from the fae.

He was the pebble that started the avalanche.

"Natural order? Freedom?" I choked, my gaze landing on all the wild-eyed people around me. Various ages, men and women, and not one even twitched. "Do they have freedom?" Disgust and anger gripped my hands. These soldiers weren't right. Slightly less feral than the ones I saw at Killian's, but something still made my skin crawl. It seemed they had improved the formula, but they were still unpredictable killing machines. "Is this what you call freedom? Did they take those pills *willingly*, Istvan?"

"You are so naïve and foolish." Though Istvan's eyes glowed almost with pride. I put all the pieces together. He valued intelligence along with cunning and shrewdness. He reasoned I had these things because of what he taught me, and maybe he was right. But now, those lessons would be turned on him. "I thought I taught you better. To see the forest, not the trees." He dropped his hands to his sides, taking a step closer. Under his breath, Warwick snarled, but I kept my focus on the general. "People don't have any clue what they really want. They want to be controlled, even when they spout about liberties. But yes, most of them came willingly. *They* understand what is at stake. What we gain if we can match the fae."

"By stealing fae essence?" I countered. "By torturing children, killing them by ripping out their magic?"

"If I must," Istvan stated. "How long have fae been stealing, raping, and consuming us for our life essence?"

It was true. They had, but it didn't make what he was doing right, either.

As if he could read my expression, Istvan wagged his head. "Right and wrong only have value from which side you stand on. I'm merely balancing the playing field."

I couldn't deny Istvan had a point. Many fae fed off humans for their energy, through sex, sins, dreams, or actually eating them. They considered it fair game and survival, so was the other way wrong?

"I've seen your lab, your sick experiments," I forced out.

"Yes, I heard of your little visit." He strolled even closer. "You should have called; I would have given you a private tour."

I huffed contemptuously, my eyes blazing. "You aren't doing this for human freedoms or peace. You're doing it to build an army. To appease your ego, your need for power."

"Oh, you wound me." He mockingly pressed his palm into his chest. The dozens of medals and patches weighing down his coat seemed to only prove my point. "And Brexley, you saw a tiny bit of what I am working on. As soon as I locate the nectar, I will be the ruler of not only the east, but I will take the west as well."

Years of training kept my face blank as I stared back at him, giving no hint of my knowledge of the nectar. If he knew how close it actually was. Not only in my backpack, but standing right in front of him.

For the first time, I was glad it was empty. If this man got his hands on it, this world would be destroyed in a war that ended all others... and us.

Even him having it without its powers could start wars.

Istvan glanced over my shoulder. "Right on time."

I whipped around to see the guards stepping to the side to allow a small group to enter.

A scream built up in my chest. Devastation swallowing me whole.

Kalaraja.

But he wasn't alone.

The guy with him was beaten up so badly his entire face puffed out, so I hardly recognized him. He stumbled forward, his arms tied, while Kalaraja tossed a woman's body off his shoulder to the ground. Her face was also almost unrecognizable, but her blue hair fanned out on the concrete, painted red near her skull.

"Kek!" I lurched, but Warwick stopped me, pressing his good arm into me, keeping me back. A whimper came up my throat as I tried to see if she was breathing. I peered at Lukas. He was barely holding himself upright, his head bowed.

"They didn't even reach the city border," Kalaraja bragged. "Though the demon had to be put out. She was starting to think she could take me."

"I can always count on you. Good job." Istvan was pleased.

Kalaraja dipped his head, stepping behind his captures. Lukas swayed on his feet, trying to stay standing. I realized his head was down because he was staring at Kek. Her body was limp, and I couldn't tell if her chest was moving or not.

Grief and guilt bruised my heart. I should have kept them here, telling them it was too dangerous. The only reason they were here in the first place was because of me. They should have never come to Budapest. If Kek was dead, I would never forgive myself. I had already watched Tracker and Ava be murdered in cold blood because of me.

Movement beside me twisted my head to Ash. We had been through a lot together so far, but I had never seen this expression before. His green eyes burned bright, like how emeralds glow in the sun. His shoulders rose. The trees along the square started to sway and creak, even though there wasn't a breath of wind.

"Ash," Warwick called to his friend, but Ash didn't seem to hear, his eyes locked on Kek's body, then rising to Lukas's, anger building in him. "Ash, don't!"

Wood cracked in the distance with Ash's rage. A sound came from him I never heard, his body lunging toward Kalaraja, the two men colliding.

The stillness flipped as gunfire and yells resounded off the buildings. Warwick swiped up his weapon, shooting a few guards down who had their weapons trained on Ash while he unlatched his claw from his back, gutting a soldier close to him.

Before I could move, I felt something press into my temple.

Click.

Istvan pressed the barrel to my temple. "I suggest you stop." His voice rang out clear and sharp. The soldiers halted instantly.

Warwick whirled to Istvan, lids narrowing, his nose flaring.

"Do not think of even trying." Istvan pressed the metal harder into my head. How blind I was that he had been inching closer to me, ready to seize me at any opportunity. "I will not hesitate."

Fury rolled off Warwick, his eyes landing on mine. I shook my head, telling him to do as he said.

"Get on your knees," Istvan ordered to my group, pushing me down to mine. "All of you." He motioned to his men. "Strip them of all weapons and items."

A guard took my weapons, my stomach sinking when he tore off my backpack. Taking our weapons, they glanced through the bags for more, then tossed them into a pile. Mine would be nothing more than a book and a tiny box, nothing of consequence… they would assume.

The very thing Istvan would destroy the world for—kill everyone here for—was only inches from his feet. The power was inside one bag, and they tossed it into a pile like rubbish.

I watched sentries move on my friends, guns to their heads, relieving them of all weapons. Ash snarled, lowering himself to the ground near Kek, Lukas next to him. One by one, they all went down, Killian being the last, going against his very being. Bowing to the human leader.

"Take off his hood." Istvan ordered a soldier next to Killian. He was the only one whose face was still covered.

The trooper over him grabbed his hood, yanking it off.

I begged for Istvan not to recognize him, to not know who they had in this square. The potential Markos held in obtaining the fae leader was strong. But I knew not to hope. The man I grew up with was meticulous and smart. Aware of every player.

The second Istvan recognized the disheveled, wounded man for who he was, his frame jerked with shock. Then he righted himself with arrogance.

"Well, well…" Istvan took a moment, then slowly stepped away from me, knowing I could do nothing. Everyone I loved was being held at gunpoint. Fae bullets pointed at their brains. "Of all the people I imaged ensnaring in my net tonight." A cruel mocking tone came from Istvan, striding over to the kneeling lord. "I never thought the *supposed* dead fae ruler would be one of them."

Killian's jaw strained, his eyes burning with fury, taking every bit of his composure not to strike Markos.

Istvan stopped right in front of him, beaming with condescension and superiority. As if he had already won the battle for this city. "Though I'm shocked and impressed your ego was willing to play dead. I will admit, for a moment there, I was disappointed, thinking I had already solved you as a problem. However, this is a more beneficial outcome for what I have planned. I dare say my night has developed exceedingly better than I hoped."

Terror gripped me as Istvan's arrogance soared, my stomach dropping at the indication of what he had planned.

"Going into hiding suggested you are smart to sense the bomb was meant to kill you." Istvan's gray brows went up with implication. I could feel it coming; we had even discussed it, but to know our theory was accurate left me breathless. "Whoever wanted you dead was one of your own… or at least aided in your demise. How awful to know someone hated you more than the thought of a human leader in charge. That night I was supposed to pluck out both the thorns in my side." Without fully admitting it, Istvan had implicated himself in my uncle's bombing, as well as Killian's. Not something we didn't already know, but to hear him so arrogantly claim it chilled me. "No matter. They will both be dealt with tonight."

Both? What the hell did that mean?

Killian's face remained impassive, though I could see the fury inching his shoulders up and down with his controlled breathing. He was a tinder keg. One more word might make him explode.

"This is all about me, for stealing the formula, for betraying you. Your ego couldn't handle that I wasn't your trained monkey." I spouted bullshit, trying to steer Istvan's attention off Killian before he got killed.

Disappointment showed over Istvan's face. "You are much smarter than you are pretending to be." He turned slightly to me. "I had high hopes for you. If anything, you were handy in controlling my son. Though I don't have much use for you now." Istvan drew back up his gun, pointing it at me.

"No!" Warwick roared, dozens of soldiers holding him back. Tension pounded in my veins, the sound of my last breaths loud in my ears. My gaze met with Warwick's, and I shook my head, telling him not to fight. To live another day. Fight this battle. Markos had to be stopped.

"I have dreamed about this for a long time." Istvan ambled up to me, the gun pressing into the middle of my forehead. "I won't lie. It will hurt. I put a lot of time and effort into you, Brexley. I thought you'd turn out even more powerful than my own son."

I was. But that secret would die with me. And somehow, I knew if I died, whatever energy was left in the nectar, if any, would die with me.

Istvan took a step closer, his finger starting to press down on the trigger.

"Father!" A voice pierced the air, so familiar it was like I dreamed him up in my last moments. Saying goodbye to my old best friend.

Istvan turned as two outlines came through the throng, my entire body freezing up with shock and confusion.

"Son. Good to see you. I'm glad you are all right." Istvan nodded formally as Caden strolled up, shaking his hand like he would a lieutenant, not a son who had been kidnapped by an enemy.

"Hanna." Istvan said her name with no emotion, but I saw his mouth turn slightly down.

"Sir." She saluted him.

Caden's eyes slid to me, but I couldn't see anything in them. I used to see through him so easily; now he had the ability to shut me out, too.

How did they escape? How was he here? The terror of knowing the answers to my questions gurgled in my stomach like acid.

"Leave her alive," Caden replied, emotionless. "Killing her now would be too easy."

"You still have a weakness for her. To become a good leader, you must cut out those weaknesses."

"Don't worry, Father. I will make her pay. She will experience everything I went through."

Went through? He was eating biscuits and drinking tea earlier. If that was the bar he set, then sign me the hell up. Had he forgotten I had been in Halálház? The House of Death, where I had been flayed open, tortured, assaulted, broken, beaten, and had to kill to stay alive. Nothing he could do to me would compare with that.

Pride hinted on Istvan's face, his head dipping with approval, lowering his gun.

My lids shut briefly with the reprieve. The echoes of screams popped them back open. My eyes caught more soldiers marching up... with hostages.

My horror was confirmed. Hanna and Caden didn't escape. They walked out.

The base had been found.

"Noooo!" I screamed. Hands grabbed me, yanking me back, but all I could see was the man they marched through, covered in blood. The guard shoved him down to his knees with force. *"Nagybácsi!"*

His head jerked to me. Deep sorrow and grief filled his eyes. *"Dragam."* I didn't know if he said it out loud or not, but I still heard it, saw it in his gaze, felt his distress in my soul.

Every person thrown down next to him cut more wounds. Scorpion, Birdie, Maddox, Wesley, Ling, and Zuz. There were others, but those were the ones I really noticed. Every breath hurt like a razor blade slicing at my lungs.

"Andris Takacs," Istvan said his name evenly, but I knew the man; I could see rage locking up his body. "It's been a while. Though I guess I wasn't expecting a reunion, as you are supposed to be dead as well."

Andris kept his chin up, looking out, not reacting.

"And this whole time, you were raising your pathetic excuse for a rebel army. From a top-tier war general, fighting for humans, to this. A fae-lover and half-breed sympathizer." He spat on him. "You disgust me. You have no honor."

"Considering what you deem is honor, I take that as a compliment," Andris replied calmly.

"You and Benet once were magnificent. Could have been the greatest war captains in the world, but look at what has become of you. One of you is dead, and the other one is at my feet like a dog." Istvan growled, the sight of his old friend and lieutenant stroking more emotion from him than I had seen in years.

Even more than seeing his own son alive and well.

"Finding out you were still alive…" For a moment, something resembling hurt flickered over Istvan. "I knew even before we learned you had Caden and Hanna. My faithful hunter found out who you were when he discovered your first base. He followed her right to you." He glanced at Kalaraja and then gestured to me. "Your weakness for her was your downfall. She led us right to you *every time*."

The crushing guilt bowed my head low, not able to look my uncle in the face. How many deaths were because of me? All the pain and devastation? I knew Kalaraja was good at his job, but now I knew all those times I felt watched, or maybe even when I didn't… he was *always* there, blending in the background, following me. I was the reason Kitty's was blown up, why the Sarkis army had been attacked, why they were all here now.

All the fae power and training in this group couldn't fight back…

Because Istvan did what Dr. Rapava never could.

He created the super soldier.

Chapter 21

"You are wrong." My uncle's voice rang through the cold night air. "You know your major fault, Istvan?" Andris kept his voice even though he slurred from a swollen jaw and cheekbone. "What you think of as weaknesses are strengths. Love, friendship, and family. They are the *reason* to fight for all of this. The single true point of life. The rest is bullshit. You were always jealous of that."

Istvan's head dropped back, letting out a dark laugh. "Jealous of what? You?"

"Of what so many could feel, and you could not. You are incapable of love or empathy. For Rebeka, friends, even your own son. You are searching to fill the gap in your soul and coming up empty each time."

"Shut the fuck up," Markos sneered.

"You think power will satisfy you? You will finally feel fulfilled? That's not how it works. You will find yourself up on your pedestal all alone, dead bodies and those you tossed away strewn around you, lonely and pathetic."

"I. Said. Shut. Up!" Istvan marched up to Andris, shoving the barrel into his forehead, his finger about to pull the trigger.

A deep protective instinct lurched me forward, but Ling's cry halted me. Ramming her shoulder into Andris, she knocked him out of the way, wiggling herself in front of him.

"Ling, no!" Urgency pitched his voice, terror in his eyes as he tried to

201

move her out of the way, but she bared down, locking down her muscles, glaring up at Istvan. Her Kitsune powers sparked over her like a current. Istvan paused, his attention entirely on her.

"Ling, is it?" Istvan's eyebrow rose. "So you are the one. The fae concubine."

"She has nothing to do with this." Andris shuffled on his knees, trying to get in front of her, the coolness he had earlier peeling away. "Your fight is with *me*."

"Is it?" Istvan tilted his head, a malevolent grin tugging his mouth. "The fae mistress you tried to keep hidden from me. Even willing to fake your own death, leave your career and your wife for?" Istvan looked at her with disgust. "If you never met her, would you still be killing them? Slaughtering them by the hundreds like you used to? Would you still be my war general? Was she really worth leaving it all for? This soulless creature who kills your own kind? You are a traitor, an abhorrent *fae-lover*."

"She has more soul in a single strand of hair than you ever could understand. That was your problem, Istvan. You didn't want to see they were like us. You wanted them to be the things you claimed, so you felt justified in killing and going after what you wanted. You are a thousand times worse than any fae you say is vile. Benet and I saw what you were becoming. I would have gotten out eventually with or without her."

"Benet. Yes, another one who greatly disappointed me." Istvan lowered his gun.

It was a minuscule moment. Andris released a breath, his lids closing with relief, thinking he defused the situation enough. That moment was all it took for him to miss the warning. The subtle shift when everything changed.

Istvan's arm went back up in a blink.

Bang!

A scream tore from my stomach, cutting through my mouth. Acid burned the back of my throat as I watched Ling's body jolt, the bullet tearing through the spot between her eyes before her brain registered, and they glossed over. Blood spurted everywhere, painting Caden's face, who stood there, unmoving.

"NOOOOOOOOOOO!" Andris bellowed, lurching for her as her kneeling body crumbled to the ground. "No! Ling! Please!" He grabbed for her, pulling her to him, her blood and brain matter covering him as he screamed. The gut-wrenching sound pierced my spine and heart, filling me with grief and despair. I tried to get to him, but his men held me back, my muscles sagging in anguish as my uncle's wails impaled the night air with his deepest sorrow. "Please, baby, wake up... please don't leave me...

Ling, my love." He rocked her on his lap, blood and tears mixing together as he bowed over the love of his life, dead in his arms.

"If one of you makes a move, you will be next." Istvan threatened, waving around his pistol. "Or possibly the person you love the most."

My shoulders bowed, my brain still not completely taking in what just happened. Andris's pain was so guttural, I felt it slam into me.

Kovacs.

Again, it was more a sensation, a heavy gaze on me, calling me. I didn't contemplate anything more than following the instinct. My eyes lifted to Warwick. Without saying a word or touching me, I could feel his strength. *Use me.* Even without our link, he was giving me his strength, letting me absorb it from him so I could keep going.

Gritting my teeth, I held back my tears, looking at the woman who had saved me in Halálház, quiet and strong, a comrade when I had none. The woman who changed my uncle's life, gave him so much happiness and peace—the woman who survived the House of Death—was now dead.

The sobs within Sarkis' army, her friends, and family were heartbreaking, but watching my uncle shredded everything from me. He whispered to her, his wails like a wounded animal, while his eyes turned dead. Shutting down from the pure agony.

"Her death is your fault, Takacs, and your punishment for going against me." Istvan gritted, wiping some of the blood off his face with a handkerchief. "I always win in the end. Always."

My uncle didn't react, though his cries quieted. His expression went blank, his stare off somewhere else, something irreconcilable curling under his skin. "You will pay for this." His voice was cold and vengeful.

"Don't sound so cliché, old friend." Istvan tucked the bloody scarf back in his pocket. "And I won't. I have been planning far longer than you could even imagine. Every situation, every player. I wasn't expecting your identity, but the plan remained the same. And even when you bombed Halálház, I adapted, and now I see you did me a favor."

"How?" Andris growled, not even sounding human.

"You will see shortly, friend." Istvan smiled cruelly, his head lifting to the army. "Let's move out. Secure all prisoners."

The soldiers' reactions were instant, turning and marching for the main street, except for those around us.

Caden still stood there, Ling's blood over him like an abstract painting, his eyes on me.

"Caden, don't stand there like an imbecile." Istvan hissed quietly to him. "Why can't you be a leader for once. Strong and resilient, not weak and pathetic."

As a guard hauled me to my feet, I saw him flinch at his father's harsh words. So many times, I had seen it happen. Caden would shut down, push me away, and storm off. Each time Istvan cracked at the sweet boy, it twisted Caden into something ugly, wanting desperately for his father's approval.

"You want the nectar?" His eyes never left mine, but he spoke to Istvan.

"Excuse me?" Istvan turned around.

Oh gods, no.

"The nectar is real. I have it. I'm not going to get into all the hows, just that I do. It's boxed up and safe right now."

My words to my family in the cafeteria slammed back into me. My cockiness in thinking my friends would never spill the secret had me forgetting some of them weren't anymore.

"Caden…" His name was barely above a whisper. *Please don't do this.* My eyes pleaded. For one blissful second, I thought he and I were still best friends, sharing bonds thicker than his duty. Than even his blood. The kids who promised they would be best friends forever, never betraying the other. It was them over everyone else.

That day was long gone. The need to prove himself to his father overrode everything.

"I don't have time for your nonsense." Istvan sneered, about to turn away.

Anger built in Caden's eyes, his shoulders rising. "Father! Stop!"

Istvan jerked around, his eyes wide with disbelief his son would be so demanding and insolent. "Don't you ever—"

"Shut up," Caden stated firmly, widening Istvan's eyes more. "You want the nectar?"

Istvan's mouth snapped shut, his expression shifting. "You know where it is?"

"It is in Budapest." Caden held his father's glare.

"Please," I whispered to him.

"You fuckin' spineless piece of shit! Think you're so tough when all you want is to beg for your daddy to pat your head like a good boy." Warwick thrashed against his captives behind me. Even with super soldiers, it took a dozen of them to keep him from attacking Caden.

Caden's shoulders tightened, his head lifting higher, like he was trying to block out the truth of Warwick's claim.

"Caden, don't." I tried again. "Please."

"I will be taken seriously." Caden cleared his throat. "Be your right-hand man from now on."

"It's all I ever wanted for you," Istvan replied. "Now tell me where it is."

"No, it doesn't work like that." Caden's shoulders rolled back. I was prepared for him to point the finger at me. "I will find it. Bring it to you. This will be *my* mission to fully run."

Wait... what?

Istvan slanted his head.

"I will be the one who retrieves it. No one else."

Istvan's eyebrows went up. For a moment, I thought he would strike Caden, punish him for his insolence.

"Of course, son," he replied smoothly. "Find the nectar and bring it to me, and you will have a place right at my side. This is your chance to finally prove yourself to me. If not..." Istvan said before departing, disappearing into the darkness.

Tension twitched a nerve in Caden's jaw. He shot me a look before he, too, walked away.

What the hell happened? Why didn't he call me out? Say that I had it? Why did he protect me when this whole time he has claimed I was a traitor? That he hated me?

My brain couldn't allow any more thoughts and questions in, full of the trauma from the last hour. Commotion rallied around me. I could see Andris wailing and clawing as they pulled him away from Ling's corpse. A soldier lifted Kek's limp body, Lukas being dragged behind. In my peripheral, Warwick bellowed for me, the vibration strumming inside like a violin string.

The guards dragged me away, my eyes going to the clothes and items being left behind.

The two most powerful objects in the world, the fae book and the nectar, were buried in the heap, discarded like garbage.

Five super soldiers hustled me out to the street, their forceful grips digging through my clothes, bruising my already burned and torn skin. My eyes opened wider. Just out of sight from the square, over six military trucks were parked at the curb, being filled with what was left of Sarkis' army.

Captain Kobak perched himself on the back bumper of the middle one, dictating where to place the prisoners, purposely keeping some apart.

Kobak's attendance didn't surprise me. The six army-style trucks did. Istvan had three pre-war ones, which had been altered to work in the new world but were always breaking down. These were fae-made and much larger… and I had seen the model before.

When Warwick and I were escaping Killian's.

"*Bazdmeg.*" *Fuck.* I muttered to myself. My body flushed as the truth of how deep Istvan was in unseating the Fae leader. He took these from the palace. Might even have taken the palace over by now. The fae wouldn't stand for it. Istvan could fight the few dozens of us, but not the hundreds of thousands in this country. He had to at least keep the appearance of the fae still being in control until he gained more power.

"Kovacs?" Warwick's voice boomed through the mass, rotating my head to the side.

"Warwick!" I called back, desperately trying to find him through the condensed crowd. Though I couldn't see him, I knew he was there. Even without our link, I could feel him. His presence tried to search for mine.

"No!" Kobak yelled, his attention over my head toward where I heard Warwick calling me. "He goes in that one." Kobak pointed to the fifth truck. "General said to keep these two apart."

The guards gripped me harder, to the point of extreme pain, forcefully pushing me toward the third vehicle, banging my knees into the metal bumper as they shoved me into the back of the truck.

"Slide back!" One ordered, cramming us in, while another came along, chaining us to the bench we were on. A few reacted to the metal touching their skin, their bodies almost going limp.

They were using iron.

If you were pure fairy or even half, it would render you inept. The purer you were, the worse it hurt. To Killian, it would be torture.

"Don't bother to even think of trying to escape." The guard barked at us. "The chains are iron and goblin made."

Basically, we were all screwed.

My heart thumped, adrenaline being burned through like dried leaves. What the hell was happening? Where were they taking us?

Rosie was tossed onto the seat across from me, her face trying to hide the terror that was racking her body. Her burned and torn flesh was barely covered by the shreds of clothes she wore, mostly destroyed in the bombing.

"Well, look at what we caught." A stocky guard leered down at her. Something about his voice grinding against my memory. "*A kedvenc kirvăm.*" *My favorite whore.* His knuckles slid over her cheek.

Recognition knifed my gut, remembering his ugly words about my friend. The guard, Kristof, who was at the market we tried to rob.

Rosie tried to jerk away, making him laugh.

"What's wrong, *kurva*? Don't you like me? I thought we had a really good time together." Kristof's hand cupped his pants, shoving it in her face. "Bet you'd like to suck on this again. Have you gagging as I shove it down your throat."

"Hey!" I yelled, my cuff clanging loudly against the metal, trying to distract him. "Stop it!"

He didn't seem to notice, pulling at her top, displaying her breasts.

"Don't touch me," Rosie sneered.

"Not what you said last time." He crudely grabbed and twisted her breasts.

Rosie glared up at him, spitting in his face.

"Te kurva kurva!" You fucking whore! He clutched her chin roughly, slamming her head back into a metal bar that lined both sides of the covered truck bed. He fully grabbed her tits. "How about I show you some fuckin' manners?"

"Stop!" I bellowed, others around me chiming in.

"Hey, knock it off, Kris." A guard stepped up to the back with another capture. "General Markos is here. Don't be doing stuff like this with him around." *Wait until he's gone to assault her.* I heard the implication clearly.

Kristof grabbed Rosie's chin again, saying something into her ear before knocking her head again into the metal, then hopping out of the truck. His physique rolled with excessive aggression, puffed up and toxic, with some exaggerated sense of ego.

"Are you okay?" I asked her. She nodded blankly, covering herself up again.

"Not the first man like that I've dealt with." She responded distantly, not looking at me. I could see her walls going up. The pain and abuse she had to live through, years of boxing it up so she could keep going on because so many men are insecure assholes who think by "putting a woman in her place," they are somehow "real" men when all they are is weak and pathetic.

Though this little demonstration proved to me these soldiers weren't robotic at all. They weren't shut down, ready to take orders. They were over-aggressive, as if the medication was burning off or this was a bad side effect.

Two more were thrown in and shackled a few down from Rosie at the very end.

"Birdie," I called to her.

Her head popped up, her blue eyes on me. Her physique was tight, ready to fight, her expression defensive, but her eyes stared at me with questions.

None I could answer, except this was my fault.

Though there was no accusation in them, more a *what the hell should we do?*

My head slightly wagged back and forth.

We couldn't do anything. Not with so many we loved and cared about, separated between all the trucks and chained in as well.

Whatever was ahead of us, we had no choice but to see it through.

The rundown roads popped us around in the back like kernels, my wrists raw and bleeding as the cuffs dug deeper with every pothole we hit. I was trying to stay focused and alert, but the jarring journey rattled my already spinning head.

This night was going from bad to worse, and with every mile the caravan took us outside the city line, my stomach filled with acid. Zuz and Wesley were also in my truck at the very end. It was a mix of women and men, but they did a good job of keeping the more powerful ones separated. I had a feeling Killian, Andris, and Warwick were being held with extra care. Not that my uncle had any magic, but he held power with his people. One word, and we'd fight.

The truck shifted gears like it was starting to head up an incline. We had a brief glimpse as we rose higher, a quick look at Budapest below. The sparse lights in HDF and the fae side sparkled in the dark.

We had crossed the river and were heading into the mountains on the Buda side.

The fae side.

Fear beat my heart, and it felt like time lasted forever in this strange state, but it also went too quickly when the truck came to a rolling stop, the brakes squeaking under us. The other trucks halted in line behind us.

Wesley, Birdie, Zuz, and I instantly sat up straight, looking at each other. The night made it too hard to see, sharpening my other senses.

Truck doors slammed, voices talking, curt and loud, some even laughing.

"All right, stop fuckin' around! Bring them in!" Kobak's order howled through the clear, cold night. I could see fire lanterns being used outside the truck, suggesting there might be no electricity out here.

Adrenaline pumped back into my veins from the terror of the unknown. Would this be where they killed us? A mass grave out in the mountains where no one would ever find us? I wasn't sure I was ready for what was coming, though I didn't think Istvan would've kept us alive just to kill us miles away. If he was keeping us alive, it was because what he had planned was the crueler choice.

A soldier jumped up into the bed of the truck, coming around with speed and efficiency, uncuffing the binds from the bar and manacling our wrists together.

"Let's go! Let's go!" Another one with a torch waved us to get out, his accent sounding Czech.

We stumbled out, and they quickly formed us into a double line, the fairies having trouble keeping upright because of the iron. Several guards were on either side, marching us forward.

I couldn't feel the cold temperature, even as I shivered violently. My subconscious understood something I hadn't yet. Or didn't want to.

With the handful of torches, I could make out a tall building in front of us, the tiers and white limestone reminding me of a wedding cake.

Inhaling, I recognized it immediately, though I had never been here, only seeing pictures in books about Budapest.

The Elizabeth Lookout Tower. The highest point on János Hill, deep in Lord Killian's territory.

My pulse tapped ferociously at my neck like morse code, air barely going in and out of my lungs. I understood what was happening, but denial was a strong force, gobbling you up with doubts and other explanations, anything to not face the truth.

A commotion from far behind me twisted my head. A man shouted, his voice familiar, but I couldn't make it out. His pitch chilled me from the inside out, pricking at the dread clogging my throat as if they foresaw what was ahead.

"Move!" a sentry yelled, shoving me forward, my feet tripping over each other. They trotted us toward the tower, but instead of going up, they took us around to where it looked like new construction was going down… inside the earth.

Guttural terror stabbed my chest, ripping away my air. My limbs went stiff, freezing in place, even as people slammed into me from behind.

"Move it now!" A guard shoved me so hard, I hit the ground, the cement grating my palms, pain throbbing at my wrists at the impact. "Get up!" He seized me, planting me back on my feet and propelling me down the long set of stairs, forcing each foot in front of the other, plunging us further into the mountain. Down, down, down… there seemed to be no end.

I felt the shift in the air instantly, and this time I recognized it. The barriers were ripping away fae power and blocking magic from entering this space.

Frantic dread clawed up from the abyss, shredding through my airways, black spots dotting my vision. I could feel it taking away my logic and understanding. It would react without my say, take over as panic consumed me. Cries from other hostages around me mixed with the desolate yells from deeper within the cave. Echoes of scraping metal banged echoed around the tunnel we entered.

"No. No. No." The single word repeated over and over in a chant, adrenaline spiking, my heart hitting so hard against my ribs, wanting to escape before it was too late. My legs dipped, not able to stop the tears from rolling down my face, my head spinning so badly I knew I was having a panic attack.

Because I fully understood what was happening.

Where I was.

I had been through this before. I vowed to never come back.

I'd choose death over this.

A stocky man stood at the end of a tunnel, waiting for the new arrivals. Seeing him caused the ground to drop out from underneath me, making me grab for the wall to stay standing. The stocky man's familiar eyes cut through the group, pinning on mine. A vindictive grin hitched up his scarred lip.

No. My head shook, making his laugh bounce off the walls. *This can't be happening.* None of it made sense.

But here he was…

Boyd.

The guard from Halálház who assaulted and tormented me. The fae guard who worked for Killian.

"Look who's back." Boyd's nasal voice pricked at my vertebrae, smugness beaming off him. "I was hoping our paths would cross again."

Vomit pushed up the back of my throat, the darkness around my eyes spreading as cries and hollers from cages below felt like a drill in my spine.

Not again. This can't be happening.

"Welcome, fishes." Boyd held out his arms. "To the new and improved prison. One way in and *no way* out."

"You think you would survive again?" Killian's voice came fluttering back to me from a conversation we had. *"There will be no escaping the new prison. I can guarantee that."*

"This is Věrhăza." Boyd motioned behind him.

"The House of Blood."

Chapter 22

My frame swayed, oxygen barely grazing my lungs.

Death would have been a mercy.

I was back in a nightmare that I barely made it out of last time. And I did only because my life was worth Eliza and Simon's. If I hadn't been, Warwick would have killed me in the pit that night.

It was bad enough to go through this once—a system that purposely killed almost everyone off. I knew I couldn't survive this again, especially mentally.

On a surface level, I comprehended what was around me, the mix of stone, iron, goblin metal, and dirt walls suffocating me. I just couldn't accept it. I was walking a see-through line of sanity and consciousness. A feral instinct to protect myself burrowed in, the place you go when terror takes over, and you are no longer in charge. The bone-grinding, gut-wrenching horror spreading across your limbs like poison.

"Come look, fishes!" Boyd sneered, motioning for us to look at our new abode. The setup was similar to Halálház, but this time it was bigger, modern, and a lot more high-tech. Instead of being square, it had circular levels with a catwalk ringing around the cells and a guard tower in the middle, which went from floor to ceiling. Every five floors, they placed a guard station from which they could watch the inmates. The doors on the cells looked reinforced, the bars thicker.

The round space stretched a block long, fitting in thousands of cells, rising at least thirty stories. The torture of the noise bouncing off the metal cells every moment of the day, with no peace, shredded into my psyche.

There were passageways leading off to locations like communal bathrooms, a mess hall, and workrooms. It may look upgraded, but it was the same. A place to come and die.

The loud clang of boots indicated a group of prisoners being led to their cells. Their faces were streaked with horror, hair wet, hands holding a blanket and toiletries, dressed in issued uniforms. Gray, blue, yellow, and red walked around a lower level.

The place had been all set up and running previously. Istvan merely had to step in and continue with only a few alterations.

Catcalls came from the few occupied cells, flicking at the trauma I tried so hard to move past. All around us were the sounds of people throwing up, sobbing, and pleading. Every sense I had was drowning in distress, robbing me of strength.

"Whoa, girl." A familiar voice sneered in my ear, hands clutching my hips as I started to drop. "Go ahead and throw up. They all do at some point." The same voice, the same sentiment—I went right back to standing at Halálház, dressed in just a t-shirt, terrified but unaware of the true horror in front of me. What I would have to do to survive.

My head whipped back to the man who brought me into Halálház last time, this time without his demon partner.

Golden feline eyes glowered back at me.

"Zion..." I croaked at the cat-shifter.

"Oh, you remembered. Guess I do leave an impression."

No words could leave my mouth, the questions being overridden by my fear. If this was still under Killian's control, I could see why they were here, but it wasn't. Did they not know that? Or worse, if they did—why were they working for a human?

My mind grazed at the thought: *Was Killian actually behind this? Was this all a ruse?*

"Don't you love the first day of camp? Brings back memories, huh?" Zion patted my ass. "And here we did all these improvements for *you*." Giving me a wink, he strolled to the front of the group, holding up his arms.

"I'm Zion, your camp check-in leader and counselor. I also help check you out if you decide you don't want to be here." Sardonic and cruel, he smiled gleefully. He motioned to Boyd. "This is Boyd. He's in charge of your camp activities. Though I warn you, he doesn't like being asked questions. Puts him in a very bad mood." Boyd and Zion shared a sinister grin. "Let's go get you guys checked in and all settled into your bunkers, so we can get to arts and crafts later." Zion motioned for the group to follow, his order reinforced by a dozen guards with guns, propelling us forward.

I tried to look back and see if Warwick had been brought down yet, but there was no sign of the next group behind us. They were making sure to keep us separated and in numbers they could handle.

"Brexley?" Rosie called out for me, my name rattling through her teeth. Through the group, my gaze caught hers. Dread was stamped across her face, her body shaking.

"Move it, whore!" a guard rammed his rifle into her back, stumbling her forward.

"It will be all right." I lied, forcing my face to look reassuring when her eyes darted back to me again. "Just do as they say."

"Liar." Birdie hissed next to me, just loud enough for me to hear. "It's not going to be all right, is it? I can't feel my magic."

I couldn't hide the truth in my eyes from Birdie.

Wesley, Zuz, and Birdie all had their expressions locked down, like they were undaunted. I came in the same way last time, believing the façade would fool those who were enduring this hell. Now, I could see how thin the disguise was, how easily it could be torn into shreds. They had no idea how quickly their beliefs and morals became the tissue they'd wipe with, flushing it away when survival became the only goal each day.

I knew too much. Only a few here understood the true horrors of this fae prison, and sadly, one of them was dead, her blood still staining Mădach Tĕr. I would wish Ling back alive, and if I had my powers, I would have brought her back. But maybe she got the better way out, the merciful way.

Swallowing, I marched forward, the panic coursing through my veins numbing me. The sharp aroma of chlorine and disinfectant drove my teeth into my lip until it started to bleed, pushing every memory I tried to forget up.

The room was almost identical to the last one, separating us into categories, though this time the staff wasn't fae... or at least they weren't at one time. Men and women wore guard uniforms, their movements precise and robotic, with extra gruffness. And once again, most I didn't recognize. There were two I recalled from the class below mine, but no one else.

Nothing was making sense.

Sliding in next to Rosie, I put myself in the human line. I was more human than I had been last time, but I also didn't want to give Istvan or anyone else an idea anything might be different about me.

"What's happening?" Rosie whispered to me. Her entire world had been utterly flipped upside down in a matter of hours. Her home being blown up, then landing in a fae prison, where even she knew you didn't get out.

Focusing on her helped my panic over knowing what was coming and the screams I heard on the other side of the wall.

"Rosie." I tried to express everything in my eyes as we got near the front. "I'm not going to lie; the next twenty minutes are going to demean you and strip you of your soul. That's what they do here."

"Move!" a guard yelled at me, shoving Rosie toward the doorway beyond.

"Find a way, carve a spot somewhere in yourself you can retreat. Don't let them have any of your power. We'll get through this."

A sad smile hinted on her lips. "Luv, I'm a whore. Men have been degrading and demeaning me since, well, even when I was married. I have a whole world I can retreat to."

"Next," a woman barked at Rosie.

I stared in awe at the human woman I met just a few months ago. Beautiful, curvy, and soft, but strong as steel on the inside. If anyone could survive this place, it would probably be Rosie.

"Name?" the woman guard snapped at me, her accent hinting at Russian or Ukraine.

My eyebrows rose at the idea she didn't know who I was, but an emptiness blanked her face.

Tempted to lie, I knew it was pointless. I already had a target on my back.

"Brexley Kovacs." I lifted my chin.

No response.

She wrote down my name, species, and details about me like she was on a mission. To do as she was ordered. Nothing more and nothing less. Though they all had an air like they were on the cusp of aggression, their physical forms robotic, energy and life hovered just below the skin with toxic vigor.

The shower stalls were basically the same style, but newer. The smell was severe, the floor wet, showing signs groups had gone before us already.

"Strip!" Four men were in charge, their forms stiff and commanding, but I could feel a wildness in them. Excitement for their duty.

Most prisoners peered around, hesitating, unsure what to do, while I started to pull off my boots.

"Guys... do it," I whispered to Wesley, Birdie, and Rosie, who were in my group.

They began too, while others stayed frozen.

"I. Said. Strip!" one bellowed, whipping out his gun and smashing the handle into the back of a woman's head with such force, I heard her skull crack. The woman, Jo, I knew had worked next to Ling, hit the floor without even a cry, blood pooling around her, her body laying limp.

"NOW!"

Everyone responded instantly, though they kept looking at the woman, wanting to go to their friend and see if she was okay.

She wasn't.

Tossing our clothes in the trash, they lined us up along the wall. Two doused us with disinfectant and soap while the other two held hoses like they were weapons, ready to gun us down.

The force of the ice water hit my wounds, opening them up again, the disinfectant sizzling screams up my throat.

"Scrub!"

Cries, shrieks, and sobs of people finally breaking down echoed off the walls. We were nothing but animals in a pen. Naked, demoralized, scared, and in pain. It didn't matter to them that there were humans mingled in here, pure or mixed. We were all faceless, soulless animals now, while our friend laid dead barely inches from us, her blood swirling around our feet.

Dressed in the gray uniform, used boots, and grandma underwear, I held my toiletries and blanket as salacious remarks were called at our group from different levels. I was right back in my hell. This time the items I had on weren't as worn, the fabric stiff and abrasive against my sensitive skin. And the number was different—Prisoner 839. Evidence the prison hadn't been open and running long.

A guard I actually knew, the kid Birdie and I fought in the alley, Samu, led us to our cells. And by the glares at Birdie and me, he hadn't forgotten.

"Prisoner 835!" Samu pointed at Rosie, then to the small cell we were passing. "You're here."

My gaze met hers as the sentry bookending us shoved her in, slamming the door with a clank. My heart dipped as the lock rolled over, her face peering through the bars.

Halfway down, directly in line with the guard station, he stopped again. "Prisoner 839. Your cell." Samu motioned me in, nodding back at the station. "So we can keep an eye on you at all times."

Empty of any fight, I stepped into the six-by-eight room, a urine hole in the corner.

A smirk hinted on his lips. "Welcome home, Kovacs." He slammed the door, the click cutting into my bones. "It will be your last."

He tapped the bars with his baton, waving the group to follow him. I watched Birdie, Wesley, and Zuz pass me. I couldn't offer them anything, no words of comfort, no smile of courage.

All my phobias and trauma tore into me, sucking out my air. I wanted to scream, to wake up, to go back and stop the night's events.

Andris, Killian, Ash, Lukas, Kek, Scorpion. My heart ached, wondering where they were, if they were okay.

But my soul screamed for him.

The man I found in House of Death.

The one who could have taken my life.

Instead, we burned that place down and rose from the ashes.

I stepped up to the bars, glancing up at the level far above where we entered. I couldn't see him, but I swear I could feel him. His eyes were on me, and even if it was to make me feel better, I could feel him wrap around me, his voice.

"Even if we have to kill everyone here and swim through their blood... we will survive, Kovacs."

Chapter 23

The shrill buzzer howled through the underground, bouncing off the thirty levels of hell and rebounding to the other side, only to hit back at us. Ping-ponging off the metal like table tennis. Grating at every nerve that survived the long night.

Very few slept. The older residents barked at the newbies to shut up, increasing their sobs and wails. I had heard it all before, the melody of agony rising and falling in a chorus. The sniffles like the sound of a tambourine, the pounding of the bars like beating drums, the wails a horn, the quiet sobs of a guitar, while they sang their fears and denials in a melancholy song.

I had stared out, looking at nothing while my mind went round and round, not landing on anything, feeling emotions of guilt, fear, and devastation. Seeing Ling get murdered. Andris. My friends. I didn't even know if Kek was alive. Where was everyone? At any second, they could be taken from me without my knowledge. Killed without a thought.

In my gut, though, there was no doubt I would know if something happened to Warwick. It wasn't a fact, merely a deep-seated gut notion. And I was afraid of what would happen if I did feel his loss. I walked the line as it was between the sides. If Istvan killed him, I would jump willingly into the depths of darkness. No conscience. No compassion.

I would become revenge.

Again, my mind conjured up the sensation of Warwick's voice. *"Same, princess. Even death would fear me."*

A baton strummed down the metal bars. "Time to get up, fishes!" Boyd's condescension resonated from close by, my muscles locking up, knowing he wouldn't pass me by. My tormentor was going to make me pay for getting away from him.

Pushing up off the cold, hard ground, bones aching, wounds screaming in protest, I rose to my feet, pressing my spine against the wall. The bag containing my toiletries in hand, like I was about to head off to school. It took all I had to keep upright. My body was finally experiencing all the pain it went through the night before and demanding to stay in bed.

I had no such luxury anymore.

Hearing his steps, I tried to build up the thick barrier you had to have here. The place in your mind where you could disappear, to keep from breaking. It was a lot harder than I thought. To know what was coming and get prepared and back in the mind frame to handle torture, to take the beatings, assaults, and starvation.

Swallowing back the whimper, the tears wanting to flood me, I lifted my chin, my expression stone.

"Well, look here." Boyd came into my doorway, blocking out most of the light, his smug, ugly face making my eyes twitch. "Up and ready to go like a good little girl. Guess some fishes can be housebroken." He ran his baton across, the sound battling my lashes faster. "How does it feel to be back home? Right where you belong?" He tipped his head, his glare full of greedy lust. He wanted to hurt. To punish. "Maybe you can show all the new baby fishes how it's done. Lead by example. Or be the example." His mouth twitched in a sneer, telling me exactly which he hoped for. "You thought Halálház was bad. Just wait…"

I tried to fight my automatic swallow, but Boyd caught it, his scarred lip rising higher. "Afraid?"

Staying silent, I understood Boyd enough that any word from my mouth would lead to a beating. He was aching for it, begging me to say something.

I wanted to ask why he was here? Why was he working for Istvan?

My mind had gone to dark places last night, almost convincing myself this was some elaborate betrayal by Killian. He was sitting somewhere watching all of this play out, not a victim at all. But the idea quickly fell apart; my soul knew he wouldn't do it. Plus, there were too many humans and HDF members here. Killian would never cross that line.

Though it seemed Istvan would.

He declared his hatred of the other species so ardently, only to want to be like them and work with them—Istvan had proved himself capable on both fronts. Somehow, when Killian went into hiding, thinking it was the best way to find out who was after him, it gave Istvan the means to take it all. No one could have seen this coming. A human brazenly taking the fae lord's land and assets without anyone knowing? That took planning, preparation, and precision, which had to be so on point, with so many situations that could go wrong. I never questioned that Istvan wasn't smart, but I didn't think he was this diabolical.

A buzz raked the air, the locks on our doors unlatching, the doors sliding open.

Boyd smirked, tapping the bat against his palm, then with the press of his finger into the end, spikes popped out of it like barbwire. He twirled it, showing how the spikes glinted in the light.

"Come on, Kovacs, the early bird gets the worm." He used the device to wave me forward.

Tucking away my pride, anger, and the need to ram the baton up this man's ass with the spikes out, I inhaled through my nose and stepped out.

"Hurry up!" He slammed his hand between my shoulder blades so hard I scrambled and stumbled, trying to keep upright in the large boots I didn't even bother taking off to sleep, barely staying on my feet.

People filled the walkways, all heading for their communal bathroom. Keeping my head straight, my feet fluidly moving, my gaze peered as far across as I could, trying to find any of my friends.

We were corralled into the large, shared restroom. It was the same setup—open showers on one side, toilets on the other, sinks in the middle, and lockers lining another wall.

Guards stood on each wall and two by the only entrance and exit.

"Get in, do your business, and get out," Boyd yelled, the only directions the new people got.

"Rosie!" I spotted my friend looking bruised, exhausted, and in pain. She hobbled toward me, her eyes lighting up a little at seeing me. "Stay close. And do what I do."

She nodded, her eyes bloodshot from crying.

Birdie, Wesley, Zuz were already there, but it was another figure I wasn't expecting to see.

"Lukas!" I ran up, throwing my arms around him.

"Brex." He held me tight, sighing deeply with relief.

"Hey! No touching!" A guard yelled at us. "No fucking talking. This isn't chat time. Shit and get out!"

"You okay?" I stepped away from him, heading to the toilets.

"Yeah. I'm healing, but since we got down here, it's been a hell of a lot slower."

"There's no magic down here."

"What?" Birdie recoiled.

"They block it. So you can't use it against the guards or break out of here."

"I thought I felt all wrong." Wesley gripped.

"Kek?" I turned back to Lukas.

"I don't know." He dropped his head. "We were attacked right at the city line. She tried to fight him. There were too many, and he was able to get her." He swallowed. "Her pulse was barely there... but I don't know anything since we got here."

"What did I say?" The same guard yelled at us again. "One more time! Just test me." He touched his baton at his side. All the guards had guns, batons which could be a mace, knives, and stun guns. They were not fucking around.

I motioned for my group to move. "Time to lose any inhibitions you had." I yanked down my pants, sitting on the toilet without hesitation.

"Good thing I haven't had those in years." Rosie scoffed, following suit.

It took the others a moment to react. I knew the feeling—watching almost half the room hesitate and debate with themselves. Their safety lines would chip away faster than they ever could imagine. What they thought of as being open and secure would be pushed far beyond their breaking point, realizing they always had a safety net. A safe space. This place shredded any resemblance of safe, of being anything more than for your base needs and survival.

My friends shadowed me, doing their business and putting their stuff in a locker before following me out. They were all formidable, badass fighters who could kill the scariest of creatures, and they trailed after me like little ducks.

The mess hall was similar to the last place, but the moment I stepped in, I knew this was where things started to change. There was no line for food or even people working behind the cafeteria-style layout Killian had built.

Everyone sat at tables. Silent and obedient. There was no mesh of different colored uniforms at tables, different alliances, deals, and payoffs to hide behind. Solid colors clumped together in different sections. Humans in gray, half-breeds in blue, fae in yellow, and demons in red. Istvan was segregating us. Keeping us with our own kind, carving the already distinct lines wider between the groups. This would cause even more hate and more violence, which would cause us to turn on each other, not the men doing it to us.

"Humans on this side!" A man's voice boomed out. "Half-breeds over there. Demons in the corner, and fae against the wall."

My eyes darted to the corner, my heart leaping up in my chest when I spotted blue hair among the group. Kek looked like shit, blood still caking her hair, but she was alive. Our eyes met for a moment. She didn't give me any emotion, which made me feel even better. Kek didn't do emotion.

"She's okay, thank gods." I heard Lukas breathe out next to me, his lids closing briefly.

"Move it!" The same guard yelled, shoving people toward their section.

My gut dropped, knowing everyone but Rosie would be parted from me.

Birdie, Wesley, and Zuz headed for the yellow tables, where I spotted Ash, Scorpion, Sloane, Kitty, and Maddox along the dozens of tables. Meeting their eyes, a simple nod from them sent relief through me, knowing they were okay.

Kitty was hardest to look at. She had been very badly beaten. Her wig, makeup, and nails were gone; she was forced into a man's appearance. I had no doubt one or more of the human guards did this to her. HDF had no understanding or tolerance for transgender. Though Kitty held up her chin with strength, I could see how much it broke her. The faraway look in her eyes. They took the base of who she was as a human being, forcing her into a role she didn't fit because it made *them* feel better.

My anger rose.

Latching onto Ash's eyes, he instantly calmed me. He held the same relief in his mossy green irises at seeing me. The same question in his expression I was asking back.

Where was Warwick?

Lukas went toward the blue, where Warwick technically should have been, but wasn't.

Nor was Andris or Killian.

My stomach twisted with what it meant.

Killian and Andris might be being tortured for information or because they are Istvan's enemy. Warwick because of who he was. What better way to make yourself a legend than by taking down the very one that even humans revered?

As I walked to the human section, a man stepped in front of me, his beefy arms folded over, a sneer on his face. "I've dreamed of this day."

Shit.

My stomach knotted at seeing Joska in front of me, the HDF soldier Birdie and I fought when he, Samu, and Elek found us in the alley. The guy who was already an extremist now had his head buzzed, an HDF symbol tattooed on his neck, and his body was even more buff, like he was taking enhancer drugs. Rage danced in his eyes like a living thing, his already aggressive nature exploding from his skin, clogging the air like bad cologne.

"You will pay for Elek's death. I will make sure you are punished severely for what you did." He stepped closer to me, his body stiff as violence emanated from him. "One step, one word out of line, and I might forgo Markos' order not to kill you," he spat.

Joska was just another bully on my list who wanted to "put me in my place," hating that I had already put him in his. Though it was this moment, looking into his eyes, I not only knew he was on the pills, but whatever barriers and spells Killian had put in place to block magic didn't block the effects of the pills. That meant every human guard here was possibly far more powerful than the fae.

The wards blocked organic magic. The human science experiments were a processed and manufactured substance, Killian's spells not recognizing it.

Istvan had his perfect world down here. Humans finally held more power.

"Get to your seat, bitch." Joska grabbed my arm, throwing me against the table, my already bruised ribs cracking against it. Biting on my lip to keep from crying out, I slipped onto a bench, Rosie settling in next to me.

"Are you okay?" she muttered.

Nodding, I peered around, noticing the two tables with humans were a mix of women and men from Kitty's, a few from Sarkis' army, and some I didn't know. There weren't a lot of us.

A table over, there were four older people in gray, which caught my attention. My mouth parted in complete shock, staring at the haggard and beaten faces.

What. The. Actual. Fuck?

No matter how dirty and gaunt they looked, I would recognize them anywhere.

Albert and Nora Molnár. Hanna's parents. The shock at seeing them pulled to my feet, my eyes locked on them, questions barreling up to my tongue.

Nora glanced over, her eyes widening at me, then subtly shook her head, petrified. But not of me.

"Sit the fuck down!" A club whacked across the back of my legs, producing a groan from my lips, dropping me back down. "Did we tell you could move?" Joska grabbed my hair, yanking my head back. "You are a disgusting traitor, exactly like them. Unless you want to be flogged as morning entertainment, I suggest you sit there until we tell you to move." He rammed my head forward, hitting it against the table.

Holding back the rage and emotion, I lifted my gaze back to them. Nora looked pained, but with one whisper from her husband, her focus went to the table, not looking back at me.

What the hell were they doing here? They were Léopold elite. Nora and Rebeka were best friends. They were respected and known, coming from old money, though Albert also made a substantial fortune by running factories in the ninth district.

My mind clicked.

Holy shit.

Blinking, a theory rolled into my head. Albert owned the very factory torturing fae and trying to produce the next superhuman drug under the factory floor. Was that the reason he was here? Did he not approve? Though I didn't see Albert caring about fae enough to put him in here. I was missing something.

Seeing the other couple, Hans and Petra, next to them was still shocking, but slightly less, only because they were very liberal in their beliefs. Istvan complained about them all the time; they were constantly a thorn in his side about politics and his leadership. But they had a disgusting amount of money, so of course, they were accepted into the top crust of Léopold. I knew Istvan always hated them.

My stomach swayed at seeing the group, really understanding how far things had advanced in a short time and the autocrat ideals Istvan was pushing forward. There was no line Istvan wouldn't cross if he needed to. He would even imprison his own people, probably taking them in the middle of the night, no one seeing anything or knowing what happened to them. But you knew without a word it could happen to you if you didn't do everything by the book and agree with Istvan completely.

Killian's "death" had given Istvan enough ego and power to become a total dictator. Having the man in his prison must have made him feel like a king. If Istvan ever got the nectar, we would be doomed. He would become a god. No one could stop him or challenge him.

"New fishes, listen up!" Zion strolled in, his voice booming. "Rule for breakfast, lunch, and dinner. You behave, you get fed. You don't, you starve… and so does everyone in your group. Easy as that."

They were turning species against each other, and they would have us killing our own if one bad seed took away food for the rest. I understood what it came down to in here. It wasn't money or jewelry. It was a scrap of toast, clean water, soap, a blanket.

223

"So better be good little boys and girls," he mocked.

The doors to the back kitchen area opened, and a dozen people brought out large pots with ladles. Paper bowls were set down next to the pots, but that was it. No utensils, no coffee, not even water.

"Oh, yummy." Zion licked his lips mockingly. "I don't even see one floating cockroach in there this morning. Lucky day!" He clapped his hands together, talking at us like we were two years old. "Okay, we start with humans today. You go first. We see anyone trying to jump line, and you all return to your seats with no breakfast."

Nora, Albert, Hans, and Petra got up, obediently walking to the counter. I made sure I was right behind them.

"What are you doing here?" I pressed as close I could to Nora, her normally golden-blonde hair like her daughters was filthy and fizzy, tied into a low bun. All the makeup, jewelry, and glamorous clothes were stripped away, making them seem even more out of place. Rich people held themselves differently, not comfortable in cheap fabrics, filth, and being around people lower than their own social standing, where others wore it like a second skin. You could smell their fear and insincerity like perfume.

Her spine stiffened, her head slightly turning, her head shaking again.

"Istvan put you in here?" I muttered so low, my eyes darting to the guards.

She didn't respond for a long time, inching closer to the food. Finally, I saw her head dip yes.

"Why?"

No response.

"How is he going to explain your absence to Hanna?"

"Hanna?" Nora jerked her head around, her eyes wide.

"I better not hear talking." Joska strolled up and down our line.

They were monitoring any communication in communal areas. Was it messed up to say at least in Halálház we had the freedom to talk and sit where we wanted? Halálház had a wildness to it, fights, brawls between groups or with guards, but in a way, the guards let the inmates control and monitor themselves. Compared to this, that was freedom within the shackles. This was far worse. Fear escalated in silence. It hung around your neck like a rope and kept the tension at an unbearable level. There was no humanity. No moment you could forget where you were.

And no coffee.

Nora's head went forward. She didn't say anything until we both were getting a single scoop of watery goop.

"Is she alive and okay?" Nora whispered out of the side of her mouth.

"Yes."

Her shoulders lowered; her whole body eased with relief. "Thank you," she uttered, her blue eyes meeting mine briefly with gratitude.

"She's back in HDF," I added.

Nora's relief flickered from her face, her eyes watering. "Oh gods. You don't know how bad it's gotten there. What has happened to—"

"What the hell are you stopping for? Move!" Joska shouted.

Nora flinched, her head lowering, and skittered back to her table.

What was she going to say? How bad was it there? What was happening in Léopold?

Turning with my paper bowl of milky water with a few grains of something in it, questions circling my mind when movement came from the doorway.

I stopped in place. Boyd, along with four other guards, walked Killian in like a dog. A gasp caught in my throat at seeing the fae lord. His face was so black and blue I hardly recognized it. One eye was closed shut, his lip split open in several places, a collar around his neck attached to a chain.

Rage turned over my stomach.

They dressed him in a yellow uniform but made sure it was ill-fitting to make him look like a fool. Istvan wanted not to just tear Killian down, but change how he was viewed by his people. To diminish the idea of him being larger than life, the grand lord you bowed to. This man appeared weak and helpless. A dog on a leash.

Boyd, who used to work for him, was now happily rejoicing in his demise, coiling my gut more, another speculation working in my brain.

Killian kept his chin high, every breath a struggle, but he held himself like the proud man I knew. Boyd roughly shoved him down onto a lone table next to the fae. "Guess what, your highness? You're gonna have to eat, shit, and work with the rest of the low-breed common folk." Boyd got close to his face, but Killian did not waver. Not responding to the turncoat. "You are *nothing special* here. No magic, no title. No amount of money can save you here. Oh, right, you don't have any now." A sneer spread over Boyd's ugly mouth.

A guard unlocked the chain but left the metal collar around his neck. I had a good idea it was probably made of pure iron, by the way Killian was fighting to keep his body from slumping. Another way to declaw the king.

"If I see one of you sit with him, help him, or even look at him," Boyd yelled, speaking mainly to his fae kin. "You won't eat for a week, and your dear liege will spend a month in the hole. He will be separate from his subjects, exactly as he likes it." Boyd rubbed his hands together. "How does it feel, *Killian*, to be locked in the very creation you made to torture and kill people? To know there is no way out because you made sure of it?"

The one eye I could see open of Killian's burned into Boyd. Killian's fury was subtle compared to someone like Warwick, but I knew it could be just as lethal. He would wait for his chance, staying still until his victim was close enough before striking.

At least, I hoped. I knew better than anyone how this place could change you. Being locked in the hole for even a day could break the strongest man, making him compliant with anything.

Chapter 24

My uniform clung to my sticky skin, sweat dripping down my back and face. Between the heat from the stoves, the room packed with people, and a bad air filter, the place stunk of body odor, smoke, and the scorching smell of iron.

My head pounded from the clanks of the machinery and hammering, drilling through the huge warehouse-size room, deep underground. We were just above the prison level, still deep in the earth, though there was a tunnel big enough to fit trucks through at the far end of the massive room. The tunnel leading out had an electrical gate and was guarded by men with machine guns and no doubt spelled and warded. It looked like a place that would have stored military trucks and brought in supplies for the prison, never to be accessed by us inmates.

Istvan had different ideas for the space's use.

Halálház used us as labor, but we were giving back to the prison, keeping it running and functioning. We hemmed our own clothes, made the meals, cleaned, and maintained. Yes, while being whipped and tortured. I won't suggest Halálház was good; it was fucking hell. But this might be worse.

Istvan was using us to manufacture items.

For war.

One side of the enormous space was set up like a sewing factory. Where—surprise, surprise—they put all the women. They packed us in at rows of long tables with outdated machines. Still divided by the color of our uniforms, we hunched over, stitching, hemming, pressing, and seaming together soldier's uniforms. Ones with a new regime insignia.

Using the block letters HDF, it was laid out diagonally, each letter getting smaller, so it appeared like a triangle… or an arrow, with a circle around it. The other shoulder had the old Hungarian flag, the one used before the fall of the wall when humans ruled. The dark green crisp uniforms felt very much a nod to the past communist history we fought so hard to end here. A time my father feared and hoped would never come back. Markos was trying to revive it, making himself the supreme leader.

The other side of the warehouse, where they put the men, was set up to make shells for bullets.

They produced thousands of iron cases, torturing the fairies who had to touch and move the slabs of iron before cutting. The machines were old, and most had to work by hand, shaping the metal after heating it in open fire stoves.

I noticed Albert and Hans were struggling to keep up. Albert was only in his fifties, but Hans had to be nearing his seventies. It was grueling work, even for the men who were young, fae, and in shape.

All of them had stripped off their shirts because of the intense heat.

Except one.

Kitty. The fact that she belonged with us didn't get overlooked. The guards taunted her, forcing her to do even more than the rest. The woman was fierce and strong, but it hurt to see her being degraded because of who she was. I did notice Ash trying to stand between her and the guards, which seemed to earn him glares from her.

For all I knew, Kitty could out sew us all while people like Birdie, Kek, and Zuz were bleeding from stitching their fingers instead of the fabric. At least I had some practice from Halálház. Rosie definitely knew what she was doing, and I noticed Nora and Petra trying to subtly help those around them catch on, as Ling had done for me.

Wiggling my aching ass, I arched my back, my head pounding from dehydration. We had already been working for five and a half hours with no breaks, and the single bowl of gruel didn't last an hour into our hard manual labor.

"I'm sorry, is there a break time I didn't know about?" Joska grabbed my ponytail, tweaking my head to look at him. "Did we say you could stop?"

"*We*, huh?" I snarled, glancing around at the other guards, half-fae. "For someone who claimed so strongly to hate fae and would kill them if he ran into one, you suddenly seem fine working with them."

There are times I really wish I thought before I spoke.

Joska's face turned deep red, his brutish appearance scrunching up with rage. His hand clamped down painfully on my roots. "Like you have room to talk, you fae-lovin' bitch!" He got within an inch of my face. "You think I want to be around these disgusting fuckers?" He spat, gripping my hair until my eyes watered. "Markos is wrong about this. But he isn't the only one with a plan. This world will be purified. I will see to it," he snarled, snapping my head forward. My forehead cracked into the sewing machine, pain exploding through my skull, the impact drawing tears into my eyes. My hand went to the source of pain, coming back red. Blood dripped from my machine.

Out of the corner of my eye, I saw Birdie's shoulders roll like she was getting ready to attack him. I glanced up, shaking my head at her. She would just make it worse.

"If I see one drop of blood on that uniform, you're going to the hole," Joska yelled at me, pointing at the red streaks on the knobs. Then he glanced up. "Back to work, all of you!"

Using my sleeve, I wiped the blood off my head and the machine, feeling nauseous and dizzy.

"How are you?" Rosie whispered next to me.

My head bounced in a reply, but it wasn't her gaze I met down the table, it was a demon's. Kek's blue eyes met mine, and I could see the same response in hers.

Fuck, little lamb… we're really back in hell.

Out of everyone at this table, she understood the most. There was no competition between the new fishes and the old, between Halálház and Věrhăza. The torment was awful no matter what, but there is an even deeper level of horror when you've already gone through Dante's inferno, barely making it out, and then finding you have to go through it again. It doesn't become old hat, especially when it's a fresh nightmare with different obstacles. You are more painfully aware of what you have to do to survive, the emotional darkness you will have to reach to cope.

I was a target in Halálház, and now I'm like a flashing neon sign in Věrhăza.

Though in my misstep, I couldn't help but feel Joska slipped up, hinting at something. He didn't like the way Markos was taking things. And I could see a faction splitting off if the General continued to work with the fae on his climb to the top. Istvan always came off as a fae-hater, so why was he working with them? Even more so, why were they working with *him*? What was each side getting out of this?

I knew I was missing something. Neither Boyd nor Zion were capable of a coup, but they were involved in it.

Glancing around, I noted the various fae and human guards. Even if I placed myself in danger, I had to get each side talking. The more I learned about Markos' plans, the better.

Something tickled at the back of my neck, a buzz moving into my chest, tugging my attention to the doorway. Two sentries dragged in a man in a gray uniform, shoving him forward.

I knew instantly in my gut who it was, like I sensed him before he even entered the room, though it took my eyes a few moments to recognize the figure. His face was beaten, bruised, cut up, and swollen, but the familiar salt and pepper hair and bushy eyebrows connected the pieces together.

"*Nagybácsi*," I whispered. The urge to run to him, to wrap my arms around him, pushed my legs off the bench. Quickly, I sat back down, knowing it would only bring more punishment for him.

Guards thrust him toward a machine, yelling at him to start working. He had been beaten so severely, he struggled to stand. Gaunt and despondent, he didn't seem to be present.

I had to wonder how badly they had hurt him since he wasn't actually human anymore. The magic running through him because of me would heal him quicker than normal.

Right under Istvan's nose were the very things he hunted and was turning this world upside down for.

The nectar—me.

The result of the nectar's power—Andris.

Through my lashes, I watched my uncle hobble to a machine. Both Scorpion and Maddox subtly moved to him, helping him pick up the process, which made my heart ease a bit. They adored him as much as I did, and I knew they'd protect him. Still, it wasn't just the physical pain I was concerned about—his grief from losing Ling had to be destroying him.

She was the love of his life. The reason he gave up his life at HDF and became the amazing man he was today. I only knew the surface level of her, but my heart ached at her loss. I kept expecting to turn my head and see her sitting next to me at the machines, nudging me along, as she did at Halálház.

"Five-minute water break," Boyd yelled out across the warehouse, motioning at several huge buckets full of water. Each had one cup for all of us to use, which, with the new influx, had to be around nine hundred if not more. "There will be no talking. Get your drink and go back to your station."

The lines formed fast, with no segregation, packing us in. I searched for my uncle, but couldn't find him as Rosie and I clustered into a line, crowds forming in on all sides.

"Brex?" a voice whispered beside me, his blonde hair tied up as sweat poured over his ripped chest.

"Ash…" Even saying his name made me want to cry, to hug him so tight, feel the love of his embrace. But we kept our heads straight, the machine noises covering up our soft voices.

"You okay?" he muttered.

"Yeah, you?"

He dipped his head. "Warwick?" he asked.

My exhale and slight shake of my head was enough of a response. I had no clue, though deep down, I knew he was alive. I believed if anything happened to him, I would know, would feel it in my soul, that tremendous disturbance he would cause in the world by leaving it.

A hand brushed my ass, jerking my head over my shoulder to see a figure behind me, a slight smile across cut lips.

It took everything I had not to respond, to cry out and wrap my arms around him too.

"Dare you to touch my ass again, *Killian*," I mumbled, keeping my head forward, our bodies crushing together in the lines.

"Believe me, *Brexley*, it's all I'd like to do right now," he whispered in my ear. The power of my name still tingled, but not even close to what he could do before.

Ash snarled, glaring back at him.

"Don't tell me; Warwick has his guard dog watching you when he can't," Killian replied, all of us acting like we didn't even acknowledge the other was there.

"Did you see him?" I asked.

"For a moment." Killian's statement had my chest clenching. "He was dragged into a room past mine when we first arrived. That was the last I saw of him."

"What happened to you?" If the fae lord was let out with us, why wasn't Warwick?

"Typical human bullshit," Killian huffed out, then cringed in pain from the exertion beneath his broken ribs. "Asking me questions I wouldn't answer and beating me. Humans really have no imagination for interrogation."

"What did they ask you?"

"What I knew about the nectar, where I had been hiding, how I survived the bombing. And some queries about the prison itself." He moved closer into the back of me. "Nothing they asked was of consequence. Though, I think it's pretty clear who helped betray me."

"Boyd." I glanced up at the man, rushing people through the line.

"He can't be alone. The guy is not that smart. And Zion would go wherever the money was. Same with most of the other fae soldiers here. They follow the paycheck, not a cause."

"We need to learn who Boyd is connected with because there has to be more fae in on this. The fae wouldn't allow a human leader to take over your property and rule."

"Unless they don't know."

"How would they not know by now?" I inched forward, treading on the back of Rosie's heels.

"To them, I'm dead. And if they have another fae noble moving in to be leader, or at least pretending to be…" Killian's voice lowered as we inched closer to the water buckets.

His theory was right in line with mine. But who would do that? Who would be willing to be a puppet for the humans instead of actually taking over as fae ruler?

"Well, that doesn't fuckin' matter if we're in here," Ash gritted back to Killian. "You designed this hellhole. How do we get out of it?"

Killian let out a sigh. "We don't."

"What?" Ash hissed.

"I made sure it was impossible after *last time*." Killian directed it at me. "I tightened the magic with Druid spells as well."

"We're so fucked." Ash shook his head.

We really were. We had a *long* list of problems.

We were forced to stop talking as we neared the bucket, the water dirty, and the single cup doing nothing to quench our thirst.

Rosie took hers, turning quickly, her head jerked slightly at seeing Killian behind me.

"Look at you, fully clothed." Killian's smooth, regal voice sounded condescending. "Barely recognized you."

She rolled her jaw. "And look at you with a dog collar." She curved her brow, stepping past him. "Finally recognized you. Fits you perfectly."

Lowering my head, I hid my chuckle.

"Ouch," Ash whispered.

"Shut up," Killian muttered.

It took everything not to laugh as I took my cup of water.

For one second, barely a blink, I felt a single bubble of relief, amusement, and joy. It's the tiny moments you have to cling to in order to stay sane here.

Because in the House of Blood, they didn't just want to burst our sanity. They wanted to obliterate it.

Achy, starving, sweaty, and gross, we were funneled from the factory down to the mess hall after twelve hours of grueling work. They gave us moldy bread for lunch, and if you didn't get that, there might be a few rotting apples, which were slimy and infested with bugs. It was all designed to break us. And with the constant influx of prisoners coming in, they would discard us like those rotten apples when we got too weak to work.

On day one, you could see who was new and who wasn't. The newbies were disgusted and thought they could hold out not eating putrid food. Barrel through the hunger for a better meal later. The rest of us knew better. If you wanted to live, you ate the rotten and moldy. Bugs meant more protein. Gross didn't even factor into it. When the line was drawn in the sand, you realized there was a lot you never thought yourself capable of when it came down to living or not.

With a lack of food and water combined with grueling work, most struggled to walk, needing assistance from their peers. We all went to our designated tables silently, like trained dogs, barely having the energy to sit up.

Killian and Andris were the only ones who had to sit by themselves. The rest of us jammed onto benches, our combined stench permeating the room.

"Humans go first." Zion was again at the front by the food being set out. It looked more like slop you'd feed pigs. His nose wrinkled with disgust, but he motioned for us to get up.

My table started to get up, and I pushed up to follow next to Rosie.

"Except you." Joska came up to me, carrying his baton. He shoved it into my chest, pushing me back. With a button, the baton turned into a spiked club.

Rosie stiffened next to me, not leaving my side, though I wanted her to. I wanted no attention on her.

"Why?" I fought to control my voice. Exhaustion had my emotions simmering just under the surface.

"Because." He shrugged with a cruel smile. "I feel like it, and I said so."

"Look at you, *Kovacs*." Boyd strolled up behind Joska, a matching smile on his face, my stomach dropping. His sneer held more meaning, alluding to the things he had done and tried before in Halálház. "Once again, you're the problem child." He carried the same baton-mace, slapping it against his palm.

Joska went rigid at Boyd's nearness, his glare shooting over his shoulder, telling him he had this covered.

"Take it easy, human. This isn't HDF camp anymore," Boyd sneered. "This is the big boys' league. And you haven't even learned to hold your baton yet."

"You take it easy," Joska snapped. "I have more power than you down here." Typical hypocrite. Mr. Human purity took the pills to become more fae.

"Then let's take this outside, shall we?" Boyd taunted, moving right beside Joska, in front of Rosie. "And I still have more authority over you, so talk to your boss if you don't like it."

Interesting. Boyd was given a higher position, even over an HDF human soldier.

Joska's expression twisted with rage, his nose flaring, creating a wider smirk on Boyd's face. To my horror, he turned his leer on the girl next to me, his eyes dancing down Rosie's figure.

"What do we have here?" He licked his lips, staring bluntly at her chest. "You're one of the whores we collected, huh?"

Fear raced up my spine like thorns. I wanted to step in between her and this sick bastard. I knew what he was capable of. Zander stopped him from raping me last time, but now he had more power and no one to stop him.

She probably understood men like him better than me, but I still wanted to protect her.

"I won't eat." I tried to deviate the attention from her, nudging her arm, telling her to go. She took only a step before Boyd grabbed her arm, flinging her back into the table.

"I didn't say you could go," he barked. "For that, you both will be punished. And everyone will get to watch." The look in his eyes told me everything. My entire body flushing with heat when he grabbed Rosie, twisting her around and slamming her face into the table, yanking at her pants.

"No!" I screamed, lurching for him, punching and kicking.

Whack!

Pain exploded as the baton struck me across the face, knocking me to the ground. I heard yells and commotion across the room and saw for a split second that guards were trying to hold Ash, Scorpion, Killian, and others back before Joska's boot struck into my stomach with force.

Pain ripped the air from my lungs, but I still tried to get up, the need to protect Rosie compelling me. Joska's boot struck again, forcing a cry from my lips, flattening me out on the ground. I started to recede from the pain, to disappear from what was happening.

And maybe this time, I'd never wake up.

A roar blasted through the room, rattling the tables and punching the walls, silencing the room with a terrified hush.

My skin tingled, feeling the heavy glare of a killer. Curving my head, my gaze landed on the man who had the power to halt everyone in their place.

The Wolf.

The legend.

Peering at me through his dark lashes, his brutal, raw aura sank into me like teeth, causing the same hitch in my breath I had the first time our eyes met across the prison cafeteria.

Through the slits of his swollen eyes, aqua burned into mine with fury and death. His body appeared as if he's been electrocuted, beaten, and tortured, but his wrath banished the idea they had broken him in any way. Warwick's shoulders rose and expanded as another chilling growl came from him.

A warning.

"Warwick!" My cry didn't even make it out before he barreled forward with a booming war cry, the eight guards around him tumbling over like bowling pins.

"Stay back, Farkas!" Boyd ordered, pulling back up his pants in a panic, fumbling for his gun.

Warwick's fist collided with Joska, the beefy man flying back onto the ground before Warwick directed himself toward Boyd.

"I'm warning you!" I could hear the slight fear in Boyd's voice as he yanked out his gun. Instead of pointing it at Warwick, he darted to me, pressing it up against my head. "I won't hesitate."

Warwick came to a jarring stop, his chest heaving, his eyes flashing with rage.

"I thought that would tug on your leash." Boyd sneered. "The great legend..." He shook his head. "Has his balls in a knot over this?" He gestured at me. "What is it with her? Her pussy can't be that great. I should know; I've *felt* it."

Oh. Shit.

Warwick could come at you like a bull, *or* a ghost, killing you before you even knew he was there.

His wrath filled the air like smoke, and he darted to Boyd in a blink, his hand clapping around Boyd's neck, lifting him off the floor, squeezing so tight I already heard popping.

"Stop! Drop him now," a guard yelled as several moved around him, striking him with their mace clubs.

Warwick howled as the spikes tore through his skin, cutting into his muscle and tissue. His hand released Boyd as more and more surrounded him, clubbing him. Warwick's blood dripped and pooled onto the floor.

Commotion buzzed around me, inmates rising up, but all I could see and hear was Warwick.

Jumping up, I leaped for the guards, trying to push them off and away from him with a shattering scream. "Stop!"

"Kovacs!" Warwick shouted as a few turned on me, striking. The agony dropped me to my knees as the clubs impaled my legs and spine. "NOOO!" Warwick boomed, trying to pull me into him, shelter me from the hits. His one hand engulfed mine, the other cupping my face, our eyes locked, and in that second, the pain ebbed and melted into the background. The fact they were going to kill us here brushed at my mind, but it didn't seem as important as long as I was with him.

In this moment, it was just us.

"Fuck that, princess. You aren't going to die here," his eyes said back into mine.

"Stop!" Boyd's voice rose above in an order, ending the brutality on us. "We were ordered to keep them alive for now." Boyd's scarred lip twitched, strolling over to us. "That doesn't mean they have to be mentally functioning." The lip rose into a smile as he rubbed his neck. "Take them both to the hole. They've been there before; they should feel right at home."

The hole.

No. No. Nononono. My head started shaking back and forth, tears filling my eyes. Terror clamped down on me as soldiers forced me to my feet, blood dripping down my legs and back, soaking into my pants. My lungs faulted, wanting to shut down.

"Kovacs," Warwick grunted, grabbing my face again. "Look at me."

Panic took over, my legs wobbling with the knowledge of what was ahead. I barely made it out last time. I would prefer death over this.

"You'll be okay." He spoke just to me as they tore us apart, roughly hauling us out of the room. "You are stronger than you think."

He was trying to comfort me when he was so badly beaten and probably as starved as I was. We weren't going in strong. He could lose himself in there as well.

"Warwick," I said his name. Only his name. It wasn't words of love or anything. We weren't like that. But my tone said it all, expressed everything I didn't say.

He just looked at me, his irises intent on me, blazing with meaning before the guards pulled us down opposite passages, leading to the pits of despair.

If it was myself trying to give me comfort, I didn't care. His voice wrapped around me. *"They didn't fuckin' break us last time, Kovacs. Whatever it takes, you fucking survive, okay? Whatever. It. Fucking. Takes."*

"Whatever it takes," I whispered before the door slammed on me, and I was left in utter darkness.

Chapter 25

Hell.

I never believed in it until I was put down here last time. It wasn't some mythical place bad people went to after death. No. If hell was a place, it was right here on earth. Only real-life beings could inflict this kind of depravity and cruelty.

I longed for death in hopes of one moment of relief.

"Hold on, princess." My sanity had curled onto itself, no longer differentiating reality from my dreams anymore. And I didn't care. I needed him; his illusion gave me the one source of strength to keep breathing.

The pit was smaller than last time, arms shackled to my ankles so I could never fully stretch or move. They left me in pitch darkness for a moment before white blinding light was pulsed so brutally, my retinas burned and my head pounded. They filled the small room with relentless ticking noises or beeps, then loud piercing chilling sounds. No rhyme or reason. No rest. No food. No relief.

"I can't," I sobbed.

"You can." He touched my face, his blue eyes reflecting in the strobe light. He felt so real, as if he were really here with me again. That our connection was alive.

I let myself drown in the hallucination.

Time no longer mattered. The starvation eating at my mind

emphasized the voices in my head. Věrhăza was chomping down on the cracks Halálház had already put in my foundation.

"You promised me, Kovacs." My vision of Warwick tugged at my face to look up at him. Oddly, in my hallucination, he looked like he was barely holding on as well. His face was sunken, bruised, and worn. *"Whatever it takes."*

"I'm trying." I swallowed. Istvan had upped the mental torture, and I was also a lot more human this time. My strength to keep fighting, no matter how much I wanted to, was lowering with each passing moment. I was ready to give over to it… either death or insanity, whichever one came first and took me away from the suffering.

"Try harder," Warwick muttered fiercely. *"You are the only thing keeping me going."* His forehead touched mine, his timbre almost vulnerable. *"Remember, we don't play by normal rules. We make our own."* My lids shut with the sensation of his skin, the feel of his hair and breath across my face as his deep voice rumbled into me. The pain eased; the nightmare stopped when he was here. *"Right here… this is how we survive. You and me. How we push through and live, sotet démonom."*

I nodded, leaning into his mirage, letting myself feel the moment of peace he gave me. Though I knew I was holding onto a thread.

It wasn't long before my delirium stopped conjuring him up. The voices no longer rattled in my head, tucking me away from the torture. I stayed curled on my side, staring at nothing.

Void of life.

Anesthetized to everything.

I didn't even move when the door did finally open. My senses were numb, my mind ignorant of what was real and what was not.

"So, how was your second time staying here?" Boyd's stocky figure filled the doorway. "You must have enjoyed it because you stayed an extra two nights this time."

Somewhere in the back of my head, I grasped I had been down here at least five days then. Five days and only five times I was dragged out to pee and given a half cup of water before being thrown back in, shackled up in a painful ball. The moment of relief when I was unchained to pee was more excruciating when they locked me back up again, my muscles and body screaming in agony. The moment of blissful silence in my ears ripped away again.

Boyd's boots struck the floor, strolling to me. "Look at you in no hurry to leave. You want to stay longer?" He bent over, unlocking the binds latching my wrists to my ankles. "I'll put a note in your file to up the ante next time. Don't want you to get too comfy here."

There would be no next time.

More men shuffled in, picking me up.

"You smell like shit and piss." Boyd waved his hand by his nose. "Toss her into the shower. The bitch soiled herself."

Flinching at their touch, I was hauled up the stairs by two guards, my senses so fried I couldn't register anything. Even as they dragged me to the shower room, tore the sullied uniform from me, and shoved me under icy water, yelling at me to scrub myself, I felt nothing.

I numbly moved as they berated and taunted me. My non-response seemed to trigger them more. They needed to feel my fear, my humiliation, my subservience to their frail egos.

I did not give it to them.

People considered "breaking" a sign of weakness. I disagreed. Bending meant you could be molded and shaped into something else. I may be full of dents, scars, and trauma, but whatever they did to me, they could not bend and form me into their idea. They turned me rigid. Titanium. I broke; I did not bend. I snapped; I did not bow. They did not twist and cast me into something different. My broken pieces could be forged together. Made stronger.

"Let's go!" one yelled, tossing a clean uniform at my naked body. I dressed and followed them out. My legs trembled, but I forced myself to stand on my own.

The cells were filled, but most were awake, appearing dirty and haggard, suggesting it was late, not early. Everyone was in for the night after a long day in the factory.

As the guards took me back to my cell, a tingle climbed up the back of my neck, my head jerking to the side, catching movement on the opposite side a story above mine.

A breath caught in my lungs, a spark of life burning through the deadness inside.

Warwick.

Our eyes caught instantly, like we knew the other was there. Though I was seeing him for the first time in a week, his image had been with me so much in the hole, it was like we had never been separated.

His hair was wet as well, and he was wearing a clean blue uniform. He was healed, but appeared weary and slightly gaunt in his face. I probably looked worse than a walking skeleton, my ribs already sticking out again.

The guards put him into a cell as my own guards shoved me into mine—straight across and one level down.

Istvan's cruelty at his finest. Putting us as far apart as possible while still being able to see each other. We could watch from afar whatever happened to the other one and not be able to do a thing. Beatings, torture… rape.

Our doors clanked shut, the guards strolling away as we continued to stare at each other. My sanity still teetering, I thought I could feel him behind me, his presence reassuring me, asking if I was okay.

"Lights out!" a guard yelled, and the place went dark. Only a few fire bulbs eased some areas like a nightlight, but I could still recognize his outline, feel his eyes on mine like hands brushing at my skin.

"We will find a way out of here, princess."

Maybe I was no longer completely sane, or Warwick had such a command, even without the bond, to push at my walls and barrel in.

Eventually, he pulled away from the bars, disappearing into the shadows of his cell.

"We will, Farkas. And we'll kill every last one of them as we do." I muttered to myself before crawling down on my blanket.

I was far past hunger. Far past simple hate or rage.

It bubbled deep inside, the heat welding my pieces back together.

Forging for a battle that was no longer hinting on the horizon or merely whispers in the dark.

It was here.

"Is she a dead fishy?" A voice stirred me.

Chirp!

"Yeah, check to see if she's breathing."

The need to sneeze tickled my nose, pulling me further from the one moment of peace I'd had in a week. I had fallen right to sleep, my body exhausted, but dreams kept jerking me back awake, filled with piercing sounds that weren't there and voices calling for me. Anxiety kept me from truly letting go, the nightmare of my torture visiting me every time I shut my eyes.

Chirp!

"You sure?" An object poked at my cheek, creating a groan from my lips. "Yep, you're right. It's alive."

Chirp.

"You are not always right. Who knew how to get us here?"

Chirp!

"Well, okay, you… but who knew how to get us down here?"

Chirp!

"Okay, well, yes, it was you too… but who was the one to dress us in these fabulous outfits?"

Chirp.

"That's right. Don't you forget it."

My head pounded as my lashes pried apart. I wanted to vomit, to go back to sleep and not feel any pain, but the awareness that my two friends were here yanked me out of the depths and actually put a smile on my face.

"Opie," I muttered, a piece of my heart feeling right again.

Chirp! Chirp! Middle fingers flew into my face.

"Yes, hello to you, Bitz."

Chirp! She huffed, flipping me off again.

"Missed you too."

"Fishy!" Opie sang with glee. "So happy you are okay. I have no idea how you survived this long without us. My little broomstick—you can't seem to go a day without a life and death event."

Tell me about it.

Shockingly, no bright or inappropriate ensembles assaulted my eyes. Today he wore a dark wool cloak with a hood, Bitzy in a smaller version, as if they were trying to go unnoticed. Which was all kinds of wrong.

"What's with the outfits?" I frowned, sitting up.

"We couldn't be spotted." Opie peered around as if at any moment someone would jump out. "Ex-master Finn is here somewhere. If I'm caught here, well, let's say being rat bait wouldn't be the worst ending."

"What?" I blanched. "You'd be killed?"

"Worse!" Opie's face crumbled, his voice pitching with terror. "He'd make me clean. Forever."

A snort caught in my throat.

"My punishment would be eternal servitude."

"And that's different from before?"

"I'd be condemned to wear a prisoner's outfit like yours… and can I say, Fishy, your skin color is blending a little too well with this putrid light gray. Not doing you any favors." He twirled his hand from my uniform to my face. "I'm mean, look at my complexion. Yes, I look good in any color, but dreary hues are so awful and don't get me started on the fabric. Ugh, my skin itches at the thought." He shivered.

"No matter what, you sparkle on the inside." I tried to smile, leaning back against the wall.

"That was my theme for today." He grabbed the cloak, yanking it open. "Ta-da!"

"There it is." I covered my eyes, a chuckle bobbing in my chest.

Under the cloak, Opie had on camo booty shorts with leather straps crisscrossing all over his torso, a studded choker made from bullet shells, and the ends of his mohawk dyed pink. I had no doubt the camo came from the uniform of an HDF soldier here, and the shells came from the factory upstairs.

"But I have to hide my fabulousness today, which is just so heartbreaking. My creations weren't meant to be hidden from the world."

"Finn is here? You've seen him?" I asked.

"Oh, he's here." Opie huffed.

Chirp! Bitzy flipped off the air.

"How did you get in?"

"We almost didn't. This place is spelled as tight as Master Finn's ass." Opie's happy mood plummeted, a scowl on his face. "But if wild rats can get in, so can we."

"What about locks?" I sat up higher. "Can you open the ones here?"

"This place is extra, extra spelled. We struggled to even find it. But even if I could, fishy, what are you going to do?" He motioned to the guard station and the dozens patrolling the catwalks. "There are hundreds of locks and spells from here to the outside. We had to scurry in through *a million* drainpipes to get down here." He pointed his finger at me. "Which shows how much we love you. Do you even want to know what is in those? My anxiety went through the roof. They are filthy and disgusting. And I did not want to clean them one bit. Nope, not at all."

Opie was right. Even if he could unlock my cell, where did it get me besides back to the hole? There were too many guards, levels, gates, and barricades between me and the outside. Plus, getting everyone I loved at the same time? Pretty much impossible. The instinct was to get out any way you could, but I needed a plan. We might get one chance at it. It needed to be exact.

A loud buzz shrilled through the prison, the lights for the day going up full blast.

"Time to get up, *kurvas!*" I heard Boyd yell from the guard station. "Today is gonna be extra special."

The excitement in his voice meant nothing good for us.

The doors clicked open, allowing us to step out and head to the bathrooms.

"Ahh, it's like we're sending her off for the first day of school again, Bitz." Opie flapped a hand by his eyes. "Our little girl is growing up so fast."

I glared back at them as I moved to the door.

Chirp! Bitzy double flipped me off, her way of saying, "Fuck you, but have a good day."

"Have fun, fishy. At least *try* to play well with others." Opie waved as I strolled out, heading down the walkway.

My eyes peered up, finding Warwick within his bustling row, his head above most. When our eyes met, I had this sense he had been in my dreams last night, too, giving me the only moments of rest.

"Whatever it takes, Kovacs," I could almost hear him say because, like me, I knew he could sense something was coming. A deep foreboding sunk into my gut.

No matter what hell we thought we were in, this place hadn't even begun to unleash its suffering on us yet.

Chapter 26

The number of people moving around me in the bathroom was jarring after coming from the pit. The low murmurings instead of the piercing noises had me unsettled and fidgety.

"Luv!" Rosie ran up to me, her arms engulfing me. I stood still, like an abused dog. The only touch I had for a week resulted in pain: my daily trips to the bathroom, the guards striking me, slamming me into walls, or throwing me down. Taunting me with food or fresh water and dumping it down the toilet before I could touch it.

"I've been so worried." She pulled away, taking in the stiffness of my frame. "Are you okay?"

"Yes." I couldn't get any more out. I hadn't spoken to anyone but my visions in over a week.

Every person who bumped my shoulder getting by me had me tightening in on myself more. The inclination to strike out or hide had me inching toward a wall for safety.

Rosie's lips pressed, eyes watering. "I am so sorry."

"For what?"

"I was the reason you went in there."

"No." I shook my head. "You weren't. They needed no reason to put me in there. Are—are you all right?" I stumbled over my words, trying to fully speak again. "Did they…"

"No." She shook her head. "They've left me alone since."

My shoulders eased down.

"You don't have to protect me," she stated firmly. "I've dealt with and suffered through what men like those need to do to feel powerful. And I survived. I'm stronger than you think."

"Without a doubt, you are." She was probably far stronger than I would be in that circumstance.

"X?" Birdie, Zuz, and Wesley gathered around me, all looking relieved and slightly shocked at seeing me. I knew I looked like hell. "Fuck, are you okay?"

I nodded at them.

"Hey! No standing around and talking," a guard yelled at us, dispersing us quickly.

"Come on." Rosie lightly touched my arm. "Let's get you something to eat. You can have my rations this morning."

"No." I shook my head vehemently.

"You can and you will." She glanced down at my figure. "Looks like you need it far more than me."

I couldn't remember the last solid food I ate. All you want when you are down there is the hunger to vanish. The pain and emptiness in your stomach drives you mad. Then it suddenly stops. You are thankful until you realize your body is not being kind—it's shutting down.

Dying.

We strolled into the mess hall, the blocks of color dividing the room into segregated groups. I hated this place with every fiber of my being. I didn't think it could get worse than Halálház, but Istvan made it possible.

I missed the talking, fighting, and the blending of people. I didn't even realize the freedom we had there compared to this.

The control and domination of Markos' reign held us down with an iron fist. The levels of hell just kept going on and on. Taking away more of our humanity, more of things we needed as beings. Stripping away the will to live.

My skin prickled with the sensation of eyes on me. My head jerked to the side, feeling Warwick's gaze like electricity, reminding me I still had fight left in me.

Sitting by himself at a table near the half-breeds, he still looked like the king watching over his people. His dark hair was tied up, his tattoos showing on his arms and under the V-neck of his shirt, his muscles trying to rip the fabric open, demanding to be released.

The man dominated the room, absorbing all the attention and charging the air with his carnal, predatory aura.

Kill.

Fuck.

He made you want them equally.

His aqua eyes met mine, and my body reacted as if I was seeing him for the first time in Halálház. The jolt of fire, the rush of desire, a connection I didn't realize then, which would bind us together beyond time and space.

He wasn't any less brutal, sensual, or dangerous, but I no longer feared the wolf. I coveted his viciousness, sought his violence, and craved his raw force.

Because I was the same.

He accepted it in me, let me acknowledge it in myself. We went to war, crawling out of the depths together. We fought. We killed.

We survived.

"My mate." The words echoed through me again, his eyes slinking over every inch of me. My body flushed as my imagination contrived the feel of him. I craved him so much, I could almost feel his tongue dragging up my thigh, parting my folds and licking through me.

"All right, ladies and gentlemen!" Zion's voice broke my gaze off the legend, twisting to see him standing at the front of the buffet area. "Because you've all been so good. There will be a special treat for you tonight. So eat up! Some of you will need it!"

His speech knotted in my stomach as our section went up to get our small bowl of gruel, which appeared a little thicker than usual.

"*Drágám.*" a voice whispered next to me in line.

It took everything I had to not respond as my uncle nestled in closer to me in line.

"How are you doing?"

He was worried about *me* when he was the one who had lost so much.

"I'm fine." I dared a glance over at him, my stomach looping into a knot. He still looked far younger than his years, his wounds healing quickly, but that was the surface. The grief behind his eyes made him look desolate, drawn, and pale, sorrow hunching his shoulders.

A thread of alarm wrapped around my lungs. He looked like a man that was only existing—no longer living. He lost his soulmate. His heart. Misery could kill a perfectly healthy person if you no longer had the will.

Grief and worry filled my eyes with tears. "Are you all right?" I felt stupid the moment I asked. Of course he wasn't. "I've been so worried about you."

"Don't worry about me."

"I will always worry about you. You are the only family I have left."

Please let that be enough.

"No." He moved his hand subtly, his finger grazing mine, squeezing, a warmth spreading through my nerves. "You have family all around you, *drágám.*" He let his scrutiny drift over the tables full of my friends, tilting his head to one. "That one especially. He loves you."

My attention flickered to Warwick.

"He might not say it, but I know firsthand when a man flips his entire world upside down for a woman…" Andris's eyes poignantly met mine. "She is it. Ling was that for me. Your father was the same with your mom." He flicked his head back at the wolf. "He would die for you."

"And I would kill anyone for him."

His lips pinned together with a nod, his head bowing. "I would have taken the bullet for her."

"I know you would have." I clutched his fingers tighter. There was no question. And I felt ashamed I was glad he didn't. The thought of losing him…

"I can't breathe without her." I heard Andris whisper, his voice quaking.

"Move it!" Joska slammed into Andris's shoulder, knocking him forward. "Fuckin' fae-lover."

Andris righted himself, moving up to the counter. He peered over his shoulder, his expression heartbreaking.

"*I love you.*" he mouthed before Joska pushed him deeper into the throng, out of my sight.

The sentiment should have been comforting; my love for Andris had become everything. He was like a father to me now. But for some reason, it only made my stomach twist into a tighter knot, filling me with trepidation.

The day continued to get worse.

My back ached, my fingers bled, and my head pounded, and this time, they had us take different water breaks, so I never got a chance to even brush by Warwick.

About an hour before the end of our day, Boyd, Samu, and two others I didn't know marched in, heading directly for us. Terror swirled in my belly, but I kept my expression impassive, already preparing for them to grab me.

Without a word, they headed for Zuz, seizing her arms and yanking her up.

"What's going on?" She struggled in their hold as the men yanked her off the bench. "No! Let go!"

Commotion drove the girls near her into a frenzy of yells and failed attempts to stop them.

"What are you doing?" Birdie asked, her pitch rising. "Where are you taking her?"

A baton cracked across Birdie's face, pitching her off her bench to the ground with a cry.

I started to rise, but I felt a hand clamp down on my shoulder. "Don't." Nora shook her head, telling me with her eyes to sit back down.

I did, watching helplessly as they carried Zuz from the room, screaming and thrashing against them.

What the hell was happening? What were they going to do with her? Why her?

"Get back to work!" Joska ordered us. "Or you will be next!"

Terror buckled everyone down, returning to sewing with shaky hands.

I saw Kek subtly help Birdie back into her seat. Blood gushed from her nose and split lip, but otherwise, she seemed all right.

We worked the next hour in utter silence, our heads down, the noises of the enormous machines across the warehouse hissing and firing as the men labored. Warwick was put on the furnaces, melting the bullet casings into shape. Sweat pooled off him, making him look like he jumped into the river with his clothes on. The cotton blend of his pants stuck to him, following his every move like a shadow.

Through my lashes, my eyes traveled over his physique, following the flex of his muscles, the curve of his ass. I could almost taste the salty sweat dripping down his spine on my tongue, the feel of sweaty skin against my own.

His head jerked suddenly, his brows furrowed, his gaze finding mine across the space.

"Get back to work!" A whip lashed across his bare back, breaking his skin. The guard struck again. A sob gurgled in my throat, but I tried desperately to hide my response. His jaw clamped down, his teeth grinding as he took the flogging. He breathed in, turning back to work, his body bristling against the submissive response.

The Wolf wanted to attack. The legend wanted to kill.

But they would hurt those he cared about. Ash, Kitty... me. I was his Achilles heel here.

"Okay! Dinner time, fishes." Joska called out, people instantly stopping, rising, and heading to the door.

"Except you." His hand wrapped around my arm, yanking me back.

"What?" My heart dropped to the ground. Not again. "Why?"

Joska didn't answer, watching everyone depart the room.

Warwick stopped, noticing Joska's hold on me.

"I meant you too, Farkas. Go." Joska sneered, his free hand coming down on my hip.

Warwick pitched forward, his icy glare on Joska. At the same time, three guards moved in his way, holding up their spike batons, guns, and switches.

"Warwick! No!" I screamed at him inside my mind, shaking my head.

He came to a stop, his eyes searching mine, while the sentries hollered and threatened him.

"Whatever you want. Take me instead." Warwick grunted at Joska.

"Sorry, direct orders." Joska shrugged maliciously. "But don't worry, I wouldn't touch this pussy if you paid me. Contaminated by your kind now."

Warwick jutted forward again, his lip curling.

Joska pulled out his gun, pointing it at me. "Don't test me, *geci.*"

"Go," I said with my eyes. *"I'll be fine. You will only make this worse."*

"No." His head did a little jerk to the side.

"Yes. Trust me… please."

He hesitated, but with one more nod from me, he very begrudgingly relented. A snarl hitching his lips, letting the guards guide him out of the room.

"Have your fae-lover potty trained, I see," Joska hissed in my ear. "Just like you had Caden. I'm starting to think you aren't human, Brexley. I see no other reason why you have all of them wrapped around your finger." He shoved me forward. "Guess we'll see tonight… see what color your blood truly runs."

I was right. This place hadn't even begun to show its cruelty.

Standing here, I was in a sick, twisted nightmare, one I lived before. Barely.

When Joska and two other guards pulled me down into a dark tunnel, I knew what was happening. The taste of my fear bled into my mouth, the same terror shook my legs, and dread locked my muscles.

Light gleamed through a locked gate at the end, exposing a dirt arena with bench seating reaching up several stories.

Oh gods, no.

Acid retched up my throat, and my body tried to purge the terror from my gut. The emptiness in my belly burned the acid down my esophagus.

No. No. No. This can't be happening again. I thrashed against the hold on me, but it did nothing as they dragged my body up to the gate.

"Nooooo!" I screamed, trying to fight my guards. Of course, Killian would build it again, but I didn't even imagine Istvan would use it as it was meant to be.

"Oh, what's wrong, Kovacs?" Boyd walked up on the other side of the gate, giddy cruelty marking his features. "Don't you like to play games? Thought you'd be excited to be picked first."

The instinct to keep fighting, to try to get away, vibrated through my bones, even though I knew I was wasting my energy. This couldn't be happening again. But it was.

Věrhăza's new amphitheater was before me, ready for the Games to start.

People were already in the stands, causing a crackle of anticipation and energy to spark the vast space. It was only half-filled now, but over time, that would change with more and more prisoners coming in.

I swayed on my legs, still weak from being in the hole and lack of food. Exactly how they wanted me. The memories of my experience last time, the blood and death—it was almost better going into it playing innocent. To not know what was ahead.

"Welcome to the Games!" Zion boomed from the middle of the pit, his voice bouncing off the walls like a speaker. His arms were up and brimming with energy, enjoying his role as a performer. "Get ready for thrilling excitement, blood, death, fame, and glory!" He pumped at each one as if it was the best thing in the world, selling everyone on the idea this was entertainment and not a way for us to murder each other, keeping us from coming together and fighting them. Sell people on a better life than they have, and they will buy anything.

"For those new to the Games, the rules are simple. Victory is declared on the last person standing." He circled the arena, taking on the ringmaster role with a flourish. The arena was larger and more elaborate than Halálház. I could also see a few fire pits, big enough someone could fall into them, being burned alive as they tried to climb out. A tally board was up high, ready to declare the winners. The seats reached even higher, with a special section off to the side, with throne chairs and plush seating. "The more you win, the more you rise in ranks of infamy. The winners will receive not just extra rations, but dishes like goulash and sweet bread, private showers, and real beds."

In a few sentences, he caught his prey. Boil down our lives to stew and bread, and they would go willingly in the hopes of it. They didn't realize most would never survive to taste any of these. It took very little output from them for us to die willingly.

"Does this not excite you?" Zion sang out. "Those who fight in here will be legendary."

Until the next fight, when your death was all but forgotten.

Zion threw up his arms. Crackles and zings filled the air as small fireworks popped above his head, awing the crowd. I could see it happening, their eyes becoming transfixed on the pretty sparkles, putting them into a trance with the presentation.

Halálház was brutal and cruel, but at least it was bold in it. This was theater, all razzle and dazzle, and sadly it worked on them like a charm.

The throng of inmates started stomping their feet, chanting and yelling. The resonance iced my body, the déjà vú tasting like metal on my tongue.

Movement caught my eye up on the side where the plush seating was, my lungs halting mid-breath. There were several figures, but I only focused on one.

Istvan.

The General stood there overlooking the exhibition and subordinates, with a smug expression on his face. He knew exactly what he was doing. He was the one who had Caden and me study the Roman Games and learn how the ruler could easily dupe the masses, taking their minds off their horrendous lives by giving them a spectacle.

He understood how simple it was to get the people focused on the superficial while taking more and more from them. Getting them to fight amongst themselves and not their true enemy. Give them more show, and they'll eat it up, asking for more, while you are boldly torturing, murdering, and starving them.

My hands shook, but I tried to steel myself. I had been here before. I survived, and I could again though my lungs fluttered in terror. One of these times, I wouldn't.

Without thought, my gaze went up into the stands, trying to find him. I couldn't see him from where I was, but I swear I could feel him watching me, finding me and blasting me with his fury. No sweet sentiment or artificial encouragement.

"You fucking kill," I swear I could hear him growl in my ear. *"You understand me, Kovacs? Whoever they have you fighting. Don't hesitate for one fucking second. You make it out. Find anything you can use as a weapon."*

Standing behind the gate, I tried to peer around the new area for anything which could be exploited, but nothing stood out except the fire, which could easily be turned against you with one push.

"Let's bring the first pair to warm you up." Zion motioned to my gate. Boyd strolled into my eyeline, a gleam in his eyes as he stopped in front of my pen, keys in hand.

"Just like the good ol' days, am I right?" Boyd smirked, unlocking my pin.

The squeal of the gate shivered up my spine, my heart thumping in my chest, terrified of who was in the tunnel across from mine. *Please be a stranger, please be a stranger.*

"One of these times, I'm gonna drag your dead body out," Boyd smirked. "Maybe tonight is my lucky night."

Samu opened my opponent's door, a tall willowy shadow stepping out.

My stomach clenched when I saw her. Long, braided dark blonde hair, a gap between her teeth.

"This is a fight… To. The. Death!" Zion bellowed, his words ringing in the pit as I stared across…

At Zuz.

Zuz's expression shut down, not allowing me to see any emotion. Her trembling body gave her away, her movements jittery and tense.

Can't say the feeling ever went away, knowing this time could be your last.

Boyd stopped by Zuz, heading for the gate. "Like I said earlier, kill her, and you can have your freedom." He smirked back at me, leaving the arena. Now I understood why they pulled her from the factory earlier. To get her ready to kill me without hesitation, giving her stakes worth fighting for.

Zuz's jaw locked down, her lids narrowing, starting to circle me.

"Zuz, he's lying to you." I countered her progression. She wasn't as close to me as Birdie or Kek, but she was still one of the group. One of Andris's soldiers. She was cared about and friends with the same people I was. "He won't set you free."

"Does it matter?" She crouched lower, her hands rolling into balls. "Only *one* of us can walk out of here, anyway. And I'm gonna make sure it's *me*."

The crowd started off with a mix of horror and excitement seeing us, as if they were aroused in their disgust. Sarkis's army only saw two friends facing off, but the thrill of the Games, the spectacle Markos was putting on, soon had the stomping of feet and chants eclipse the ones who were crying foul.

"Blood-ing!" was chanted out like a battle cry. The mantra corroded my stomach, tapping my pulse against my neck with hot and cold chills of the past.

Adrenaline from the crowd pumped into the air, crackling the tension between us. Nervous energy pushed her to act first. Springing for me, I slipped by her, twisting as she passed. My fist colliding with her temple, stumbling her to the side.

Her eyes blazed, as if her ego was embarrassed that I got the first knock. Her fae sensibility wasn't used to it.

Ego could get you killed here. It didn't matter who got the first hit. It was the last that counted.

Zuz came for me with a grunt, swiping her arms at me. I barricaded against her attack, moving quicker than I thought I could around her, my knuckles cracking into her kidney, forcing her to falter again.

Fury contorted her face, and she barreled for me with a cry. Grabbing my arms, yanking me in, she slammed her head into my face. Blood instantly gushed from my nose. The crowd "ooh'd" with the first sight of blood, the cheers growing louder.

Wiping my nose with my arm, I stepped back, and we circled each other again. While we were striking out with punches and kicks, which didn't connect, the masses grew louder in their need for more action.

Zuz was no different from some of the others I fought in the Games, getting caught up in wanting to win the crowd's favor over blocking them out and surviving.

I used it to my advantage.

Letting her get a hit in, they chanted her name, pulling her focus.

Darting closer, my fist smashed into her throat. Zuz's head snapped back, gasping. Her body flew back, hitting the dirt. I leaped down for her just as she rolled, knocking me over onto my side. Her boot kicked out, slamming into my stomach. Pain exploded across my abdomen as she kicked again.

"Get the fuck up, Kovacs. Find a weapon and kill her." As if a tendril of a ghost brushed the back of my neck, my head jolted to the crowd. Did I imagine his voice?

I didn't get time to reflect. Zuz leaped on me. As we wrestled, I saw her reach up into her hair, yanking something out.

A hairpin—and not any normal one you used to set your hair. This one had a dagger point, sharp and long enough to kill.

We had been stripped of all items when we arrived, left with nothing that could be used as a weapon. This was given to her here… and I had no doubt by who.

Boyd.

Acute pain pierced my shoulder as she stabbed the sharp prick into my muscles, tearing through my skin and nerves.

255

"I'm going to walk out of here," she seethed, yanking it out and pointing it at my heart. "And if I have to kill you to do it, so be it."

This had always been a fight to the death, but something switched at that moment.

I had been hesitating. As if there was some slim chance I wouldn't have to kill again. To go to the place inside myself, even I feared. That was no longer an option.

Clutching her arm to keep her from stabbing me again, I popped my elbow up, whacking her across her face. It halted her for a moment.

It was enough.

With all the energy I could muster, I flung her off me, scrambling up to my feet.

I no longer heard the crowd. No longer saw anything but her. The monster roared from the depths of my body, crawling from the mud and muck, dragging itself back up to the surface.

I kicked her in the face with a crack, driving a cry from her lips, her body tumbling over into the dirt.

The hairpin tumbled from her fingers.

As I learned before, it was kill or be killed. I would not die tonight.

Jumping for the weapon, her legs shot up, tripping me. My face hit the dirt with a thud, sliding the pin farther from us.

It was a millisecond. We looked at each other and then at the hairpin. Clawing and scrambling, we lunged for it, kicking, punching, and hitting each other to get it first.

My fingers wrapped around the cool metal.

"No!" Zuz growled, jumping on me to get it as I rolled over to face her.

She quickly realized her mistake.

The dagger point sliced through her ribs, stabbing through her lung like a popped balloon.

Her body froze, her eyes widened, peering down at the end of the hairpin sticking out of her chest, and then looking at me with wild disbelief and horror.

Pushing her off of me, I ripped it back out, climbing up to my feet.

Her palm covered over the hole in her chest, her frame shook with each breath, still staring at the wound as if she was couldn't believe what happened. Until the shock wore off and her raspy breaths became wet gasps.

"Kill! Kill! Kill!" The crowd roared.

With one lung heaving with a rasping inhale at their chant, Zuz realized who the death call was for this time. A guttural whimper wheezed from her as she tried to crawl away from me.

The sickness of what I had to do screamed through me like I was the one about to die. My chin trembled as I strode over to her as her body tried to suck in oxygen. She would die anyway, but that didn't make it easier.

"Kill! Kill!"

I shut down. I could not show weakness. This place preyed on it, sucking on it until you had nothing left.

I spent so long hiding from the memories of the Games, turning away, ignoring the truth of myself. It was the only way to survive the day. But now, I had to both face them and sink into them, wrap the talons of horror and death around me, and become the monster once again.

With the force of an axe, I came down on Zuz, the sharp hairpin piercing her chest with a sick wet sound, sinking into the walls of her good lung before I yanked it back out.

Her mouth opened in a wheezy cry, all the air leaking from her lungs. Her form withered and fought against the invisible force claiming her life, along with the sounds of her gasping and struggling for air. Wet. Raspy. Then the fight left her body. A tear slid down her cheek before she stopped moving, her eyes blank.

Zuz was dead.

Fury and grief collided, huffing out my nose. I was forced to kill another comrade, used for entertainment, doing their own dirty work.

Slowly, I lifted my head to Istvan, staring at him with an unrelenting gaze. Covered in gore, grime, and sweat, my fingers wrapped around the hairpin, blood dripping from it onto the dirt. The object that was supposed to kill me. My jaw clicked together, my head tipping at him just enough for him to recognize my challenge. The girl he had trained to become a soldier...

Turned into a warrior.

And she would not stop until she took him down.

Istvan stepped up to the railing of the balcony. His arrogance pulsated off him, the stench of his ego stronger than the blood drenching the ground.

"Bravo, my dear." Istvan's voice filled the arena, his voice thundering, the crowd hushing in an instant. All eyes on the new king of Věrhăza. "I always knew you were a good fighter, one of the best in your class if I recall, but it was breathtaking to watch you kill a fae." He looked positively giddy at Zuz's dead body. "There could be hope for you yet in my regime."

A wave of nausea curled in my throat. It was survival. I learned that the first time. Zuz would have killed me. It was her or me. Though I could feel with each life I took, I became more of the person he was trying to create.

A soulless monster.

And I would not bend to his image.

"No." I sneered.

Istvan's head tilted. A look I used to see when Caden and I bucked his authority, a sign of the punishment he would come back with later. He never hit us; that would have been too easy. Istvan's abuse was psychological. Making us choose between causing pain to ourselves or the other. We always chose ourselves, but it mentally messed with the other one, anyway.

Istvan loved games.

"I think you will change your mind." He smirked at me.

A figure came up beside Istvan, looping her arm with his, pulling my focus at the massive diamond engagement ring glinting off the lights. She was dainty, with long dark hair and delicate features. Her lips pursed, peering down at me like garbage before smiling adoringly up at Istvan.

My body jolted, watching him turn to gaze down at her. His smile was empty, but he leaned over, kissing her.

The woman was *not* Rebeka, but Olena, the princess of Ukraine. The woman engaged to Caden. Or had been.

What the hell was going on? Where was Rebeka?

My chest sucked in at seeing Olena snuggle closer in, whispering in his ear like lovers, her cruel superiority over everything written on her face.

He gave her a nod, his grin appearing more genuine, his hand rubbing over hers.

"My soon-to-be bride enjoyed watching you fight so much she would like an encore," Istvan announced, nodding down at the gate. "Bring out the next."

Soon to be bride?

Next?

"This one will be very interesting." He lifted a brow, patting her hand absently.

My head darted to where Istvan gestured. Boyd strolled to the pit gate with the same malicious sneer slid over his face I recalled from one of my previous times fighting in the Games. The elation he got in making me fight two at once. One person he specifically had picked for me: Aron.

My stomach twisted into knots as I watched a form being dragged down the passage, the terror of who they were bringing wracked through my body.

A bag was over the person's head as they kicked and thrashed against the guards, but I could tell it was female.

Boyd opened the gate, the squeal of the hinges piercing through my ears. The taste of adrenaline, sharp and metallic, caked on my tongue.

My heart slammed against my ribs. The guards shoved her forward, her body hitting the ground. Boyd reached over, ripping the bag from her head.

No… oh gods, no.

I heard the scream inside my head, the tears burning behind my lids, the agony of what Istvan was doing. The cruelty of his punishment.

"Nooooo!" I heard a woman wail from the stands, the pain and agony of a mother's cry shredding through me.

Hanna Molnár, my friend, my comrade since our early teens. The one I would have fought to the death to protect… was now the one I would have to kill.

Watching her rise to her feet, her blue eyes locked on mine with confusion and fear, but a formidable strength most pretended to have.

The girl was not the same as the one I fought in class. She had changed. Her time at Sarkis's had woken something in her.

"No," I yelled up at Istvan. "I won't play your fucked up games."

His brow curved. "We'll see, won't we?" He nodded again at Boyd.

Nausea spun my head as I watched him open the gate again, another form being shoved through.

My heart dropped out, flipping around on the dirt, no longer wanting to be in my body, the pain too deep.

"Scorpion…" His name trembled out of my mouth.

His gaze went from me to Hanna. "No!" He belted out, his head shaking.

"If I'm not mistaken, the rules of the Games are if you don't participate… you *all* die," Istvan stated.

Boyd nodded his head, his glare locking with mine, knowing I understood this firsthand.

Fury broke through Scorpion as terror washed over Hanna, her mouth parting.

"Wasn't he your tormentor when you were being held prisoner? Didn't you say you wished you had the chance to kill him?" Istvan addressed Hanna, motioning to Scorpion. "I am giving you that chance."

"I-I… that's not…" Her head shook slightly.

"I thought you would be happy to kill your fae captor."

Hanna's head darted to Scorpion and then to Istvan. The sureness I had seen in her at Sarkis's base, her disgust of fae, her righteousness, wasn't there.

"I can't fight them," she croaked.

"Oh, don't worry. I made this competitive enough. I wouldn't throw you in without giving you an even playing field." Istvan smirked, making my stomach drop. "Every meal you've had since returning has been doused with fae essence."

"What?" Terror exploded over her features.

Oh fuck, no. I jerked to her. She blinked in confusion, peering at her hands, as if at that moment she felt the drug running through her veins.

He had given Hanna the formula.

Fuck...

That meant there were two fae in this ring, and I was the one who held no power now.

"As your Emperor of Věrhăza and soon to be Sovereign King of the East," Istvan boomed, Olena's smile widening in pride at the thought of being his queen. "I declare the tournaments of death officially open." His cold eyes turned to me.

"Let the *Games* begin..."

Blood Lands #5 Available Now.

Thank you to all my readers. Your opinion really matters to me and helps others decide if they want to purchase my book. If you enjoyed this book, please consider leaving a review on the site where you purchased it. It would mean a lot. Thank you.

About the Author

USA Today Best-Selling Author Stacey Marie Brown is a lover of hot fictional bad boys and sarcastic heroines who kick butt. She also enjoys books, travel, TV shows, hiking, writing, design, and archery. Stacey is lucky enough to live and travel all over the world.

She grew up in Northern California, where she ran around on her family's farm, raising animals, riding horses, playing flashlight tag, and turning hay bales into cool forts.

When she's not writing, she's out hiking, spending time with friends, and traveling. She also volunteers helping animals and is eco-friendly. She feels all animals, people, and the environment should be treated kindly.

To learn more about Stacey or her books, visit her at:

Author website & Newsletter: www.staceymariebrown.com

Facebook group: www.facebook.com/groups/1648368945376239/

TikTok: @authorstaceymariebrown

Instagram: www.instagram.com/staceymariebrown/

Facebook Author page: www.facebook.com/SMBauthorpage

Sex, Lies, & Blank Pages Podcast: https://linktr.ee/sexliesandblankpages

Goodreads: www.goodreads.com/author/show/6938728.StaceyMarie_Brown

Pinterest: www.pinterest.com/s.mariebrown

Bookbub: www.bookbub.com/authors/stacey-marie-brown

Acknowledgements

The love for this series has seriously been beyond anything I expected! Thank you all so much for living the Savage Lands Series as much as I loved writing it!

Kiki & Colleen at Next Step P.R. - Thank you for all your hard work! I love you ladies so much.

Mo & Emily– You both make it readable! Thank you!

Jay Aheer- So much beauty. I am in love with your work!

Judi Fennell at www.formatting4U.com- Always fast and always spot on!

To all the readers who have supported me: My gratitude is for all you do and how much you help indie authors out of the pure love of reading.

To all the indie/hybrid authors out there who inspire, challenge, support, and push me to be better: I love you!

And to anyone who has picked up an indie book and given an unknown author a chance.

THANK YOU!

Printed in the USA
CPSIA information can be obtained
at www.ICGtesting.com
LVHW022151141023
761116LV00005B/120